The Biology of Music Making

MUSIC AND CHILD DEVELOPMENT

Proceedings
of the
1987 Denver Conference

Edited by

Frank R. Wilson
Franz L. Roehmann

MUSIC AND CHILD DEVELOPMENT
Frank R. Wilson and Franz L. Roehmann, editors

Cover design: Jim Johnson
Printer: BookCrafters, Inc., Ann Arbor, Michigan
Second printing: October, 1997
Printed in USA
ISBN: 0-918812-58-5

For further information and catalogs, contact:

MMB Music, Inc.
Contemporary Arts Building
3526 Washington Avenue
Saint Louis, MO 63103-1019

Phone: 314 531-9635; 800 543-3771 (USA/Canada)
Fax: 314 531-8384
e-mail: mmbmusic@mmbmusic.com
Web site: http://www.mmbmusic.com

Acknowledgments

Music and Child Development, the second of a series of three Biology of Music Making conferences, could not have taken place without the considerable support of a number of groups and individuals. As was the case in 1984, the Denver Center for the Performing Arts, the University of Colorado, Denver, and a number of individuals from the Denver community provided encouragement and essential assistance from the inception of the project to its completion. The warm and friendly atmosphere of the meeting was the most prominent effect of their continuing care and attention.

We acknowledge with special thanks the contributions of Glendon F. Drake, Chancellor of the University, and Donald R. Seawell, Chairman of the Board of Trustees at the Denver Center for the Performing Arts, who provided critical guidance and support, and a seamless liaison between the two institutions. Personal thanks go to Harold Levin and the staff of the Executive Tower Inn, who managed once again to turn their hotel into our home; and to Meryl Orlin, who always makes Denver seem like home. We were most fortunate to have the services of Contemporary Forums of Danville, California as conference manager, and continue to receive favorable comments about the conference because of the hard work of their extremely capable staff. Robert L. Meissner, Publicity and Promotions, Wilmington, Delaware, handled press relations energetically and imaginatively before and during the conference.

We owe a great deal to the financial supporters of the conference and of these proceedings. We acknowledge in particular the extremely generous support of the National Association of Music Merchants, whose substantial grant made it possible to transform the plan for the conference into a reality. We extend thanks, as well, to other friends in the music industry who have been with us since the beginning and who continue to support and encourage this work: Yamaha Music Corporation, USA; Baldwin Piano and Organ Company; G. LeBlanc Corporation; and Gemeinhardt. We also thank Wells Music of Denver, who supplied the piano for Denny Zeitlin's concert; Davis Audio-Visual, who made it possible for us to offer video presentations at the conference; and Les Stephensen and Bryan's Music, Tallahassee, Florida, for providing synthesizers and computers for Carol DeGuire's workshop.

We note here, with great sadness, the death of Thomas D. Barna, a young pianist, a loving father, and our warm and faithful friend at Hammell Music in Livonia, Michigan. His love for children and for music will always remain an inspiration and a cherished memory.

The planning for the conference was greatly aided by the active collaboration of both the Music Educators National Conference and the Music Teachers National Association, and by the International Association of Music for the Handicapped. We are particularly indebted to Paul Lehman in Ann Arbor, Dolores Zupan in St. Louis, Rosalie Pratt in Provo, Helen Myers in Hartford and Roy Ernst in Rochester for their special contributions to the design and continuity of the conference program.

Plans for this *Conference Proceedings* began well before the meeting itself, and work on the manuscript has demanded considerable time, energy and good will of the faculty, who have graciously and patiently collaborated in the long process of transforming a collection of conference papers into an integrated monograph. Whatever success the book may achieve in articulating and advancing the thesis stated in the Preface is theirs to claim.

We are deeply indebted to Bob and Sherry Berschauer, and to the IBM Fund for Community Services, and to Alan Kay and his staff at Apple Computers in Los Angeles for providing the tools we needed to prepare the book for publication. Norman Goldberg, our publisher, has worked tirelessly on the manuscript and on a host of technical concerns. His friendship and support have been, as always, invaluable. Finally, we acknowledge with profound gratitude the dedication and professionalism of Patricia Wilson, without whose unstinting efforts neither the conference nor the book could ever have come into being.

Conference Faculty

John Baily, Ph.D.
School of African and Asian Studies
University of Sussex
Brighton, England

Children's Music in Afghanistan
The Role of a Motor Grammar in Musical Performance

Jeanne Bamberger, M.A.
Associate Professor of Music
Massachusetts Institute of Technology

The Mind Behind the Musical Ear

Paula Bernstein, Ph.D.
Assistant Clinical Professor of Psychiatry
University of Colorado Health Sciences Center

Moderator: Session on Early Childhood Development

Bob L. Berschauer
President, Micro Business Instruction
Pleasanton, California

Workshop on Computers in Music Learning,
Teaching & Research*

Jon-Roar Bjørkvold
Professor of Musicology
University of Oslo
Oslo, Norway

Canto — Ergo Sum

John Blacking, Ph.D., DLitt, MRIA
Professor of Social Anthropology
Queen's University
Belfast, Northern Ireland

Music in Children's Cognitive and Affective Development

Alice G. Brandfonbrener, M.D.
Director, Medical Program for Performing Artists
Northwestern Memorial Hospital, Chicago

A Former Prodigy Looks Back: Filmed Interview with Yo-Yo Ma

Max W. Camp, D.M.E.
Professor of Music
University of South Carolina

Rhythmic Control and Musical Understanding

Richard Colwell, Ed.D.
Professor of Music and Secondary Education
University of Illinois at Urbana-Champaign

Is There an American School of Music Education?

David Darling
President, Music For People
Litchfield, Connecticut

An Evening Workshop on Improvisation*

Carol A. DeGuire
Piano and Synthesizer Studio
Perry, Florida

Synthesizer Accompaniment for Solo Piano (Demonstration)*

Martha B. Denckla, M.D.
Chief, Section on Autism and Related Behavioral Disorders
Neurologic Institute, National Institutes of Health

The Paradox of the Gifted/Disabled Child

Diana Deutsch, Ph.D.
Research Psychologist, Department of Psychology
University of California, San Diego

*Individual Variation in Melodic Perception***

Roy Ernst, Ph.D.
Chairman, Department of Music Education
Eastman School of Music, University of Rochester

Moderator: "Breaking 100 in Music"

Donna Brink Fox, Ph.D.
Associate Professor of Music Education
Eastman School of Music, University of Rochester

Workshop: Bringing Music to Infants and Toddlers

Prof. Dr. med. Hans-Joachim Freund
Director, Department of Neurology
University Hospital
Düsseldorf, West Germany

Timing Mechanisms in Skilled Hand Movements

Robert Garfias, Ph.D.
Dean of Fine Arts
University of California, Irvine

Language and Music Acquisition

Gary S. Gelber, M.D.
Assistant Clinical Professor of Psychiatry
University of California, San Francisco

    Moderator: Session on the Musically Gifted Child

Edwin E. Gordon, Ph.D.
Carl E. Seashore Professor of Research in Music Education
Temple University

    The Role of Developmental and Stabilized Music Aptitudes

Barbara J. Grenoble, M.M.
Instructor in Music Education
University of Colorado at Denver

    *Workshop: Orff Teaching in the Primary Grades**

Stewart H. Hulse, Ph.D.
Chairman, Department of Psychology
The Johns Hopkins University

    The Acquisition of Pitch and Rhythm in Songbirds

Elizabeth Jones
Director of Instruction, Yamaha Music Education System
Buena Park, California

    What Children Teach Us About Learning Music

Sharon Jones
Former Chairperson, Department of Piano
Harlem School of The Arts, New York City

    Teaching Music for Life

Paul R. Lehman, Ph.D.
Professor and Associate Dean, School of Music
University of Michigan

Moderator: Session of Concepts and Controversies in Music Education

Richard Lewis
Director, The Touchstone Project for Children
New York City

The Role of the Arts in Childhood Education*

Victoria H. McArthur, Ph.D.
Center for Music Research
Florida State University

Analysis of Pianist Movement using Biomechanics*

Randal McChesney
Music Education Department
University of Southern California

Workshop Demonstration: Music Therapy with Children*

Helen Myers, Ph.D.
Consultant on Ethnomusicology
The New Grove Dictionary of Music and Musicians
London, England

Children's Music: The Cross-Cultural Perspective

Peter F. Ostwald, M.D.
Professor of Psychiatry
University of California, San Francisco

Music and Emotional Development in Early Childhood

Ann Pick, Ph.D.
Institute of Child Development
University of Minnesota

*The Development of Perception of Melodies and Musical Events***

Rosalie Rebollo Pratt, Ed.D.
Coordinator of Graduate Studies
Department of Music, Brigham Young University

Moderator: Session on Music Education and Handicapped Children

Roy A. Pritts
Acting Resident Dean
College of Music, University of Colorado, Denver

*Workshop on Computers in Music Learning, Teaching & Research**

Kyle D. Pruett, M.D.
Clinical Professor of Psychiatry
Child Study Center, Yale University

Coping With Life on a Pedestal

Franz L. Roehmann, Ph.D.
Professor of Music
University of Colorado, Denver

*Moderator: Session on Perceptual Psychology;
Conference Co-chair*

Sally J. Rogers, Ph.D.
Assistant Professor of Psychiatry
University of Colorado Health Sciences Center

Theories of Child Development and Musical Ability

Chava Sekeles, M.A., R.M.T.
Department of Music Therapy
The David Yellin Teachers College
Jerusalem, Israel

> *Case Report: Music Therapy in a Neurologic Disorder*

Anne Dhu Shapiro, Ph.D.
Associate, Department of Music
Harvard University

> *Music in the Service of Ritual Transformation*

Patricia K. Shehan, Ph.D.
Associate Professor of Music
Butler University

> *Movement in the Music Education of Children*

Donald J. Shetler, Ph.D.
Professor of Music Education
Eastman School of Music, University of Rochester

> *The Inquiry into Prenatal Musical Experience*

John A. Sloboda, Ph.D.
Department of Psychology
University of Keele
Staffordshire, England

> *Music as a Language*

Lauren A. Sosniak, Ph.D.
Associate Professor of Education
University of Illinois at Chicago

> *From Tyro to Virtuso: A Long-term Commitment to Learning*

William Starr, M.M.
Professor of Music
University of Colorado, Boulder

Workshop: The Suzuki Method of Music Teaching

Dale B. Taylor, Ph.D.
Director of Music Therapy Studies
University of Wisconsin-Eau Claire

Teaching Rhythm, Melody and Pitch to Handicapped Children

Jack A. Taylor, Ph.D.
Director, Center for Music Research
Florida State University

The Development of Music Performance Skills in Children

Michael G. Wade, Ph.D.
Director, School of Physical Eduction and Recreation
University of Minnesota

Motor Skills and Music: Contrasting Styles of Control

Cecilia Wang, Ph.D.
Coordinator of Music Education
University of Kentucky, Lexington

A Microcomputer System for Teaching Singing Skills to Children*

Christopher A. Waterman, Ph.D.
Assistant Professor of Music (Divison of Ethnomusicology)
University of Washington, Seattle

The Junior Fújì Stars of Agbowo

Frank R. Wilson, M.D.
Associate Clinical Professor of Neurology
University of California, San Francisco

> *Moderator: Session of Psychomotor Development;*
> *Conference Co-chair*

Dennis J. Zeitlin, M.D.
Associate Clinical Professor of Psychiatry
University of California, San Francisco

> *Conference Banquet Recital**

Dolores N. Zupan
President, Music Teachers National Association
St. Louis, Missouri

> *Moderator: Panel on Music Education*

*   Presentation not published.

** Presentation published elsewhere; contact author for details.

Editors' Preface

The second Biology of Music Making conference was held at the University of Colorado, Denver, in July, 1987. While it might seem unnecessary to cite the impetus for a meeting concerned with the relationship between musical experience and child development, it is worth stating that this particular conference came about largely as a response to the growing concern (alarm is perhaps too strong a word) among music educators over the declining support for music programs in the American public school system. It is difficult to be certain about the magnitude of this problem, however there have been persuasive recent signs — both public and private — that many people who have devoted their lives to music education feel the future of their work to be in serious jeopardy. One sign that such private distress exists on a large scale is the prominence of advocacy programs developed by associations of music educators (The Foundation for the Advancement of Education in Music, for example).

From our perspective, the most eloquent expression of such private anguish has been the recurring, invariably urgent, telephone call from a music teacher, typically as follows: "Please send me the research that proves that music is important for children; the school board meets next week and I have to come up with something or I lose my job."

Those familiar with the first Biology of Music Making conference will recall that Robert Freeman, Director of the Eastman School of Music at the University of Rochester, described something of a paradox in the educational and professional worlds of "serious" music in the United States today:

> "We have some of the world's greatest soloists, born and trained in the United States. We also have people coming to the United States from all over the world, not only from Western Europe, but from Asia and South America as well, to study music composition, scholarship and performance. Musically, we have much to be proud of, including some of the world's great orchestras, some of the world's greatest chamber music societies and groups, wonderful library systems, and an emerging group of very good critics. We also have some problems as well. Among them is the great oversupply of profes-

sional musicians and the as yet fairly limited demand for what some people call 'serious' music.

It is unfortunate that many young musicians in this country are trained in a rather narrow way. Many of them are deficient in nonmusical, cognitive skills, possibly because musical training so often begins at a time when young people are scarcely in a position to make a determination about what they want to do with their lives. Consequently, many professional musicians find themselves at age fifty or sixty frustrated with their lot in the professional world."[1]

At the conclusion of the 1984 conference, we suspected (as we still do today) that Dr. Freeman's statement not only states the paradox, but explains it. The difficulty appears to stem from the remarkably one-dimensional view of musical life prevalent in our society. What we have arrived at, without examining either our reasons for doing so, or the full range of consequences of such a happenstance policy, is the conviction that musical ability is a special skill requiring intense cultivation in particular children who show special promise. We try to identify these children at an early age, to begin their training as soon as possible, and to shield them from the distracting influences of ordinary childhood experience. The corollary of the above is that we generally try to spare other children the waste of time and the frustration of laboring at an activity for which we believe them to be ill-suited.

That this is the true state of affairs was confirmed at the 1987 conference on Music and Child Development, reported in this volume. Adverse consequences fall equally upon those who are "talented" and those who are "spared." It is, therefore, not only fair but critically important to ask ourselves what we really believe to be the role of music in human life; without a clear sense of what music is *for*, we can hardly expect to have a clear sense of what music education ought to be, or how and for whom it should be provided.

The concern of American music educators over public attitudes about music education could be excessive. To decide this question would require studies specifically protected from the influence of institutional anxieties, and we are unaware of the existence of any such studies. Still, one of us (FR) was particularly struck by a sign suggestive of neglect while browsing in a Denver bookstore, thinking about the 1987 conference and about the preparation of this Preface. Curious about what might be found there on music, he strolled over to the children's section, an enormous collection of books occupying most of the store's third floor. What would be in this collection, not only about music, but in stories written for children about music? And would there be anything about music in the books sold in *Parenting,* a subsection of the children's collection?

Collections of songs composed by adults on subjects that adults believe are important and relevant to the child's world were abundant. Within the children's book collection (which included a surprising amount of poetry, endless books about dinosaurs, travel, occupations and fantasy) there were only occasional references to music, usually as a minor incident in a non-musical story line, and usually in the context of music as an adult activity with children participating. And in *Parenting?* Music was rarely mentioned, and then only in passing — for example, referring to the sense of peace a mother feels singing to her child. There were no collections of songs written *by* children, and no books depicting the musical experiences of children from a child's point of view.

Whether or not the above anecdotal sampling reflects an important underlying cultural reality, it provides a helpful backdrop for the work reported in this volume. Regardless of the background or perspective from which the reader approaches this material, it will be evident that music is far more influential in children's lives than one would infer from a casual visit to the bookstore.

It seems to us that this faculty has delivered a strikingly clear message that deserves the attention of an enormous community of parents and educators: musical experience has a *profound* influence on language, social and emotional maturation of children, beginning in infancy (that is, long before music "training" begins). Moreover, as contemporary neurophysiology and psychomotor research discover more about the nature of rhythmic organization in movement, it is likely that musical experience will be shown to have important effects on motor skills development as well.

Children themselves, regardless of where they live, and entirely independent of adult instruction (or intrusion), regularly engage alone and in groups in a variety of musical activities appropriate to their personal, peer-group and family circumstances. There exists, in other words, a rich and dynamic world of musical experience in the lives of all children, nourishing what Dr. Paula Bernstein calls "the musical self," often bearing little relationship to the adult goals and standards of music performance. All that babbling, cooing, humming and sing-song that babies and young children indulge in, we discover, has both meaning and weight for the developing child. It is not until later that they fall under what Jon-Roar Bjørkvold refers to here as "the Mozart shadow."

Perhaps our adult ideas about music are so deeply entrenched (and the musical self each of us harbors is so completely muted) that we cannot bring ourselves to take a serious look at musical experience from the child's perspective. It is time we did.

The reader of this book is invited to consider the relationship between children and music from developmental, cultural, anthropologic, cognitive, physiologic, therapeutic and educational points of view. It is only by permitting ourselves to look comprehensively at this issue (which requires most of us to suspend our own personal, culturally and experientially determined opinions) that we have any real hope of seeing what is there, or *could* be there.

Frank R. Wilson
Düsseldorf, West Germany

Franz L. Roehmann
Denver, Colorado

December, 1989

Reference

1. Roehmann, F., Wilson, F., eds. 1988. *The Biology of Music Making: Proceedings of the 1984 Denver Conference.* Page 243. St. Louis, MO: MMB Music, Inc.

TABLE OF CONTENTS

IV. Teaching the Child With Special Educational Needs

V. Teaching the Gifted Child

VI. Current Concepts and Controversies in Music Education

Section I

Music and Early Childhood Development

Theories of Child Development and Musical Ability

Sally J. Rogers
Department of Psychiatry
University of Colorado Health Sciences Center

Introduction

The trouble with theories of child development when applied to young children's musical development is that traditional theories do not easily account for the proclivity with which young children learn the melody, rhythm, and lyrics of typical nursery songs and musical games, as well as more sophisticated musical skills.

One reason that such theories do not deal with music learning is that the major theories of child development are Western theories, built upon Western culture. Theorists have studied what is important to the Western mind: logic, numbers, language, reasoning, information (Gardner, 1983). In all the 3822 pages of Mussen's current source book on child development, there is only one index listing concerning music, and that refers to a 27 word sentence describing an adolescent social group of musicians (Hartup, 1983). Western culture does not expect (therefore teach) specific music skills to young children, and Western theories have not looked at or considered musical development as an important area to be integrated into a general theory of child development. Those cultures which *have* valued and taught sophisticated musical skills to young children are quite distant from Western cultures, far removed from Western theorists. Thus, the only clear-cut examples of early musical ability in young children which occurred in Western literature were prodigies, savants, or children from intensely musical families, and these children were accounted for in terms of genetics or "accidents of nature."

A second reason is that the *zeitgeist* of the times for the major theory builders was for global theories that explained huge areas of learning with a few elegant concepts: i.e., Piaget's concepts of concrete and formal operations; learning theory concepts of operant and classical conditioning; Erikson's seven stage theory. Musical ability is a more discrete area of ability than general concept formation, problem solving, or social learning.

Thus, music was not well suited for inclusion in global theories of child development, and it did not present the kind of global learning problem that most appealed to the Western theorists.

Current Premises Concerning Musical Aptitude

In his book, *Frames of Mind* (1983), Howard Gardner has drawn from a wide body of knowledge to provide us with a new framework for thinking about musical ability. He points out that cross-cultural evidence from Asian and African cultures has broadened our knowledge of early music abilities. In the Anang culture in Nigeria, very young children are taught the songs, drum skills, and dances of their culture. By age five all the children in the culture have a repertoire of hundreds of songs, complex drum skills, and intricate dance movements. The Venda culture of Northern Transvaal teach their young children movement patterns rather than songs. (May, 1980; Gardner, 1983). In contemporary Hungary, China, and Japan, considerable emphasis is placed on children's' musical development (Gardner, 1983). The proficiency with which all young children learn nursery songs and rhymes, and the skill with which young children can be taught sophisticated music skills has lead to a new set of premises concerning young children's musical aptitude, well articulated by Gardner. In this way of thinking:

a. Musical ability is seen as a discrete area of ability, not particularly associated with general, global intelligence (i.e., IQ), or with language, mathematics, motor, or visual/spatial skills. The reasons for this position are several. First, musical development is not synchronized with another major area of development. Second, it does not co-vary with IQ, motor skills, language, math, or visual/spatial skills. Thus, it is sometimes intact in people who demonstrate severe impairments in most other intellectual areas. Likewise, it can be completely undeveloped in people who are otherwise bright and capable people. Finally, it appears to be processed in the brain separately from non musical auditory stimuli (Deutsch, 1975).

b. Musical awareness is observable very early in life. Gardner states that it emerges the earliest of all the different kinds of intelligence. The Papouseks, highly respected developmental researchers from West Germany, report that infants as young as two months can match the pitch, intensity, and melodic contour of the mother's songs, and at four months infants can match the rhythmic structure as well. These researchers feel that infants are even more predisposed to these aspects of music than to speech (Papousek, 1982). There are similar data from the field of auditory perception. Current researchers have found that infants between five and eight months of age can discriminate pitch differences of less than a half tone (Olsho, Schoon, Sakai, Turpin, & Sperduto, 1982). However, Werner reported that not until ten *years* of age could a majority of school aged children discriminate a half tone difference in pitch (Werner, 1957). Since the studies used vastly different methodologies, these studies can only be loosely compared. Nevertheless, the infant work certainly demonstrates the sensitivity of young children to musical elements.

c. Because young children are quite attuned to music, musical experience in early childhood will result in greater musical development. This premise draws its support from evidence of increased musical development in those children who have received considerable musical experience in early childhood. In addition, there are other areas of development in which stimulation has maximal effects when the biological capacity is rapidly developing. This is quite evident in language development, in the ease with which a young child masters whatever languages surround the child. It is also evident in motor skills, demonstrated in McGraw's work with twin boys (McGraw, 1935). In mammals, the impact of early versus late experience on visual and social systems is well known, (Reisen, 1947; Suomi & Harlow, 1971; Held & Heim, 1963; Scott & Fuller, 1965). Finally, the cognitive theorist Kurt Fischer has demonstrated that during the time of cognitive spurts, children's "innate" problem solving is enhanced *400%* by practice and by praise from an adult. As he states, "when the time is right," high practice and support can tremendously accelerate learning skills (Fischer, 1987).

Thus, music appears to be a discrete area of learning, available for development and growth quite early in life, rather unrelated to other developmental accomplishments of young children (i.e., language, motor skills, social skills), but quite dependent on environmental stimulation and training in order to develop fully. While global theories of child development do not account for or even consider the young child's aptitude for musical experience and development of musical skills, global theories can help us consider what qualities of the environment will aid children's musical development.

Psychological Theories of Child Development

Psycho-dynamic theories of child development probably provide the most help in answering the question, "Why is music so important to people and so salient to young children?" The emotional qualities of music and the emotional state that music creates in listeners and participants is the meat of psycho-dynamic theories. Also, the transmission of music from parent and teacher to young children depends heavily on the adult-child relationship, which psycho-dynamic theories help illuminate.

An infant's early experiences of loving parents' songs imbues music with an emotional connection to these loved parents, and the child's own music may create a feeling of connectedness which can last a lifetime. Winnicott (1971) states that for infants whose mothers sing to them, the songs may be part of the same phenomenon as early social games and transitional objects — a most important area of infant-mother dialogue and shared experience which allows the child to recreate the feeling of being with mother even when separate from her. In this way, music comes to evoke the child's feelings for the mother. Gardner points out that music serves no instrumental function for humans. Since we don't need it for communication or for survival, why is it so important and so central to the human experience? The answer probably lies in the stream of emotion which music makes available to its participants.

It is difficult to overemphasize the role of emotion in music. Even the cognitive theorist Vygotsky (1971) underscores the decisive role that emotion plays in music and other "lyrical arts," those of music, architecture, and poetry, in which emotion is generated by the form and structure of the work, not by the cognitive content. Vygotsky emphasizes that the lyrical quality of music cannot be taught, that it is achieved only by feeling. This access to one's stream of feelings requires that one be more attuned to one's internal state than to external reality, and young children are much closer to this than older children and adults. The psychology of music depends on perception, emotion, and imagination— the realm of the young child.

Sally J. Rogers

Providing young children with enhanced musical experiences, whether from singing, dance and movement, or instruments may well allow the connections between one's feelings and their expression through music to develop more fully. This is certainly a strong component of the Suzuki method, of Dalcroze, of Orff Schulwerk and other early childhood music curricula. The sensitivity to emotional aspects of music may be a particular strength of young music learners.

For the young child who is learning music, the psycho-social dynamics between self and parents, and self and teacher, are important to consider, particularly when structured music training occurs. Erik Erikson (1963) describes several characteristics of the young child in interaction with parents and other key adults which will affect music teaching.

During the ages two and three, the child's main interpersonal issues focus on acquisition of independence and control, acquisitions which are constantly threatened by the child's self doubt due to his or her small size and limited capabilities. Mastery motivation is very high for independent learning. Successful teaching works within the child's own framework, emphasizing independent mastery and success, while downplaying requirements for cooperation with the adult.

The four and five-year-old child has a strong desire to be like the parents and to please the parents, particularly through skill mastery. Joining the parent and teacher in musical activities is much more appealing at this age, and levels of cooperation are reached that were previously unattainable. Peers are important and the social elements of group music are strong motivators. Although the child of this age seems quite competent linguistically, with good memory and motor skills and a clear desire to please, it is important to remember how emotionally immature children in this age group are, and how much parental support and involvement they continue to need.

Learning Theories of Child Development

Learning theories of child development, with their emphasis on operant and classical conditioning techniques and natural consequences of behavior, do not easily account for the seemingly innate musical propensity and interest of very young children. Other early learning accomplishments like language, motor skills, and self care skills result in clear positive consequences for the toddler. Unlike these skills, early songs result in no new control over the environment and no clear and immediate environmental rewards. Although the social aspects of mother-child songs and games seem rewarding, the young child often uses learned songs and games without a social partner. Thus, there appears to be something "internal" about infant music learning that learning theories do not address well.

When one looks at music learning one must take into account the socio-cultural aspects of music learning and teaching. As Levi-Strauss (1969) has pointed out, music is as integral a part of a culture as the culture's language. Singing to and with children is an acculturation process, and the social aspects of music are its very first function. Parents are the transmitters of cultural experience and the young child's experience with music cannot be separated from the child's social experience with parents, nursery school teachers, and others who are contributing to the child's musical development.

It is social learning theory (Bandura, 1977) which emphasizes children's learning of social behavior via imitation and observational learning. Social learning theory also demonstrates the importance of peer models and adult models whom the child perceives as warm and responsive. Since music is a cultural phenomenon, transmitted socially from adults to children and from children to other children, social learning theory should offer us some powerful ideas regarding social music teaching.

Social learning theory highlights how much children want to imitate other children like themselves, the power of the peer group. It also highlights the impact of an older child's behavior on a younger child, and how much older children can become role models for younger children. Providing music training in a group situation provides a strong motivation for young children to acquire the skills being taught. Exposing young children to somewhat older children who have already mastered some musical skills provides another powerful motivation for children to become like the older child, and to define his or her future self as a child who is competent with music. Another important contribution of social learning theory is that of observational learning — the idea that children learn from watching others even when the child is not engaging in the desired behavior. Observing the musical activities of other children is a powerful learning experience in its own right. Finally, social learning theory has demonstrated that children learn not only the modeled behavior through observation, but they also learn the consequences or contingencies surrounding behavior. Children who observe the positive

Sally J. Rogers

consequences of other children's musical activities are learning that such activities lead to positive consequences.

Other learning theory concepts which should aid us in developing teaching approaches to music for young children include the following:

   a. the idea that consequences of a behavior determine whether and how frequently it will be repeated;

   b. the concept of gradual approximation, or shaping, which refers to accepting a crude imitation at first and slowly working to refine it;

   c. the mirror concepts of task analysis and chaining, which refer to analyzing a behavior and breaking it down into its smallest and simplest components, and then teaching the task by chaining these small steps together in their logical sequence. In this way, very complex behavior can be broken down into extremely simple motor movements.

Through the concepts of task analysis and chaining, learning theory can explain how very young children can produce the complex and differentiated motor movements which are required for complex musical tasks. Learning theory also does away with the concept of "readiness," and assumes that almost any skill can be taught to anyone, provided it is taught correctly. Thus, while learning theory does not answer the question, "Why is music so readily and easily learned by young children?", it is of great assistance in helping parents and teachers design teaching methods for young children.

Cognitive Theories of Child Development

The final major area of child development theory is cognitive theory, and Jean Piaget is the best known of the cognitive theorists. Piaget does not discuss music learning in any depth, and his view of young children's minds tends to emphasize the illogic and magical thinking of the young child. Because young children do not have abstract principles for understanding the way the world works, they are extremely attuned to sensory and perceptual qualities of the world around them. This intense attunement to perceptual qualities of stimuli meshes well with the kind of absorption of music that young children display.

Piaget, Vygotsky, and others also emphasize the development of imagination, seen in the child's symbolic play and imaginative comments during the preschool years. Piaget discusses how young children use symbolic play as a vehicle for emotional communications and emotional expression. Thus, the preschooler's mind is quite adept at using imaginative activity to express emotions. Since, in music, emotion is generated by the form and structure — the perceptual content, not cognitive content — the young child's mind is very well equipped to respond to music (Vygotsky, 1971). Vygotsky goes on to point out that music, as one of the lyrical arts, induces an emotional response that feels real but is actually released by one's imagination, which has been stimulated by the music. Thus, for Vygotsky, music represents the union of emotion, perception, and imagination — the world of the young child.

Other contributions of cognitive theory include the concept of mastery motivation and the role of repetition. Piaget points out that young children enjoy repeating a newly learned skill many times, and that the pleasure they experience is intrinsic to the act of repeating the newly mastered skill. This feeling of pleasure at having learned something new is basic to the concept of mastery motivation. Piaget also underscores for us that teaching techniques for young children should not rely on verbal or concept teaching, but rather on motor, imaginative, and perceptual experiences. Young children learn music through seeing, hearing and doing. Passive instruction in which the child is physically moved by another is much less effective than instruction which results in an attentive child attempting a movement by him or herself. Young children are very concrete learners, and they are helped by physical props — tapes on fingerboards, marks on fingers — so that the task becomes extremely visible. Young children are also imaginative people, and the use of stories is quite helpful to induce the emotional quality of music.

Conclusion

None of the major theories of child development can account for the musical development which young children demonstrate. Humans appear to have a special aptitude for music learning which is maximally available for development when stimulated by the environment in early childhood. However, each of the current major global theories — psycho-dynamic, cognitive, and social learning theories — have important contributions to make as we try to uncover the emotional, perceptual, cognitive, and social experiences which form the core of early music development. As we look closely at young children who become accomplished with music, we can learn more about how to stimulate the music aptitudes of all young children.

References

Bandura, A. *Social learning theory,* Englewood Cliffs, NJ: Prentice Hall, 1977.

Deutsch, D. "The organization of short-term memory for a single acoustic attribute." In D. Deutsch & J.A. Deutsch (eds) *Short-term memory,* New York: Academic Press, 1975.

Erikson, E. *Childhood and Society,* New York: W. W. Norton, 1963.

Fisher, K. "Cognitive developmental levels and biobehavioral shifts." Paper presented to the Developmental Psychobiology Research Group, Denver, 1987.

Flavell, J. H. *The Developmental Psychology of Jean Piaget,* Princeton, NJ: Van Nostrand, 1963.

Gardner, H. *Frames of Mind,* New York: Basic Books, 1983.

Hartup, W. W. "Peer relations." In P.H. Mussen (ed.) *Handbook of Child Psychology,* V.4, New York: John Wiley & Son, 1983.

Held, R. & Heim, A. "Movement-produced stimulation in the development of visually guided behavior," *Journal of Comparative Physiology and Psychology,* 56:872-876, 1963.

Levi-Strauss, C. *The Raw and the Cooked,* New York: Harper and Row, 1969.

May, E. *Music in other cultures,* Berkeley: University of California Press, 1980.

McGraw, M.B. *Growth: a study of Johnny and Jimmy,* New York: Appleton-Century, 1935.

Olsho, L.W., Schoon, C., Sakai, R., Turpin, R., & Sperduto, V. "Auditory frequency discrimination in infancy," *Developmental Psychology*, 18:721-726, 1982.

Papousek, M. "Musical elements in mother-infant dialogues," Paper presented at the International Conference on Infant Studies. Austin, Texas, March, 1982.

Reisen, A.H. "Arrested vision," *Scientific American,* 183:16-19, 1950.

Scott, J. P. & Fuller, J. L. *Genetics and the Social Behavior of the Dog*, Chicago: University of Chicago Press, 1965.

Suomi, S.J. & Harlow, H.F. "Abnormal social behavior in young monkeys," In J. Helmuth (Ed.) *Exceptional infant: studies in abnormalities.* Vol. 2., New York: Bruner-Mazel, 1971.

Vygotsky, L.S. *The Psychology of Art,* Cambridge, MA: MIT Press, 1971.

Werner, H. *Comparative psychology of mental development,* New York: International Universities Press, 1957.

Winnicott, D.W. *Playing and Reality,* London: Tavistock, 1971.

Music in the Organization of Childhood Experience and Emotion

Peter F. Ostwald
Professor of Psychiatry
University of California, San Francisco

I will be referring to a study that Delmont Morrison and I recently completed, which is called Music in the Organization of Childhood Experience. Dr. Morrison is a child psychologist and clinical professor of child psychiatry at the University of California. The study will be published in *Imagination and Cognition in Childhood: The Psychological Organization of Early Experience*, by Baywood Publishers in New York. You will notice that our emphasis is on early childhood. In fact we will be talking a lot about infants and very young children.

I thought since this was the beginning of the meeting, I would be very arrogant and try to define what music is, since we'll be talking about music. We all know of music, we play it, we love it. A definition of music that I like very much comes from a book called *In Search of Beauty in Music*, written in 1947 by a really fascinating man and a pioneer in this field of ours.

> "From the beginning music, as the expression of emotional life not reducible to logical language, has been a medium for communicating ideals or urges as contrasted with ideas. It has been the language of mysticism, going far beyond the idealizations as expressed in poetry. It has expressed an attitude toward the gods and the spiritual world as a whole. As in the behavior of birds, it has expressed the sexual urge in all its rationalized and idealistic forms. As music for music's sake, it is a sort of dream language which carries the performer and the listener far beyond the routine of daily life."

For me, Seashore's definition really captures the essence of music, its emotionality, its idealism and its capacity to transcend reality.

Music has long been recognized to be of importance in the lives of children, especially in the contact that children have with the world of adults. Infants respond to the musical quality of their mothers' voices. Toddlers will play with musical toys, and enjoy musical games. Teenagers, of course, indulge in numerous musical activities — singing, dancing, playing instruments, collecting tapes and records, attending concerts. Music also is used widely, often expertly, in many programs of education. And yet, there seems to be little in the way of an organized body of knowledge about music in childhood. We have tried in our paper to organize the knowledge that is available into three large domains. First, the field of biology, with its exploration of relations between music and the brain; second, the domain of psychology with its emphasis on the development of musical abilities and intelligence; and third, clinical studies about music and musicians and children through case reports and psychoanalysis and psychobiography.

Biological Aspects

Let me begin with the biology of music-making. Investigation of the anatomical and physical underpinnings of musical behavior in childhood has been very difficult. There are methodological and technological problems, not to mention the ethical limitations placed on research with human subjects, particularly with infants and children. As a consequence, almost everything that we know today about the limbic system and the hypothalamus and the other parts of the brain involved in the control of moods and emotions derive from animal research or from the study of adult brains.

Similarly the role of the neurotransmitters, which regulate moods and emotions chemically has been elucidated largely through work in the laboratory using animals or adults rather than the direct study of children. Even the most modern studies, for example the techniques of positron emission tomography, deal primarily with diseased or abnormal children. Nevertheless, there is evidence from recent PET scans that the sensorimotor cortex and the cerebellum of the infant are quite active at birth, while the visual areas are not. I am referring to a study published last year by Chugani and Phelps in *Science*. These kinds of findings reinforce a belief that I've held for many years that musical development may actually start before the baby is born.

In a paper published fifteen years ago, I emphasized that a sense of rhythm probably is of biological origin, beginning when the fetus inside the uterus produces rhythmical heartbeats. It starts to make chest movements, and it begins to move its trunk and its limbs in a rhythmical fashion. These are innate movement patterns. By the third trimester, the sixth to the ninth month of pregnancy, the fetus also seems to respond to acoustical stimuli. Pregnant singers, for instance, often report a change in fetal activity —

usually the baby seems quieter — when they sing. Pianists and other instrumentalists who are pregnant often will notice that the fetus becomes more active while they are playing music or shortly afterwards. Fortunately we have an expert in this field, Dr. Donald Shetler, who will bring us up-to-date on this important topic.

I'm impressed with the fact that the middle ear and the inner ear of the human fetus attain practically adult size by the fifth month of gestation, long before birth. Furthermore, it has been demonstrated that sounds produced at levels similar to normal conversation from outside the mother can reach the amniotic sac inside the mother with relatively little attenuation, as do the sounds of the mother herself, including her eating, swallowing, breathing and intestinal noises. Here again, these researches are done using animal models, lambs in particular. In the study by Armitage and colleagues, lambs were selected, because of their similarities to humans particularly with respect to the pulsations of the great vessels in the abdomen, the aorta, and the large arteries in the pelvis close to the uterus, which provide rhythmical and other sonic information about the mother.

What does the fetal brain do with this information? Here I think we have to face one of the very fundamental conundrums in development neurology. As you know, there are scientists who regard with skepticism the idea of preformed or specialized areas in the brain that subserve higher mental functions such as symbolization, language, or music. I refer here to studies by Critchley and others. These neurologists would emphasize the importance of musical experience, of listening and playing as being the most important factor leading to the production of neural networks in the brain.

The opposing view is that musical talents or gifts are in some way predetermined genetically or anatomically. And here we refer to studies of brain localization, cerebral dominance and the genetics of absolute pitch.

I happen to believe that an appreciation for acoustical nuances is built into the human brain during its embryonic development. I think that much of the new research on language acquisition points in that direction. I also believe that the capacity to produce certain sounds which have musical properties is innate, and that these sounds are linked to the experience of primary affect such as pain and pleasure. We have spent considerable time at the Langley Porter Institute in San Francisco studying the crying and cooing of babies. Newborn babies produce sounds that have melodic structures and rhythms which seem to be fixed by the neurophysiological and respiratory apparatus of the infant. And studies throughout the world, in Sweden, Great Britain,

Russia and so forth, have demonstrated the similarity of neonatal crying and its associations with emotions of discomfort and distress. We also know of certain abnormalities, for instance, genetic abnormalities, which markedly alter the cries of infants. The trisomy disorders lower the pitch of the cry and prolong its duration and really wipe out the melodic pattern of the cry. The aptly named, *Cri du chat,* (the cat-cry syndrome) which produces abnormally high pitched mewling sounds, is another example. We know that deprivation of oxygen to the brain during pregnancy or shortly thereafter, as well as certain metabolic and endocrine diseases, will also interfere with the development of these innate musical patterns.

Psychological Aspects

I'll be getting back in a moment to the role of the mother and the father in the caretaking environment, who guide the infant's subsequent musical and emotional maturation. Before I do that I want to touch on a delicate problem, that of musical genius, which many of us intuitively feel is also somehow connected to biological issues and to heredity. Erwin Nyiregyhazi, for example, became the subject of a very interesting study published in 1925 by G. Revesz, who was the director of the Psychological Laboratory in Amsterdam. He believed that this boy had a personality which resembled markedly the infant Mozart. Erwin was born in Budapest and his family had been connected with music for at least two generations. Both of his parents were musically talented, and their chief interest was centered on the boy in whom they saw a future maestro musician. Before Erwin was a year old he seemed to have the ability to imitate songs. In the second year of his life he could correctly reproduce melodies sung to him. Absolute pitch was discovered in his third year, and at the beginning of his fourth year he began to play at the piano "everything that he had heard." He also began to compose original melodies. And when he was five years old he started to have music lessons. At age six he was enrolled in the Budapest Academy of Music. Quite an accomplishment for a six-year-old child. From that point on Professor Revesz personally could observe his development until age twelve.

Revesz did tests of mental development. He used the first set of Binet-Simon test. These were given to the boy when he was seven. The tests included vocabulary, counting, digit memory, drawing of a rhombus and object and pattern recognition. Revesz reports that Erwin "did more than was to be expected from the average eight-year-old child," and also answered correctly

Peter F. Ostwald

all tests in a series for nine-year-old children and many in a series for older children.

Revesz concluded that Erwin's general mental development was at least three years in advance of his age. Unfortunately Revesz was not able to do a follow up study of this musical genius because as it turned out, Erwin Nyiregyhazi did not become a successful musician nor did he become world famous as one might have expected. He did give a Town Hall recital that was well received, but thereafter his career went steadily downhill. For many years he did not perform at all, and none of his compositions (and he wrote over 700, very much like his countryman Franz Lizst) are known or played today. The man lived in obscurity in a single room in a Los Angeles slum and he didn't even have a piano. Only when he was seventy years old was this musical genius rediscovered and invited to make a few recordings, which display his astonishing virtuosity. They are available on Columbia Records.

Why did Erwin *not* make it into the pantheon of musical greatness, along with Schumann, Mozart, Liszt and other men of genius? Some have blamed Nyiregyhazi's predilection for alcohol. Others attribute it to his marital problems. He had ten wives — possibly a world's record for a musician. His life suggests that musical intelligence may be a form of special intelligence which is not necessarily related to general or practical intelligence. The problem is that measures of musical intelligence were developed within the same theoretical framework as measures of general intelligence. They share similar strengths and weaknesses. For instance the Stanford Binet tests that were applied to Nyiregyhazi were originally developed as a quantified system to select those children who would be assigned to special classes because they were intellectually incapable of benefiting from regular instruction. This is hardly a good way to select a gifted child. Considerable effort was made to construct a measure with acceptable reliability and validity which would define normal intelligence according to what normal children do at different ages.

This approach to the measurement and definition of intelligence has received considerable criticism. For example, one should be aware that the use of a mental age, or an IQ, or any measure referring to a mean and standard deviation, is a kind of average in which success on each test item in a battery can substitute for success on any one of the others. These metrics imply a constant level of intellectual development across ages and they obscure what we know about the structural and the hierarchical nature of the developing abilities of each individual child. In addition, such scores do not adequately reflect the importance of the integration of various abilities that truly reflect intelligence. (For those of you who want to go more deeply into this question, I'd strongly recommend Howard Gardner's excellent book, *Frames of Mind*, which deals centrally with the issue of specialized versus general intelligence.)

I want to say something at this point about the work of Jean Piaget, which is relevant to the psychology and the testing of musical ability. Piaget emphasized the importance of play in emotional as well as intellectual development. In his theory, the sensorimotor period which lasts from birth until about 24 months is described as the child's active exploration environment. Through what Piaget terms the circular reactions, exploratory behavior of the environment results in consistent information being produced and in the development of coordinated abilities such as visual-motor and auditory-visual integrations. A major shift occurs in information processing with the development of memory and representational thought. Piaget felt that this cognitive development at about age two marked the beginning of what he called pre-operational thought, which is dominant until ages seven or eight. From a musical perspective it would be important for a child to have pleasurable and reliable experiences with sensitive musicians and music teachers at this stage of development. Musical ability appears to be related to the capacity for the pre-operational child to establish stable concepts of melody, rhythm, harmony and form, for which education is essential, particularly in establishing what the Piagetians have called the laws of conservation regarding musical elements. (In our paper we discuss the laws of conservation that have been worked out by Pflederer, who works along Piagetian lines, as well as the very important new work on cognitive psychology of music which John Sloboda has published in his splendid book, *The Musical Mind*.

No discussion of emotional development in childhood could proceed without a tribute to ethnomusicology. Clearly, we must all be aware of the enormous importance of culture as it dictates not only the sorts of musical instruments children learn to play and the styles of music that they enjoy, but also the attitudes which are adopted toward music as a form of work, leading toward professional careers versus music as something simply to play and enjoy as an avocation. I shouldn't say "simply," because I believe that musical play is a very important part of musical development. But a child growing up in a Balinese village, for example, and exposed to the daily activities of Hindu ceremony with gongs and chimes and gamelan orchestras, and dances is surely going to have perceptions and cognitive development that differ from those of children raised in a metropolis like London or a college town like Berkeley.

As a psychiatrist and a musician, I was deeply impressed with the results presented in Lomax's book, *Folk Songs, Style and Culture*. Alan Lomax and his associates studied folk songs from many different cultures around the world to analyze their structure in terms of text, and the vocalization patterns and musical patterns, and at the same time to study in quite some detail the patterns of child rearing and social processes within each of these cultures. It fascinated me to find that there was a strong positive correlation between the amount of stress that children are exposed to and the tonal range of songs that are heard in songs in their communities. In a society where babies are circumcised, or innoculated, or subjected to ritual scarification before two years of age, for instance, the tonal range of songs was found to be significantly greater than in societies where such stresses do not take place or are delayed until after age two. Lomax also demonstrated that voice qualities used in singing may be related to patterns of child rearing in different cultures. For instance, in those cultures where children are encouraged to be highly self assertive, one hears more of vocal "rasp," especially among boys. In cultures where sexual behavior is markedly inhibited, singing tends to be more nasal and narrower in range. Surely, findings of this kind point the way to a better understanding of the musical and emotional development of young children in specific cultures.

We must remember that ethnomusicological data reflect mass effects. These may be of limited value in accounting for individual differences that are so striking when we observe particular children, especially highly musically gifted children. In order to study and appreciate these individuals, and to know more about the child with his or her special inclinations or disinclinations toward music, we really need a case orientation, psychobiography, and related clinical work.

Clinical Approaches

Psychoanalysis, as you know, originated in turn-of-the-century Vienna, which had been a musical capital and home of Schubert, Brahms, and other major musical figures. Sigmund Freud himself often mentioned that he was not particularly sensitive to music, but if you go into his writings you find at least forty times that he referred to music. It seems clear that he and his early disciples discussed music frequently and even treated some of the leading musicians of Vienna, including Gustav Mahler, Bruno Walter and Alban Berg.

To understand psychoanalysis it is necessary to realize that this has been and continues to be a conflict theory of the mind, in which competing forces struggle for recognition, where behavior is expedited or inhibited according to how conflict is handled. The unconscious, for example, may contain libidinal and aggressive tendencies that are unacceptable to consciousness. Tension, anxiety and other unpleasant affects result from unresolved conflicts which seek resolution through dream symbolism symptoms and special forms of behavior.

One of the first efforts to explain psychoanalytically how music may keep the mind in harmony was by Heinz Kohut in 1951. He indicated that music provides excitement and relief of tension, and pointed out that this satisfies what psychoanalysts at that time called the *id*, which is that part of the mind dealing with the basic biological drives for aggression and survival. Kohut also pointed out that the acquisition of skills needed to appreciate and to perform music is very satisfying to the *ego*, which is a Freudian term for cognition, reality testing and the other social skills. Finally, through associated cultural and aesthetic values, it gratifies what the Freudians call the *super-ego*, that part of the mind which represents the sources of conscience.

Psychoanalysis has always had a strong developmental perspective, which became particularly prominent through the work of Anna Freud, whose research focused on the emotional development of children. Richard Sterba, who together with his wife wrote a very interesting book called *Beethoven and his Nephew,* pointed out that "the gratification which music provides is based on a deep regression to the earliest states of extra-uterine mental development." According to Sterba, "music reaches back to a period of development before the establishment of ego boundaries and the separation of inside and outside world." But, paradoxically, the regressive and narcissistic pleasure of music, "organized by the highest synthetic functions of the ego," is a "safeguard" against regression. This combination of and interaction between deepest regression and highly developed organization makes music a unique experience. It creates the inner illusion of ego-world identity, which brings the cosmos under the domination of the self.

Another important contribution to our understanding of music in childhood, and the development of emotions has been by Pinchas Noy, a psychoanalyst working in Jerusalem who has very critically evaluated the entire body of literature about the psychodynamics of music. (For those of you interested in that, I refer you to a number of issues of the *Journal of Music Therapy* that carry these studies.) Pinchas Noy believed that there are auditory hypersensitivities at birth or shortly thereafter which allow some children to respond more readily to the musical properties of the mother's voice, such as changes in loudness, rhythm and timbre. At the same time, the child may be overly sensitive to intrusive noises from other sources, and gradual mastery of the auditory perceptual field will involve focusing on desirable sounds, while undesirable ones are screened out. This process presumably initiates a special interest in music.

Noy insists, and I tend to agree with him, that when we study musical behavior it is important to make a fundamental distinction between:

1. Creative musicians, artistic persons, composers who have the capacity for creating new musical structures and who find original forms of expression in this musical language;

2. the performing artists who know how to articulate the language of music by making its signs audible and intelligible;

3. the listeners who are sensitive enough to hear and understand and enjoy music, but do not become musicians.

Obviously, we know of individuals who are all three of these, but in general, I think this is a good scheme to keep in mind.

Over the years, psychoanalysis has moved closer to what is called an object-relations theory, which has to do with the concern of the way children build up inside their minds various representations of their parents, siblings, teachers and other objects of love and hate. A primary contributor to this line of investigation has been Donald Winnicott, a psychoanalyst who had been a pediatrician. When he worked with mothers and children, Winnicott observed very carefully how babies are able to reduce the anxiety they experience due to separation from the mother or from other caretakers. Often Winnicott observed how babies will hang on to some physical objects from the customary nursery environment, something that the baby can actually touch, see, feel or smell. When the baby begins to do that and to incorporate this experience into his mind, Winnicott called it the "transitional object" experience. He gave examples of transitional objects such as pillows and blankets, toys, dolls, even just a piece of fluff or material from the crib. You know of the famous security blanket of Linus in the cartoon *Peanuts*, which is a wonderful example of transitional object use. These transitional objects seem to bridge the gap of separation between mother and child.

Music, I think we will all agree, is a very physical thing. Not only is it sound, which vibrates and can be felt, but also musical instruments can be seen and touched and smelled. (I was polishing my violin the other day and I noticed what a wonderful smell it had.) So I think music and musical things are very much capable of being used in this transitional way. We can observe the fragments of sound, or humming and tunes that babies make while falling asleep. And often, as McDonald observed in a wonderful paper about transitional tunes, these transitional bits of music are taken from what the mother or the father or some other loving person in the environment has given to the child. These tunes become the child's first musical possessions, paving the way for further attachments to people and things in the environment.

Many children outgrow the need for transitional objects by developing internal psychological resources, like fantasies and thought. Here the transitional object and the security that it represents can remain in the mind symbolically when it is no longer present in actual reality. For these children, music may suffice just as something to listen to or to imagine, but at times children, in order to feel comfortable, must be actively humming tunes or whistling melodies or beating out rhythms. In these cases, simply listening to or imagining music isn't enough; they want to have a physical experience in the body. And finally we come to that extraordinary phenomenon, the child for whom music becomes the most fascinating and exciting thing in the world, who needs music, the sounds, the musical instrument and the continuity of the musical experience as a matter of life or death, much as an infant needs a mother.

Let me quote a few successful musicians looking back and describing the vivid animating experience that music had in their early childhood.

> **A cellist**: "I stood for hours at the piano when I was three or four. Each note had a character of its own, and playing combinations of sounds I found that some tones would fight with each other while others were peaceful."

> **A pianist**: "Whenever I listen to Clara Haskil's recordings, they create an immediate thrill. Her playing has such a caressing quality. I remembered my mother and how comfortable I felt when she would hold me."

Peter F. Ostwald

A composer: "I grew up in a chaotic household. The only security I knew was playing the piano. It was a Rock of Gibralter."

An orchestra musician: "My father died when I was very young. I loved him. And I love the trombone, which I inherited from him."

An oboe player: "The sound of my instrument is like a voice and I think of my older sister who sang beautiful lullabies and made me feel so good."

The latest trend in psychoanalysis has to do with aspects of the self. Here I would like to draw your attention to an important contribution by Daniel Stern, whose book, *The Interpersonal World of the Infant*, I find particularly useful in understanding the development of musical emotions and cognitions of early childhood. Stern delineates four cumulative self-developments between birth and three years of age. The first stage of self-development, beginning at birth, is called the "emergent self," during which the child establishes its basic perceptual and motor organization. There is yet no clear differentiation between the inner and the outer world; perception is "amodal" in the sense that information from one sensory modality is easily translated into another modality. For example, sound may be seen visually or felt motorically, in addition to being heard acoustically. Feelings, too, are global and undifferentiated in this phase. Stern talks about a powerful "vitality" affect which is felt as rushing or waves of emotion, very much akin to the oceanic feelings experienced later on during trance states, orgasm, or intense esthetic pleasure.

The second stage of self-development that Stern describes is from 3 to 8 months. Here the child establishes a sense of the "core self," the feeling that he or she is a separate physical entity with a will and existence apart from other people, specifically the people who previously had been taking care of him or her. It's during this phase of separation and the beginning of individuation that the healthy child, as mentioned earlier, may create a transitional object by filling the gap between himself and his previous caretaker or continuing caretakers. These physical things include such things as pieces of cloth or snatches of songs or tunes, as well as the rhythm and intonation of babbled speech.

The next stage is called the "subjective self." This is the period from 8 to 15 months when children begin to sense how others feel about them, and how they feel about others. The term "attunement" is used here to depict the process whereby the child and his caretaker achieve mutuality and empathy. Stern also speaks about the feeling of "evoked companionships," that can be achieved through memory and fantasy, a feeling of playful togetherness, even when the child is alone. I suspect that the evoked companionships of this early developmental stage are precursors for those moments later on when the musical child is practicing alone or composing music, and has memory fantasies of bygone interactions with certain teachers, other musical children, or audiences that he or she has performed for. Here is also where the dreadful feeling known as stage fright or performance anxiety may arise, because I think it fundamentally relates to fear of strangers which so many children exhibit between 8 and 15 months.

The fourth and very important stage for the understanding of musical development is from 15 months until approximately age three. It is what Stern calls the development of the "symbolic self," a time for the acquisition of language and unspoken rules of non verbal communication which children require for transcending reality. Symbolic behavior enables the child to go beyond real time and space into the imaginary world of dreaming, fantasizing and play-acting. This change, I think, is the underpinning of creativity and art. After age three music can leave the arena of purely personal or narcissistic enjoyment to become socially relevant. Good role models are very essential here in the form of recordings, live concerts, or personal interactions with family members, neighbors, friends or music teachers. This is how we can achieve, and stimulate positive identifications toward music. But a word of caution. The symbolic self is like a double-edged sword. On one side it can cut into the area of outstanding achievement and artistic development. On the other side, the symbolic self can run into delusion-formation and even psychopathology.

Finally it is through the study of *psychobiography*, which is becoming a very interesting field, that we can begin to see the development of extraordinary intelligences and musical ability. We can also observe how musical ability can be coupled with abominable clumsiness and even disability in other spheres of behavior. Take the case of Scriabin whose musical genius as a composer was fostered by his indulgent grandmother and a host of really outstanding music teachers in Russia. Scriabin's life development was maimed by extraordinary eccentricities, grandiosity and promiscuity. Another example is Anton Bruckner, one of the most intelligent musicians of the 19th century, who led an extremely ritualized and asexual life, plagued by morbid preoccupations and suicidal depression. Regrettably, it seems,

Peter F. Ostwald

musical excellence in childhood does not confer immunity against emotional breakdown and disease. My biography of Robert Schumann goes to considerable length in documenting the coexistence of extraordinary musical genius along with a malignant bipolar affective disorder. Clinical work with gifted musicians often shows how much pain and frustration must be endured before the joy of music can be realized by an individual.

In this paper I have given a sort of overture to the drama of music in the lives of children. I've sounded a few of the main themes — the musical brain, the musical genius and the musical environment — which seem necessary for developing a musical child. In the literature of biology, psychology and psychoanalysis, we have the beginning of a new science about music-making. Let's nurture it, so we may discover new ways of promoting and preserving that very precious form of art called music.

Suggested Reading

Arlow, J.A. "Disturbances of the Sense of Time, with Special References to the Experience of Timelessness," *Psychoanalytic Quarterly* 53:13-37, 1984.

Armitage, S., Baldwin, B., Vince, M. "The Fetal Sound Environment of Sheep," *Science* 208: 1173-1176, 1980.

Bergman P., Escalona, S.K. "Unusual Sensitivities in Very Young Children," *Psychoanalytic Study of the Child* 3/4:333-352, 1949.

Bever T.G., Chiarello, R.J. "Cerebral Dominance in Musicians and Non-musicians," *Science*, 185:537-9, 1974.

Binet A., Simon, T. *The Development of Intelligence in Children*, Williams and Wilkins, Baltimore, 1916.

Chungani, H.T., Phelps, M.E. "Maturational Changes in Cerebral Function in Infants Determined by 18FDG Positron Emission Tomography," *Science* 231:840-843, 1986.

Critchley, M. *Aphasiology and Other Aspects of Languages*, Arnold, London, 1970.

Damasio A.R., Damasio, H. "Musical Faculty and Cerebral Dominance," In *Music and the Brain — Studies in the Neurology of Music*, M. Critchley, and R.A.Henson (eds.), Heinemann, London, pp. 141-155, 1977.

DeCaspar A., Fifer, W. "Of Human Bonding: Newborns Prefer Their Mother's Voices," *Science* 208:1174-1176, 1980.

Elkind, D. "Children's Discovery of the Conservation of Mass, Weight and Volume: Piaget Replication, Study II," *The Journal of Genetic Psychology* 98: 219-227, 1961.

Freud, S. *Collected Papers*, Hogarth Press, London, 4:257, 1948.

Gardner, H. *Frames of Mind — The Theory of Multiple Intelligences*, Basic Books, New York, pp. 99-127, 1983.

Gutman, R.W. *Richard Wagner: The Man, His Mind, and His Music*, (For an historical depiction of these debates and the major protagonists) Harcourt, Brace and World, New York, 1968.

Guttman, S., Jones, R.L., Parrish, S.M. *The Concordance to the Standard Edition of the Complete Psychological Work of Sigmund Freud*, Hall, Boston, 4:306-307, 1980.

Hunt, J. McV. "The Utility of Ordinal Scales Inspired by Piaget's Observations," *Merrill-Palmer Quarterly* 22:1, 31-47, 1976.

Jones, R.L. "Development of the Child's Conception of Meter," *Journal of Research in Music Education* 24:142-154, 1976.

Kaufman, A.S., Kaufman, N.L. *Kaufman Assessment Battery for Children*, American Guidance Service, Circle Pines, Minnesota, 1983.

Kohut, H. "The Psychological Significance of Musical Activity," *Music Therapy*, no pagination, 1951.

Lange-Eichbaum, W. *Genie, Irrsinn und Ruhm: Eine Pathographie des Genies*, W. Kurth, (ed.), Reinhardt, Munich, 1961.

Larsen, R.L. "Levels of Conceptual Development in Melodic Permutation Concepts Based on Piaget's Theory," *Journal of Research in Music Education* 21:256-263, 1973.

McCandless, B.R. *Children: Behavior and Development* (Second Edition), Holt, Rinehart and Winston, New York, Chapter 7, 1967.

McDonald, M. "Transitional Tunes and Musical Development," *Psychoanalytic Study of the Child* 25:503-520, 1970.

Meyer, A. "The Search for a Morphological Substrate in the Brains of Eminent Persons including Musicians: A Historical Overview," In *Music and the Brain — Studies in the Neurology of Music,* M.Critchley and R.A. Henson (eds.), Heinemann, London, pp. 255-281, 1971.

Meyer, L.B. *Emotion and Meaning in Music,* University of Chicago Press, Chicago, 1956.

Milner, B. "Laterality Effects in Audition," In *Interhemispheric Relations and Cerebral Dominance,* V.B. Mountcastle (ed.), Johns Hopkins Press, Baltimore, p. 177, 1962.

Murray, F.B. *The Impact of Piagetian Theory,* University Park Press, Baltimore, 1979.

Norton, J.L. "The Relationship of Music Ability and Intelligence to Auditory and Visual Conservation in Kindergarten Children," *Journal of Research in Music Education* 1:3-13, 1979.

Noy, P. "The Psychodynamic Meaning of Music," *Journal of Music Therapy* 3:126-134, 1966; 4:7-23, 45-51, 81-94, 117-125, 1967.

Noy, P. "The Development of Musical Ability," *Psychoanalytic Study of the Child* 23:332-347, 1968.

Oremland, J. "An Unexpected Result of the Analysis of a Talented Musician," *Psychoanalytic Study of the Child* 30:375-408, 1975.

Ostwald, P.F. "Musical Behavior in Early Childhood," *Developmental Medicine and Child Neurology,* 15:367-375, 1973.

Ostwald, P.F. *Schumann — The Inner Voices of a Musical Genius,* Northeastern University Press, Boston, 1985.

Pflederer, M. "The Response of Children to Musical Tasks Embodying Piaget's Principles of Conservation," *Journal of Research in Music Education* 12:251-267, 1964.

Piaget, J. *The Origins of Intelligence in Children,* International Universities Press, New York, 1952.

Pollock, G. "Psychoanalysis of the Creative Artist: Gustav Mahler," Fifth Regional Conference Report, Chicago Psychoanalytic Society, 82-156, 1976.

Revesz, G. *The Psychology of a Musical Prodigy*, Harcourt, Brace and Co., New York, 1925.

Rider, M.S. "The Relationship Between Auditory and Visual Perception on Tasks Employing Piaget's Concept of Conservation," *Journal of Music Therapy* 14:126-138, 1977.

Rider, M.S. "The Assessment of Cognitive Functioning Level Through Musical Perception," *Journal of Music Therapy* 3:110-119, 1981.

Roehmann, F., Wilson, F. (eds) *The Biology of Music Making*, Conference Proceedings, 1984, MMB Music, Inc., St. Louis, 1988.

Schiller, F. "A Mobius Strip — Fin-de-Siecle Neuropsychiatry and Paul Mobius," University of California, Berkeley, 1982.

Schwartz, D.W. "Rossini: A Psychoanalytic Approach to 'the great renunciation,' " *Journal of the American Psychoanalytic Association* 13:551-569, 1965.

Seashore, C.E. *Psychology of Music,* Dover Publication, New York, 1967.

Sloboda, J.A. *The Musical Mind: The Cognitive Psychology of Music,* Clarendon Press, Oxford, 1985.

Solomon, M. *Beethoven,* Schirmers Books, New York, 1978.

Stern, D.S. *The Interpersonal World of the Infant*, Basic Books, New York, 34, 1985

Sterba, R. "Psychoanalysis and Music," *American Image* 22:96-111, 1965.

Terman L.M., Merrill, M.A. *Stanford-Binet Intelligence Scale*, Houghton Mifflin, Boston, 1973.

Uzgiris I.C., Hunt, J. McV. *Assessment in Infancy: Ordinal Scale of Psychological Development,* University of Illinois Press, Urbana, 1975.

Wechsler, D. *Manual for the Weschsler Intelligence Scale for Children — Revised (WISC-R)*, The Psychological Corporation, New York, 1974.

Weissman, P. "Early Development and Endowment of the Artistic Director," *Journal of the American Psychoanalytic Association* 12: 59-79, 1964.

Werthem, N. "Is there an Anatomical Localization for Musical Faculties?" in *Music and the Brain — Studies in the Neurology of Music*, M. Critchley and R.A. Henson (eds.), Heinemann, London, pp. 282-297, 1977.

Wing, H.D. "A Factorial Study of Musical Tests," *British Journal of Psychology* 31:341-355, 1941.

Winnicott, D.W. "Transitional Objects and Transitional Phenomena," *International Journal of Psychoanalysis* 34:89-97, 1953.

Wittenberg, R. "Aspects of the Creative Process in Music: A Case Report," *Journal of the American Psychoanalytic Association* 28:439-459, 1980.

Zatorre, R. J. "Musical Perception and Cerebral Function," paper given at the Fourth Annual Symposium on Medical Problems of Musicians and Dancers, Aspen, Colorado, July 31-August 3, 1986.

Music as a Language

John A. Sloboda
Department of Psychology, University of Keele
Newcastle, Staffordshire, England

Introduction

I guess that all of us are here because, in one way or another, we love music. It is that love which has led us to become teachers, performers, researchers, concerned to deepen our awareness and effectiveness in ensuring that music and musicians are held in high esteem by society and given society's best resources.

But as well as bringing love with us, most of us also probably carry a deep puzzlement; despite our deep familiarity with it, music still remains at many levels a mystery to us. We don't really understand what music is, how it comes to have such a profound effect on us, why it moves us, fascinates us, brings us back to it again and again.

To many of us, the mystery is part of the love. As in any love affair, it is the sense of never ending discovery which gives impetus to the love. Once we feel that we have found everything out about the other, the love dries up. It is, I am sure, for this sort of reason that many of us have a deep aversion to the scientific analysis of music. It seems that if we could reduce music to a set of explicit categories or formulae, if we could derive an all embracing theory, then music would lose its mystery and power.

I very much respect this intuitive aversion. I think scientists labour under a constant temptation to replace what they are studying with theories about what they are studying, and then talk about their theories as if they were the total reality of the situation. To overcome this tendency to narrow the sights, I believe that every scientist who studies music has a duty to keep his or her love of music alive, and be constantly aware of what escapes the net of particular theories.

On the other hand, I believe that science has much to offer musicians. One thing that it does is attempt to make theoretical assumptions explicit, and thus open to discussion and test. Everybody, whether scientist or not, is operating on theories and assumptions. Whatever else scientists may or may not do, they can offer people new ways of looking at old issues. And sometimes these new ways are more profitable. They can also offer hard data to replace speculations.

Let me give one example of what I mean. Recently I attended a conference on what in Britain we call "ear training" or "aural training." There was a lot of talk among the teachers there about "developing a good ear" for music, and some rather sterile controversy about whether some people had better ears than others. As a psychological scientist, I was able to remind them that the ear as such is not the problem. Most people's ears function excellently, and there is nothing anyone can do to enhance their functioning. Everyone's ear is constantly sending to the brain highly sophisticated, fine grain information about all sounds received. It is what the brain does with it that determines musical differences between people.

As a result of a large amount of experimentation and theorising in cognitive psychology, we are now able to say rather precisely what needs to happen to produce the behaviour that musicians would associate with "a good ear." First, the relevant dimensions of the sound have to be *attended* to, then the listener requires some method of *coding* or *categorising* the individual sounds. Thirdly, the listener must be able to hold the various sounds together in some *structure* or *pattern*. Finally, the listener must be able to translate what has been received into some form of *response*. Many unfortunate people have been labeled "tone deaf" because they can't sing in tune. The analysis just outlined shows that the problem could be entirely one of response; the other stages may have been completed perfectly.

I believe that the four stage theory of musical awareness is more useful to practitioners than an unarticulated theory about "the ear." It allows us to ask at what stage a problem might be occurring, and it gives us better ideas about what we might do to overcome the difficulty. All these stages are known to be susceptible to profound alteration through learning and experience. The theory does not solve all a practitioner's problems. The business of teaching and learning is still largely an art; but I contend that the availability of such ways of thinking will enhance a practitioner's functioning, by providing better and more varied tools to tackle particular problems.

It is in the same spirit that I offer some observations on music as a language. I do not claim that thinking of music as a language is a completely satisfactory way of accounting for everything about it. Indeed, some of the most important things about music seem to arise from the ways it is different from a language. But it offers a way of thinking about music which is, I believe, useful and illuminating.

Like music, the primary medium of language is sound. We can capture and measure the various physical dimensions of speech sounds through the many sophisticated measuring instruments we have. In themselves, however, these sounds are just sounds, with various physical characteristics such as pitch, amplitude, and timbre. They are not language. What makes them language is what human brains do with them. And it seems that what human brains do is to attempt to map these sounds onto internal structures. When some kind of match has been made with these structures, then language can be said to have come into existence. These internal structures seem to be divided into these types: *phonological, syntactic,* and *semantic.* Generally, some contact has to be made at each level for speech to be understood or created.

Phonology

Phonology describes the way in which the brain parcels up continuously varying sounds into discrete and separable units. These units constitute the basic building blocks of a language. It seems clear from studies on language that phonology is learned. Different cultures place phonological boundaries in particular places. What are taken as two separate speech sounds by users of one language are heard as the same by users of another.

There are some dramatic scientific demonstrations of the way that phonological mechanisms transform the raw sound. One of these is the phenomenon of *categorical perception.* We can take two naturally occurring speech sounds, such as "da" and "ba," and artificially synthesise them. We discover that what distinguishes them physically is the frequency of the initial burst of sound When it is high we hear "da"; when it is low we hear "ba." What happens if we synthesise a series of sounds which move from "da" to "ba" through small steps of frequency change? How are they heard? The common sense view would be something like this. The sound definitely starts as "da." Gradually it becomes more and more ambiguous until a point is reached where it sounds like neither, or an amalgam of the two. Then it gradually becomes more and more like "ba."

Experimental evidence (e.g., Liberman, Harris, Kinney, and Lane, 1961) shows that this common sense view is wrong. What actually happens is that we hear a series of apparently indistinguishable "da's," and then, quite suddenly, the perception flips, and the experience is of "ba." Our brains categorise intermediate sounds, and make it very difficult for us to notice

John A. Sloboda

any difference between two sounds falling within the same category. Then, as some internal boundary is crossed, the perception quite suddenly changes, as the sound is assimilated to a new category.

What, then, of music? The best evidence we have (Locke and Kellar, 1973) is that similar categorisation processes go on for most of us. That is, we tend not to perceive every slight change in sound dimensions, but assimilate to broad categories. One example of this is the musical scale. If we take a major triad, and change the third note of the chord in several equal small steps from major to minor, then many people experience an effect analogous to the language experiment. There seems to be a rather sudden shift from major to minor somewhere in the middle of the sequence.

We can find analogous effects in the time domain. If, for instance, we ask people to reproduce rhythmic patterns, there is a tendency for the reproductions to be inexact but categorical. That is, if the ratio of two notes in the original is roughly 2:1 then the reproduction will tend to be roughly 2:1. We have internalised categories which tell us that durations tend to be whole number multiples of one another. We find it hard to hear truly ambiguous rhythms as ambiguous. We try to fit them to one or other definite category.

When comparing to language, we need to make two important caveats. One is that the degree of categorisation tends to depend on musical experience. In most of the published studies "musicians" (however defined) tend to show stronger categorisation effects than "non musicians."

The second caveat is that even when we do categorise, we are still able to be aware of the differences within a category. So, for instance, a musician will be able to say "that $C^{\#}$ is flat." This shows both categorisation (an identification of the note as in the category $C^{\#}$), and the awareness that the note differs from an ideal central pitch. Sometimes we are simply aware that two notes within the same category differ in some way, without being able to consciously identify the difference. So one finds musicians who say "I know that the note is badly pitched, but I can't tell whether it is sharp or flat" (Siegel and Siegel, 1977). The same phenomenon also explains why we are able to find two performances of the same notes different. We judge performance A to be livelier, clearer, more satisfying, than performance B, but cannot precisely identify what it is that makes them different. In general, these differences are due to minute expressive deviations within categories.

Syntax

The second level of structuring in language is syntax. This concerns the ordering of the basic phonological building blocks. In all languages, and in music, it is not enough to notice which sound categories (be they phonemes or notes) are present; their combination and ordering contains the crucial information. Most languages (and many musical styles) seem, at least in principle, describable by a grammar. This is a set of rules which is capable of generating (or recognising) all sequences which are acceptable, and fails to generate (or rejects) sequences which are not acceptable.

There are many types of evidence that people handle language through syntactic structures. One is that it is much easier to remember word sequences that conform to grammatical order than the same sequences that have their order scrambled. This is so, even when the sentences make little or no sense. For instance, it is easier to remember *Colourless green ideas sleep furiously* than *deep green furiously ideas colourless.*

In music, it is easier to remember sequences which conform to conventional rules of tonality than those that don't. This is increasingly so as one becomes more experienced with a particular musical culture. For instance, there are studies which suggest that the memory advantage for tonal sequences does not develop until about age seven in the average child (Zenatti, 1969).

In my own research (Sloboda, 1985) I have been interested in the growing ability of children to reject what we would judge to be illegal musical sequences. At age five, most children I tested seemed unable or unwilling to reject gross chordal dissonance as wrong. By the age of nine, they were overtly laughing or screwing up their faces at the "wrong" chords, and scoring at an adult level. In another test, each chord was tonally coherent in itself, but the ordering of the chords could be either tonally conventional (e.g., ending with a cadence) or scrambled (e.g., ending without resolution). On this test children did not achieve adult levels of performance until the age of 11. I was particularly interested to find that these abilities seemed to develop regardless of formal music tuition. Children who had regular lessons did not develop these abilities earlier than other children. It seems that mere exposure to the standard musical culture is enough for children to build grammatical structures.

John A. Sloboda

Semantics

I take semantics to be the systematic set of processes whereby the symbols of a language are able to be mapped onto, or represent, objects, states of affairs, and events that are not part of that language. To be a full language user it is not enough to recognise a sequence as grammatical; one has to understand it. This means at least two things: identifying what the individual words refer to, and identifying what kind of event or proposition is being described.

I see semantics as the driving force behind language acquisition. Children don't learn the meaning of their first words until they are already familiar with the objects and states that the words represent. Similarly they cannot learn to express relationships between objects (such as wants, movements) until they know and experience such relationships. Their map of the world and their understanding of it undoubtedly develops as a result of becoming language users, but the whole process would never start unless they first had something there before language.

There was once a belief, generated through some of Chomsky's ideas, that children might have a "language acquisition device" which would build up competence through mere exposure to language. Most experts would now reject this idea, emphasising instead the necessity of a child's embeddedness in the social and physical worlds as the major stimulus to language development.

The study of semantic aspects of language development has proved rather fruitful. This is because it is relatively easy to determine a child's understanding through practical behaviour. We know that the child understands the concept "under" if she is able to carry out the request to "put the green block under the red one." We all know the domain (or one important domain) onto which language has to be mapped. It is the public world of social and physical action that we all inhabit.

When we come to music, we have a difficulty. I think we would find it very difficult to agree on a set of criteria for demonstrating that a person had "understood" some music. The domain, if there is one, onto which music maps is not wholly (and some may argue not even partly) public. Although there is general agreement that it has in some way to do with emotion, feeling, or affect, there are scant hard data to constrain our theorising.

What little research has been done has tended to focus on the ability of listeners to verbally identify the general character of different pieces of music. Hevner's (1936) pioneering work still stands as the major contribution in this area. She showed that within our culture, adults tend to generally agree which adjectives best describe the character of a musical excerpt, that is, whether it is happy or sad, lively or solemn, restful or agitated. Gardner (1973) has more recently shown that this ability develops slowly through childhood and into adolescence.

The ability to describe and talk about music is clearly an important aspect of the awareness of musical meaning, but it is not primary. Anyone who has had any significant musical experience will know that the words to describe it are not always at hand. This will be particularly so for children. We should not take what children *say* about music to fully reflect their experience of it.

Another thing which limits many studies is their mode of data collection. Subjects are played several brief extracts in an experimental context. In contrast, real musical experiences are embedded in rich social and personal context. If we wish to understand more about how musical meanings are acquired, we need to turn to the everyday real-life acts of musical involvement that make up a child's musical life.

With substantial resources, I guess one would want to observe directly many children over many years. With fewer resources, I have had to adopt a different approach, but one which is nonetheless turning out be be rich and promising.

The Autobiographical Memory Study

I have been asking people to write down the details of any autobiographical memories they could access which involved music in any way, from the first 10 years of their life. To date I have collected 113 usable memories from about 70 adults, ranging from professional musicians to people with little or no current involvement in music.

Despite the apparent indirectness of this approach, it allows us to answer questions not addressed by earlier research. First, we get the responses of people to the naturally occurring musical events of their lives, rather than to contrived experimental situations where a response is forced. Secondly, we can get some indication of the effect of such events on subsequent musical development. Thirdly, adults often have the words to describe, in retrospect, an experience that as a child he or she would have been inarticulate about.

It seems to me that for there to be any kind of consensus in a culture about musical meaning there would have to be fairly general kinds of experiences with music shared by large numbers of children in a culture. Furthermore, these experiences should be expected to generate regularly the same kinds of affective responses. I would not, for example, expect crucial experiences to occur very often within formal musical training. Such training is only given to a minority of children and could not account for wider cultural patterns.

I am aware of two great shortcomings of my study. One is that few people are able to access specific memories before the age of three or four. If the crucial experiences occurred in the first three years of life then my study will not capture them. The second shortcoming is that memory is selective, biased and inaccurate. I cannot guarantee that this sample of memories would necessarily give the same picture as a sample of observations on the subjects of children.

It is however, possible to argue that a memory study actually highlights the kind of event we are looking for. This is because memory for specific events very often seems linked to a high emotional tone. For instance, almost everyone of an appropriate age remembers exactly what they were doing when they heard the news of John F. Kennedy's death. If the meaning of music is connected to affect, then specific memories related to the acquisition of this meaning should be high in affect, so more likely to be remembered. Memory should act as a sort of filter or concentrator.

Although my volunteers were asked to write freely, I offered them 10 questions as cues:

1. How old were you?
2. Where did the experience take place?
3. Of what event did the music form a part?
4. Who were you with?
5. Can you identify the piece of music, or say anything about it.
6. If you can identify it, have you experienced it recently, and do you know it well?
7. What significance or meaning did the experience have for you at the time?

8. Did the experience influence your subsequent behaviour or attitudes in any way?
9. How often, if at all, does this memory come to you?
10. Any other comment.

After subjects had finished the recall task, they were asked to provide information on:

1. Current level of involvement with music.
2. Amount of formal music tuition received prior to the age of ten.
3. The degree to which experiences such as that reported determined current level of involvement with music.
4. The number of other memories available which were not written down.

On examination of the results, a coding scheme was devised so that quantitative statistical analysis could be carried out. It very quickly became clear that events could have two distinct types of significance. Firstly, the music itself could have some effect on the person. This I have called the *internal* significance of the event. Secondly, the context in which the music was taking place could have some effect. This I have called the *external* significance.

In the initial classification, I coded each memory on each of these two dimensions according to whether the significance was positive, neutral, or negative. Table 1 shows the frequency breakdown for all combinations of internal and external significance. Several points are of interest. First, there are almost no cases of negative internal significance. People rarely remembered events where the music itself was disliked or aroused negative affect. This is not simply a reluctance to recall negative experiences or some form of repression, since plenty of memories with negative external significance were recalled.

Secondly, the number of events having neutral classification on both dimensions was rather small (17% of the total). Thirdly, there are almost no cases of positive internal significance where the external significance is negative. One way of interpreting this is to say that you can't enjoy the music when you are not enjoying the circumstances in which it takes place.

John A. Sloboda

Table I

RATED SIGNIFICANCE OF 113 MEMORIES

INTERNAL   **EXTERNAL**

	Positive	Neutral	Negative
Positive	16	25	3
Neutral	25	19	24
Negative	0	1	0

I would like to give a few examples of specific memories illustrating the main categories of response. Here is one which shows positive internal significance but neutral external significance.

> *Subject 42: age twenty; regular private performer; tuition from seven.*

> "I was seven years old, and sitting in morning assembly in school. The music formed part of the assembly service. I was with my friends Karen, Amelia, Jenny, Allan. The music was a clarinet duet, classical, probably by Mozart. I was astounded at the beauty of the sound. It was liquid, resonant, vibrant. It seemed to send tingles through me. I felt as if it were a significant moment. Listening to this music led to me learning to play first the recorder and then to achieve my ambition of playing the clarinet. Playing the clarinet has altered my life; going on a paper round and saving up to buy my own clarinet; meeting friends in the county band...Whenever I hear clarinets being played I remember the impact of this first experience."

I would like to give one further example in this category to make a specific point:

> *Subject 49: age nineteen; regular private performer; tuition from six.*

> "I was about ten years old, at school with the teacher and the other kids. The music was a very sad song about the loneliness of the people which we learned in a music lesson. The music

made me very sad. I haven't heard it recently and don't know it well. I loved this piece so much that I bought some music instruments and played them every night. I used to think of this song very often, but then I forgot it almost totally until this experiment."

What this memory shows is that sadness in music can be a positive and sought-after experience, even for children. The next example shows positive external significance, but neutral internal significance.

Subject 23: age twenty; occasional private performer; tuition from seventeen.

"I was about ten years old. I was singing in the school choir for the school carol concert. We were in the school hall. The carols were some more unusual ones. I can't remember them now. I remember being pleased at missing history lessons, and also because it was a really cheerful occasion. This memory returns occasionally, but I don't think the event had any particular influence on me."

The final example shows negative external significance with neutral internal significance. It is sadly by no means unique in this set of memories.

Subject 31: age fifty; occasional listener; tuition from seven.

"I was five years old. I was at the local Infant School, and a music lesson was being taken by the Infant Head Teacher, Miss Linkler. She played a piece of music. I have no idea what it was called. I don't think I was ever told the name of the piece. The class had to listen to the music, and then beat out the time. Suddenly the teacher pounced on me, screaming that I was beating 3/4 time to a 4/4 piece of music. She then produced a battledore and gave me six smacks on the back of my thighs. At the time I ran home, and my mother had the greatest difficulty in making me go to school after that. As far as the music goes, I have always considered that I am not musical, and for many years I refused to sing or do anything connected with music..."

Since most volunteers provided a wealth of information about the social context of their memories, it has been possible to isolate factors which are associated with positive internal significance. The most significant of these are:

Place: When in a concert hall, church or at home, over 60% of the memories had positive significance, as opposed to only 29% of events at school.

Event: 59% of events where the subject was listening to music were positively significant but only 17% of events where the subject was performing were positively significant.

With: When with family and friends, 50% of memories were positive; when with teachers only 27% were positive.

All this suggests that the occasions when significant meaning was transmitted were mainly informal, relaxed occasions when the person was not being evaluated, and was in the company of loved ones. A stepwise discriminant analysis revealed that the *event* was the only one of these variables to enter into the discriminant function. This suggests that listening is the crucial factor. It just so happens in our culture that opportunities to listen to music are provided more often away from school and teachers.

Positive internal significance is also predictive of indices relating to subsequent behaviour:

Status: 53% of people currently claiming to be regular performers of music produced a memory of positive internal significance; whereas only 26% of those not regularly performing did so.

Influence: Positive memories were recalled by 68% of those who claimed that the memory had an enhancing influence on their subsequent musical involvement. Such memories were only recalled by 14% of those who claimed a neutral or negative subsequent effect.

It seems, therefore, that children experiencing events with positive internal significance were more likely to pursue a high level of involvement with music in later life. Interestingly, this was not true of external significance. Positive external significance did not go with a higher level of subsequent involvement in music. People will not pursue musical activity just because they have experienced positive events around music. The positive experience has to come from the music itself.

Finally, it turns out that the amount of formal music tuition received before the age of ten relates weakly to experience of positive internal significance.

If, however, we compare the age of the positive experience to the age of starting lessons, we find that the experience often precedes the start of lessons. Of the 36 events for which full information was available, only 9 (25%) occurred after the beginning of formal music tuition. It looks as though such experiences are spurs to a child seeking lessons, rather than the lessons providing a basis for such experiences.

On the sample I have so far it is hard to conclude a great deal about specific types of music eliciting these experiences. Sometimes people could not name the piece in question, and when they did, they covered a vast range of classical, folk, and popular pieces. The one thing which has emerged so far is that memories of nursery rhymes, hymns, and carols (of which there were a significant number) almost never carried positive internal significance. My explanation for this is that it seemed to be usually the *first* experience of a piece which led to the most profound effects. Many of the rhymes and hymns will have been repeated many times in the child's life, and the first experience of them may well have been before the age of concrete memories.

A similar analysis was carried out to see what factors seemed to be responsible for *external* significance. The picture here is simple. Negative significance is most often associated with performing situations (56% of cases), almost never with listening (4% of cases). It often occurs in a formal educational setting with teacher and/or other children present and almost never with parents or friends. Experiences with positive significance are spread roughly across all categories of occurrence.

The main negative experiences are of nervousness, embarrassment, humiliation, and criticism (either feared or actual) associated with the performing situation. These negative events almost invariably (85% of cases) had a negative influence on the subsequent involvement of these subjects with music, inhibiting either performing or listening involvement. These results will not be surprising to anyone familiar with the research literature on motivation, but they do remind us of the immense care that teachers need to take when asking children to perform. They confirm the reports of a recent British study which roundly condemned music competitions for their damaging effects on the development of young talented musicians.

To conclude the brief treatment of these results, I would like to turn back to the data on internal significance and look more closely at the content of these experiences. What kinds of things did respondents say about the musical experiences? I found that people's statements were of two kinds; statements about the *feelings* that the music evoked in them (e.g., "The music made a deep impression on me," and *judgments* about the characteristics of the music itself (e.g., "the music was very lively"). I tabulated such statements according to similarity of meaning , and also according to the age at which the music was experienced. A statistically significant age progression was found on both the feeling and the judgment dimensions.

Adults who reported no particular feeling associated with the music had an average age of 4.8 years at the time of the memory. An *enjoyment* cluster (including words such as *love, like, enjoy, excited, elated, happy*) came from children with an average age of 6.2. Then followed a cluster which I have categorised as *wonder*. (It includes such words as *enthralled, incredulous, astounded, overwhelmed, awe-struck,* etc.) The average age associated with such feelings was 8.1. Finally a small cluster of *sad* feelings (e.g., *melancholy, sad, apprehensive*) was experienced by children with an average age of 8.7 years.

A similar progression was observed in *judgments*, although fewer memories contained judgment elements overall. The average age for events containing no judgment element was 6.7. A cluster of memories used what I have called *emotional neutral* descriptive words (e.g., *fast, loud, simple,* and the anodyne *nice*). The average age of such events was 4.8. The remaining memories all occurred at an average age of around eight years. They were mainly *emotional/sensual* (e.g., beautiful, romantic, liquid, funny) but with a few memories mentioning particular imagery or qualities of the performance itself.

Although the number of memories is as yet rather small for definite conclusions, a suggestive pattern has begun to emerge. At around four years of age, children begin to remember music for its general level of activity (*fast, loud, simple*). Such characteristics are capable of evoking memories of general excitement (*happy, enjoy, elated*) by around six years of age. By the eighth birthday, children are remembering music for its sensual and expressive characteristics (*liquid, funny, beautiful*), and by the age of nine are regularly remembering feelings of wonder or sadness as a result.

It looks as if the memories I have gathered reveal an evolutionary process in the acquisition of musical meaning. Music has meaning at many different levels. Excitement at the activity, movement, and energy of music seems to precede wonder at the sensuous and expressive qualities of music. The age of seven seems to signal the progression to the new awareness. It is useful to look at what other changes in the awareness of music as a language are taking place at this age. Evidence mentioned earlier suggests that the age of seven is when the grasp of tonal syntax becomes particularly apparent. It is at this age that a memory advantage of tonal music emerges, as well as the ability to reject non-tonal chords. I suspect that the syntactic and semantic developments are not unrelated.

This study has been exploratory. It has shown a number of things:

1) The autobiographical memory technique is a rich and workable one.

2) Significant musical experiences are most likely to occur in particular contexts (relaxed, informal listening).

3) Such experiences have long-lasting effects on musical behaviour and involvement.

4) Negative environmental factors generally preclude the possibility of the music itself acquiring positive significance, and can inhibit the level of subsequent involvement with music.

5) Positive environmental factors do not in themselves lead to an increase in involvement with music.

6) The general nature of the experiences does not seem to depend upon the amount of prior formal tuition. Most memories with high internal significance precede formal tuition.

7) Changes occur between the ages of six and eight in the nature of the emotional and judgmental responses to music. They move from responses related to energy and excitement towards ones of wonder and beauty.

We have a long way to go before we can explain precisely what features of music are capable of eliciting these early significant responses, but we now know they are common, deeply influential, and we know something about the situations likely to encourage them. I think this is crucial information for any attempt to build an understanding of musical semantics.

References

Hevner, K. "Experimental studies of the elements of expression in music," *American Journal of Psychology*, 48:246-68, 1936.

Gardner, H. "Children's sensitivity to musical styles," *Merrill-Palmer Quarterly of Behavioural Development*, 19:67-77, 1973.

John A. Sloboda

Liberman, A.M., Harris, K.S., Kinney, J.A. and Lane, H. "The discrimination of the relative onset time of the components of certain speech and non-speech pattern," *Journal of Experimental Psychology*, 61:379-88, 1961.

Locke, S. and Kellar, L. "Categorical perception in a non-linguistic mode," *Cortex*, 9:355-69, 1973.

Siegel, J. and Siegel, V. "Categorical perception of tonal intervals: musicians can't tell sharp from flat," *Perception and Psychophysics*, 21:399-407, 1977.

Sloboda, J.A. *The Musical Mind: The Cognitive Psychology of Music*, Oxford University Press, London, 1985.

Zenatti, A. "Le developement genetique de la perception musicale," *Monographs Francais Psychologique*, 17, 1960.

The Inquiry into Prenatal Musical Experience:

A Report of the Eastman Project 1980-1987

Donald J. Shetler[1]
Professor of Music Education
Eastman School of Music[2]

My interest in the study of prenatal and postnatal response to musical stimuli began as a result of my association with the Japanese musician and educator, Shinichi Suzuki. It was Suzuki who speculated about the possibility that the unborn child was able to respond to recorded violin repertoire. Conversations with him during the research study "Project Super" I directed at the Eastman School of Music from 1966-1970, and subsequent consultation with audiologist Lawrence Dalzell of the University of Rochester Medical School, encouraged me to embark on the investigation of prenatal response to musical stimuli discussed in this paper (Shetler, 1985).

It was after reading Dr. Thomas Verny's book *The Secret Life of the Unborn Child,* (1981) and listening to a graduate student describe the movements her in-utero child was making while she was playing the piano, that I began in earnest to investigate the phenomenon of in-utero sensory response in earnest.

The observation that the prenatal infant responds to external stimuli is not a recent one. In early oriental societies, in China and Japan, a child's age is reckoned to be one year at birth. Sir Thomas Browne, 17th century physician and philosopher wrote:

> "Every man is some months older than he bethinks him, for we
> live, move, have being, and are subject to the elements and the

---

1   Dr. Shetler is now Professor Emeritus.

2   Note: Much of the work on the report of this project was completed during a Bridging Fellowship to Psychology awarded by the University of Rochester in 1986. Thanks to Irving Phillips, Irene Yang, Robin Panneton, Brent Logan, Tom Verny and Richard Aslin for their assistance in obtaining sources.

malices of diseases, in that only world, the truest microcosm, the womb of our mother." (cited in MacFarlane, 1977, p. 5).

Review of research by Sontag (1935), Sontag and Wallace (1935), Sontag and Newberry (1940, Forbes and Forbes (1927), Grimwade (1970), Grimwade, Walker and Wood (1971), Sakabe (1969), Bench (1968), Read and Miller (1977), produced ample evidence that the issue of prenatal auditory response had been an increasingly important area for scientific investigation.

In addition to the studies reported by obstetricians and other medical professionals, questions of in-utero activity, including the fascinating issue of prenatal memory and learning, have been explored by a growing number of psychologists since the 1940's. Most prominent among empirically based reports are those by MacFarlane (1977), Annis (1978), Ferreira (1960), Montagu (1962), Spelt (1948), Salk (1960, 1962, 1966), Liley (1972), Wedenberg (1964, 1970), De Casper and Fifer (1980), Smotherman (1982), Eimas et al. (1980, 1982, 1984), and Panneton (1985).

Among the questions that would interest a music psychologist — or an educational researcher — are those that focus first on the physiology and neuroanatomy of the fetus. Correlated issues that call for investigation are those that deal with the ontogeny of primate auditory and cortical systems as they impinge on memory and learning.

1. Can the fetal infant hear?
2. What does it hear, and how does it respond?
3. Does the prenatal infant respond differently to a variety of stimuli?
4. Is music a feasible stimulus source?
5. Is the fetal cortical response to auditory stimuli measurable?
6. How early in postnatal development does the infant respond to auditory stimulation?
7. Is it possible to detect specific differentiated behavioral response to musical stimuli in the postnatal infant that refer directly to prenatal stimulation with music?
8. To what extent is it possible to track the musical development of the young child in the first twenty-four months?
9. Do the available research findings support a hypothesis that prenatal learning takes place?

10. Do current musical development theories take prenatal
auditory response to music stimuli into consideration?

Following is a brief summary of the research results that bear on the forego-
ing questions. In each case, publication data and significant findings that
relate to the questions are provided.

1. Peiper (1925) reported evidence that the fetus of five weeks responded
with sudden movements to loud sounds originating outside the body of
the mother. Sontag (1969) produced evidence that the fetus was
responsive to a 120 Hz vibratory stimulation and responded by patterned muscular activity and cardioacceleration. The prenatal infant
in the second trimester possesses the physiological structure that permits hearing. (See Figure 1.) The infant differentiates stimuli between
frequencies of 20-12,000 Hz. Best responses reported were to lower
frequencies (200-4,000 Hz).

2. The environment of the fetus resembles the aquatic environment of
sound transmission to the ear. Rubel (1984) reports research by
Saunders and his colleagues indicating that conduction of sound to the
external and middle ear follows principles of vestibular and cutaneous
transmission of audio signals.

3. Cochlear function, basilar response and development of inner and
outer hair cells permitting transmission to the eighth cranial nerve
(the first to fully develop in the fetal brain) is present by the 5th to
7th month. Responsiveness is first to low frequencies and then to
higher frequencies (Rubel, 1984). (See Figure 2.)

4. Animal research indicates imprinting of the maternal heartbeat in all
primates. The human infant "memorizes" the sound along with others
originating in the gastrointestinal system of the mother.

5. In a pioneering study, Spelt (1948) reported conditioning the fetal infant to an external auditory stimulus during the final two months of
gestation. This included extinction, recovery, and retention of the
response as well as significant agreement with records of fetal movement and maternal reports of fetal movement.

6. The imprinting (long-term memory, autonomic SR driven) of the
mother's normal heartbeat, and the implications for normal health of
the fetus, were investigated extensively by Salk (1960, 1962, 1966). He
observed that rhythm in all societies, from the primitive drum beat to
the patterns heard in the symphonies of Mozart and Beethoven, bear
"startling similarity to the rhythm of the human hearts." The perinatal infant responds to the adult heartbeat rhythm with less anxiety

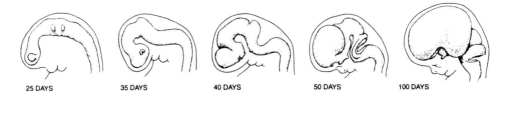

25 DAYS   35 DAYS   40 DAYS   50 DAYS   100 DAYS

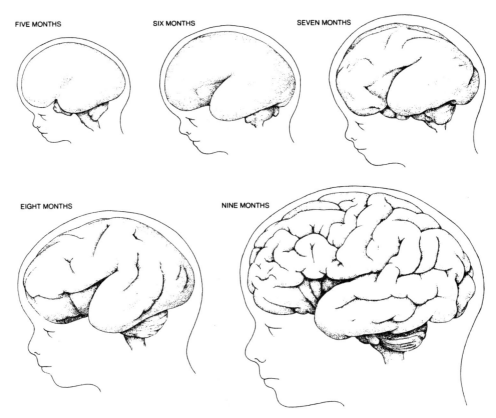

FIVE MONTHS   SIX MONTHS   SEVEN MONTHS

EIGHT MONTHS   NINE MONTHS

Figure 1

The human brain in its development sequence

The human brain shown in its developmental sequence starting at twenty-five
days and progressing through birth. Early in our brain's development, the neural
tube expands to form three prominent structures, the hindbrain, midbrain, and
forebrain. As the cerebral hemispheres develop from the forebrain, the midbrain
unites it with the hindbrain, which develops into the pons and medulla. (Restak,
1984, p. 43)

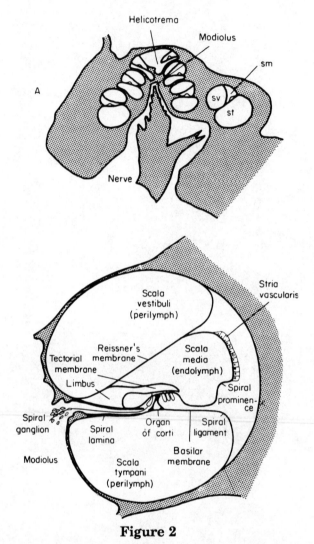

Figure 2

Cochlear structures in the prenatal infant

Cochlear structures involved in perception of musical signals present in the prenatal infant. The eighth cranial nerve is the first to become fully functional. (Pickles, 1982, p. 26)

and more stable sleep habits. Salk suggests in a later study that this phenomenon lends credence to the idea that later learning is enhanced by the imprinted — or learned — response. He further states: "For this reason we must explore further the elements of prenatal sensory

Donald J. Shetler

C

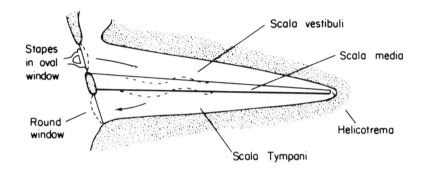

Scala vestibuli

Scala media

Stapes in oval window

Round window

Helicotrema

Scala Tympani

D

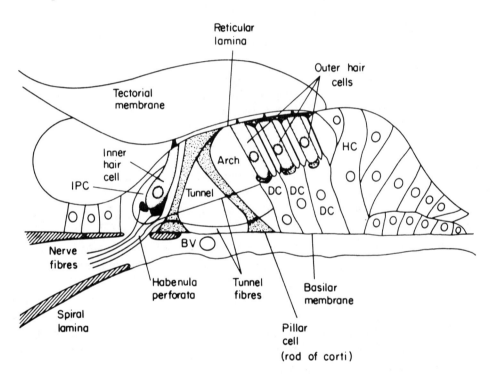

Reticular lamina

Outer hair cells

Tectorial membrane

Inner hair cell

Arch

HC

IPC

Tunnel

DC DC

DC

Nerve fibres

BV

Habenula perforata

Tunnel fibres

Basilar membrane

Spiral lamina

Pillar cell (rod of corti)

Figure 3

C. The path of vibration in the cochlea.

D. A cross section of the organ of Corti as it appears in the the basal turn. (From Pickles, 1982, p.27) experience in the human. Perhaps conditions may alter the sensory and intellectual thresholds, resulting in variations in intellectual capacity or in emotional stability." (Salk, 1966, p. 302, See Figure 3)

7. The early anecdotal reports by mothers that the fetal infant responded to external musical sounds is referred to in a number of articles. A.W. Liley (1972) reports data on FHR (fetal heart rate) response to both pure and complex tones. Likewise, Wedenberg (1970) observes that the fetus is "listening all the time after the 24th week." (Karolinska Institute, Wedenberg et al., 1985.)

8. Grimwade (1970) and Grimwade et al. (1971) report direct differentiation of FHR to a wide variety of frequency stimuli. In addition, differentiation of response to sine tones and percussive sounds is reported. Sakabe, Arayama and Suzuki (1969) report AER (auditory evoked response) in the fetal brain. Thus, it appears that the stimulus is transmitted to the brain, and it can be concluded that it is perceived and stored in memory.

9. Investigations of fetal well-being by Read and Miller (1977), Bench (1968), Grimwade (1970) and Scibetta (1971) using auditory response data further support the observation that the prenatal infant "hears" and responds to a wide variety of external sound sources. It is not possible at this point in research history to conclude that long-term memory for specific rhythmic and tonal patterns is detectable. One of the central objectives of the present study focuses on that issue. It is hypothesized that only by longitudinal tracking of postnatal developmental response can it be determined that prenatal stimulation may enhance prenatal learning.

In his recent book, *The Infant Mind,* Richard Restak (1986) speculates that memory in the "wide sense" is achieved, before birth at full term. He reviews the work of Hamburger and Harrison who learned that during normal fetal development about 50 percent of cortical neurons die. Those surviving cells continue to develop connections and to differentiate for years after the baby is born. Very little is known about the process of early neuronal organization (Restak, pp. 50-57). (See Figure 4.)

Current research efforts by De Casper, Eimas, Trehub, Aslin et al. (1983) in the area of speech perception may have much to offer us in our search for answers to the important questions of differentiation of response in infants.

Rene Van deCarr (1985) has suggested that prenatal infants are in a "prenatal university." He exposes in-utero infants to music, poetry, and mother's

Timing of Developmental Processes

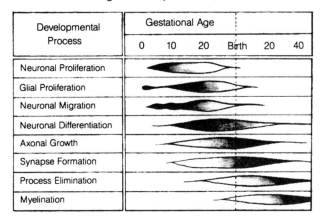

Developmental Process	Gestational Age					
	0	10	20	Birth	20	40
Neuronal Proliferation						
Glial Proliferation						
Neuronal Migration						
Neuronal Differentiation						
Axonal Growth						
Synapse Formation						
Process Elimination						
Myelination						

Figure 4

From the Infant Mind (Restak, 1986)

Formation of the brain can be plotted as a function of age in weeks. For example, at ten weeks neuronal proliferation is active whereas synapse formation has hardly begun. At twenty weeks just the opposite situation prevails: neuronal proliferation is well on the way to completion whereas synapse formation will continue at a hectic pace until birth and beyond. Many developmental processes overlap and therefore injury to the brain at any time is apt to interfere with concurrent processes. The diagram is only approximate since the timing often differs between components of the nervous system. In other instances the details are not available concerning the precise timing for all events.

and father's reading *The Cat in the Hat*. He and his subjects' parents report dramatic developmental differences between first and second children, and between siblings when only one child experienced systematic stimulation. (1986)

The Eastman Pilot Study: 1980-1987

It was after reading the intriguing anecdotal reports that had appeared in Verny's 1981 book, and reviewing the available published research findings, that we decided to investigate the phenomenon of in-utero auditory response to musical stimuli in a more scientifically controlled fashion.

Although medical researchers had used tones and clicks as stimuli, only one report indicated the identification of what we would regard as "real music," that is, recorded excerpts of instrumental selections or orchestral works, as stimuli to be administered in any systematic design. That work came to my attention shortly after I started my research project at the Eastman School.

Although his research had been cited in other publications, a brief report in *Science Digest* (February, 1984) on the work of Dr. Clifford Olds that referred to the same use of recorded music sources employed in the same prenatal environmental placement on the mother's abdomen that I was beginning to use. Further, Olds reported his developmental observations of the infant for some time past the perinatal period.

Since 1981, and those solitary, early beginnings, I have been contacted by many doctors, mothers-to-be, and young parents who have forwarded anecdotal reports of in-utero response to external music stimuli of a wide variety. At this point, however, it is my perception that no other formal studies of the sort I will describe are underway. Indeed, there are many valid reasons one might cite in choosing *not* to investigate the issue of prenatal response to musical stimuli — or the even more tenuous issue of prenatal learning:

1. In spite of the findings reported by Eimas (1978) and De Casper (1980), among others, musical signals are very different in physical energy content than those of normal adult speech. It is this difference in acoustic complex wave forms, that renders some types of musical patterns (both tonal and rhythmic) ideally suited for research involving fetal response, and even the potential for in-utero learning.

2. Until we have documented specific measurements of differential post-natal developmental behavior due to the treatment variable (musical stimuli), it is not appropriate to report anything but a tentative cause-effect relationship. It is this critical factor in the design of my studies

that I hope will produce data that will generate a proto-col for others to replicate.

3. Many unsubstantiated reports have been published by musicians and psychologists that border on the bizarre, resulting in negative reaction from professionals in the field.

Beginning with one mother and prenatal infant in 1981, I established a protocol for exploring the phenomenon in a pilot study that continues to the present. Following are some of the most critical factors, or controls, I have exercised, and some observations on my findings.

1. The mother is a volunteer. She usually contacts me as a result of reading about the study in a paper or magazine, or discussing our work with someone who has been a subject in the study. Many are musical, or come from a family with a history of higher education.

2. Mothers, fathers or both parents make an initial appoint-ment to discuss the project and their potential involve-ment. The importance of record keeping, consistent use of the music selected, and follow-up visits is stressed. Only two of over thirty who considered joining the study did not choose to participate. I have not always been able to accept those who wanted to join.

3. After the first interview and discussion of music matters, we select a "stimulative" piece and a "sedative" work. The selection process involves instruction on time for use of the music, position of the mother, record keeping, and the general medical history of the mother-to-be. Visits during pregnancy are usually once every 6 to 10 weeks.

Note: The reason for using two contrasting musical selections is that we are interested in differences in motor response that might occur. Measurement of fetal cardioacceleration and AER (audio evoked response) have not been reported when these widely contrasting types of music have been used ex-cept for those reported by Olds (1984) in two informal monographs.

4. During the in-utero stimulation period, music is presented to the infant by means of high fidelity stereophonic earphones, removed from the headpiece frame, placed directly on the abdominal skin without any clothing or obstruction. Although the stimulus may be

recorded in stereo, the signal (amplified to about 90 dB) is monophonic. The listening period — or in-utero stimulation time — is between five and ten minutes, no longer. Some mothers use one stimulus in the morning hours and the other in the evening.

Note: Studies recently reported by Gagno and his associates at the St. Joseph Hospital in London, Ontario indicated that external sounds of 110 dB at the skin surface are attenuated 40 to 50 dB in the uterus. Thus, there would appear to be no damage to the fetal hearing system. It should be noted that 90 to 110 dB levels are peaks.

In my studies, 10 of the 30 subjects have reported differences in response to the two types of music:

    a.   The infant tended to respond with more sharp, rapid or agitated movement to the stimulative selection, and

    b.   With more rolling or soft, muted motor movement to the slower, "sedative" selection.

This supports the speculation made by Olds (1984, 1985) that tempo — the temporal variation — may be the earliest and most primitive musical stimuli possible. Responses may be a predictor of personality and, eventually, of competent speech acquisition as well.

    5.   My first appointment with the mother and new baby is always within the first 4 to 6 weeks after birth. At this first visit a routine is established that we have continued, with minor variations, up to the present time.

The appointments, or clinical observation periods, are designed to be very low in stress to the mother and child; the same office, a small seminar room in the music department, is always used. Music is presented by means of records or tapes played on high-quality equipment and stereo speakers, or by real instruments and toy-like music sources. No more than one additional observer is in the room. Sessions are audio or videotape recorded. I take brief observational notes for the subject's cumulative folder. The sessions normally last about 25 to 35 minutes.

A major music behavior I am trying to assess is that of vocal production (singing or cooing) in addition to early babbling or speech acquisition. The research on infant vocal behavior is rather new and the corpus very small. I refer here to those studies that attempt to measure the singing, or presinging behavior of the infant before 24 months (Fox, 1982). It is quite possible that the infant of less than 12 months can match pitch and echo intervals as well as rhythmic patterns. At present, in light of the small sample of mothers and infants participating in the study, and with many environmental variables uncontrolled, I am not suggesting that prenatal musical stimulation has promotive, or direct cause-effect impact on behavior of the infant between 1 and 24 months. It is the period after this — that of 24-60 months — that interests me even more.

It appears that after the child attains spoken language and the cognitive skills that support language, he or she "remembers" much more than one might have imagined. I am just beginning to learn about this most intriguing phenomenon in my studies of cognition and memory. One of the findings I have reported in brief articles and interviews about the study, is the early development of highly organized and remarkably articulate speech of those children who have been exposed to prenatal music stimulation.

Video Case Studies

Following are a brief descriptions of color video recordings of four subject clinical sessions. All children received prenatal musical stimulation.

I. Female 27 months

The child sings the popular Christmas song *Rudolf, the Red Nosed Reindeer* from beginning to end. The song is thirty-two measures long. It contains intervals of an octave, chromatic intervals, key changes. Her parents cue her twice. Noted are speech clarity, gestures and expressive dynamics.

II. Male 46 months

(This is the oldest subject in the study.) Mother is a singer and teacher. He had not been to a clinical session for over two months. He listens to recorded synthesized sounds, identifies them and displays creative, innovative responses; excellent articulation, and expressive verbalization. (These recorded sounds are heard only during clinical sessions.) He plays a small xylophone, imitates tonal patterns, dynamic contrast replicated. He wants to compose (improvise) his own songs. He imitates rhythmic patterns played by his mother on a small wood drum. He interchanges right and left hand, discriminates like and different patterns. He also plays the Fischer-Price® drum toys. Although he sees these instruments only every two or three months, he remembers the names of the instruments and plays each of them correctly. He plays the kazoo, sings the *ABC Song* and plays the piano with his mother.

III. Female 30 months

This Chinese child is being raised by her grandmother as well as her natural mother who is a singer and teacher. She sings in two registers, a loud low register and a soft high register. She sings over fourteen songs by memory. During this video sequence she sings *This Old Man, Twinkle, Twinkle Little Star,* and *Rain, Rain, Go Away*.

She replicates triadic and intervalic patterns that are played on an instrument or sung to her. She responds to synthesized sound by creating gestures and is very attentive to the novel auditory stimulus. She also plays the xylophone, the drums, the kazoo and and the Projectone®, an electronic instrument. At her first exposure to the Projectone®, she "played" a song and experimented with sounds of short and long duration. This girl may be gifted. She exhibits remarkable attention and motor integration.

IV. Female 21 months

This is a first child, with one younger sibling. She is in a day care center most of the day. The mother was a music teacher who took a year's leave. I had not seen her in the clinical sessions for 69 days. (The audio stimuli are regarded as novel for most normal children if they are not exposed to them at least every three weeks.)

The girl sings *Jesus Loves the Little Children* in the correct key with no melodic or rhythmic errors. She sings 12 songs by memory. She played the Fischer-Price® drum toys, xylophone, wood drum and kazoo. She also plays the piano with independent fingering. Often she will sing while playing. This child has excellent verbal articulation. She verbalizes in complete sentences.

You may wonder why I have not systematically employed the same music for the longitudinal, or tracking, observations that was used in pre-natal sessions. I did that with my first three subjects — and for the first two or three visits. The infant responded with instant motor movement, fixed gaze at the source of the music, and in one case, by reaching out to the sound source. A decision was made to use another selection, and to introduce a novel series of synthesized musical sounds, in order to assess the infant's ability to transfer or generalize the response behavior to many types of music appropriately. Not surprising, subjects tended to respond to almost all musical selections of the same type in a generalized way. I am still investigating the stimulus value of comparable music selections among the more critical variables in this phase of the study. In addition, I am now recording a series of short melodic patterns for use in a future study.

Finally, I want to emphasize a most important point — even a tentative conclusion — of the studies now underway. This is a pilot experiment. It utilizes music in the sense that humans, not animals, recognize it as an aesthetic object and a man-made artifact. Because of the unique characteristics of the stimulus and its cultural significance, and because of the host of environmental variables that pour in on the postnatal infant beginning with the moment of birth, we are reluctant to advance the hypothesis that musical stimulation of the in-utero infant will have significant behavioral effects on development. However, the data we have collected, and the tentative conclusions reported, encourage us to continue the research and to urge interested professionals who share our curiosity to join us. As indicated in my article written for the Music Educators Journal in 1984, who knows when life begins, and who can state when musical life of a child is first experienced? I hope our research will help provide at least some of the answers to those questions.

NOTE: Since the first formal presentation of this study in the summer of 1986, I have added three subjects. We hope soon to be able to add ultrascan videos to our data now available. I continue to follow my subjects and record their musical and cognitive development. (July, 1987)

References

NOTE: This is a highly abridged version of an extensive list of sources. A complete list appears in the *Pre- and Perinatal Psychology Journal*, Vol 3. No. 3, Spring, 1989, pp. 185-189.

Annis, L. *The child before birth*, Ithaca, NY: Cornell University Press, 1978.

Araki, S. "Studies on the sound response of fetus and newborn infants," *Journal of the Japanese Gynecological Society*, 24:267-275, 1972.

Arayama, T. "Intrauterine fetal reaction to acoustic stimuli," *Journal of Otolaryngology of Japan*, 73:1885-1907, 1970.

Argal, S., Rosen, M., and Sokol, R. "Fetal response to sound," [Special Issue], *Contemporary Obstetrics and Gynecology*, 5, 1975.

Aslin, R.N., Pisoni, D. and Jusczyk, P. "Auditory development and speech perception in infancy." In P. Mussen (Ed.) *Carmichael's Manual of Child Psychology*, 4th ed., Vol 2: *Infancy and the Biology of Development*, M.M. Haith and J.J. Campos (vol 2 Eds.), (pp.574-614), New York: Wiley & Sons, 1984.

Bench, J. "Sound transmission to the human fetus through the maternal abdominal wall," *Journal of Genetic Psychology*, 113:85-87, 1968.

Brierley, J. *The growing brain: Childhood's rucial years*, Windsor, England: NFER 1985.

Chusid, J. & McDonald, J. "Correlative neuranatomy and functional neurology," Los Altos, CA: Lange Medical Publications, 1967.

DeCasper, A.J. and Fifer, W.P. [News note], *Science*, 208:1174, 1980.

Eccles, J., and Robinson, D. *The wonder of being human: Our brain and our mind*, New York: Free Press, 1984.

Eimas, P.D. "Developmental aspects of speech perception." In R. Held, H. Leibowitz, and H.L. Teuber (Eds.) *Handbook of sensory physiology: Perception* (Vol. 8), Berlin: Springer, 1978.

Eimas, P.D., Siqueland, E.R., Juszyk, P., and Vigerito, J. "Speech perception in infants," *Science*, 171:303-306, 1971.

Eimas, P.D. "The equivalence of cues in the perception of speech by infants," *Infant Behavior and Development*, 4:395-399, 1985.

Fernald, A. "The perceptual and affective salience of mothers' speech to infants." In L. Feagers, C. Garvey, and R. Golinkoff (Eds.) *The origins and growth of communication*, (pp. 5-29), Norwood, New Jersey: Ablex, 1984.

Ferreira A. *Prenatal environment*, Springfield, Illinois: Charles C. Thomas, 1968.

Field, Tiffany. "Supplemental stimulation of preterm neonates," *Early Human Development, 4:301-314, North Holland: Elsevier Biomedical Press*, 1980.

Forbes, H.S. and Forbes, H.B. "Fetal sense reaction: hearing," *Journal of Comparative Psychology*, 7:353-355, 1927.

Fox, Donna Brink. "The pitch range and contour of infant vocalization," *Dissertation Abstracts International*, 43:8A-506, 1982. (University Microfilms No. 83-00,247).

Gardner, H. "Do babies sing a universal song?" *Psychology Today*, 14: 70-76, 1981.

Grimwade, J.C. "Response of the human fetus to sensory stimulation," *Australian and New Zealand Journal of Obsetrics and Gynaecology*, 10: 222-224, 1970.

Grimwade, J.C., Walker, D., and Wood, C. "Human fetal heart rate change and movement in response to sound and vibration," *American Journal of Obstetrics and Gynecology*, 109:86-91, 1971.

Howell, P., Cross, I., & West, R. (Eds.), *Musical structure and cognition*, London: Academic Press, 1985.

Johnson, J. "Making life in the womb more interesting, Unborn babies get lesson in music, voice," *U.S.A. Weekend*, p. 31, November 8-10, 1985.

Kolata, G. "Studying learning in the womb: Behavioral scientists are using established experimental methods to show that fetuses can and do learn," *Science*, 225:302-303, 1984.

Liley, A.W. "The foetus as a personality," *Australian and New Zealand Journal of Psychiatry,* 6:99-105, 1972.

Logan, B. *Patient specification and drawing: Prenatal audio player,* Unpublished manuscript, 1985.

MacFarlane, A. *The Psychology of Childbirth,* Cambridge, MA: Harvard University Press, 1977.

Manshio, D.T. "Lactic dehydrogenase of fetal ear fluids under ambient high intensity sound," *Research Communications in Chemical Pathology and Pharmacology,* 14(2):385-388, 1976.

Montagu, A. *Prenatal Influences,* Springfield, IL: Charles C. Thomas, 1962.

Moore, B.C.J. *An Introduction to the Psychology of Hearing (2nd ed.),* London: Academic Press, 1982.

Neff, William D. (Ed.). *Contributions to Sensory Physiology,* Vol. 6, New York: Academic Press, 1982.

Nijhuis, J.C., Prechtl, H.F.R., Martin, C.B., Jr. and Bots, R.S.G.M. (Eds.) "Are there behavioral states in the human fetus?" In *Early Human Development (Vol. 1)* pp. 177-195, North Holland: Elsevier Biomedical Press, 1982.

Olds, C. *Fetal response to music,* Wickford, Essex: Runwell Hospital, 1984.

Olds, C. *A Sound Start in Life,* Wickford, Essex: Runwell Hospital, 1985.

Panneton, R.K. *Prenatal auditory experience with melodies: Effects on postnatal auditory preferences in human newborns,* Unpublished doctoral dissertation, University of North Carolina at Greensboro, 1985.

Peiper, S. "Sinnesempfindungen des Kindes vor seiner Geburt," *Monatschur. F. Kindehl,* 29:236, 1925.

Peiper, S. *Cerebral function in infancy and childhood,* (B. Nagler & H. Nagler, Trans.), In J. Wortis, (Ed.), *International Behavioral Science Series,* New York: Consultants Bureau, 1963.

Pickles, J.O. *An Introduction to the physiology of hearing,* London: Academic Press, 1982.

Ray, W. "A preliminary report of a study of fetal conditioning," *Child Development,* 3:175, 1932.

Read, J.A., et al. "Fetal heart rate acceleraton in response to acoustic stimulation as a measure of fetal well-being," *American Journal of Obstetrics and Gynecology,* 129,(5):512-517, 1977.

Restak, R.M. *The Brain,* New York: Bantam Books, 1984.

Rubel, E. "Special topic: Advances in the physiology of auditory information processing," *Ontogeny of the Auditory System, Annual Review of Physiology,* 46:213-229, 1984.

Sakabe, N., et al. "Human fetal evoked response to acoustic stimulation, [Special issue], *Journal of Otolaryngology,* 252 (Supplement 29), 1969.

Salk, L. *The effects of the normal heartbeat sound on the behavior of the newborn infant: implications for mental health,* Technical paper presented at the annual meeting of the world Federation of Mental Health, Edinburgh, 1960.

Salk, L. "Mothers' heartbeat as an imprinting stimulus," Transactions: Journal of the New York Academy of Sciences, 24 (7):753-763, 1966.

Scibetta, J.J. "Human fetal brain response to sound during labor," *American Journal of Gynecology Annuals,* 109:82-85, 1971.

Shetler, D. "Prenatal music experiences: Prelude to a musical life," *Music Educators Journal,* 71(7):26-27, 1985.

Sloboda, J. *The Musical Mind,* Oxford: Clarendon Press, 1985.

Sontag, L.W. & Newberry, H. "Normal variations of fetal heart rate during pregnancy," *American Journal of Obstetrics and Gynecology,* 40:449-452, 1940.

Sontag, L.W. "The fetal and maternal cardiac response to environmental stress," *Human Development,* 12:1-9, 1969.

Sorokin, Y., & Dierker, L. "Fetal movement," *Clinical Obstetrics and Gynecology,* 4:25, 1982.

Spelt, D. "The conditioning of the human fetus in utero," *Journal of Experimental Psychology,* 3:338-346, 1948.

Spiegler, D. "Factors involved in the development of prenatal rhythmic sensitivity," *Dissertations Abstracts International,* 28:3886, University Microfilms No. 68-2696), 1948.

Trehub, S.E. "Reflections on the development of speech perception," *Canadian Journal of Psychology*, 33:368-381, 1979.

Van de Carr, F.R. "The prenatal university," *U.S.A. Weekend*, p. 32, 1985.

Veny, T. *The Secret Life of the Unborn Child*, New York: Dell, 1981.

Walker, D., et. al. "The acoustic component of the fetal environment," *Journal of Reproduction and Fertility*, 24:125-126, 1971.

Webster, D. "Neonatal sound deprivation affects brainstem auditory nuclei," *Otolaryngology*, 103:392-396, 1977.

Wedenberg, J.B. "Measurement of tone response by the human fetus," *ACTA Laryngology Supplement*, 57:188-192, 1964.

Wedenberg, J.B., Westin, B., & Johansson, B. "When the fetus isn't listening," *Medical World News*, 4:28, 1985.

Windle, W. *Physiology of the Fetus: Origins and Extent of Functions in Prenatal Life*, Philadelphia: W.B. Saunders, 1940.

Section II

Children's Music:

The Perspective of World Culture

The Child's World of Music

Helen Myers[1]
Consultant in Ethnomusicology
The New Grove Dictionary of Music and Musicians
London, England

It is a great honor and pleasure for me to have been invited to convene this session at our second Biology of Music Making Conference. In this session the members of the panel will address fundamental questions ethnomusicologists have asked about the the child's world of music. You will be visiting, through these six papers, children in faraway countries — children who grow up in cultures unfamiliar to you. You will see how these different settings have affected the world of the child and the child's world of music.

Ethnomusicologists feel particularly comfortable in such a forum as we have here assembled this afternoon, one that includes physicians, psychologists, and physiologists as well as scholars of music. It was in just such a setting that the discipline of ethnomusicology was born 100 years ago. A group of psychologists at the University of Berlin, interested in aspects of human perception, particularly hearing, set out to collect samples of music from all parts of the world for comparative study. The most famous member of this circle, Erich von Hornbostel, analysed hundreds of wax cylinders recorded by German ethnologists, and drew on this data for his psychological research, particularly the theory of binaural hearing. These cylinders became the basis of the Berlin Phonogrammarchiv, today a center of ethnomusicological study and one of the largest collections of non-Western music in the world.

Children's music has not been a popular topic in ethnomusicology, indeed many published studies which claim to treat the entire music of a culture fail to make any mention of children's music. There are very few studies that deal exclusively with the children's music of different cultures. Therefore, I am particularly pleased that we have with us today six scholars whose work reflects the high value they place on the study of children's music.

---

1 Professor Myers is currently at the Department of Music, Trinity College, Hartford Connecticut

We begin our global tour in southern Africa with Professor Blacking's talk on the Venda, a rural people of the Northern Transvaal. We then move several thousand miles northwestwards to Nigeria, for Dr. Waterman's discussion of a completely different African culture and musical tradition, popular *Fújì* music of Yoruba children. We then make a leap eastwards with Dr. Baily's report from Afghanistan, a country now closed for ethnomusicological study. We will continue with Professor Garfias' very recent fieldwork from the many cultures in which he has conducted research. We next move close to home, on the Mescalero Apache reservation of New Mexico, where Dr. Shapiro has just conducted further field work on the very special music which accompanies the closing moments of childhood for Apache girls. We conclude our global survey with Professor Bjørkvold's exciting recent work on children's songs in Norway, the Soviet Union and the United States.

The function of this panel is not to provide answers but to raise issues, and to draw your attention to the diversity of musical behavior amongst the world's children. I would beg you to keep your minds open. Much of this information inevitably will be new to you; I hope you will allow it to challenge your thinking. I am particularly pleased that this session has been scheduled early in the week, so that the issues raised by a global perspective will be on the table from the start of our discussions. Inevitably you may be tempted to search for unifying themes (perhaps in vain) to search for "universals" that link the children's music of these cultures to our own children in Europe and the United States. Perhaps it would be helpful in listening to the papers to bear in mind some fundamental questions about children's music that have been raised by ethnomusicologists:

Firstly, do children have a separate musical repertory? What is the relationship between the child and the adult repertory?

Secondly, is children's musical learning directed exclusively by adults? Is it aimed exclusively at learning the adult repertory? What kinds of music do adults select for children to perform?

Thirdly, are there any special characteristics of children's music that may be considered universal? Some universals that have been suggested are simplicity of form, repetitive forms, short forms, and limited melodic range.

Finally, how does children's music reflect social structure and cultural norms?

In closing I would like to thank Frank Wilson and Franz Roehmann and to applaud their open-mindedness and eagerness to enliven this meeting with contributions from ethnomusicologists, knowing full well — as they do — that the data that they are about to present from various corners of the globe may obstruct any simple conclusions about the child's world of music.

Music in Children's Cognitive and Affective Development: Problems posed by ethnomusicological research

John Blacking
Department of Social Anthropology
The Queen's University of Belfast, Northern Ireland

I want to spend the first half of my talk discussing one or two general issues that arise from ethnomusicological research, and incidentally arise from my own work, because I do not regard ethnomusicology as the study of other musical systems, but rather a way of looking at all music-making in society at any time. The point is that ethnomusicological research has created very considerable problems for the psychology of music and for studies of music and child development, because it challenges many of the definitions and concepts with which most research has been carried out. Nevertheless, I do not think we need to adopt a completely relativistic approach, which would make cross cultural comparison almost impossible. On the contrary, research into different musical systems can expand the scope of work already done in western musical traditions and explain some of the phenomena that have been reported.

I'll illustrate this very briefly by referring to the work of three distinguished scholars who are contributing to this symposium. Dr. Deutsch will be reporting that there are striking individual differences in how simple musical patterns are heard, and that these differences do not relate to musical training. In an article published in 1980, Jeanne Bamberger demonstrated that better musical results were often obtained from people who performed by ear and were unrestricted by notation and relied on intuitive knowledge. In his book, *The Musical Mind*, Dr. John Sloboda argues that the way in which people represent music to themselves is a central issue in understanding how musical ideas are expressed and appreciated.

If we look at any three or four or more musical systems from Asia or Africa, we will find that not only individuals but whole groups acquire very different ways of representing music to themselves, as Dr. Sloboda points out, and these affect the ways in which they make sense of musical and other sounds, bearing out Dr. Deutsch's point.

We can also discover what kinds of intuitive knowledge they bring to bear on music making by examining the different social and conceptual contexts of their performance, which bears on Dr. Bamberger's point. So you see that some of the material of ethnomusicology can help and expand what is already being done in the psychology of music and child development and at the same time raise a number of critical issues. It is some of these that I want to discuss very briefly.

I want to draw together some of the problems and conclusions that have arisen from research in ethnomusicology. When we are considering human musicality there are two major problems that emerge. First of all, what is human, in an evolutionary perspective? There are some facts about the evolution and workings of the human brain which we need to know (see, for instance, Ornstein, 1986). In the course of biological evolution the brain has become a lot of separate systems lumped together. The brain's basic job is to mind the body and it is well equipped to respond to emergencies, but very bad at dealing with long-term problems. The brain is tuned to adaptation, not thought, and as animals, human beings are exceptionally incoherent. The part of the brain making judgments often operates independently of the part that is behaving. People get nervous and blush when they don't want to, so that from a biological point of view, as Paul Ekman has pointed out, lying would be regarded as a remarkable human achievement.

Although the organization of our minds may be hierarchical as a result of our culturally conditioned uses of the brain, the organization of the brain itself is not hierarchical. It is not helpful to talk of "memory," for instance, as a general category as if it covered all kinds of memory. We know, of course, from our own experience that each of us has a good memory for different things. We should not think, therefore, of taste memory or visual memory, but rather of taste information and visual information. So the brain is an organizational system which does modular analysis. Milgram's famous experiment in persuasion was a powerful example of the manipulation of the brain's basic incoherence. He persuaded decent people to inflict increasing quantities of pain on others and so demonstrated that violent action can be induced in individuals outside the normal context of violence and in marked contrast to habitual behavior through willingness to conform and obey.

Even more striking examples of the brain's incoherence are found in the cases of so called *idiots savants*, or clever imbeciles, who are mentally retarded but show extraordinary ability in one particular skill such as drawing, mathematical calculation and most significant for us, music (see

Gardner, 1985, and Sloboda et al., 1985). They lack the coherence which is necessary to use their brains as truly human minds. Similarly, autistic children, whether they are bright or mentally retarded, lack the sociability necessary to break out of what Bettleheim has called their "empty fortress" and become fully human.

So these problems, the problem of the brain and its evolution, are very important, and what is even more important for us as ethnomusicologists, and I shall come back to this in a moment, is the fact that the first two species of humans — homo erectus and homo sapiens Neanderthalensis — who have produced culture's coherent systems of communication, were not, it seems, able to speak a language. They had other methods of communication, chiefly nonverbal, gestural and so on. One begins to wonder, therefore, whether perhaps homo erectus had the same kind of brain capacity of *idiots savants* and what kind of role musical thought or musical intelligence (and kinesthetic intelligence, dance intelligence) may have played in the building up of the mind or the brain that we now have, with what is known as the bi-cameral mind (with two hemispheres and so on). There is not time to go on any further with that, but just these few general remarks on what is human.

The second point about human musicality is, what is music? I don't know whether or not John Baily will be talking about the problem of Quranic chant. In Afghanistan and other Islamic countries, what sounds musical to many of us in this society is not regarded as music. This, for example, amongst the Venda is music (see musical example 3 and Figure 6 in Blacking, 1973, pp. 28 and 70). It is contained precisely within a musical framework which is complete in itself and which can be repeated many times without rests. There is no concept of rests. Once you move into "music" you are moving into a special transcendental world in which there are no rests. Here is another Venda song which may sound more to us like music (example). It is less "musical" in Venda terms than the other chant. Why? Because if you were to speak these examples without the melody, you would hear that the former is quite different from speech. But when I sing the second example, it is very like speech, with the intonation of speech. What we expect to be music in Venda society is not always so musical to their way of thinking. Similarly, if we take the Nigerian definition of music, *egwu* is not just music. It is costume, dance, drama, ritual, the whole nexus of activities all combined.

Let me sum up four major issues that ethnomusicological research has shown very clearly. First, a general definition of music is problematic.

Secondly, sounds defined as music by different people are the products of many different processes and some of those processes may not be strictly musical: that is, equal spaced holes, or equal spaced frets on instruments may be the basis of a scale system because of visual aesthetic concepts, but they will not produce acoustically "regular" intervals. Patterns of thumb movement on a Venda instrument are the basis of melodic patterns. Patterns of finger movements on a flute are the basis of tonal shifts, and so on (Blacking, 1973, pp. 11-19). And then symbolic requirements in rituals or mathematical order lead to musical sounds. The bases (or deep structures) of many musical structures are not always strictly musical.

The third problem raised by ethnomusicological research is that the effects of music are not determined solely by musical sounds, something to which Dr. Sloboda referred this morning. I have done a considerable amount of research on dance music and possession — how the same music affected people differently according to where they were and who they were on different occasions (Blacking, 1985b). On some occasions they would be "possessed" by the music and on others they would not. Why was this? Because people are not cultural dopes to whom music *does* things; they are conscious agents in social situations, making sense of music in a variety of ways.

Fourthly, the processes of an orally transmitted performance do not differ fundamentally from the variations of performances of written music. Music is available for use and exists only in performance. As with speech, listeners make sense of music, creative listening if you like, no less than performers make sense of it when they actually produce or create the sounds. There is a very fascinating article by the sociologist Alfred Schutz (1951) on making music together and on this problem of resonance, asserting that listeners are as important to making music as performers. I'll talk about this in a few minutes in connection with reinforcement.

So then, we have to consider rather carefully what we mean by music. I would suggest a provisional distinction between, firstly, the enormous range of "musics" which members of different societies categorize as special symbol systems and kinds of social action — that is to say, musics as cultural systems — and, secondly, an innate, species-specific set of cognitive and sensory capabilities which human beings are predisposed to use for communication and for making sense of their environment — that is, music as a human capacity.

In analyzing musical performance and musical composition, we need to distinguish between those processes which are based on reasoned argument in terms of the rules and parameters of a given musical system from those which are derived from the innate musical or esthetic or other primary intelligences of human beings. That's a distinction between musical thought and musical intelligence, that is, the distinction between explanations of music in terms of *talas*, *rags*, *bols*, scales, keys, tonality, harmonic sequences and so on, and explanations in terms of intuition, inspiration, divine guidance, the unconscious and whatever. The point is that these latter quasi-mystical explanations are the really important ones in musical analysis, because they refer to the structures of the innate musical intelligence of all human beings, which can also account for the possibility of trans-cultural communication in music. These kinds of structures are referred to in a wonderful book by Victor Zuckerkandl, *Man the Musician* (1976). And that's why I think we need to distinguish musical thought from musical intelligence.

Let me sum up how I divide these: musical thought is composing, performing, listening to and talking about music as parts of the processes of making sense of the world through and with music. Musical intelligence is the cognitive and affective equipment of the brain with which people make musical sense of the world.

I hypothesize that not all organized sound is composed exclusively with musical intelligence or even at all with musical intelligence, and that musical intelligence may be used for organizing other cultural phenomena that would not be described as musical, such as architecture, mathematics, ($x^2 =$ x, for instance), rhetoric and poetry. Musical intelligence is not related specifically to the acoustical laws of sound or even to any specifically musical parameters at all. It is a more abstract system of ordering, and the use of musical intelligence, as of all human activities in the cultural sphere, has not proceeded in an evolution from low to high, simple or complex. That, again, is one of the most important discoveries of ethnomusicology, although in a sense we knew it long ago. We know very well that Saint Saens was not a better composer than Bach. Nevertheless, people go on talking as if European music is better than Balinese or something like that, which is absurd.

I don't have time to go into any more detail about this issue of musical intelligence, but what I'm getting at is the kind of argument that people like Martin Heidegger refer to when they say that science does not think, and Paul Feyerabend referred to when he argued that scientific knowledge has been advanced by intuitive thinking in the affective mode. All these people are referring to a mode of thought in human activity and in human creativity which I personally believe is very close to what I am trying to describe as musical intelligence.

Therefore, I suggest that in studying music and child development, we think in terms of pure artistic action and thought as the infrastructure of practical life rather than as an embellishment of it. It is not that children transcend reality with music, but that they create reality transcendentally.

Just as the earliest human cultures were created by people who did not have speech as we know it and must have used a kind of gestural language and other nonverbal modes of communication, so the neoteny and ontogeny of infants suggests that the human gait and speech presuppose dancing and singing. For instance, have a look at this! (Shows a slide of a four-week-old baby being held up and taking a step). Doctors and nurses and medical experts refer to that as the stepping reflex and infants do it very well when held up during the first six weeks of life. They cannot develop the ability further, for a number of reasons, and they lose it altogether and have to relearn it when they can stand up. Now I don't call that the stepping reflex. I call it *dancing*.

It's not a new idea. The philospher Vico said that man danced before he walked, and women, too. Similarly, infants seems to discover, by accident, a lot of proto-musical activities but cannot remember how they did them, and so lose the ability, perhaps for good. I have found that it doesn't necessarily help if these are reinforced. For example, one five-month-old baby whom I've been studying, began to sing and then suddenly discovered the muscular coordination necessary for going "da da da da." In spite of enthusiastic reinforcement by parents and older siblings, she lost the ability in three days as fast as she found it. Two and a half weeks later, quite independently, she produced the sounds once more.

Now I find no problem about that in terms of a theory of performance and resonance, that is, listening and making sense. What was done to her by her parents and siblings was not reinforcement, because she was not able to comprehend what they were doing. She hadn't a clue. The ability to make music and to speak depends on being able to comprehend precisely what is happening around you. She didn't know what "da da da" was, so she wasn't being reinforced. She was not able to listen to it intelligently. It remained her own discovery, not a result of communication with others. I have a suspicion that at that age babies probably respond better to recordings of other older infants of about 12 months or less. It is because of this kind of problem that I wish to draw the distinction between musical thought and musical intelligence. When we are discussing, as we did this morning, pre-natal and post-natal musical stimuli, or even musical stimuli during infancy, I wonder if we can or should use the word "musical," since the infant has no conceptualization of musical sound. By using the word musical, we are im-plying that there is a continuum between these experiences, which may pos-sibly be exercising musical intelligence, and later experiences in which musi-cal thought is being exercised.

So, the intelligence of musicians and musical intelligence in general, and musical thought — the exercise of these musical intelligences — seems to depend very much on social context and the ways in which people in society recruit their musicians and what they expect of them. It seems that there are some societies where musicians are regarded as intellectuals and others where they are exceptionally "thick" in everything but music. When I start talking to musicians in some societies, people say, "You are already talking to our intellectuals." I go to another society and I talk to musicians, and they say, "Why are you wasting your time talking to those people? They know nothing except music." That is a very interesting point. Different societies attribute different kinds of intelligence or ideas to their musicians and so one wonders how other people would fare in that society. What would a person like Wagner have done in the time of Bach? What would Bach have done in the time of Wagner?

Ethnomusicology has quite a simple explanation for these contradictions be-cause it argues that the roles that people play are consequences of the varieties of ways in which music is conceptualized and made.

And now I want to show some pictures of various social contexts of music in Venda children's lives, just to show you in what sorts of situations children acquire music and musical experience.

Here are pictures of a girls' initiation school where the older girls are going through initiation and the women are teaching them. They are all participat-ing and the children are having an opportunity to soak up quite a lot of what is happening. In view of the fact that these children often fall asleep while they are listening to music, they may really be taking in a lot more music than you'd think — I refer to the theories of sleep-learning, which hold that people can learn well while falling asleep.

Here is another example, the child of a potter, with the child playing around and "drumming" with the seed pod which is used for pottery (see. for ex-ample, illustrations in Blacking 1973, p. 56). When infants start making a noise in this society, parents and others do not say "Stop it, do not make such a noise." What they do is to convert the noise into music. When this little girl here was going *bang, bang, bang* on the plate and I was getting a little exasperated, another person came along and tapped out a rhythm and made it into music. This was a very good way of turning noise into music.

Finally, more formal education takes place in teaching pounding songs, being trained by a master of initiation, and so on. Daily life was full of opportunities for every child to participate in music making. Music was a part of normal social life and its performance was a necessary feature of most institutions. Children were encouraged to sing and dance by their peers, no less than by adults. Nobody was excluded from musical activity, since musicality was regarded as part of the human condition. Even the physically handicapped could join in. One of the best dancers in the girls *tshigombela* team which I studied in 1957 was a hunchback.

Although the Venda assumed that all human beings were musically competent, they did not expect all to perform equally well, or necessarily to be creative in the musical medium. Excellence could only be attained through commitment and hard work and the motivation to do this was often socially determined. For instance, during the early rehearsals of the *tshigombela* dance in 1957, I found it very difficult to discern differences in the performance of the newest and youngest recruits, and my views were shared by other spectators. But as rehearsals continued, certain of these girls began to emerge as better than the others. It was no coincidence that those girls were known personally by members of the regular audience at the chief's place where they were dancing. Therefore, they tended to be singled out for praise by name while they were playing, and this personal attention spurred them on to greater efforts.

Venda people frequently suggested that exceptional musical ability ran in families, and they often drew attention to the antics of infants, or the momentary virtuosity of an older girl by referring to the performance of her parents or grandparents. But nobody argued that exceptional musical ability, as distinct from ordinary musical competence, was biologically inherited. Although commitment and hard work were considered essential for developing musical talent, nothing permanent could be achieved without a satisfactory relationship with the spiritual world, and the most likely candidates for direct guidance were the spirits of deceased members of the mother's or father's lineage. So the fact that music appeared to be inherited was not a biological concept. It was essentially a religious concept and a social concept.

Although singing was the most important and most pervasive musical activity in Venda society, the first recognized signs of musical activity were in motor movement — in dancing, or in trying out instrumental skills. This was consonant with the belief that the body should be moved by the spirit, and that this experience could be acquired by the exercise of certain musical skills with the help of others. One of the most elementary musical skills which Venda children had to learn or wanted to learn was playing two rhythms in polyrhythm. It's more difficult to do it with another.

This discovery of self-in-community was a very important milestone, not only in the acquisition of musical skills, but in the discovery of something about the self. This cognitive development had to be assessed in terms of Venda concepts about growth, motivation and intelligence. In traditional Venda society each individual birth marked the return of an ancestral spirit in human form, and the death of every identifiable, fulfilled person marked the birth of a new ancestral spirit. Thus every human being began life as a reincarnation of a deceased person who maintained his or her autonomy as an ancestral spirit and could eventually become an independent ancestral spirit in his or her own right.

So the Venda theory of personality and cognitive development began with the assumption that the child is an active rather than a passive participant in his or her own development and that a person could only become a person through social interaction with others. The second assumption was that of the interactionist position in developmental psychology. If an infant survived the first physically dangerous year of life, the innate characteristics of the deceased's ancestral spirit lodged in the child's body would gradually be modified by the different social experiences of the new person, who could eventually develop a strong and independent personality. Much of this discovery of self, discovery of "other," discovery of "real self," that is, ancestral self and at the same time, the spiritual reality of self, was achieved through quite systematic musical training.

The experiences of music making were a source for understanding the true nature of these facts of life. In Venda, children acquired this knowledge by means of a process in which they perceived and remembered pieces of music successively as schemata, symbols, concepts and rules. So one of the first songs that all Venda children acquired, as a recognized musical skill, was the four tone counting song, Potilo (See Blacking, 1973, p. 90).

Between the ages of 24 and 36 months most children produced first an erratic melody, unstable words and rhythmic movements that were regular but did not necessarily coincide with the melodic phrases, and they then graduated effortlessly to coordinated performances that were publicly accepted as correct. By the age of three they also appreciated the symbolic significance of Potilo and other similar schemata as counting songs. And so gradually they began to learn the significance of musical categories in their society as a whole (see Blacking, 1985a).

During my field work between 1956-1958, children between the ages of five and eight years taught me concepts and rules relating to their music. Not only could they outline the classifications of different types of children's song and several different musical styles, but they had grasped the essential difference between speech and song. They had also discovered the rules of music-making to the extent that they could correct my mistakes and could adapt a given melody to new words, because they understood the principles of the interaction of melody and speech tone. They grasped the basic principles of harmony and could recognize two different melodies as transformations of a single harmonic framework. They understood the principles of repeating rhythmic patterns and also appreciated that repeated melodic patterns could be transformed by the organizing principles of tonality and mode.

I discovered all this simply by working with them over a period of two years and giving them my impromptu tests. All the European tests that I gave were a complete disaster (see Blacking, 1973, p.6). But children's keenness to participate in musical activities and to excel was initially ensured by the pleasure of association with neighbors and kinsfolk and often the praise and encouragement of appreciative audiences of adults. As they grew up they realized that musical experience was an important key to self knowledge and understanding of the world. The variety of contexts in which children experienced or tried to perform music and dance helped them to understand the relationship of artistic skills to social institutions and to value them as means of communication no less important than speech.

They learned how to think and how to act, how to feel and how to relate. And they did this first in an informal way and then through the formal instruction of initiation. Emotion and reason, affect and cognition throughout this process were not separate but integrated aspects of their social life.

References

Blacking, John. *How Musical is Man?* Seattle: University of Washington Press, 1973.

Blacking, John. "Versus Gradus Novos ad Parnassum Musicum: Exemplum Africanum," in *Becoming Human Through Music,* D. McAllester, ed., The Wesleyan Symposium on the Perspectives of Social Anthropology in the Teaching and Learning of Music (Middletown: Wesleyan University and Music Educators National Conference), pp. 43-52, 1985a.

Blacking, John. "The Context of Venda Possession Music: Reflections on the Effectiveness of Symbols," 1985 Yearbook for Traditional Music, pp. 64-87, 1985b.

Gardner, Howard. *Frames of Mind: The Theory of Multiple Intelligences,* London: Paladin, 1985.

Ornstein, Robert. *Multimind,* Boston: Houghton Mifflin, 1986.

Schutz, Alfred. "Making Music Together, Social Research," 18(1):76-97, 1951 (Reprinted in Arvid Broderson (ed.), *Collected Papers II: Studies in Social Theory,* 159-178, The Hague: Martinus Nijlhoff, 1976.

Sloboda, John. Hermelin, B., O'Connor, N., "An Exceptional Musical Memory," *Music Perception* 3(2):155-170, 1985.

Zuckerkandl, Victor. *Man The Musician,* Princeton, NJ: Princeton University Press (Bollingen Series XLIV, 2, 1976.

The Junior Fújì Stars of Agbowo:
Popular Music and Yorùbá Children

Christopher A. Waterman
Division of Ethnomusicology
University of Washington

What have ethnomusicologists to offer colleagues in other disciplines interested in the study of music and child development? Two potential contributions come immediately to mind: first a body of empirical evidence that may be used to test the universality of hypotheses concerning musical cognition and behavior; and second, the "naturalistic" ethnographic methods characteristically employed in field research. The dominant scientific methods for studying human musical development have traditionally fallen into two broad categories: laboratory research, which tells us about patterns of musical perception, cognition, and behavior under controlled, and therefore artificial, conditions; and classroom-based studies providing detailed information about musical learning and the effectiveness of teaching techniques within a restricted set of institutional contexts. Much has been learned from the application of such methods, but they do not by and large address a crucial issue: that the total musical development of children, in any society, is not restricted to labs or school buildings. Ulric Neisser's (1974:2) assertion that theories of perception and cognition should be ecologically valid, that is, that they should account for "what people do in real, culturally significant situations," finds some support in the ethnomusicological literature,[1] and in two recent overviews of music cognition research, each of which draws to some degree upon cross-cultural data (Sloboda 1985; Dowling and Harwood 1986).

---

1 The ethnomusicological literature concerning children's music and the role of music in cognitive and social development is, it must be admitted, not extensive. [Exceptions include Waterman 1955; Nettl 1956; Blacking 1967; Smith 1987, and in two recent overviews of music cognition research, each of which draws to some degree upon cross-cultural data, Sloboda 1985; Dowling and Harwood 1986.]

My field research consisted of a total of eighteen months in Ibadan, the largest indigenous city in sub-Saharan Africa. My inquiries focused upon the urban popular musics produced and patronized by the roughly twenty million Yorùbá of southwestern Nigeria. As an anthropologist, I was particularly interested in the relationship of musical ideas, values, and practices to other domains of urban life, including economics, ideology, and social identity. My core informants were men ranging in age from 20 to 70, practitioners of such popular musical styles as *jùjú* and *fújì*. I also asked everyone I could, from taxi drivers and traffic cops to clerks and professors, what they thought about music, what they listened to in live performance, whose records they bought, what band they would hire for a naming ceremony or funeral, and so on. I hung around with the children in my neighborhood, playing with them and noting the impressive diversity of their musical knowledge — most kids past the age of six could competently parody various genres of Yorùbá popular music, Christian hymns and Muslim occasional music, imported music ranging from reggae to country and western, Indian film themes, and television and radio jingles. Nonetheless, I regarded children as relatively peripheral to my research aims.

I was awakened one bright morning at 8:00, after an arduous night on the Ibadan nightclub circuit, by a stream of sound emanating from a building under construction next door. Upon such investigation as my tender condition allowed, I concluded that a group of boys were ensconced therein, beating cardboard boxes and creating a dense, rumbling texture penetrated on occasion by one or two voices, an inept rendition of a traditional iron gong pattern played on a Fanta bottle with a nail, and a shrill whistling sound, repeated at irregular intervals. With characteristic alacrity, I rolled over and pulled a block of mattress foam over my head.

I was later visited that day by the leader of this ensemble, Kazeem Salawu (age twelve), and his self-described "right-hand man" Maruf Ganay (age fourteen. Knowing of my interest in music, Kazeem said that he thought it best that I record them before they became famous. "We want our name to be great in this Nigeria," said he, with the forthright self-confidence typical of an empire-building entrepreneurial people. We made plans to meet the next afternoon in my flat for a taping session. The *Junior Fújì Stars of Agbówó* consisted of eight boys between the ages of ten and fourteen. All of them were Muslims, and all had experience performing *wéré* or *ajísáàrì* music, a genre performed by groups of young men during Ramadan to wake the faithful for their morning meal. The largest *wéré* groups include a singer/declaimer who intones Quranic texts and praise songs, several chorus singers, and an eclectic selection of drums and idiophones. Organized competitions between groups representing area mosques became popular in the 1960's.

Although the first commercial recordings of *wéré* music were made in Lagos in the late 1920's, the genre was not fully professionalized and detached from the Islamic sacred calendar until the mid-1970's, with the emergence of *fújì* music. The etymology of the term *fújì* is uncertain, although informants suggest linkages with *orin fáàjì* (songs for enjoyment), used as a stylistic designation on recordings during the 1950's and 60's, and the term *fújà*, "to show off or give a lavish display." The first popularizer of the style was Sikiru Ayinde Barrister, a former *wéré* musician born in the crowded central district of Ibadan. Barrister claims to have developed *fújì* music in the early 1970's while a soldier in the Nigerian Army, and to have taught it to his major competitor, Ayinla Kollington, a native of the northern Yorùbá town of Ilorin. Both Barrister and Kollington, now wealthy Alhajis, had won major *wéré* singing contests in their youth, and thus achieved some degree of notoriety before becoming full-time professional musicians. Despite the widespread association of professional musicianship and praise-singing with low status, the Horatio Alger-like career stories of these two superstars evoke traditional Yorùbá values: the importance of God-given destiny, conceived as a spiritual force seated in the individual's head (*orí*), and the necessity of hard work as the basis of entrepreneurial success and status mobility. Barrister and Kollington, based in the cosmopolitan economic center of Lagos, provide role models for young men preparing themselves to eke out a living within an unpredictable urban informal economy.

Professional *fújì* bands may include *dùndún* and *gángan* pressure drums; *sámbà*, a square wooden frame drum; *sákárà*, a circular ceramic frame drum; *igbá*, calabashes beaten with ringed fingers; *sèkèrè*, bottle-gourd rattles, and Afro-Cuban derived maracas; *agogo*, iron gongs; various single-headed conga-type drums (*àkúbà, ògido, agbámbolé*); and *double-toy*, or bongos, derived from Cuban dance music. Stylistic norms encourage experimentation with both old and new instruments, including the *bàtá* drum, symbolically associated with the powerful god of thunder (Sàngó); the long ceramic *kàkàkí* trumpet, a traditional prerogative of northern Yorùbá sacred kings; police whistles, inspired by Afro-American funk music; and the Western trap set or "jazz drums." The lyrics of *fújì* generally praise wealthy patrons, and abuse the enemies of the band leader. *Fújì* singing style is tense and nasalized, and melodies are often melismatic and microtonically-ornamented, features derived from and symbolically associated with the genre's Islamic origins.

The members of the *Junior Fújí Stars* had gained some experience performing *wéré* music during Ramadan season. They were eager to become professional, and began practicing in the deserted building to develop their repertoire before seeking employment at naming, wedding, or funeral ceremonies, the most common venues for live *fújí* performance. None of the boys were from wealthy families. Kazeem's father was a lineage-trained *dùndún* talking drummer. Ganay, the second-in-command, was the son of a butcher, who had also worked as a drummer to supplement his earnings. Three of the other boys' fathers were butchers, one a *makalíkí* or "bush mechanic," another a lorry driver, and the last a traditional healer. Although Kazeem admitted that his father wanted to "leave drumming" and become a trader, he was adamant about his own desire to be a *fújí* musician. He had organized the group, prodded the members to attend rehearsals, and owned the only drum used in their performances, a *sámbà* drum given him by his father. More expensive local and imported instruments were, for the moment at least, out of the question.

To substitute for the instruments used by adult groups, Kazeem incorporated readily available materials; a set of three cardboard boxes of varied size, chosen in keeping with the traditional notion of hierarchically-organized drum "families;" a soda bottle; a small tin can filled with coarse sand; and a pair of plastic Biro ballpoint pen caps, fastened together with scotch tape and used as a whistle. Each band member was immediately able to offer an imaginative homologue for the instrument he played; one cardboard box was a *dùndún* "talking drum"; the second, an *ògido* or large conga; and the third, a *bàtá* drum; the sand-filled can was a *sèkèrè* rattle; and the Fanta bottle an *agogo* iron bell. The pen-cap aerophone was modeled upon a type of whistle used by Yorùbá children. Lacking the resources to equip their band with traditional instruments, the *Junior Fújí Stars* incorporated the detritus of urban consumption, creatively fashioning musical instruments from materials found in trash heaps.

The performance I recorded that day was largely based upon *fújí* recordings by Barrister and Kollington. It began with a non-metric vocal recitation, a typical feature of the genre. Important stylistic features included shifts between duple and triple meters, call-and-response singing, and occasional dramatic pauses for group recitation of proverbs and slang phrases. As in almost all Yorùbá social dance music, the rhythmic infrastructure was generated from the interlocking of relatively simple and repetitive patterns, which together formed a complex polyrhythmic aural gestalt. Any sound instruments producing three distinct pitches or timbral qualities may be used to imitate the tonal contours of spoken Yorùbá. In the *Junior Fújì Stars*, the largest cardboard box was used — albeit somewhat ineffectively — as a "talking drum." When I played the tape for adult Yorùbá informants they noted that the box was used to "say" a proverb, although the lack of clear pitch distinctions made it difficult to interpret.

Clear distinctions were drawn among sociomusical roles, the two boys whose fathers were drummers filling the apical positions of leader and "right-hand man," and the others constituting the *ègbè* (chorus, literally "supporter" or "protectors"). The construction of the song text, a *bricolage* of segments snatched from commercial recordings, was an impressive example not only of the children's imaginative involvement in mass-reproduced music, but of their knowledge of the social rules governing Yorùbá musical performance.

Kazeem began the performance with a non-metric solo vocal phrase drawn from a Kollington album, and used to abuse a competitor:

> *agbóko lówó, agbáyá lówó alyá*
> The husband-stealer, the wife-stealer

On a signal from Kazeem, played on the *sámbà* drum, the three cardboard boxes, coffee can, and soda bottle established a rolling 12/8 pattern, and the chorus sang:

> *Alàbí tí gbé'se re dé-o*
> Alabi has brought your thing, oh [i.e., what you like to do].

They repeated the phrase over and over, inserting the names of various band members ("X has brought your thing to you, oh"), a typical introduction and group boast. After about two minutes, the rhythm shifted to a four pulse 16/8 pattern, and Kazeem sang an excerpt from Barrister's *Family Planning*, a song urging adherence to the federal government's population control program:

> *gbogbo èyin bímo-bímo, e wá gbó òrò kékeré kan o jàre*
> All you people who have repeatedly given birth to children, come
> and listen to one little word, o.k.?

The lyric continued, "When praying to God for children, pray for children that will go to both the Western and Islamic schools, and who will become doctors, lawyers and judges and bring money home." Interestingly, a strategic omission was made from Barrister's original text: all references to birth control were discarded, and only the section about good children — reflecting, of course, on the performers themselves — was deployed.

The drumming then shifted to a brisk 16/8 pattern, and Kazeem launched into a rendition of Barrister's hit song about his visit to "Destneyworld"

E tétí, e gbó! America ti mo rè, ojo mi lójú
Open your ears and listen! The America I visited is very impressive

èmi pèlú Alájì Kamoru, a jo sere lo sí America, ni Florida, ni Orlando
Alhajo Kamoru and I, we went on a spree in America, in Orlando, Florida

Kazeem continued, "We entered a lift when the light was off, and then got inside something that was not really an automobile or a plane, it wasn't clear to us at all. The white people who were there numbered more than four hundred. I was shouting, 'My mother, Osere Sifau!' ; the whites were screaming 'My mother!' " Suddenly the drumming stopped, and the whole band shouted in unison:

kò s'éni tó mó pé Magic Kingdom!!
Nobody knew that we were in the Magic Kingdom!!

The fast 16/8 pulse was established again, and Kazeem began a refrain that was picked up by the others:

Olórun tó dá Raji eléwé ló dá Rabiu aláta, certainly!
The same god that created Raji the herbalist also created Rabiu
the pepper-seller, certainly [i.e., the same God created all human beings].

To close the performance, the percussionists returned to the opening 12/8 rhythm, and Kazeem sang the phrase that was used to introduce the band, with the term *òyinbó* (white man) inserted in the opening position.

òyinbó ti gbé's e re dé-o
White man has brought your thing, oh.

My adult Yorùbá informants regarded this performance as *aríwò* or "noise," humanly disorganized sound. Perhaps they, like many adults in our society, no longer had access to the wellsprings of imagination that turn cardboard boxes into talking drums. From my (non-Yorùbá) point-of-view, the *Junior Fújì Stars* clearly knew a great deal about the essential norms of Yorùbá music-making and text construction, and the pragmatics of performance. The overall structure of the performance paralleled in all essential respects the commercial recordings of Barrister and Kollington, with a vocal introduction,

the subsequent entrance of the percussion instruments, abrupt shifts between duple and triple metric schemes, and pauses for group recitation of
proverbs and slang phrases. The basic structural scheme of an open-ended
string of sections characterized by contrasting rhythmic schemes, and sometimes separated by dramatic pauses, is typical of *fújì* and other styles of
Yorùbá popular music.

The organization of the ensemble group also reflected the performers'
sociomusical knowledge. Yorùbá models of social and musical order are
predicated upon a cardinal conceptual distinction between a leader and his
supporters. In musical contexts this distinction is verbalized in terms of a
distinction between *elé and égbè*, which in terms of performance roles may
be glossed as "leader" and "chorus"; in musical terms as "call" and
"response"; and which, literally translated, might be rendered as "that which
drives something into or ahead of something else" versus "that which supports, surrounds, or protects." This conceptual dichotomy was clearly
reflected in the performance behavior of the *Junior Fújì Stars*. Among the
instrumental roles, the leader/supporter distinction was clearest between
lead cardboard box (the imaginary talking drum, fulfilling the traditional
role of the "mother drum") and supporting percussionists. At one point in the
performance, after the section described above, Kazeem looked at his "right-
hand man," Maruf, and sang *od'ówó onílù mi Ayansola* ("I pass it to the
hand of my lead drummer Ayansola"), Ayansola being the name of
Barrister's famous lead drummer. Maruf then took a solo, slapping the
cardboard box sharply to create a cracking sound that cut through the texture of the band. Relationships among the supporting parts were not as
clearly articulated. One adult informant commented sardonically that the
agogo player was either the world's greatest musician or a complete idiot,
since he stuck to his own pattern without adjusting to any of the others. The
"time-line" played on *agogo* is musically crucial, and it is interesting that the
part was given to one of the least experienced musicians in the group. Independence and variability are characteristic of the highest levels of social and
musical organization; repetitive supporting patterns are generally given to
lower-status individuals.

Fújì music is essentially praise music, sung to boost the reputations of
powerful sponsors, and this performance shows a keen understanding of this
fact. The fashioning of texts appropriate to particular social contexts is a
primary focus of Yorùbá aesthetics. The lyric I have described here, made of
of seemingly disconnected segments about adulterers, good children, Dis-
neyworld, herbalists and pepper-sellers, was in fact a refined application of

traditional rhetorical techniques, strategically aimed at a particular individual. After the introduction, the band introduced itself, member by member, and claimed to have their patron's "thing." They then portrayed themselves as morally upright children who attend school and take money home to their parents, and recounted a wondrous incident in what they knew to be my country of origin. An *ìjìnlèe* (traditional, literally "deep") Yorùbá proverb culled from a vinyl disc was used to assert the ontological connection of all human beings, regardless of external appearance. Kazeem gave the performance a sense of closure by returning to the opening refrain, and substituting the term *òyìnbó* ("white man") for the band members' names, a textual strategy that reinforced our relationship while emphasizing its inherent inequality, clarified whose "thing" they had, and, most importantly, compelled me to respond with a monetary "dash."

The excerpt I have schematically described here, a little less than six minutes in length, is the initial segment of a continuous thirty-minute performance. It is the music of children emulating adult models of performance; but it is also *children's* music, a distinctive form of creative *bricolage* drawing upon the resources available in a socially heterogeneous, economically precarious urban context. The acquisition of musical knowledge begins early in Yorùbáland, and is inextricably intertwined with the internalization of cultural values and social norms, and the formation of self through interaction with others. In Ibadan, as in Calcutta, the South Bronx, and Mexico City, children who, by virtue of their age and class position, are doubly excluded from dominant forms of musical technology, create vital music from the precipitates of industrial production. Yorùbá popular music flows from the margins of power as well as the center, and from poor children like Kazeem and Ganiyu as well as the wealthy adult superstars created by the music industry.

Our understanding of what happens when humans learn music "in the world" would be enriched by applying the ethnographic methods utilized by anthropologists and ethnomusicologists, including participant-observation, open-ended interviewing, and detailed description of musical behavior and interaction across a broad range of contexts.[2] Children learn to interpret and

---

2   In Western Europe and the United States these might include not only schoolroom, but also living rooms, tree houses, playgrounds, and bathtubs.

produce musical sounds as part of a more inclusive process of orientation in time and space, within a given cultural universe of knowledge, value, and affect, and a constellation of social relationships.

Bibliography

Blacking, John. *Venda Children's Songs*, Johannesburg: University of Witwatersrand Press, 1967.

Dowling W., Harwood, Jay and Dane L. *Music Cognition*, Orlando: Academic Press, 1986.

Neisser, Ulric. *Cognition and Reality: Principles and Implications of Cognitive Psychology*, Chicago: W.H. Freeman, 1976.

Nettl, Bruno. "Notes on infant musical development," *Musical Quarterly*, 42:28-34, 1956.

Sloboda, John. *The Musical Mind: The Cognitive Psychology of Music*, Oxford: Clarendon Press, 1985.

Smith, Barbara B. "Some interrelationships of variability, change and the learning of music." Seeger Memorial Lecture, 31st annual meeting of the Society for Ethnomusicology , (Rochester, NY).

Waterman, Richard A. "Music in Australian Aboriginal Culture: some sociological and psychological implications." *Music Therapy*, 1955:40-50, 1956.

Patterns of Musical Enculturation
in Afghanistan

John Baily and Veronica Doubleday
Department of Music
Columbia University

Introduction

The study of musical enculturation is one of the keys to understanding musical systems as cognitive phenomena, for it shows how cognitive schemata are built up and reveals the kinds of information necessary for their development. It thus illuminates the nature of musicality and allows for differentiation between innate biological components and those that are socially generated. Our account of musical enculturation in Afghanistan focuses on the musical environment of the child, and examines its crucial impact on the development of competence in musical performance. Afghan society is firmly based upon the home and family and the musical skills of an Afghan child are directly related to the abilities of the adults that immediately surround it. We are concentrating upon musical development as a *social* process, one that is intimately bound up with the musical role that the child will be expected to play in adult life.

The data upon which this article is based were collected in the city and environs of Herat during the 1970's. Herat may be considered as representative of provincial Afghan towns and cities. As in other areas of Afghan life, conditions in Kabul, the capital city, were in some ways rather different. Since the time of our research Afghanistan has been invaded by the Soviet Union, and Herat — the third largest city in Afghanistan — has been devastated by war. Many of its inhabitants have been killed or have become refugees in Iran, Pakistan and other countries. While the broad outline of our analysis would undoubtedly apply to present conditions, we prefer to use the past tense in this discussion as a reminder that there has been considerable disruption in all aspects of Afghan life — including, and perhaps especially in, music-making.

The Place of Music in Herati Society

It is necessary to mention several general aspects of the socio-cultural milieu within which musical development took place in Herat, and which were also in one way or another related to Muslim beliefs and practices.

1. The Afghan definition of "music" differed in some ways from the European. What we are treating here as music is not necessarily what the Afghans would classify as music. According to the Afghan folk view, music (*musiqi*) was produced by playing musical instruments, especially melodic instruments. Unaccompanied singing was not classified as *musiqi*, and this applied to both religious singing (most obviously heard in the call to prayer of the *(muezzin)*, and to the singing of women, even when accompanied by the frame drum *(dāireh)*. But for analytical purposes we would include such phenomena in the category of music. (See Sakata, 1983, chapter 4 for further discussion of the Afghan concept of music.)

2. The people of Herat constituted a traditional Muslim society in which purdah, the strict segregation of men and women, was strongly enforced. Men dominated public space while women moved largely within the privacy of the domestic sphere. All social occasions, apart from intimate family gatherings, were segregated, and this was also a strong feature of musical performance. Outside the theatre, with its courtesan singers, it was rare for boys and girls or men and women to make music together. At weddings — the the prime occasion for singing, dancing and playing musical instruments — men and women gathered in separate spaces, often in neighbouring houses. There were important differences between men's and women's musical styles, instruments, repertories, and knowledge of music theory. Purdah therefore had musical consequences.

3. Music occupied an ambiguous place within the Herati value system. There was a general consensus that music played an appropriate role in rituals and celebrations, but that for other purposes such as entertainment it was disapproved of by religious authority. Orthodox mullahs (Hanifi Sunni) preached

that *musiqi* — playing musical instruments — was a worthless and even sinful activity. This stern, puritanical view was counterbalanced by popular and Sufi traditions which emphasised the positive spiritual values of music (describing music as "food for the soul"), and in certain contexts music was even used for devotional purposes.

4. An important distinction was made between amateur and professional musicians (Baily 1979). The performance of music at public or semi-public gatherings, such as wedding parties and concerts, was in the hands of hereditary professional musicians, call *sāzandeh*. Urban male *sāzandeh* sang and played the *armonia*, the small hand-pumped harmonium so common in South Asia, the *tabla* drum pair, and the *rubāb* (a plucked lute), and sometimes other chordophones such as the *delrubā, tanpurā* and *sormandel*. As musicians they had an ambiguous status. On one hand, they were admired as artists (*honarmand*), equivalent to poets, painters and calligraphers, and in this sense had acquired something of the prestige of the former court musicians of Kabul. On the other hand, they were stereotyped by others as *jats*, (low ranking rural barber-musicians) accused of a variety of practices contrary to Islamic precepts. Urban female *sāzandeh* in Herat sang and played the harmonium, *tabla* and *dāireh* (frame drum), but not the chordophones of the men. As women whose work regularly led them to break the rules of purdah they had an unambiguous low social status, mixed with fame and notoriety, and were stigmatised as "easy women," if not as prostitutes. Male amateurs strove to disassociate themselves in the public eye from *sāzandeh*, emphasising that they themselves played and sang because of their compulsive love of music, not merely to make a living; they invoked the status of *shauqi* (enthusiast) — despite the fact that some earned their livelihood from music. (See Slobin 1976:23-24 for further discussion of the term *shauqi*.) Female amateurs were not faced with this problem; their performance did not fall into the Afghan domain in music, and they were in no danger of being confused with female *sāzandeh*.

5. Music education was not part of the traditional or modern school curriculum. The traditional mosque school offered a

John Baily and Veronica Doubleday

basic education; not surprisingly, given the attitude of mullahs, music had no place in the curriculum. Music was not taught in modern secular schools, which also failed to recognise or exploit music as a useful tool for learning through songs or action games. There was a formal music theory in existence, called the "science of music," but this was the domain of the urban male *sāzandeh* and not public knowledge. It included the Indian *sargam* system of oral and written notation (comparable in many ways to tonic sol-fa). Only the male children of hereditary musicians had direct access to this formal knowledge, apart from a few cases where parents took the unusual step of arranging private music lessons for their children.

Four Patterns of Musical Enculturation

Herati children did not have a distinct musical culture of their own in which children created their own songs. There was little in the way of a distinct children's musical repertory. Nor was there a large body of songs for adults to sing to children. As music makers, Herati children were principally involved in the musical imitation of adults. The songs they sang were mainly currently popular radio songs, and their dances were like those performed by men and women at wedding parties.

The lullaby was one early musical experience common to virtually all Herati children. Women sang lullabies to their swaddled babies and small children while they vigorously rocked them to sleep in their cradles. The singing was highly rhythmic at its most basic an extended repetition of the phrase *Allā Huwa* (He is God), but sometimes the mother sang a long selection of suitable verses.

We will now examine the process of learning music by looking at four distinct categories of children, distinguishing between girls and boys and between children from ordinary (non musician) families and those from hereditary musician families. It is necessary to point out that the number of *sāzandeh* in a city like Herat was very small, about thirty women and twenty men in this case.

Girls From Non Musician Families

Girls participated in, and learned to perform, what we may call here *women's domestic music*. This consisted of singing, either solo or in a group, accompanied by the *dāireh*, the only important instrument for women, a large frame drum fitted with pellet bells and rings inside the frame. This drum was also used to play the rhythms of a number of distinct dances. Women were required to perform this kind of music in connection with happy occasions, such as betrothal, engagement or wedding parties, and on the seventh night after the birth of a new baby. Girls usually joined in eagerly with music-making at these times, clapping together with the *dāireh*, particularly when encouraging solo dancers, and joining in the choruses and refrains of songs. Some songs were traditional, others were the recent popular songs from Radio Afghanistan or Iranian radio. Such occasions afforded ideal circumstances for girls to listen, learn and actively participate in music-making with gifted and motivated adult performers.

Children, particularly little girls, played this kind of music as a game, on their own or under the supervision of older girls or women. If the family did not possess a *dāireh* one was borrowed from next door, or girls made do with a metal tray or even imitated the *tabla* drums of the women's bands with an upside-down washing bowl and bucket. Drumming and clapping were an integral part of these singing and dancing sessions, and rhythms were learned from an early age. Little girls were encouraged to dance almost as soon as they could walk and they were sometimes called on to display their precocious talents in front of guests. The *dāireh* clearly required some performance skill, but the women did not consider that this was something that had to be deliberately learned; it was a skill that was taken for granted. Girls heard the various *dāireh* rhythms from an early age and learned how to execute them by watching others.

Before reaching puberty girls had a good deal of time for music and often developed a passion for this pastime. As they approached puberty, music making was discouraged; it was necessary to become more responsible, modest and hard working. Musical skills were not forgotten, but there were fewer opportunities for performance and any desire to perform had to be curbed. Girls knew that they would soon be married and that older women were already judging them for their manners and domestic skills with the prospect of selecting daughters-in-law. A strong interest in musical performance could be interpreted as a sign of flightiness and reluctance to work hard.

Boys From Non Musician Families

Boys were also exposed to women's domestic music and participated in it to some extent. They might sing and take part in the dancing, but they shunned the *dāireh* as a girls' instrument. In villages there was a tradition of solo singing whilst at work in the fields. A specific occasion for boys' group singing occurred during the evenings of Ramadan, the Muslim month of fasting, when boys went from house to house singing special Ramadan verses and begging for treats.

A few boys made toy instruments, such as long-necked lutes (*dutār*) out of wooden spoons and drums out of tin cans. Few boys had access to the musical instruments played by adults, which were not common objects in the households of Herat. Instruments were expensive, delicate, and even slightly shameful, and were kept well out of the hands of children. The *dutār* was perhaps the commonest instrument played by amateur musicians in Herat, both solo and to accompany singing. Research on the way adult *dutār* players had acquired their instrumental skills (Baily 1976) showed that they usually claimed to be self-taught and were proud of the fact. They usually began to play the *dutār* at about the age of twelve, and learned by copying another performer, normally a relative or friend, without revealing what they were doing. They would listen and watch, and then practise in private. To gain access to an instrument they often had to borrow it surreptitiously, when the owner was out of the house. Acquiring a *dutār* of one's own, usually an old instrument bought from the *dutār* maker, made all the difference to the aspiring *dutār* player. Boys were often discouraged by their relatives from learning music, being told it was sinful. They had to overcome many obstacles to learn to play the *dutār*.

Boys had more freedom than girls to extend their knowledge as they grew older. They would get together as groups of friends to play music, which provided another type of learning situation, involving participation. A few amateur musicians went for formal paid lessons, usually from hereditary musicians, to learn particular compositions and to find out more about music theory.

Girls From Hereditary Musician Families

In some hereditary musician families both men and women worked as musicians, while in others only the men followed this occupation and their women were kept in strict purdah. Girls from those families where the women were musicians were brought up in a family life oriented around the performance of music. A women's band usually had four or five members, and performed popular radio and traditional Herati songs and dance music at wedding parties, with harmonium, *tabla* and one or more *dāireh*s. As wedding festivities lasted for a twenty-four hour period, women musicians took their babies and young children with them — day after day during the peak seasons, but less frequently at other times of the year. Their children received frequent exposure to musical performance from the earliest stages of life. Small girls ran errands and minded their younger siblings, and it was recognized that they learned a great deal through watching and listening to their mothers, aunts, sisters and cousins.

At about the age of ten, girls began performing solo song-and-dance routines at weddings in response to requests from the hosts, who rewarded them with small gifts of money. Rather than being barred from music-making and told to behave modestly like non musician girls of their age, these girls competed for attention and were rewarded if they were outward-going and confident performers. Soon after this the girl would be given opportunities to play the *dāireh* and sing in a band, which was organised flexibly so that any member could drop out to rest or to feed a baby when necessary. The girls were recruited into these bands through kinship or marriage and all acquired an acceptable level of competence in *dāireh* playing and singing.

Next the young female musician aspired to master the *tabla*. *Tabla* rhythms were a transformation of *dāireh* technique and the flat-handed strokes they used were rather different from those used in the classical Indian styles of the men. Their drums (which were imported from Pakistan) were of poor quality, and the women made no attempt to tune them. Some girls never became good enough to play the *tabla*, and remained in a subordinate role as singers and *dāireh* players. From playing the *tabla*, a few girls progressed to playing the harmonium, teaching themselves, and picking out familiar tunes. In the early stages such a girl might play only dance pieces; later she would learn to combine the role of lead singer with her harmonium playing. A talented girl would be able to lead a band, select songs and structure a half-hour programme of music by about the age of fourteen, and by the age of sixteen or seventeen could be an accomplished musician and independent band leader.

No great emphasis was placed on technical finesse as instrumentalists (in contrast to urban male hereditary musicians) and there was no tuition, apart from the correction of faults. Women encouraged and praised learners in the bands, but ultimately motivation was left to the individual, who had to strive for herself to learn through imitation. While it was expected that anyone could join in the singing, and play the *dāireh*, the *tabla* and harmonium were instruments that had to be *learned*, even though by oneself. A more detailed account of the lives of women musicians in Herat is given by Doubleday (1988).

Boys from Hereditary Musician Families

Boys raised in musician families grew up in a musically more complex world. Urban male *sāzandeh* played the popular music repertory performed by women, but they also performed various genres of art music (closely related to the "classical" music of India and Pakistan) that women did not know. One of the distinguishing features of male hereditary musicians was their music theory, essentially a variant of Hindustani music theory with its *rāg*s and *tāl*s. They believed that music should be learned through the medium of notation and emphasised the importance of the master-student relationship, through which musical knowledge should be transmitted. But despite these ideals, it seems that these boys learned music in the same way as *sāzandeh* girls, "by ear," through exposure to the sounds of music, imitation of musical performance, and individual trial and error in a social environment in which every encouragement was given by family members. There was no formal musical training, no exercises of the type used to learn Hindustani music, and little notion of sitting down for a "practice session."

Male musicians had some interesting ideas about musicality and its development. They recognised that some individuals were naturally musical, and thought this had to be nurtured, like blowing on smoldering embers to make them burst into flame. They believed that *early exposure* to the sounds of music was especially important in the development of musical ability, and used to take their young sons with them from an early age to sit upon the bandstand with the musicians. Even if the child slept they believed the sounds of music were still absorbed. A boy often showed a lively interest in a particular instrument at a quite early age (five or six) and would be allowed to experiment with it. Of course, there was parental intervention in this process, more in giving encouragement at what was right than in active discouragement of what was wrong, but it seems that despite all the talk about how one *should* learn music, boys in musician families actually learned principally through imitation. Boys in families in which the women were also musicians had the additional experience of going with their mothers to wedding engagements when young, just like the girls, and even lent a hand with the music, especially playing *tabla*. This came to an end when they reached puberty.

By about the age of twelve, when young amateur musicians were starting to learn an instrument, the young *sāzandeh* musician was ready to start his professional career, going out as a member of a band. Once he was a regularly active performer in a group there was an opportunity to develop more advanced skills from playing with others. A young singer-harmonium player of twelve might be able to lead a band for a set of songs, and by the age of sixteen he could be the full-time leader of a band. A musician was identified as the player of a particular instrument; often he could play others, though not usually in public, and this was taken as a sign of musical maturity.

There were some non-musician men amongst these musician families. They were not necessarily "un-musical," but chose, or were encouraged, to go into some other profession. *Sāzandeh* bands tended to be organized as family businesses and there was only work for a rather small number of full-time professional musicians. Boys tended to learn the instruments that were going to be required in the family band some years in the future. A fuller account of the lives of male musicians in Herat is given in Baily (1988).

Discussion

Perhaps the most interesting aspect of the data presented above is the contrast between children of musician and non-musician families, which shows that the former developed more advanced musical abilities, in terms of cognitive and motor skills, and repertory. This difference did not arise from a distinction between what one might term "formal" and "informal" modes of music learning. One could not really talk about "music education" in this context, nor about "training in music," for these terms imply a "directed learning process" (Merriam 1964:146), an intention to create a learning situation in which to impart information, which was hardly the case in Herat. *Musician and non-musician children learned in the same way,* through imitation and participation, in what one might describe as a course of "self-paced self-instruction." The difference in the musical abilities of the two groups of children must have been the result of their exposure to different social environments. The learning situations and the learning processes were inherent in the family life of musicians and non-musicians.

Imitation has not received the attention it deserves as a method for learning music. Merriam (1964) was surely wrong to see the role of imitation as simply a "first step" (*ibid* 147), to say that "special skill requires special training," or that "formal training is required to become a real musician" (*ibid* 150). In Herat, imitation would seem to have been the central part of the learning process. Imitation implies learning in a situation in which the child attempts to reproduce the thing itself. Acquisition has not been separated off as a course of instruction, systematised for pedagogic purposes. Visual information is very important; it is often necessary to see how things are done in order to understand how to do them. Imitation requires the child to work things out for itself; there are no explanations. The difference between children of musician and non-musician families in terms of ability lay in the musical resources available to be imitated and the way that imitation was encouraged.

A number of factors enriched the musical environment of the child in a musician family:

1. There was frequent exposure to the sounds of music from the earliest age.

2. There was strong encouragement to engage in musical play activities, with access to musical instruments.

3. There were models for emulation, frequent opportunities to watch adults and older siblings playing musical instruments, and to observe closely their instrumental skills.

4. There was the opportunity to participate actively in the performance of music by adults.

5. Musician children grew up in a social world in which playing music seemed to be what life was all about.

These differences in musical environment are sufficient to explain the apparent differences in the musicality of musician and non-musician children and there is no need to look for explanations couched in terms of, for example, genetic factors.

Learning by imitation has important consequences, for it really means that the child inevitably reproduces what is going on around it. This is an example of culture as "a setup for *learning* behaviour of very complex and specific types." (Gillin, cited by Merriam *ibid,* 162) This principle is clearly shown by a second contrast in the data, between girls and boys. Gender relations in Herat were clearly manifest in musical terms, where women's access to material goods and information was restricted. Women had access to a smaller variety of musical instruments than men; indeed, most women had access to only one instrument, the *dāireh*. They knew very little about formal music theory. They were not faced with tuning problems; they did not play the chordophones of the men, which required fine tuning of sympathetic strings, and they did not tune their tablas. Their music was structurally (melodically and rhythmically) simpler than the music played by men. It was altogether closer to a method for reciting poetry, the text being the main focus of attention, not the "musical setting" of the text. Women had no access to the genres of art music.

Women's domestic music, the simplest of the adult musical styles we have mentioned in this paper, was also the most widespread. There were far more women performers than men amongst the non-musician population of Herat. We see this music as the main enculturating experience for Herati children, the basic "reservoir" of music. It is significant to find that this was the style that constituted children's music, a relationship maintained by constant interaction between children and their elder kinswomen. Moreover, this was a type of music making sanctioned by religion, and, therefore, suitable for children. The separate worlds of men's and women's, and of amateur and professional, music were anticipated in the musical life of the child, who learned through imitation from an early age to perform the role that would be expected of it in adult life.

Acknowledgments

This research was supported by a post-doctoral research grant from the Social Science Research Council to John Baily while a research fellow in the Department of Social Anthropology, The Queen's University of Belfast, 1973-78.

This paper was originally presented at the conference on Music and Child Development by John Baily under the title "Children's music in Afghanistan. It was rewritten in collaboration with Veronica Doubleday, who collected the

John Baily and Veronica Doubleday

data relating to women's music making in Herat, for publication in French under the title "Modeles d'impregnation musicale en Afghanistan," in *Cahiers de musiques traditionelles 1. De bouche à oreille*, Genève, Ateliers d'ethnomusicologie, 112-124, 1988. We wish to express our gratitude to Laurent Aubert, editor of *Cahiers de musiques traditionelles* for permission to publish the English version of the paper in this volume of conference proceedings.

References

Baily, John. "Recent changes in the *dutār* of Herat," *Asian Music*, 8(1):29-64, 1976.

Baily, John. "Professional and amateur musicians in Afghanistan," *World of Music*, 21(2):46-64, 1979.

Baily, John. *Music of Afghanistan: Professional musicians in the city of Herat*, with accompanying audio cassette, (*Cambridge Studies in Ethnomusicology*), Cambridge: Cambridge University Press, 1988.

Doubleday, Veronica. *Three Women of Herat*, London: Jonathan Cape, 1988.

Merriam, Alan P. *The Anthropology of Music*, Evanston: Northwestern University Press, 1964.

Sakata, Hiromi Lorraine. *Music in the Mind: The Concept of Music and Musician in Afghanistan*, with two accompanying audio cassettes. Kent: Kent State University Press, 1983.

Slobin, Mark. *Music in the Culture of Northern Afghanistan*, Viking Fund Publications in Anthropology, No. 54, Tuscon: University of Arizona Press, 1976.

Thoughts on the Processes of
Language and Music Acquisition

Robert Garfias
Department of Fine Arts
University of California, Irvine[1]

Drawing on my own experience in the study of several different music cultures and almost as many languages, I shall endeavor to make a virtue of my lack of deeper study of the questions at hand and to share some personal speculations concerning the processes of language and music acquisition which have of late intrigued me. In the course of studying different musics and different languages, it began to occur to me that there might be strong parallels between the process of language and music acquisition which are more than fortuitous. I have come to the belief that the roots of each different music structure are inherent and inseparably linked to the structure of spoken language and that the two are, in fact, a single system which is acquired from the earliest stages of infancy throughout the infant's constant processing of the sounds of human voices around him.

The acquisition of one's culture through the process of language acquisition is something we largely take for granted and yet the parameters of this process become more vivid as we learn of the seemingly infinite number of variations through which this is accomplished as we move from one language and culture to another. We assume that things are done differently in other cultures but do not usually imagine the magnitude of such differences until we experience them at first hand.

While much of their activity may seem random and unfocused, children are constantly engaged in the process of absorbing and rejecting from all that they experience each day. Through this process they are constantly selecting and developing a vast repertory of responses, both positive and negative, sets of likes and dislikes, attitudes which generate approval and disapproval,

---

1   Dr. Garfias is now Professor of Anthropology, University of California, Irvine.

all of which eventually enable them to become the responsible, rather rigid and conforming adults which every society expects and demands.

While we all like to think that we have played a unique role in determining the patterns of our own individual cultures, of our likes and dislikes, much of what we choose has, of course, been predetermined. The choices are in fact limited but we do not see these limits since we feel that we operate freely within our range of choices. The free choices in one culture might not reasonably be expected to occur in another.

On my first trip to India many years ago, I recall my quiet astonishment at the process by which mothers put their babies to sleep. Mothers in India usually sit and lay the baby across their knees while vigorously tapping the heel up and down causing the baby's head to bounce rhythmically. The babies do quickly drop off to sleep. Certainly this is antithetical to the Western idea of lulling the baby into a state of quiet which leads to sleep. The Western concept of the lullaby certainly bears this out. In Romania the classic prototype of the *Cintec de Leagan*, the lullaby, has strong ties to, and may have eventually led to the folk love song of Romania, par excellence, the *Doina*. [Taped example 1]

But this is a decidedly Western view of the matter. Among the Aymara speaking Indians of the Puno region of Peru, the lullaby takes on a different nuance. [Taped example 2] While the primary purpose of the lullaby is still to draw the infant into sleep it no longer serves specifically to lull the infant into a state of drowsiness. It provides the infant with a sense of the mother's presence as she continues to work. As long as the infant hears the voice of the mother, the necessary sense of security pervades and sleep can then safely follow. It was apparently this same reaffirmation of the presence of the mother that was going on between the mother in India and her infant. While lulling, comforting, and soothing sounds may be what the Westerner believes to be essential in the raising of a healthy infant, what the survival of the species requires is, in essence, sleep, and this can only come about when a sense of safety and security has been established. The species does survive because of the various traditions of all those mothers, while each — the Westerner, the Aymara Indian, the Gujarat and Tamilian, and the Japanese — will, no doubt, insist that her own method of child-rearing is innately superior.

The lullaby is in a sense a convenient metaphor for all of the earliest communications to the new infant from those already established members of its society. In the lullaby and other sounds made directly to the infant, as well as those sounds which it hears as the adults communicate with each other, are also transmitted the essential sound patterns — the formulae of stress, tone and accent — which serve both as the structure of the spoken language and which underlie the fundamental structure of the music of the group as well. After several years of hearing the speech patterns of his language and of his music around him, the Indian child in Peru finds it natural and reasonable to sing within the boundaries of this same system. [Taped example 3]

I believe, however, that several kinds of information are being transmitted during this very early process of speech/music exchange between the infant and those around him, all occurring long before language as we usually think of it has even begun to formulate itself for the Beyond the formal structural information about both speech and music which is communicated, and the emotional communication which takes place through the interpretation of tone and pattern in speech and music, there is also a broader and more general effect which these speech and musical interactions may have on the infant, and which must certainly influence and alter development.

Ideally, the associations with speech sound and music sound for the infant should suggest comfort, warmth, security and protection. Whether it be a mother's quiet singing, or a thirty-man Balinese Gamelan orchestra which the child grows accustomed to hearing as he falls asleep in his father's or mother's lap at an all night performance, these sounds come to be associated positively with the sense of peace and well-being. The Balinese infant is granted a sense of security and peace while listening to his mother sing an artistically sophisticated lullaby. [Taped example 4] Later in life he or she may recall some of that same sense of peace while sitting, half drowsing, through an all night performance of the *Gambuh* theater, hearing the names of ancient fabled cities and of kings and princes whose dialogue on stage is so classical and archaic that he cannot fully comprehend it. [Taped example 5]

A Shona child growing up in rural Zimbabwe is soon accustomed to hearing the rich sound of several *Mbira* as they are played almost continuously for two or three days at a time in the huge smoke-filled *banya*, or meeting house. It becomes natural for him in later life to associate this sound with a sense of well being, and of unity with his community. Eventually he will probably begin, as most others in the village also do, to become absorbed in the process of picking out various combinations of sounds in the music. He may perhaps even become entranced by the music and use it as a link, to communicate with the ancestors through dreams of music. [Taped example 6]

Such group experiences serve as an excellent means of communal bonding, at the same time reinforcing the cultural values of the group. In these examples, the overt pattern of music to the outsider seems simple and repetitive, but those who have been culturally prepared for it have the opportunity for gaining much more depth — the complex layers of character definition and historical reference in the Balinese *Gambuh*, the complex and ever-changing pattern of kaleidoscopic sound in the Zimbabwe *Mbira* music. Among the Tarahumara Indians of Northern Mexico, the music for the *Matachines* is played by a group of eight or nine violins. While the overall impression is one of an incessantly repeated melody played by all the violins, the musicians and listeners become entranced by listening to the subtle interchange of variations between one musician and another. [Taped example 7]

I would like to return now to consider something about the specific content of the early levels of music and language acquisition. I believe that the process of transmission of both language and music pattern may encompass much more than we generally consider. There are several groups of languages in which the pattern of speech can be abstracted from the phonemic structure of its verbal message and used as the basis for music, e.g., African languages from south of the Sahara, and Chinese and other tone specific languages of Asia.

It occurs often and in many different cultures that a child of two or three years of age says something which seems entirely unintelligible but which is then interpreted by a sibling a year or two older. On such occasions there is often general disbelief from the adults. These certainly cannot be cases in which the children have developed a consciously separate language of their own. The younger children, still engaged in the early stages of language acquisition, rely more heavily on hearing stress and pitch pattern and contour than on pure phonemes in understanding speech. There is also the important factor of expectancy which must aid in this level of communication. Here, "He says he wants bubble gum," is a much more predictable message to be transmitted between speaker and listener than "If I install the 80386 chip should the new 80387 co-processor be set to 'no wait' mode?"

Reliance on speech and contour pattern in spoken language communication plays an important role in defining the underlying accent and contour pattern in the music of the same culture. Of the hundreds of illustrations which might be cited let us consider but a few. The natural stress in Hungarian is on the first syllable of multi-syllabic words. This has generated a characteristic and easily recognized pattern in Hungarian music. It is interesting that of all the Slavic language speakers of Europe, it is the nearest neighbors of the Hungarians, the Czechs, who also make use of the first syllable accent and whose music also shares the characteristic "Hungarian snap."

There is an interesting predilection among Japanese singers trained in the Western art music tradition, to prefer French *chanson* over German *lied*. While this preference could be interpreted as the result of a number of changed historical and cultural factors, it seems significant that while Japanese and French are, as languages, as dissimilar as English and Chinese, both French and Japanese avoid heavy stress and marked accent in speech and song pattern. In fact, this even string of unstressed syllables and general "unmelodious" quality of French *chanson* is the bane of many English and German-speaking connoisseurs of Western art vocal music. French song seems to lack the strong contour and pattern expected by English and German speakers and yet seems to work just fine for the Japanese.

The speech and melodic contour patterns of our language are embedded in our system of recognition and conceptualization very early on. The anthropologist Edward T. Hall suggests that this language imprinting begins within a few hours after birth as the newborn begins hearing others around him speak. The patterns of spoken language, with their inherent implications for music, thus begin developing from a very early period and continue incessantly as the years go on. Rather than thinking of this very earliest stage of cultural acquisition as a prototype for either spoken language or music, I have begun to think that the distinction between language and music might better come at a much later stage, and that perhaps, even then, the distinction is one that becomes exaggerated by our need to create taxonomy and order. If it is correct to assume that earliest communication between the infant and his or her society occurs at the level of stress and tone pattern perception and recognition, rather than recognition of the relationship between phoneme and morpheme, then we must consider much more carefully the communicativity of the basic sound patterns of speech.

If from the metaphoric lullaby, or perhaps meta-lullaby, the infant learns that it is safe to sleep, then from this earliest stage there is an emotional message received along with the sound and, in such cases, it is precisely that message which the sender wishes to be perceived. It takes a great leap forward from this observation to go on to say that verbal communication in these early stages also transmits emotional messages and that these gradually expand their verbal specific referents to such a degree that eventually we learn to read verbal messages in print and to infer the emotional tone embedded in the style without reference to the actual sound of the writer's voice.

I would like to believe that the tone, or emotional content, is vital in verbal communication even when one is reading from a printed page. In our tendency to separate sound from signal and meaning from message we have lost sight of the important capacity for emotional communication which humanly produced sound *as sound* can carry. What the child learns in his earliest years as a speaker of the language of the surrounding adults is not simply more words — a greater vocabulary by which to express his or her feelings, desires, and thoughts — but rather a vast repertory of subtle emotional coloring and nuance, the shades of meaning by which these "words" can be more effective in getting the message across.

The structural principles of spoken language help to determine the fundamental approach to pattern structure in the music of the speakers of this language. The very close relationship between language and music in these early periods of acquisition may be much more than only a reflection of the process. For most of us there is music which has very strong positive emotional associations. Some of these positive associations may go back as far as we can remember. We have been convinced by many, many years of indoctrination that music, as an aspect of our culture is, a cultural refinement, an enrichment of our daily lives, etc. Given the very strong positive position which music has in every known society in the world it is certainly a likely vehicle for more than enrichment and refinement. I believe that it is very likely that it serves a function vital to the continuation of our very complex species. The manner in which we learn music — to listen to it and to participate as we can in its production — serves to constantly refine and expand our vocabulary of spoken expression. It does so by refining and enhancing our sense of emotional coloring as expressed in minute shadings of tone and stress pattern heard in music. I believe that music may be man's primary means of sustaining a process of socialization.

Music in the Service of Ritual Transformation

The Mescalero Apache Girls' Puberty Ceremony [1]

Anne Dhu Shapiro
Department of Music
Boston College

I am going to talk to you today about an extraordinary event, which takes place in the mountains to the Southeast of Albuquerque, New Mexico, and in which music is used in a powerful and important way to shape a ritual central to the identity of the Mescalero Apache tribe and the adolescent females in it.

Before I begin my paper, though, I would like to take a moment to tell you how I, a classically trained harpsichordist and musicologist with research specialties in British-American folksong and theater music, began to work with native-American music. It began with the serendipitous visit of a colleague to my class, Dr. Inès Talamantez, a Professor of Religious Studies at the University of Santa Barbara, California, and herself a woman of Apache heritage. As visiting professor at Harvard for the year, she came to a seminar in ethnomusicology which I was co-teaching there, hoping to gain some insight into how the music of the ceremony about which she was writing could be comprehended. I taught her something, I hope, but became intrigued with her background, and accepted with enthusiasm her invitation to come to the Mescalero Apache reservation to see the ceremony over the fourth of July weekend of 1980.

With the aid of her knowledge, and with the advantage of her contact, I began to be drawn into the wonderful ceremony which I will shortly be describing, and I began to attend the public ceremony every year. At first I

---

1 Portions of this talk have already been published in Shapiro and Talamantez, *The Mescalero Apache Yearbook of the International Council for Traditional Music*, 18, (1986), 77-90.

did so just out of curiosity. Then, slowly, as I began to see and hear more and more, I gained the conviction that here was a kind of music with the utmost beauty and dignity, capable of holding together a four-day long ceremony. This music has been sustained by a vitality sufficient to last in the memory for centuries. Virtually unknown to the outside world,[2] Inès and I began to collaborate on an article, which has subsequently appeared in the *Yearbook of the International Council for Traditional Music*, and on a section of her forthcoming book on the ceremony.

As I became better acquainted with the people, I also was invited to come to private ceremonies, and this year had the good fortune to be invited to a highly traditional ceremony held for a girl whom I had known since she was eight years old. While I have enjoyed extraordinary advantages as the guest of my Apache friends, I and any other researcher who respects the culture, operate at what most ethnomusicologists would hold to be a great disadvantage as well — the banning of the use of tape-recorders and cameras by outsiders. I explain this to you now, so that you will know that I have depended on commercial recordings, authorized tape-recordings of insiders, and their slides as well for any audio-visual material I have.

After describing the ceremony to you with the aid of tapes and slides, I'll discuss some theories concerning its impact on the girls and other tribe members. Music is just one aspect of the ceremony, but a very important one, and its role is, I think, profound.

The Mescalero Apache reservation is found in Southwestern New Mexico, in the mountains just above White Sands desert, which used to be part of Apache territory. The reservation, occupied by the Mescalero since the 1860's, (except for their enforced encampment at Fort Stanton in the 1870's) is beautiful and replete with natural resources. These range from their sacred mountain, the 12,000-foot Sierra Blanca, which also serves as a ski resort, to the White Sands desert, once a part of their territory and now a

---

2 The ceremony has been written about by various other scholars; among them Claire R. Farmer, "Singing for Life" in Charlotte J. Frisbie, (ed.) *Southwestern Indian Ritual Drama* (Albuquerque, 1980), Dan Nicholas, "Mescalero Apache Girls' Puberty Ceremony," *El Palacio* 46 (1939), 143-204, Morris E. Opler, *An Apache Life-Way* (New York, 1941).

government testing site, where certain Mescaleros still have herb-gathering rights.

Once a year, around the fourth of July, the tribe as a whole celebrates their central ceremony, *Isdzanadl'eshde*[3] *Gutaal,* roughly translatable as the *sing* or feast of *Isdzanadl'esh*, or white-painted woman, the most important deity of the Apaches. During the ceremony several girls who have reached puberty are given the ceremony by their parents, as once *Isdzanadl'esh* was given it. It is believed that the ceremony is what returns the goddess to youth and strength. When she begins to feel old, she has only to walk Westward and meet a girl running Eastward at the end of her ceremony in order to renew her youth. During the ceremony, the girls participating become *Isazanadl'esh*, are called *Isdzanadl'esh*, and are deemed to have all the healing powers belonging to her. When they run East at the end of the ceremony, they rub off the white clay which has symbolized their identification with the goddess, and thus begin their womanhood.

Increasingly, individual families also hold private feasts for their daughters, an incredibly burdensome undertaking, since this involves not only preparations for a complicated ritual, but also feeding virtually the whole tribe three meals a day for four days. I will describe the ceremony as it is held for an individual girl, since that is the most traditional form of it.

Preparations for the ceremony begin in advance of the onset of a girl's menarche. The family committed to traditional ways, for instance, knows to begin collecting the sacred pollen each year during the season when the cattails are ready, as well as the other objects which will be necessary for the ritual. A singer or medicine man and a respected woman sponsor are secured in the proper ritual manner (four gifts must be given, the correct words exchanged).

The girl is taught proper Apache ways by her sponsor; her doeskin dress is prepared with elaborate symbolic beadwork and with metal cones on the fringes which represent the sun's rays, and which give a gentle jingle as she dances. All of this initial rite is carried out privately within the family during the year preceding her feast.

---

3   Students of Apache lexicography should be aware that we adopt here the English "a" as a cognate for ą.

As the feast day approaches, friends and family gather, supplies are stored, temporary tipis and cooking arbors are erected, and preparations are made to feed the many who will come to the ceremony.

Prior to dawn of the first day of the ceremony, the girl is separated from her friends, installed in her own tipi, where she is instructed and where she will eat and sleep for the next eight days. Her hair is ritually washed with yucca soap, her legs are wrapped, and she is dressed in the ceremonial garb. She is ritually fed traditional Apache foods and is provided with a special straw through which to sip water, as well as a scratching stick which hangs from her dress.

While all of this is going on, the singers and families are preparing the sacred tipi in which the ceremony will take place. It is built of twelve fresh-cut evergreens, with their green tops left on. Approximately at dawn after each pole has been blessed with pollen, they are raised in turn, the four main ones representing the four directions, then another eight are added. All of these actions are accompanied by singing on the part of the medicine men. Once the tipi has been erected and filled in, the top wrapped in canvas, and an entryway constructed from more trees, the girl is brought out by her sponsor. She carries a blanket and a buckskin which are laid down in front of the tipi. The initiate has been blessed with pollen and she in turn blesses members of the tribe by marking them with pollen. After the blessing the initiate is "molded," that is, massaged by her sponsor to insure a healthy body and a long, fruitful life. On the buckskin the medicine man draws four footprints using pollen, and while the sacred basket is put in place to the east of the tipi, the initiate steps into each of the prints and is "trotted off" to make a run around the basket. Four times the basket is moved closer to the tipi and four times the girl runs around it as four verses of the ritual song are sung, accompanied by a long, high-pitched sound, emitted by the sponsor as she runs. After her four runs, there is a "giveaway": candy, fruits and presents are thrown out of trucks into the crowd.

All of this activity takes about three hours, during which time at least twelve songs are sung. After this initial early morning ritual, the girl appears in public only at night for the next four nights. During the day she is enjoined from normal social contact with her friends, and is visited in her tipi only by her relatives and by those who wish to be blessed.

When dusk arrives, a large central fire is lit, and the *Gaahe*, or Mountain Spirits, dance, blessing the initiate, the ceremonial grounds, the tipi, and the fire. The *Gaahe* dance in teams of four, each with its own drummer and group of singers. They dress in deerskin kilts, fringed with tincone jingles, and they have been ritually painted black with bold designs on back and front, black cloth masks hiding their human identities; yucca headdresses and long flat sticks complete their impressive costumes. They are trailed by one or more *Gaahelbaye* (sometimes called clowns or fools), who are usually apprenticed *Gaahe*. They all bless the fire by bowing toward it and making owl and turkey cries.

As the *Gaahe* dance vigorously around the fire, the initiate, her sponsor, and female relatives, in groups determined by clan, come to dance around the outskirts of the *Gaahe's* circle, in a solemn, stately, dance, as restrained in movement as the Gaahe are bold. The *Gaahe* will continue until about midnight, but the girls and sponsors retire.

By about 10 p.m., the initiate reappears with her sponsor and singer at the ceremonial tipi. The first night the initiate is led into the tipi with an eagle feather, each of four verses of the song marks a large step by the whole group toward the home of *Isdzanadl'esh*, the interior of the tipi, where, facing the fire, the girl and her sponsor sit on deer hides. The singer and his assistants sit on the other side of the fire, backs to the opening of the tipi, and prepare their ritual smokes, long prayer sticks, and rattles.

Following that single song for entering the tipi, all songs are sung in groups of four, as the initiate dances back and forth across the deerhide, looking only at the fire. The songs, accompanied by the light, regular pulse of faunhoof rattles held by each singer, last from four to six minutes. Between songs, the girl rests for three to four minutes. Sometimes instructions are given by the head medicine man; usually there is silence. At the end of each set of four songs, a short formula is sung to mark the group of songs. The singers light hand-rolled cigarettes of ritual tobacco, and a longer break is taken, during which the girl is sometimes given water through her drinking tube. After four or five groups of songs, a set of four ending songs is sung, and the girl and her relatives retire to her tipi. The dancing of the *Gaahe* may continue, however, and after that social dancing around the bonfire often continues well into the night.

Except for the leading-in song of the first night, each of the succeeding three nights proceeds in much the same way, although with different songs each night. The first night songs celebrate the earth and all things on it, the third with all things that fly. I can't provide you any slides of the sacred dancing; all picture-taking is forbidden.

Anne Dhu Shapiro

On the fourth night the girl must dance all night, with only a short break before dawn. For each song sung this night, a wooden marker specially carved by the girl and her family is driven into the ground around the fire. By dawn, the circle is complete; the special dawn songs are sun, just as the first light hits the markers. The main singer paints his hand with the image of the sung, and holds it up just as the sun hits the tipi, while singing the following words:

> They have made the tipi poles of Galena,
> They have made the tipi poles of Red Clay,
> They have made the tipi poles of White Clay,
> They have made the tipi poles of the Rays of the Sun.
> Long life! Its power is good.
> Long life! Its power is good.
> They traditionally make it so for her.
>
> He will paint you with Galena
> Its power is good.
> Long life! Its power is good.
> He will paint you with Red Earth Clay.
> Its power is good.
> Long life! Its power is good.
> He will paint you with White Earth Clay.
> Its power is good.
> Long life! Its power is good.
>
> He is holding up his hand
> Painted with the sun pollen.
> He is holding up his hand
> Painted with the rays of the sun;
> The sun has come down,
> It has come down to the earth,
> It has come to you.
> He will paint you with Red Earth Clay
> He will paint you with White Earth Clay.
> Long life! Its power is good.[4]

---

4   Translation of the song text by Inès Talamantez.

He presses the sun image onto the head of the girl, and paints her with white clay. As this is happening, the branches and cloth covering the sacred tipi are being removed, so that only the four structural poles remain. Within this skeleton structure, the blessing and healing of the entire tribe takes place. The singer, with red clay beside him, blesses every member of the community by marking them with red clay, taking special pains for young children, the elderly, and anyone who is ill.

Following the blessing, which can last over an hour, the final ceremony takes place — a sort of reversal of the activities of the first morning. The girl is led out of the tipi with an eagle feather; footsteps are once again painted on the buckskin; and the sacred basket is once again placed at a distance to the East of the tipi equivalent to its position on the last run of the first morning. Again, the girl takes a position in the footsteps and is "trotted off" to the four verses of the song and accompanying ritual noise made by the women. This time, the basket is moved further to the East for each of the four runs. On the last run, the girl runs to the basket — now far away to the East — and as she runs she rubs the white clay from her face and goes to her private tipi. *Isdzanadl'esh* has returned to her youth, and the girl in turn has become a new Apache woman.

Simultaneously, amid shouts and excitement, the rope of the tipi is undone, and during the last run, it falls to the ground with a great crash. During all of this, the singers continue, accompanied by their rattles. The crowd, however, versed in the traditions of this ceremony, has moved toward the cooking arbor, where pick-up trucks have driven in, laden with candy, fruit, and kitchen goods, which are thrown to the crowd as gifts from the family. The effect of the simultaneous dismantling of the tipi, the last run, and the give-away, with all the shouts of excitement accompanying it, is to break the sacred sense of time decisively and to return the participants to normal tribal life, except for the girl, who will remain secluded in her tipi for the next four days to contemplate what she has been through.

The music ends at this point. The singer and his assistants have sung over one hundred fifty songs during a five-day period. What is its impact on the participants and on the tribe as a whole? The obvious functions of the music during the ceremony are first to shape the ceremony and to carry the sacred words — a function very much akin to that of almost any religion's ritual music. Here we can notice that while the songs are rather rigid, their application is flexible, and they provide time-boundaries and connectors for events. During the first morning, the music serves to unite disparate actions; during the long nights of dancing in the tipi, their grouping marks the time of otherwise undifferentiated activity. Even when something interrupts the dance, the songs continue. This year, for example, the girl's beads broke, and she had to stop dancing while they were collected. The singers continued uninterrupted to the end of the song, though. The song, like almost any piece of performed music, had a course to run, no matter what else occurred.

Second, the music creates accompaniment for the dance of the adolescent girl. For this function, it is particularly important that the music is repetitious in nature. Far from this being an unintentional "primitive" trait, it is deliberately and skillfully done in the service of creating a special environment and an almost trance-like experience for the girl. Repetition, which is a feature of almost any music, is here highly organized and important at every level: from the pulse-beat maintained by the rattle, to the repetition within each refrain and verse, to the fourfold repetition of the verses themselves, and finally the fourfold repetition of the same tune for four different songs. The repetitions lull the listener, giving the effect of timelessness. The singers themselves often have trouble keeping track — the noise emitted by the sponsor, besides being a sacred "calling out" of the goddess, also functions as a sort of ritual marker for the verses, and one sometimes sees the sponsors and singers holding up fingers to signal the number of verses remaining. On the last long night, the wooden markers placed around the firepit help keep track of the number of songs done.

During a complete song one can have the effect of losing oneself, just listening. But it is also easy to keep track of the structure by noticing the refrains, which have strongly profiled contours, (and which repeat both words and music), and the verses, (which repeat music only, where extra syllables may be accommodated. The structural scheme of a complete song can be seen in Figure 1.

During the ceremony, this same tune will normally be sung four times in a row, with different words for the refrain and verse. The sense of stability created by such repetition, as well as by the back-and-forth dancing movement of the girl, contrasts with the images created by the words — images of the entire natural world outside the tipi — and with the instructions given by the medicine men for the girl to think of movement, for example of walking the sickness of a family member away over the mountain. The stability of the music perhaps allows the roaming of the thoughts it accompanies, much as the repetitive nature of an action such as walking or jogging often allows the mind to roam freely.

Figure 1

Refrain:	AABB AABB AABB ABBB
Verse:	CCCCCB
Refrain:	AABB AABB
Verse:	CCCCCCCB
Refrain:	AABB AABB
Verse:	CCCCCCB
Refrain:	AABB AABB
Verse:	CCCCCB
Refrain:	AABB AABB AABB AABB

This is music that literally seems to hold time still, the more so since we know it is music that has been handed down for a great many years with very little change. I have listened to cylinder recordings made in Mescalero in the 1930's and have found exactly the same kinds of structures and singing styles used fifty years ago. Since the ceremony represents a recreation of the original mythical ceremony of *Isdzanadl'esh*, the songs *should* be unchanging — perhaps an impossibility in oral tradition, but nonetheless the ideal. The changes in the ceremony that I have witnessed over my six years of visits have mainly to do with reduction of the number of tunes by some singers because the rest have been forgotten.

Besides functioning to make the ceremony seem timeless, the music also creates associative memory in the girls. These tunes, with their strongly profiled contours, repeated many times, are made to order for memorability. The girl is told by the singer to remember the ceremony, to remember how it felt to be the goddess, and to remember the songs. In fact, at the end of the all-night singing, the girl is asked which were her two favorite songs; these are repeated as the last ones to which she will dance.

It is clear when one listens in the tipi, that it is not only the medicine men and sponsors who know the songs, but also the women (and some of the men) who can be heard humming along with the songs. When interviewed, many of the older women who had had feasts of their own said they could still remember the sound of their songs. Of course, it is also a memory which may be renewed at every feast which they attend subsequently.

The tipi dance songs are not the only music heard, of course. In fact, at the same time, as you may have noticed in my example, the *Gaahe* dancing is going on — with a different style of singing and drumming accompanying it. Here children are actively encouraged to participate in the music; small boys arrange themselves in front of the singers and drummers, and, using a large piece of cardboard, drum along. Even the smallest girls join their female relatives in dancing; and I think we have to realize that the dancing *is* musical participation on the part of the women, who, although they do not sing the *Gaahe* songs, are considered a necessary part of the whole. Elsewhere I have called this the silent music of the women.[5]

The importance of music in the ceremony places demands on the singers — and one finds extraordinary musicians among them. I have worked most closely with a medicine man of fifty-one, who has been singing the ceremony for forty-five years — that is, since he was six years old! He started learning the songs from his grandfather at the age of three, an experience of which he has vivid memories. Considering that a whole ceremony involves memorization of nearly two hundred songs and that they must be done correctly or the ceremony is invalid, he seems to be a clear case of a child prodigy — a sort of Mescalero Mozart, absorbing huge amounts of material from a father figure and able to perform fearlessly under stress at an extremely early age. He is today also a consummate musician, able to discuss his songs intelligently and to teach them to anyone willing to take the time. He will not, however, allow himself to be recorded. It is his view that music should be learned from people, not machines.

His assistant this year at the ceremony was a girl of about eighteen, who was taking the role of apprentice usually taken by an adolescent boy. She already knows many songs, which she sings quietly along with the others using their high baritone range. The tribe seems to accept her in this role, and her mother supports her religious activities. I will be watching her development with interest, since I do not know of any women singers in the history of this tribe.

In summary, the girls' puberty ceremony of the Mescalero Apaches clearly has great impact on the tribe as a whole. They have taken pains to ensure its preservation; they take great pride in it, and its observance is on the rise,

---

5   In an article "Silent Music in the Role of Women in Native-American Ceremonial Music," *Music and Gender*, ed. Barbara L. Hampton, in press.

with as many as sixteen girls going through either private or public ceremonies this spring and summer. From my observations and interviews, I
would say that while music is obviously one of the most important elements
in the ceremony, it is not singled out by the tribe members as an object of
particular interest. Its role for the tribe, and even for the adolescent girls, is
more subliminal, becoming part of the whole sensual background of the
ceremony — the surrounding mountains, the sacred tipi, the smells of
Apache cooking and of smoking sacred tobacco. It is impossible not to feel
the appropriateness of the songs — the very contours of their melodies, with
octave leaps and boldly triadic melodies — seem to echo *both* the natural
surroundings and their symbols, as painted on the Gaahe and incorporated
into the tipi decorations.

For the singers, of course, the music is of vital importance in shaping the
ceremony and in keeping its flow. It literally carries both the meaning and
the structure of the ceremony in its words and forms. I hope I have managed
to convey some idea of its power to you in this talk.

Canto—Ergo Sum

Musical Child Cultures in the United States, the Soviet Union, and Norway

Jon-Roar Bjørkvold
Department of Musicology
University of Oslo, Norway

The books of the Swedish author Astrid Lindgren truly belong to the heritage of child literature. In her most recent book, *Ronia the Robber's Daughter*, there is a passage in which the young Ronia, roaming in the woods, suddenly discovers her beloved Birk:

> And there was Birk, as he had promised. He was stretched out on a flat rock in the sunshine. Ronia did not know if he was asleep or awake, so she picked up a stone and tossed it into the water to see if he heard the splash. He did, and he sprang up and came towards her.

> "I've been waiting a long time," he said, and once again she felt that little spurt of joy because she had a brother who waited and wanted her to come.

> And there she was now, diving headfirst into spring, It was so magnificent everywhere around her, it filled her, big as she was, and she screeched like a bird, high and shrill. "I have to scream a spring scream or I'll burst," she explained to Birk. "Listen! You can hear spring, can't you?"

"I have to scream a spring scream or I'll burst!"

Ronia's inner urge to express herself musically, in sound, is so fundamental that she could not make life without it. And millions of children, all over the world, seem to share this musical need of using the music of the voice to express life experience.

Did Ronia sing beautifully — satisfying the standards of the *bel canto* tradition? Did her "spring scream" kind of song reveal a talent, predicting a future opera star?

This is an adult way of thinking, deplorably common in traditional music education. It misses, however, a crucial point: The beauty of children's spontaneous singing is primarily a question of the dynamics of life existence, not of refined aesthetics. Children sing spontaneously not in order to perform, but in order to survive: *Canto — ergo sum! I sing — therefore I am!*

The Myth of the Muses

Ronia's musical urge is in full correspondence with the original concept of Music in the history of ideas in Western society. This is the old myth about the creation of the Muses:

> Zeus had created the world, and the Gods viewed in silent admiration all its beauty and magnificence. Then Zeus asked if something was still missing. And the gods answered that one thing was still missing: The world was lacking a Voice, the ultimate voice which in words and sounds had the gift of expressing and praising all this magnificence. To make such a voice sound, a new kind of divine being was necessary. And thus the Muses were created, as the children of Zeus and Mnemosyne.

Here the existential aspect of musical expression even accounts for the very introduction of musical beings on earth. It is my conviction that the children of today, producing their play, rhythms, words and songs — from Denver to Leningrad and Oslo — all are true descendants of the Muses of Antiquity. Starting with the primal cry of the new born baby, they all possess the old Greek *mousiké techne*, the musical ability of letting the voice of the Universe sound, again and again.

The Ngoma of Child Culture

Is the very concept of music, as we traditionally use it today, a useful and manageable tool in dealing with children's musical expressions in contemporary research and education? Professor John Blacking emphasized this very point in his lecture earlier at this conference. We, the music educators and researchers, are too often not rightly tuned in. We too often listen to children with the preconceived adult notion of Western art music.

In the musical cultures of children, however, there is no well defined, specialized concept of music as such — children's spontaneous singing is an intrinsic part of a contextual whole, in which song, body movement, rhythm and words are one inseparable mode of expression. Its most usual context is play. The analytical splitting apart, putting song, words, body movement and rhythm into different and convenient categories for investigation, threatens the basic validity of the actual field of research. The ethnomusicological perspective, so highly brought to the fore at this Denver conference, is in this connection a useful one.

Take the rich musical life of Tanzania, in which song is as functionally rooted in everyday life as is the song in child culture itself. Does a Swahili dictionary contain a reference to "music?" Yes, it does, laconically relegating "muziki" to "Western European Art Music." In other words, "muziki" gives you no idea of Tanzania. There is a word, however, stemming from their own cultural idiom of musical thinking: *Ngoma,* meaning "dance-ritual-song "— inseparably molded together. No song without dance, no dance without ritual.

Child culture does not possess a dictionary of its own. But *if* it had, I am fully convinced that a children's dictionary would have relegated "music" to adult art music of the Western World, just as the Swahili dictionary does. In a way, there is a *ngoma* in child culture, too. The *ngoma* of play, words, song, dance, body movement and rhythm, are universally shared by American, Russian and Norwegian children alike.

In the first, basic years of life children develop much the same way all over the world. Child culture, therefore, seems to go beyond some of the boundaries of national cultures, manifesting cross-cultural traits. To what extent does this cross-cultural core of child culture manifest itself in terms of musical expressions, gradually being influenced by the predominant cultural values and standards of so dramatically different countries as the U.S., the Soviet Union and Norway?

> **The United States**: the superpower of the Western World, an enormous cultural melting pot, with free enterprise capitalism and a relatively short history, both politically and culturally speaking (at least in Southern California where I did my field observations!)

> **The Soviet Union:** the superpower of the Communist World, also an enormous cultural melting pot, with a strongly controlled cooperative socialism, a long history and proud cultural traditions.

> **Norway:** a little country, politically insignificant, a homogeneous welfare state with a long history and deep cultural roots.

Despite major differences of influence, the children of these three countries still seem to share a repertory of musical universals, a *musical mother tongue* of clearly cross-cultural significance. Their spontaneous singing, brought to life in everyday play and communication, clearly exhibits common patterns both in form, use and function. In the following, I will present some major characteristics of this musical mother tongue in some more detail.

Our Musical Mother Tongue — Worldwide

The child is innately a social being. It is through conscious contact with people and surrounding objects, smells and sounds that the child's potential for communication is developed in a steadily growing repertory, with the possibility of social contact as the principal goal.

The social child becomes by necessity a playing child, a *homo ludens.* In fact, children seem to organize their social and cultural relations through play all over the world. Their play is rooted in the distinctive traditions of national culture and at the same time exhibits obvious cross-cultural patterns. It is within the context of cultural rules, codes and values of play that a major part of the life experience of the child unfolds, with language as one basic tool.

This language of the child is, as we know, very complex. Dawning verbal language is integrated with a variety of body expressions — not the least, singing — into an organic whole. When I speak of singing, I am not thinking of the kind of song we adults specifically urge children to sing for us as a kind of entertainment, and which in many cases is the only kind of children's songs we ever happen to notice. I am rather thinking of singing within the context of child culture itself: the kind of singing children spontaneously resort to in their everyday life, either alone or together with other children. The type of singing I am referring to is usually very short, often with children's original words to it, produced to satisfy the needs of the moment. I am sure most of us are familiar with the following intensely teasing utterance of the little child:

You ain't gon - na get me!   You ain't gon - na get me!

Children express their spontaneous singing within the specific context of a certain sign system, that is, the *musical codes* of child culture, passed down through generations. What I am referring to is, in fact, a functional form of communication with some clear linguistic features. This song language, our musical mother tongue, is of fundamental importance in the first, formative years of life.

My first material was based upon observations of Norwegian preschool children. This material very much applies to a more general *Scandinavian* tradition of child culture. Later on this material was cross-culturally extended in two ways:

- In the fall of 1985 I had the opportunity of studying the spontaneous singing of Russian preschool children (four to six years of age), mostly in Leningrad;

- in the fall of 1986 and spring of 1987, I observed American children's spontaneous singing in kindergartens of the Los Angeles region and the beautiful Orange County of Southern California.

Since the American media expert, Neil Postman, fairly recently boldly announced to the world that children's plays and child culture had been wiped out in the United States by extensive viewing of television (*The Disappearance of Childhood,* 1982), a closer look at American children's playful singing was a special challenge to an alarmed European musicologist. And I can reassure you — American child culture is still there, vigorously keeping its traditional play alive!

In order to approach an understanding of the distinctive character and meaning of children's spontaneous singing, it is, in my opinion, of fundamental importance to look at it in the light of its natural context, i.e., within the framework of the common codes of child culture itself. Common code familiarity among children, the understanding of norms and values of their culture, constitutes the very frame of reference for meaningful social and mental development. Let me illustrate this with just a simple figure in which our subject, the children's spontaneous singing is put into focus. (Figure 2)

The triangle is meant to illustrate how the *social situation* in which the children's singing is triggered, as well as the use and form of this kind of singing as interdependent, complementary aspects of musical communication — as different parts of a socio-musical whole. Decisive to the song's form, at the same time, is a culturally specific musical code fellowship, a set of intersubjectively understandable musical structures which the children sys-

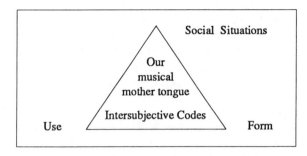

Child Culture with Common Codes of Values
and Ideas

tematically employ among themselves. As tradition bearers, children know the deep emotional power and semantic secrets of their singing, treating them with virtuosity, poignancy and creativity in the developing of their own lives.

Song Use

Song is a basic aspect of children's play. Music and play simply make magic. Take a teaspoon, a very ordinary teaspoon, stainless steel. Put song and play to it and see what happens:

Ba - bu - ba - bu - ba - bu.

goes the little boy—and the teaspoon is all of a sudden turned into an ambulance. And every child intuitively agrees. Of course it is an ambulance! The next moment, however, the King Midas of Music might touch the teaspoon once more, with the left hand holding around its neck, the right hand rhythmically starting to make movements up and down. And what happens? The little, insignificant stainless teaspoon is all of a sudden turned into the most wonderful, electric rock guitar! Just listen, with your playful heart:

One, two, three o'clock, four o'clock rock!   Five, six, se-ven o'clock, eight o'clock rock!

What an experience! What a feeling! Do we still remember how we did it, way back in childhood?

A: Sound play (Analogous imitation)

Let us now, more systematically, consider how children use their song in daily life.

The four-year-old boy is playing with his paper plane. The long sliding glissando of the voice follows the movement of the arm which mirrors the diving of the plane towards the floor.

Song and physical movement imitate each other and are complementary analogies in one total mode of expression — like the little boy with his teaspoon rock guitar. With one simple grasp the child is able to convey his thoughts, sensations and feeling of form. Far from being abstract and non-tangible, the spontaneous singing acquires object quality in the play. The

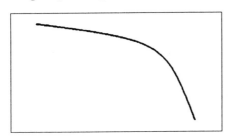

glissando of the song is part of the paper plane's physical plunging towards the floor. Imagine a rising song glissando to a falling paper plane. It would be absurd and cause mental disturbance!

As long as song is used as pure sound imitation in play, the analogous connection between song and play is pretty obvious to observe. But it turns out that spontaneous singing of young children is used to elaborate upon a wide range of emotions, in which the analogous form congruency does not manifest itself as clearly as when the song glissando reflects the descending curve of the paper plane. But analogies of expression are still there. Song fluctuation materializes the abstractness of the emotions in a kind of musical paraphrase. The song improvisations become an integral part of the mood. Like the following song monologue, where the quiet distress of a little, lonesome girl might be depicted like this in a kind of contemporary musical

graphics. A kind of solitary song monologue, tracing the labyrinths of the heart. It all opens tentatively, then increases in volume and slurring intensity, before fading out in a pianissimo kind of relief. Song and emotion being just two sides of the same coin.

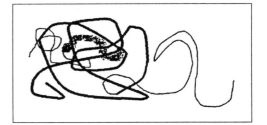

B: Musical speech acts
(Teasing, calling, relating, commanding, asking, answering in terms of spontaneous song; symbolic representation

Do you remember the teasing formula that I just sang for you:

You ain't gon-na get me! You ain't gon-na get me!

In Norway, by the way, it goes like this:

Dum-me, dum-me, deg!____ Dum-me, dum-me, deg!____

(You are silly)

This is the so-called "Ur-motive" of child culture.

With this kind of use the singing of children has moved from the objective to the symbolic level. The song formula above is a symbolic representation for teasing. Its structure is no longer that of the paper plane imitation analogy. It is rather a distinct song word, in which digital characteristics serve to separate it from other song words. The syntax of melodic elements in itself makes the symbol teasing. This understanding is predominant in child culture, also when no words are added. The song formula connects to an inter-subjective reference of meaning, partly cognitively and partly emotionally defined. It is this decoding to an intersubjective reference of meaning, that makes a formula like this a linguistic symbol in its own right. (Figure 2)

This type of song communication is, however, not restricted to the important field of teasing. Using song words with different and very specific intervalic structure and syntax, the children, in the U.S., Russia and Norway may call upon each other, tell each other things, bully each other around, ask questions and answer them — all in terms of song formulas — boys and

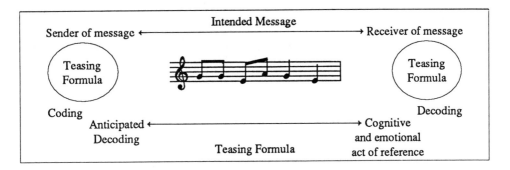

Figure 2

Social context of intersubjectivity in child culture

girls, four-year-olds and six-year-olds alike. This is a fascinating aspect of cross-cultural communication.

C. Song accompaniment
(Song as part of the contextual frame of play)

Finally we may observe another, widely common way of using spontaneous singing among children: that of the more loosely attached musical accompaniment to play activities. The five-year-old Bruce Springsteen fan is building a sand castle on the beach and starts humming one of the latest hits:

Here the making of the sand castle is the key point of the play, not the Bruce Springsteen humming as such. But still the singing is an important part of the play, as an aspect of the reference frame and emotional back-up. The singing is a play accompaniment with analogous significance, producing impulses of action and emotions directly, without any specific semantic reference. It has the function of a linguistic *signal,* as opposed to that of a linguistic *symbol.* Let it be that this type of song use does not possess the intersubjective reference of the song formulas. But within the total context of play, a self-produced musical accompaniment is, of course, as important for the children as are the semantic significance of the B-formulas and the analogous song play of the A-category.

To sum it up: in child culture, spontaneous singing is used on different functional levels of children's play:

Song Form

When children, triggered by a certain event in everyday life, start singing,

- from **A**: being the very sensual object of play, either in its own independent right or in analogous interplay with other aspects of expression

- to **B**: constituting an intersubjective linguistic symbol in the process of playing

- to **C**: being an important part of the underlying context that makes play thrive and prosper

Singing as pure sound play and fantasy	Singing as symbolic representation	Singing as part of the context

their song must necessarily be structured in one way or another. This structuring does not happen by chance. It is governed by the rules and intersubjective standards of child culture itself, with its own children as the virtuoso experts. The children know pretty well what they want to achieve and how to achieve it. What could sound like unpleasant noise to an untrained ear of the adult, often turns out to be a rather sophisticated system of spontaneous song communication.

The first form of song that the children use as part of their expressive development, is a kind of *fluid/amorphous* song. It starts out when the child's experiences of the surroundings are still "global and multifunctional," to use the Russian psychologist Vygotsky's terminology. The amorphous song has no fixed formal structure in terms of intervals, melody and rhythm. Changing microintervals and glissandi without any traditional tonal basis are typical. The free, improvisational introspection of the little girl pre-

Jon-Roar Bjørkvold

viously referred to, is one obvious example of this kind of song. Fluid/amorphous song was found in all the countries where I did my observations.

The amorphous song, the kind of song most daringly different from traditional song tonality, seems however to get lost at an earlier stage in the U.S. than in Norway and the Soviet Union. This obviously has something to do with American children starting school at a significantly earlier age than do Norwegian and Russian children. The earlier children get into school, with its dramatically different set of cultural priorities, the more forcefully the children are socialized into the adult way of learning and, consequently, into conforming with the school world's formal way of understanding music. The intense parental ambitions focused on the American superbaby, which lead to an early or, if you like, premature socialization into the norms of adult culture, do not seem to encourage the further unfolding of childhood spontaneity and creativity.

The specific *singing formulas,* the next stage of spontaneous song development, have a more fixed structure. The teasing motive, previously referred to, is one example out of many. I might add that I was not able to find this particular formula, the "Ur-motive," confirmed in current use in the Soviet Union. But Russian children did use other formulas extensively, which are cross-culturally shared by Norwegian and American children.

The singing formulas are characterized by half tones and whole tones. A certain amount of variation in intervalic pitch is fairly common, especially in connection with falling thirds. Typically, their form is highly standardized, due to their mainly extroverted purpose to communicate as effectively as possible a specific message to others, both friends and enemies. These singing formulas are usually picked up, as part of cultural tradition, from two to three years of age. There seem to be about 12 standardized song words in current use, at least in *Western* cultures. (Figure 3)

Cross-cultural analyses show that the same song formula can be used to convey different meanings within the same group of children. The implicit semantic potential of the "Ur-motive" (Formula 1) thus covers both the provocative, the narrative and even the descriptive. In practical use, though, the least neutral mode of expression, the teasing, here comes out as the predominant alternative. Likewise, the two falling thirds (Formulas 2 and 3) can be used both as a means of calling to someone and of telling about something. The calling mode is obviously the basis of both, and even more one-sidedly so in the case of the falling major third (Formula 3). With a clear nucleus of predominant meaning, nearly every song formula turns out to be

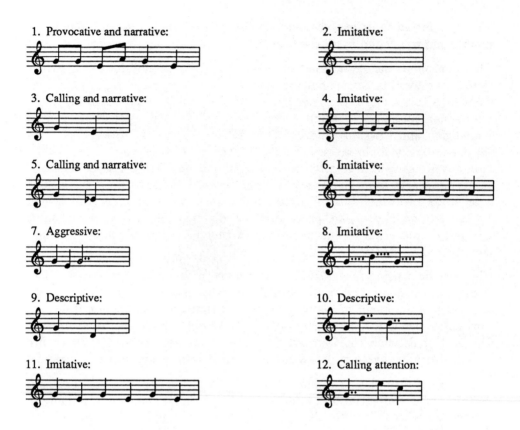

Figure 3

more or less homonymic. All the way through, however, it is the understanding of the total social context of a given setting that always decides what interpretation to deduce, as is the case with the abundance of verbal homonyms as well.

Finally, we have the *preset songs*, already composed by an adult, or simply songs in the anonymous oral tradition of folk culture. These songs are, at the outset, musically determined as regards intervals, melody, rhythm, form and words. In these respects they are totally opposite to the amorphous singing of the children. Children like to use such songs as a starting point for their own flights of imagination, both musically and in terms of words. At the same time it is clear that children normally use only fragments of these songs in their spontaneous singing activities. Still, such short phrases, lasting for only a few seconds, are clearly based on older, traditional songs. A

Jon-Roar Bjørkvold

tune like "Happy Birthday to You," was used with a different text in all three countries where I made my observations:

The Norwegian girls were baking a loaf of bread out of sand:

Jeg ba - ker et brød, jeg ba - ker et brød.

(I'm baking some bread ...)

American boys were playing with planes, pretending they were the "Blue Angels":

I'm fly - ing a plane, I'm fly - ing a plane!

And the Russian kids, who also happened to know this song (a symptom of the rapidly growing American impact on Russian society?) went like this, playing sort of a party:

Ya sly - sal teb - ya, ya sly - sal teb - ya!

(I heard you, I heard you!)

Not only are these musical utterances based on the same melody, but the way they are transformed into genuine children's comments upon daily life activities offers us a glimpse of how the very process of spontaneous singing seems to be cross-cultural and universal. Usually, however, children of different nations tend to use their own national song repertory when it comes to the preset song improvisations. Take, for instance, American children.

They don't hum the Stephen Foster tunes that much any more. But the musical slogans of the television commercials may do as well.

Have you dri- ven a Ford late - ly!?!

Or the following example, where some young girls were sort of doing their hair nicely—in front of an imaginary mirror:

Feel- ing beau- ti- ful, nothing less than beau- ti- ful. No thing less than Fin esse!

These musical outbursts would, of course, be unthinkable in Leningrad, with the non-commercialism of Russian television. The traditional Russian song repertory is very different, indeed. But the very attitude and process of spontaneously connecting songs with everyday activities is uniquely and cross-culturally the same.

In terms of developmental psychology, the child's full mastery of this type of song could be referred to as a third stage of development, in which the concepts of functional linearity and musical syntax are introduced. But here there is every reason to emphasize that fluid/amorphous singing, song formulas and improvisations based upon preset songs are all found *simultaneously* in the song culture repertory of children, from 2-3 years of age onwards. The different levels of spontaneous musical expression cover different areas of use, both psychologically and culturally. They meet different, and to some extent complementary, needs of the children themselves, governed by an interaction between the inner urge for different kinds of self-expression and the code repertory of child culture as such.

Jon-Roar Bjørkvold

The Interrelationship of Use and Form

Within the existing rules and codes of child culture the children systematically link specific categories of song use with specific categories of song form. Not that the different use categories coincide with the different form categories on a one-to-one basis. As it turns out, the children's preferences rather exhibit manifest inclinations and tendencies, following certain cultural patterns, cross-culturally confirmed. Some of these are briefly outlined in the following.

The *amorphous song* is primarily connected with the kind of song use that I called *analogous imitation*. This kind of song is used both in solitary and social play, as could have been the case with the paper plane example. Most typically, however, the amorphous song is used as a means of introspection, as was the case with the song fantasies of the little girl. Here the song can forcefully penetrate into the deeper layers of feelings, dreams and thoughts within, without anyone interfering. The code is basically *intrasubjective*, being the child's own special song idiom. The subjectivity and non-conforming essence of the amorphous song makes it the very private medium we all need now and then for therapeutic relief.

The *song formulas*, with their clear cut style, serve quite another main purpose: that of communicational poignancy. After all, if you want to tease somebody and do it vigorously at that, you need to hit the bull's eye right away! Thus, the song formulas are primarily related to the B category of musical speech acts. Here song *intersubjectivity* is of major importance.

A closer analysis of the interrelationship between the song formulas and their actual use also reveals a positive connection between the extent to which certain formulas are used on the one hand and the social maturing of children in terms of group dynamics on the other.

Although this connection has not been verified in earlier research, the point seems reasonably obvious; when a new year in kindergarten starts, the children do not usually know each other very well. The social network within the group is not elaborately developed in any way. But after a year of social growth, with friendships and fights, laughter and tears, things are very different, of course. This gradual socializing of the group, for better or for worse, is reflected in the children's use of song as a means of expression and communication. Thus the communicative song formulas show a steady increase in frequency of use as the year passes by. The more the children are involved in the friendships and the fights (an inevitable aspect of child group development), the more they seem to need these powerful song formulas to find their way through. And for young children, even small doses of melody often prove far more effective than the rhetoric of the words alone.

If we take a look at the *preset songs* as a point of departure for personal expression and musical communication, we find that they are fairly evenly applied to all three use categories. It is used both for emotional introspection, extrovert communication purposes and pure contextual related accompaniment. The twisting and creative reshaping of the words, or the omission of words altogether, is the decisive factor which makes this kind of song idiomatically suitable for its specific purpose in a given every day setting. Much striking humor and even touches of creative genius can be observed in this kind of children's musical improvisations, indeed.

Functional Significance

A human voice is uniquely personal. Every voice on earth is a personal voice, different from every other voice in the world. Its timbre and "soul," its registers and vocal fluctuations, its idiolectic intonations, tempos and dynamics all reflect the very breath of life of each individual. With the human body itself as a vibrating and resounding instrument, such a musical means of expression more often than not falls short of the aesthetic standards of a too-intellectualized adult society.

A crucial part of children's musical mother tongue, its communicational power and significance, is rooted in this deeply personal basis, with musical features transcending formal language structures. The very development of human verbal language, as we know, emanates in part from this sensual and musical potential of man, from the fetal stage onwards.

Being so deeply rooted in the child's personality, the musical mother tongue concerns every level of identity formation, as does the verbal language of the child. As one of the common codes through which child culture manifests itself, children's singing will obviously contribute to the constant consolidation of *cultural identity*. Sociometric analyses of the characteristic group dynamics of spontaneous singing can further explain how this singing also is important for establishing *group* identity as well as *sexual* and *individual* identity.

Children's singing is found in contexts which convey the entire spectrum of human emotions, from joyous laughter to heartfelt tears. Singing can be a means of expressing and conveying feelings, and of arousing feelings in others, not the least in situations in which word alone would be inadequate.

An important aspect of the *emotional function* of the children's singing is its *therapeutic* role. I am not thinking of professionalized music therapy with functionally disabled children, but rather of the kind of therapy which children in general spontaneously come to use among themselves as part of everyday life. It can generously contribute to the solving of conflicts as well as to the releasing of individual tensions.

As part of its communicative potential, children's singing evidently functions as an important aid in *establishing contact* with others. Contact is created through the entire range of feelings which singing can relate. And, highly neglected in adult appreciation, it also promotes social contact through its semantic powers of intersubjective communication. The *informational function* of children's singing is a basic aspect of its significance, the more so since the often subtle blending of music, emotions and information makes its rhetoric especially persuasive. All this music belongs to the socializing of the child. And the child's singing plays not a minor part in that general process. The expression of life experiences, the acceptance or rejection of the countless challenges of every day life, is part of the growing into adult culture, for better or worse.

These song processes seem to be universally shared by children in the United States, the Soviet Union and in Norway. These children also share the use of amorphous song and the singing formulas. The national ethnocentric flavor to this cross-cultural song tradition first specifically manifests itself in the repertory on which children base their preset song improvisation. Where as Norwegian children normally will resort to Norwegian material, so will American children and Russian children normally resort to the national song heritage of their countries for preset song improvisations. But the inner urge is even here universally the same: to express life experience through song.

Remember the little boy with the teaspoon rock guitar? His name was Arnie. He was five years old. He had long lagged behind in verbal development and could hardly pronounce his own name. But he constantly burst into song, in his own sort of idiom. His favorite tune was about the butterfly. The song is built on the musical idioms of Norwegian folk music and goes like this. (See next page)

The perfect rendition of this rather complicated song was, of course, far beyond the powers of young Arnie. But Arnie was absorbed by the melody and the words. And so Arnie sang the butterfly song his way, in small fragments, caressingly, carefully. Never mind all his trouble with verbal language. What happened? The rock guitar teaspoon in his hand turned into a butterfly. We could all see it. The whole little boy turned into a butterfly through song, so deeply felt, so dearly needed. Arnie's butterfly song expressed the same fundamental urge that Ronia, the robber's daughter, felt in the forest — a fundamental urge shared by all children in all child cultures in the world.

I have to sing or I'll burst: **Canto — ergo sum!**

In this common musical heritage lies a hope for the survival of mankind in a "star war" society of tomorrow.

Jon-Roar Bjørkvold

Literature

Bjørkvold, Jon-Roar. *Den spontane barnesangen — vårt musikalske morsmål,* Oslo, 1985 (Children's spontaneous singing — our musical mother tongue)

Bjørkvold, Jon-Roar. *Det Musiske Menneske (Man is musical),* Oslo: Freidig Forlag, 1989.

Lindgren, Astrid. *Ronia, the robber's daughter,* New York, 1983

Vygotsky, Lev S. *Thought and language of the child,* Cambridge, Massachusetts, 1975.

Section III

Auditory and Psychomotor Aspects of Musical Development

Comparative Psychology and Music Perception

Stewart H. Hulse
Department of Psychology
Johns Hopkins University

I would like to thank some students who helped with the work I shall be discussing. They include Dr. Jeffrey Cynx, John Humpal, and Stephanie Polyzois, who were there when the project started, and Suzanne Page and Richard Braaten who are working with me now. They also include many Hopkins undergraduates too numerous to mention. Without their hard work, I would not be here today.

I should like to begin by describing a fascinating experiment. Then I have a few remarks to make about the comparative approach to the study of behavior. Comparative principles have some important implications for the study of music perception and its development from infancy to adulthood. Next I want to tell you about some research we have done on relative and absolute pitch perception in songbirds. That research illustrates how the comparative approach can be useful as we try to understand the sources and development of human music perception.

Let me begin, then, by describing a remarkable experiment that was done recently at Reed College by Debra Porter and Allen Neuringer (Porter & Neuringer, 1984). These psychologists wondered, quite simply, if birds could be taught to discriminate between the music of Bach and Hindemith. People can, why not birds?

Offhand, this might seem a rather silly question. Why should it matter to anyone if birds can distinguish Bach from Hindemith? Why should it matter at all, especially when the birds were common ordinary pigeons? It turns out, however, that there are very interesting issues raised by Porter and Neuringer's questions. Let's see what they did.

One-minute taped excerpts from J.S. Bach's *Prelude in C Minor for Flute* and P. Hindemith's *Sonata, Op. 23, No. 1* for viola were used as stimuli. Hungry pigeons were trained to peck at a disk on a wall in a conditioning chamber. When the Bach selection played, pecks were occasionally rewarded with food from a food hopper. When Hindemith played, pecks were not rewarded. If pigeons could discriminate between Bach and Hindemith, they should peck at the key when Bach played, but not bother to peck when Hindemith played because they got food for Bach, but nothing for Hindemith. And that is exactly what happened.

But suppose the birds were attending to some isolated cue in each excerpt to make the discrimination — instead of the general musical picture painted by the two composers. Perhaps they were listening for the loudness or frequency of a certain tone. To control for that possibility, another experiment was done. Here, much longer, 20-minute excerpts from a different Bach composition, the *Toccatas and Fugues in D Minor and F* for organ were used. These were compared with excerpts from Stravinsky's *Rite of Spring* for orchestra. Note that in this experiment, Stravinsky substituted for Hindemith. On any given test, a 1-minute excerpt was drawn randomly from the 20-minute Bach or Stravinsky pool, so selections from each composer varied from trial to trial. Also, *two* response disks were used. When Bach played, a peck on one disk was occasionally rewarded with food. When Stravinsky played, a peck on the other disk was occasionally rewarded.

Once again, the discrimination was readily learned. When Bach excerpts played, the pigeons pecked the Bach disk; when Stravinsky excerpts played they pecked the Stravinsky disk.

But now, Porter and Neuringer did something else. They wondered if pigeons could *classify* music that was, to human ears, "Bach-like" or "Stravinsky-like." To find out, they occasionally introduced into standard test sessions a different Stravinsky piece and taped excerpts from the music of Buxtehude, Vivaldi, Scarlatti, Eliot Carter, and Walter Piston. A variety of musical instruments and coloration appeared in these excerpts — organ, harpsichord, violin, chamber ensemble, and full orchestra.

What did the pigeons do? In a word, they pecked the "Bach" key when they heard Buxtehude, Vivaldi, and Scarlatti. They pecked the "Stravinsky" key when they heard Carter, Piston, and the new Stravinsky excerpt. What did *people* do when asked to make the same judgments? They classified the composers just like the pigeons.

So pigeons can discriminate between the music of different composers, and like humans, they can judge which composers write music that is, in some sense, similar.

What are we to make of this? On what basis do pigeons distinguish one musical excerpt from another? On what basis do they perceive different musical excerpts to have something in common? For that matter, how do people do the same thing? I suppose we would all agree that Buxtehude, Vivaldi, and Scarlatti wrote music that is more similar to Bach than to Stravinsky, but how do we know? How do we see the similarity so easily? The problem calls for analysis.

The Comparative Approach to Music Perception

Music is a rich, multidimensional collection of serial acoustic information. What features of that information do people use to distinguish one musical selection or one composer from another? Do people from different cultures use the same features? What features might be especially important in the *development* of music perception in infancy and childhood? These questions define major targets for a *comparative* psychological study of music perception. They also define a major theme for a symposium such as this one.

The idea of fundamental musical features acquires new, fresh overtones if we adopt a comparative viewpoint. You might think that the study of musical sensitivity in animals would be rather fruitless because, to the best of my knowledge, no one has ever heard an animal produce an original, well-formed melody. The only candidate I can think of is the famous parrot that appeared on the Johnny Carson television show a while back singing a rendition of *I Left My Heart in San Francisco*. The parrot was a late-night TV success, but I doubt the bird will every bring its limited repertoire to the concert stage.

Remember, however, that people were skeptical when psychologists set out to teach a language to chimpanzees. No one had ever heard a chimpanzee say a word. We have learned a great deal from the efforts to teach language to chimpanzees, however. For one thing, we have learned that they are not very good at it. Assuming that chimpanzees are using language at all, the best of them may have acquired language skills approximating that of a very young child.

For another thing, and this is by far the most important matter, we have been stimulated — even forced — by chimp language experiments to study our own human language with a new, fresh perspective. That is especially so for the *acquisition and development* of language. In order to conclude that apes could not learn a language very well, we had to study and decide what it was they could or could not learn. The result has been a significant advance in the way we conceptualize the syntax and semantics of human language and the way these things develop in childhood. There have been important contributions to anthropology and linguistics, to say nothing of psychology.

I believe much the same case can be made for a comparative study of musical capacity. The musical skills of Porter and Neuringer's pigeons notwithstanding, it would astonish me to find that nonhuman animals can become very accomplished musicians. But a search for the things that animals can and cannot do musically could be very important. In particular, it could serve to uncover the psychoacoustic features of raw, serial, sound patterns that turn them into the music we *humans* know and enjoy. We might even discover that animals and humans do share certain musical capacities. After all, pigeons could discriminate among the music of different composers and — just like people — classify music into similar-sounding categories.

Musical Features

What psychoacoustic features turn a collection of sounds into music? The list is potentially enormous, of course, and perhaps it is presumptuous to ask the question at all. But given the comparative viewpoint I have adopted, where might one start? Here are a few suggestions in no particular order. They are relevant to the research I want to discuss in a moment.

First, like language, music consists of sounds arranged in time; that is, music has a serial, temporal order. When the temporal order becomes formally organized, we have rhythm. In fact, it was the old problem of perceiving stimuli in serial order that led me to a comparative study of music perception. Both animals and humans certainly perceive the serial order in which events occur.

Second, music stresses the constancy of *relations* among sounds. Within *temporal* structure, music emphasizes relational constancy among temporal durations and intervals. Rhythmic structures remain perceptually equivalent over a broad range of tempos, for example. Within *pitch* structure, constant relationships appear between serial intervals in melodic contours. Relational constancy also appears between vertical intervals in chord structures. It is the constancy of such tonal relationships that accounts in a major way for the perceptual invariance of tone chroma across tone height and key change.

Stewart A. Hulse

Third, in *contrast* to relational properties, music places *little* emphasis on the *absolute* properties of sounds, such as their exact temporal duration or their precise pitch. It is the rare person, for example, who has absolute or "perfect" pitch. In fact, we often neglect absolute pitch when we consider music perception, precisely because absolute pitch appears so rarely in perception. Those who possess absolute pitch are special rather than ordinary.

Fourth, we humans place great emphasis on the relational as opposed to the absolute properties of sounds to *remember* music. We have a keen memory for musical melody or harmony, but a relatively poor memory for tone chroma, tone height or key.

Finally, music has an *emotional* quality. There is joyous music. There is sad music. The major mode is light and gay. The minor mode is depressing and dolorous. With one or two exceptions I can think of (jazz-accompanied funeral processions in New Orleans, for example), composers rarely write marches in the minor mode or funeral dirges in the major mode. I mention the emotional character of music because emotion and other aesthetic qualities hold great significance for musicians and composers. Also, as we have heard, emotional characteristics of music are central for ethnomusicologists. However, I also mention emotional considerations because, for now, I want explicitly to exclude them from a comparative musical analysis. The reason is simple. We have valid techniques to study an animal's perception of the formal properties of music, that is, music's rhythmic, melodic, or timbral features, as you will see shortly. But as yet we have no valid methods for evaluating how an animal "feels" — whether it likes or dislikes something, for example.

Universal Features

All this raises the question of the *universality* of musical features. Psychologists, musicians, and others have wondered whether there are musical universals — common modes of perceiving musical structures — that transcend compositional styles, cultures, and so on. A comparative approach to music adds something new to this idea. It wonders whether there are universals that transcend both cultures and *species*. For human music makers, that may be an appalling prospect indeed.

But it need not be. Suppose we define a musical universal to mean common perception of psychoacoustic features of the type I have just identified — absolute and relative pitch, and so on. Then music becomes, in a major sense, the artful combination of such psychoacoustic features. Put the other way around, music becomes universal to the extent that its psychoacoustic features do indeed share a common perception among listeners.

In this context, a comparative analysis can become very interesting. Suppose we assume for argument's sake that animals respond to psychoacoustic features just like humans. That is a daring assumption, but it leads us to ask questions we might not otherwise ask. Suppose our assumption is true. If and when it is, we will have discovered perceptual capacities, acoustic universals if you will, that humans and animals share.

On the other hand, when animals don't respond like humans, we will learn at least two things. First, of course, we will discover something new about complex acoustic information processing *in animals*. We will better understand how they hear. That is important. From a comparative viewpoint, however, we will also discover a characteristic that distinguishes *human acoustic perception*. That may seem less important at first. But remember the lessons learned from attempts to teach language to chimpanzees. The successes — and especially the failures — of the chimps led us to better define the uniqueness of human language. In the same way, successes and failures in the perception of acoustic features by animals can lead us to sharpen our definition and understanding of music as we humans know it.

Let me summarize briefly to this point. There is a bit of evidence that animals perceive some as yet undefined properties of music as we humans understand it. Remember Porter and Neuringer's pigeons. This suggests a detailed comparative study of music perception might be useful. Such a study will teach us about animals' perception of the complex acoustic patterns that combine to form music. We may be led to the discovery of true musical universals not only across cultures, but also across species. Just as important, however, the fresh questions and the contrast afforded by a comparative study will help us to learn about the things that are uniquely *human* in music perception. That may be especially true for developing infants and children.

Problems and Procedures

Let me turn now to some research that has come from the ideas I've discussed thus far. Specifically, I want to tell you about some work on the perception of relative and absolute pitch. As I have indicated, the ability to process relative pitch is fundamental to human music perception. On the other hand, sensitivity to absolute pitch is much less important for people. How do animals process relative pitch? Do they also tend to ignore absolute pitch?

Species

In starting a comparative research program, one of the first tasks was to choose a suitable animal for study. We were going to work with non-natural complex sounds, and that suggested the use of songbirds as subjects, mimicking birds in particular. Birds use sound extensively in their natural communication so we know they pay attention to complex sounds. If they also mimic, that gives good evidence that they can hear and discriminate complex *arbitrary* sound patterns. Accordingly, we chose to work with the European starling. This is a mimicking songbird that has proved to be a marvelous, tractable species for behavioral work in the laboratory. Starlings have another advantage: everybody hates them (rather unfairly, I might add).

We posed our birds a very simple relative pitch problem, the simplest we could think of. We asked them to tell whether a series of successive tones went up or down in pitch. The ability to discriminate rising from falling pitch patterns is, in fact, a relative pitch discrimination based on formally-defined pitch relations between neighboring tones. If the birds could learn the discrimination, we would have major evidence for relative pitch processing in nonhuman animals.

Stimuli

Figure 1 shows the patterns we used. They were 4-tone patterns constructed from computer-generated sine tones. Their pitches were selected according to an arbitrary rule from 6 equal intervals on a whole-tone, log scale of frequencies shown on the left axis of the figure. With the constraint that all tones occurred in a one-octave range cf frequencies, 4 sequences rose in pitch, while 4 fell in pitch. Each rising and falling sequence began on a different pitch, but their frequencies overlapped extensively. Many patterns had absolute frequencies in common.

The pitch patterns had an organized temporal structure. The birds heard a series of repetitions of each 4-tone pattern. Each repetition lasted about three quarters of a second, and there was a three-quarter-second rest between each repetition. The idea was to use temporal structure to *configure* and emphasize perceptually the rising and falling pitch relations in the patterns.

The animals were trained and tested in a wire mesh acoustic cage, one foot on a side, that was suspended from the ceiling of a sound-proof chamber. The cage had a loudspeaker overhead and a panel with some disks in a horizontal row on one wall that the birds could peck. The panel has three disks, but we used only the center and the right disk in the research I'm describing today. A hopper that brought food within reach when the bird did the right thing was located directly below the disks. The bird pecked on the disks to indicate its choices.

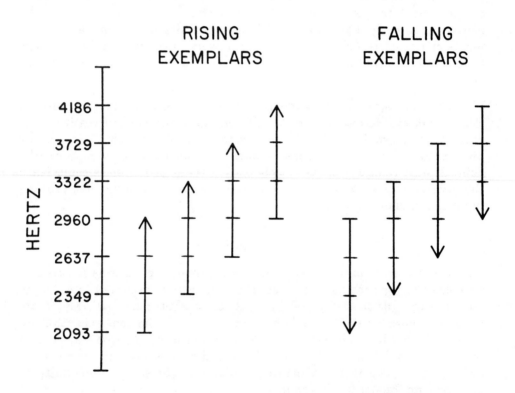

Figure 1. The eight 4-tone exemplars used in initial rising/falling pitch pattern discrimination. The exemplars appeared in a one-octave frequency range marked on the ordinate. Each frequency was separated from its neighbor by a whole tone.

Stewart A. Hulse

The procedure we used was very similar to that used by Porter and Neuringer with their pigeons. A learning trial began when the center disk lit up. A peck on that disk darkened it and started either a rising or falling pattern that continued for a minimum of 4 seconds. No pecks on any disk had consequences during that listening interval. But then, the right disk lit up. If the patterns on that trial fell in pitch, a peck on the right disk ended the sound pattern and raised the food hopper so the bird could eat for 2 seconds. If the pattern rose in pitch, a peck on the right disk produced no food and the birds had to *withhold* a peck for 4 seconds to start the next trial. With this *go/no-go* procedure, birds should learn to peck quickly for falling pitch patterns and slowly, if at all, for rising pitch patterns. As the birds learned the discrimination, the difference between go and no-go response latencies should become steadily greater.

Starlings were trained in daily sessions with this procedure until behavior settled down. In other words, they learned well. They produced response latencies to ascending patterns that were all about 4 seconds long and latencies to descending patterns that were all about 0.6 seconds long, so they discriminated with great accuracy. Apparently, because they readily discriminated rising from falling pitch patterns, the birds were sensitive —like humans — to *relative* pitch structure. So far, so good.

Transposition of the Relative Discrimination

Next, we explored another possible capacity of the birds to manage relative pitch. We asked them to *transpose* the relational discrimination to a new set of tone frequencies higher or lower than the original set. Suppose, for example, we doubled or halved all the tone frequencies in the patterns, but kept their formal ascending or descending pitch structure intact. Would the birds transpose the discrimination to the new stimuli?

Humans make such transpositions readily. They do so by responding to constant pitch *relations* between neighboring tones in pattern — showing *perceptual constancy* of a relative pitch discrimination. Furthermore, this capacity appears to be a musical universal as I have defined it. It represents a psychoacoustic feature that underlies, for example, the common perceptual constancies associated with transpositions of tone chroma across tone height and key change.

Generalization of Relative Pitch Discrimination: Downward Shift

To explore the capacity for transposition, we simply divided the frequency of each tone in our test series in half and shifted the absolute pitch of the 4-tone patterns down one octave. Everything else remained exactly the same. When first exposed to the octave transposition, the birds reacted instantly. Suddenly, they failed utterly to discriminate rising from falling pitch patterns. Figure 2 shows the relevant data.

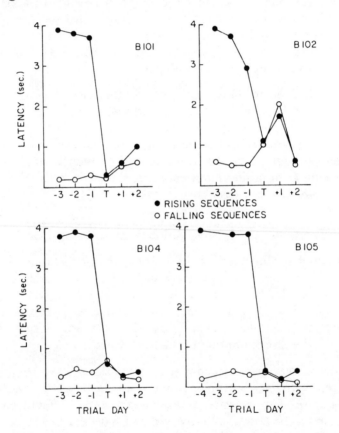

Figure 2. The discrimination (long as compared with short latencies) between rising and falling pitch patterns (on Days -3, -2, and -1), and the loss of the discrimination (on Day T) with the shift of pitch frequencies down an octave for four starlings. The starlings' failure to discriminate the patterns continued for more than two days (Days +1, +2) after the shift.

Stewart A. Hulse

For several days before the octave transfer, marked -3, -2, -1, there was a large difference between *go/no-go* latencies for ascending and descending patterns — good discrimination. On the day of the downward shift, marked "T," the latency differences disappeared completely. The birds simply pecked as rapidly as they could for all patterns, a trend that continued for a good many days.

Upward Shift.

Most birds slowly relearned the discrimination in the new pitch range. Sometimes, relearning took just as long as original training. When returned to the initial training stimulus frequencies, however, all birds *recovered* the discrimination immediately. So a shift to a new range did not produce some catastrophic memory loss for the original discrimination.

Next, we tried a transposition to a stimulus range an octave *above* the initial training range. To do this, we simply *doubled* the frequency of the original stimuli.

That stimulus transformation produced exactly the same result as the downward octave shift. The birds lost the discrimination immediately. The data looked exactly like those you see for the downward octave shift in Figure 2.

Gap Transfer

But we still did not give up. In a continuing search for robust transposition, new birds first learned to discriminate rising and falling pitch patterns in both a high *and* a low frequency range. The two one-octave ranges were separated by a *gap* of unused frequencies not quite an octave wide. After the discrimination in the high and low ranges was well learned, the birds were shifted suddenly to rising/falling stimulus patterns built from tones in the novel gap. If transposition were possible at all, surely it would occur under these conditions. Discrimination within the gap would be supported by identical, well-learned discrimination with frequencies both immediately above and below the gap.

Performance averaged across ascending and descending patterns in the high and low training ranges was excellent as before. The birds discriminated ascending and descending patterns very well. However, there was no evidence for transposition of the relative pitch discrimination into the gap at all. In the gap, where we would expect long latencies for ascending patterns and short latencies for descending patterns if the birds had transposed successfully, the birds' response latencies were virtually identical for the three pairs of 4-tone ascending and descending patterns that were tested.

Familiar Range

By this time, you must all be asking yourselves an obvious question. Could the birds transpose the discrimination to *any* new frequencies at all? To answer this question, we transferred birds to patterns *within the original one-octave training ranges*. We did this by shifting the frequencies of the patterns up or down a semitone. This meant that pitches of the new stimulus patterns were located half way between the pitches of the original stimulus patterns. With great accuracy, the birds immediately discriminated the new ascending and descending pitch patterns.

Why did the birds have such difficulty transposing a relative pitch discrimination they learned quite easily to unfamiliar pitch ranges? We can get a clue by looking again at the rising and falling pitch patterns displayed in Figure 1.

Notice that although there is considerable overlap in the tone frequencies across the patterns, each pattern does have at least one combination of frequency and frequency location unique to that pattern. For example, with one exception beginning on 2960 Hertz, the frequency of the first tone of each pattern appears only in that pattern. Thus, a tone of 3729 Hz appears in 4 patterns, but there is only one pattern that *begins* on 3729 Hz. That is the falling pattern second from the right. So, although there are many common frequencies across patterns, the birds could code each pattern by remembering the *absolute pitch* of the first tone. We tried to reduce the availability of absolute frequencies as potential cues when we designed the patterns, but we may have failed.

In fact, when we designed the patterns, we may have exhibited our own human predilection to use *relative* pitch and to ignore *absolute* pitch. With human hubris, we assumed it wasn't necessary to completely remove the confound between absolute and relative pitch in the patterns. We'd mixed things up enough. The birds would never figure out how to remember any particular frequency out of that big collection of sounds.

Well, maybe we were wrong. To find out, we did a simple test. One day, the birds went into the test chambers as usual, but instead of rising and falling

Stewart A. Hulse

patterns, they heard four tone patterns that simply repeated the frequency of the initial tone. In other words, we *removed* rising and falling relative pitch cues and asked how the birds would do if all they could hear was the frequency of the first tone. Figure 3 shows the results of that test.

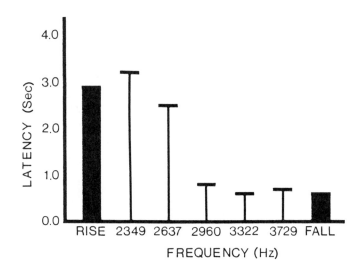

Figure 3. Response latencies when relative pitch information was removed, and the starling heard just one frequency on a test trial. Baseline performance on patterns that *did* rise or fall is shows at the left and right of the slide for comparison. The starlings discriminated very well when they heard just one frequency; they gave long latencies for low frequencies and short latencies for high frequencies.

Data averaged over all rising and falling baseline exemplars are shown at the right and left of the figure. You can see that, as usual, latencies were much longer for rising exemplars than they were for falling exemplars. But, as you can also see, the birds showed sensible performance when all they heard was the initial frequency of exemplars in the range. If tested with a high frequency they responded with the short latencies characteristic of falling patterns — because falling patterns all began with high frequencies. On the other hand, if tested with a low frequency, the birds responded with long latencies characteristic of rising patterns — because rising patterns began on low frequencies. So the starlings varied their performance *without* the rising and falling pitch cues. They appeared to be paying attention just to the frequency of the initial tone in a pattern. In spite of our attempt to reduce absolute pitch cues — an utterly inadequate attempt in hindsight — the birds learned to use them anyway.

We might conclude that the starlings did not learn anything about relative pitch at all in these experiments. Perhaps they and other songbirds are incapable of perceiving the acoustic world in relational terms. That conclusion is possible, but is premature.

For example, we tried some tests with the rising and falling patterns in which a pattern began on, say, a high frequency like 3322 Hz (see Figure 1), but "went the wrong way," and rose instead of falling from that frequency. If the birds responded on the basis of absolute pitch, they should give short-latency responses. That is so because high frequencies marked the beginning of falling patterns which the birds already knew produced food. If the birds responded on the basis of relative pitch, however, they should give long-latency responses because they had already learned to withhold responding for rising patterns.

In a word, the starlings gave long latency responses: they responded on a relational basis. We have evidence therefore, that relational responding is possible within pitch patterns, although relational perception may not be the strategy of choice.

Even more to the point, there is evidence implying that some birds use relative pitch perception in birdsong, their own means of communicating with one another (Ratcliffe & Weisman, 1985). Black-capped chickadees have a simple song composed of sinetones that shift from just one pitch to another. Usually, chickadees sing just one pair of frequencies — about two whole tones apart. Sometimes, however, they shift to another pair. When they shift, they maintain the exact ratio relationship between the two frequencies involved. Starlings are not chickadees, of course, but this evidence in nature for the use of relational pitch processing is significant and worth pursuing. Perhaps our starlings would do better if we asked them to respond to relational transpositions of their own song.

Summary

What are we to make of all these data? It is quite clear that perception of *absolute frequency* plays an extremely important role as starlings discriminate among arbitrary serial pitch patterns. Unlike you or I, birds depend a great deal on memory for the absolute pitch of the sounds they hear in the patterns. That dependence shows up most clearly when birds are asked to transpose a pitch pattern discrimination to a new *frequency range*. We have called this the *frequency range constraint*. To a songbird, a shift of a pitch pattern from one range of absolute frequencies to another appears to create an entirely alien pitch experience. That pattern must be learned anew — even though the formal, relational organization of the pattern is identical from one range to the next. Imagine how you would respond if the opening lines of Beethoven's *Fifth Symphony* were completely unrecognizable if I were to simply transpose them up an octave. Apparently, that is just what songbirds experience.

Although they may even show a preference for using absolute over relative pitch perception, don't forget our evidence that songbirds do use relative pitch processing under some conditions, conditions that we don't yet fully understand. Remember, for example, that they could transpose their discrimination between rising and falling patterns if the stimulus frequencies remained in a *familiar* pitch range.

We are vigorously pursuing research on the tradeoff of absolute and relative pitch perception by songbirds. We would like to know, for example, how well songbirds would do if we were to test *directly* their capacity for absolute pitch perception. How many frequencies can they learn to distinguish and "name" individually? In other words do they have "perfect pitch" as we humans understand the term? In work going on now in the laboratory at Johns Hopkins, Sue Page has shown that starlings can learn to classify at least 14 frequencies into high and low categories with ease, and the birds are still going strong.

Let me summarize the things I have discussed this morning and add a few final thoughts. If you will recall, a comparative approach to music perception starts with the assumption that animals, songbirds in our case, respond to musical features just like people do. Then experiments are done to find out the extent to which that is true. How do humans and songbirds fare in such an analysis?

First, it seems that songbirds do share sensitivity to some feature of the serial acoustic patterns we humans organize to make music. Like people, under some conditions that we don't yet fully understand, birds are sensitive to *relative* constancies in pitch structures.

However, the striking observation from our research shows birds' relative pitch perception to be heavily modulated by a potent *absolute pitch constraint*. Under the conditions we've used to date, anyway, birds were quick to use a perceptual strategy based on absolute, not relative, pitch. We found no evidence for octave generalization or for the transposition of other pitch relationships outside a familiar range of frequencies. We did find evidence that the birds remembered pitch patterns by coding the absolute frequency of individual pattern tones. In this sense, birds differ markedly from people.

But do they? Our discovery of a range constraint in birds opens the possibility that a similar constraint may hold for humans if we only look for it. When we started, our birds were musically naive. This suggests that the place to look for absolute pitch constraints is in the development of music perception in infants and young children. Perhaps infants come into the world with a well developed sense of absolute pitch which they have to *unlearn* or abandon if they are going to perceive music the way adults do. Perhaps the absolute pitch mechanism is tied to rapid neurological changes that occur in early development.

In a very real sense, human development is a problem within comparative psychology, too. For purposes of analysis, we can think of infants and children as other species to be compared with human adults. Of course, some parents are quite sure that children — on at least some occasions — are alien species from some other planet for sure! But that is beside the point. The point is that if we adopt the comparative approach I have advocated, we will be led to ask some important questions that might otherwise be overlooked.

For example, my impression is that the developmental literature on relative pitch perception is often inconsistent. Some excellent experiments with infants — by Ann Pick, for example, from whom you will hear shortly — show evidence for octave or pitch contour transposition, but other experiments do not. We need to explore this problem vigorously.

Then again, how do animals, infants, and adults compare on time and rhythm perception? I would be surprised if we find there are no differences among humans and animals, adult or otherwise. I would also be surprised if we don't find some unexpected similarities. In fact, in research I simply don't have time to tell you about today, our starlings do transpose temporal discriminations across changes in rhythmic tempo. That is a constant relational perception for sure.

Finally, let me add a further word about something I just touched upon. There are some possible implications of our work for developmental neuropsychology and the role of the brain in mediating psychoacoustic perception.

Stewart A. Hulse

As you may know, there are some interesting parallels between the functional organization of the human and the avian brain. For example, as Peter Marler and others have pointed out, birdsong and language show interesting developmental parallels. Furthermore, just as human language is mediated in a dominant brain hemisphere, so is the production of birdsong. And Fernando Nottebohm at Rockefeller University has been developing a beautiful description of how steroid hormones control the growth and regression of brain nuclei that control song production in adult birds.

However, none of this work has been directed toward comparative neurological parallels in the psychoacoustic features that are typical of music perception. If parallels exist, that could be very interesting. Birds might provide an excellent animal model for work that could lead to further understanding of how the human brain mediates the complex serial acoustic patterns we know and enjoy as language and music.

In any case, I hope that I have interested you in a comparative approach to music perception. I believe the comparative approach leads not only to new data, but even more important, to new ways of thinking about things. If I have stimulated some new thoughts, I will be pleased. Thank you.

References

Hulse, S.H., Cynx, J., Humpal, J. "Absolute and relative pitch discrimination in serial pitch perception by birds," *Journal of Experimental Psychology: General,* 113, 38-54, 1984.

Hulse, S.H., Humpal, J., Cynx, J. "Processing of rhythmic sound structures by birds," In J. Gibbon, L. Allan (eds), *Timing and time perception* (pp. 407-419). New York: New York Academy of Sciences, 1984.

Hulse, S.H., Humpal, J., Cynx, J. "Discrimination and generalization of rhythmic and arrhythmic sound patterns by European starlings," *(Sturnus vulgaris), Music Perception* 1. 442-464, 1984.

Hulse, S.H., Cynx, J., Humpal, J. "Pitch context and pitch discrimination by birds," In P.D. Balsam, A. Tomie (Eds.), *Context and learning* (pp. 273-294). Hillsdale, NJ: Erlbaum Associates, 1985.

Hulse, S.H., Cynx, J. "Relative pitch perception is constrained by absolute pitch in songbirds," *(Mimus, Molothrus, and Sturnus). Journal of Comparative Psychology* 99, 176-196, 1985.

Hulse, S.H., Cynx, J. "Interval and contour in serial pitch perception by a passerine bird, the European Starling," *(Sturnus vulgaris). Journal of Comparative Psychology* 100, 215-228, 1986.

Cynx, J., Hulse, S.H., Polyzois, S. "A psychophysical measurement of pitch discrimination loss resulting from a frequency range constraint in European Starlings," *(Sturnus vulgaris). Journal of Experimental Psychology: Animal Behavior Processes, 12, 394-402, 1986.*

Porter, D., Neuringer, A. "Music discrimination by pigeons," *Journal of Experimental Psychology: Animal Behavior Processes* 10, 138-148, 1984.

Ratcliffe, L., Weisman, R.G. "Frequency shift in the *fee bee* song of the black-capped chickadee," *Condor* 87, 555-556, 1985.

Motor Skills and the Making of Music

Michael G. Wade
School of Physical Education and Recreation
Center for Research on Learning, Perception and Cognition
University of Minnesota

Irrespective of how we arrived on this planet, movement is a fundamental aspect of almost everything we do, in an endless variety of contexts and places, and is accomplished with varying levels of skill. Watching sporting events we perhaps wonder at the skill with which a player hits or passes a ball, or projects his or her body in a particular form; skilled athletes often inspire us to go out and try such activities ourselves.

Sport is just one of the contexts in which we regularly note not only the activity itself, but the level of skill of the performers. We do the same thing at concerts, marveling at the skill of a pianist, a violinist, or for that matter any instrumentalist or vocalist. As parents, we delight in the growing repertoire of our own children's motor skills such as walking, running and catching a ball. A persistent question in all of these activities is how does the organism contrive to coordinate the joints and muscles to produce the skilled activity? This question is valid for both the fine movements of the fingers and the movements of the large joint muscle groups of the lower limbs or shoulder girdle.

In approaching the question, I will first outline some of the theories concerning acquisition of motor skills, and then discuss how such theories might be applied to the study of musical skills. An important first step is to review models of motor skill acquisition developed in the past 15 to 20 years to see what theoretical perspectives have to offer in accounting for motor skill acquisition in general. I will then discuss some of the limited research available in the area of musical instrument playing.

There seems to be very little developmental research focused on the motor skill aspects of playing musical instruments, and I suspect this is so for two reasons. First, the investigation of motor skill learning is a relatively young endeavor, still in the process of developing a theoretical and methodological base. Second, the majority of research has focused on laboratory based tasks which have little relevance to the real world. Some inferences have been made to practical situations, but the study of natural biological motion and everyday activity has been largely ignored until quite recently.

Research on motor skills was being conducted by the end of the 19th century, but until the Second World War the majority of this research was theoretical, designed to test the general psychological models of the day. World War II created an urgent demand for individuals skilled in the operation of complex engineering systems such as aircraft, large tanks and guns; coincidentally, and extremely important for the development of our understanding of movement, the war created a critical need for the military to understand the principles of target tracking.

The field of engineering psychology spawned by World War II had an enormous impact on the evolution of motor skills research. During the post-war period from 1945 to the 1960's, an increasing number of engineers and psychologists became interested in motor skills research for both its industrial and military applications. At the same time, individuals in the field of physical education began using the scientific method to study skill in sport. By the late 60's the foundation had been laid for shifting motor skills research to a movement-oriented theoretical perspective. This transformation has brought us much closer to the research domain of motor system physiology, and is likely to have significant application to the study of musical development.

A good starting point for us on this brief theoretical journey would be the publication of a closed loop theory of motor learning by Adams (1971) at the University of Illinois. This was the first data-based operational theory of motor learning.

Adams' Theory

One example of a closed loop system found in everyday life is the temperature controller used in heating and air conditioning systems. The thermostat compares the difference between desired temperature and actual temperature; when they are not the same it generates an error signal (too high or too low by so many degrees) to cause the output system to produce warm or cold air until the error is zero — to bring the actual temperature to the desired level. Adams suggested that, in place of a thermostat, the motor system possesses an error detection and correction capability based on the internal neurological monitoring of ongoing activity. This so-called "feedback" gives the organism instantaneous knowledge of results (KR) of the

Michael G. Wade

status of any intended movement from the time it is initiated, and thereby permits modifications in the control signals driving the muscles. Error reduction occurs until there is a match between the response and the desired activity.

Adams viewed KR as something more than a reward protocol. KR consisted of information the individual could use to solve the motor problem — the performer using KR is tracking errors in order to form hypotheses about the task to be learned. Adams also sought to explain how individuals develop this detection capacity. The theory postulated two memory states: first, an approximate representation of the intended activity; second, a task-related perceptual trace operating in the feedback loop used to reduce errors during learning to permit the desired outcome.

From an historical perspective, Adams' theory was a powerful motivating force for movement scientists interested in motor skills research. It led to a large number of empirical studies focusing on the many questions that the closed loop theory of motor learning posed. There were one or two studies that investigated the use of KR by children in acquiring a motor skill; however, little of this research was related to children or to other developmental questions, nor was there any significant examination of the developmental aspects of motor skill relative to the closed loop model of movement control.

There are several limitations to the closed loop theory, and I would like to mention two of the more important ones here. First, the theory focused almost entirely on slow, linear positioning responses. These activities are not representative of the many motor skills that we see in everyday life. Further, Adams' insistence that rapid movements can be governed by feedback mechanisms is contradictory to much of recently published data. There is considerable evidence that organisms deprived of all sensory feedback from limbs can, in fact, respond skillfully and even learn new skilled actions. A major weakness of the Adams theory is that it fails to account for what are called "open loop" processes in movement learning and control.

A second problem concerns the issue of the perceptual trace in relation to variable practice. It has been shown that when the subject practices around a criterion target, it is not necessary to experience the criterion — to hit the bull's eye — in order to learn how to produce consistently accurate movement toward that specific target. Adams' theory claims that such experience is critical to the development of the perceptual trace, however the work of Shapiro and Schmidt (1982), in contradiction to Adams' model, clearly demonstrated that variability of practice and success can produce successful learning of a criterion target.

Although Adams' theory may not have given a correct account of motor skill acquisition, it was unquestionably both a step forward in theorizing about motor skill learning and a driving force behind a great deal of empirical activity and thinking in the 1970's.

Schema Theory

Due in part to his dissatisfaction with Adams' conclusions, Schmidt (1975) developed his own theory of motor learning, the "schema" theory. The schema idea is not new (the term was used by the British psychologist, Bartlett, in 1932 and later by the Swiss biologist, Piaget, in 1952); Schmidt's contribution was to formalize the idea into a specific theory. Just as Adams' closed loop theory of motor learning posited two memory states, one to generate the initial movement, and a second to refine the movement to the desired target response, schema theory also posits two memory states: a *recall memory* responsible for the production of the initial movement, and a *recognition memory* that permits response evaluation. The schema notion contradicts the idea that movement commands and their consequences are stored uniquely in memory, postulating instead a storehouse of abstract generalizations of many classes of motor actions. This is an intuitively inviting notion when one begins to consider realistically the limitations on the brain's information storage capacity.

Both Schmidt and Pew (the latter, in some earlier ideas on schema published by Pew, [1974]) attempted to adapt the schema notion of the nervous system to what was then known about motor control. Schmidt's schema-based approach still gives closed loop responding a place in motor learning. The theory postulates that, after the movement is initiated from a generalized motor program, the individual briefly compares four items:

1. the initial conditions (bodily position, weight of thrown objects, etc.) that existed before the movement;

2. the parameters, or range and characteristics of movement, available from within the generalized motor program;

3. the outcome of the movement in the environment (usually a change in the location or condition of the object being acted upon);

Michael G. Wade

4. the sensory consequences of the movement (how the movement felt, looked and sounded).

Information included in these categories is not retained permanently — this would lead to a serious storage problem. Rather, it is stored only long enough to enable the performer to abstract the relationships among them. Two such relationships, or schema, are thought normally to be defined by this process. They are:

I. **The Recall Schema.** This is concerned with the production of the movement. When the individual produces a movement, the comparison of any parameter and the movement outcome produces a "data point." With repeated responses, using different parameters and producing different outcomes, other data points are established and the individual begins to define a relationship between the parameter and the nature of the movement outcome.

II. **Recognition Schema.** This is for response evaluation and is formed and used in a similar way. Here the schema is comprised of the relationship between the initial conditions, the environmental outcomes and the sensory consequences. The recognition schema is used in a way analogous to the recall schema. Before the response, the individual decides which of the movement outcomes is desired and determines the nature of the initial conditions. Using the recognition schema, he then can estimate the sensory consequences that will be present if that movement outcome is produced. According to Adams' theory, incorrect movements would degrade the perceptual trace, which was the main influence in development of the response. In Schmidt's schema theory, by contrast, incorrect movements provide additional information as to how the body is functioning, and thus are beneficial rather than disruptive. Two important predictions from Schmidt's schema theory were:

1. That variability of practice was an advantage in building up the strength of the schema. The more the subject knows about the range of activities that surround the specific skill, the better the individual will be at producing the skilled movements. The first practical tests of Schmidt's schema theory were experiments that focused on the *role of variability of practice*. The results suggested that variability of practice and a schema theory explanation of motor skills applied more to children than to adults. The schema appeared more capable of modification in children than in the adult, where the

schema may have already been fully developed. For adult subjects, then, the schema idea has been less well supported.

2. The schema theory gave theoretical importance to novel responses. A particular movement need not previously have been produced by the subject; a novel response can arise from the general rules of parameter selection related to any similar set of movements in the same class. In other words, motor learning may be primarily rule-learning, rather than the learning of specific responses.

Schema theory has some relevance to research focusing on the acquisition of musical instrument skills. But before considering why this is so, let us turn to some general criticisms of both the closed loop theory and the schema theory. Having discussed some of these, I will present a more contemporary view of motor skill acquisition and the associated problems of coordination and control. Finally I will review some research on the playing of musical instruments and discuss some of the problems and issues related to the above theories and the developmental research in acquiring instrument skills.

Criticism of Schema and Closed Loop

Adam's theory and Schmidt's theory both represent traditional cognitive viewpoints. Orthodox cognition, from which these traditional theories come, has its philosophical foundation in the writings of the philosopher John Locke, in that the development of motor coordination is presumed to be explained by a special class of "things" that act as an intermediary between the world and the organism. Locke referred to these "between things" as *ideas* and saw them as interfacing the organism and the environment. Contemporary cognitive theorists who address motor learning issues (into this category I place Adams and Schmidt) refer to these "things" as "representations," "programs" or "reference schemas." Irrespective of what they are called, they refer to an intermediary mechanism between the organism and the environment.

For those who adhere to a more contemporary view of the acquisition of coordination and control, this creates some particular problems. Contemporary psychological thought traces its roots back to the ideas of the Russian physiologist Nicolai Bernstein (1967) and views motor skill acquisition as dynamic activity. An "action theory" view takes an important point of departure philosophically from Locke in its commitment to realism. This view dis-

Michael G. Wade

cards the Lockean notion of "ideas" and promotes a direct relationship between the organism and the environment. Thus, for the realists, the model construct for coordination and control is that it is *autonomous, self-organizing* and possesses no "between things."

During the period of the 60's and 70's, the overriding model for all cognitive and motor skills (if they can indeed be separated) was the computer analogy. The development of information theory, and of computers themselves, produced a way of thinking of the central nervous system and the brain as acting, in large part, like a computer. This metaphor places the motor system under the control of a higher executive, an "in the head" device which issues commands to the lower levels via the spinal cord and out to the muscles, which ultimately generate the action. This idea has driven research in neuroscience and motor skills for 25 years. Current research on artificial intelligence and robotics continues to adhere in large part to the idea of executive control in a so-called top-down representation.

As you can see from Figure 1, the little person (or the "motor executive") uses movement scripts which it takes off the shelf then "plays" down the system to the joints and muscles. This is the traditional computer analogy for the motor system. Schmidt (1975), in formulating his schema theory of motor learning, noted: "The schema theory does not specify from where the motor program comes. This is an important problem, but the level of knowledge at this time does not allow much to be said about this process." This argument adheres to the idea that there is a higher order executive. Schmidt recognized the problem inherent in any theory invoking the notion of a general motor program: *How is the motor program put together and where is it located?* The traditional argument places it in some central location, while the more contemporary view takes issue with the general motor program view and the computer metaphor. A major criticism of earlier cognitive models has asked how the "executive" can realistically control all of the parameters involved in a particular skilled movement. This is often referred to as the "degrees of freedom" problem.

The Degrees of Freedom Problem

I searched long and hard for an example of the degrees of freedom problem that might serve an audience interested more in music than sport. The following illustration (Figure 2) is not mine, but that of a colleague, Professor Claudia Carello, (Michaels and Carello, 1981) of the University of Connecticut.

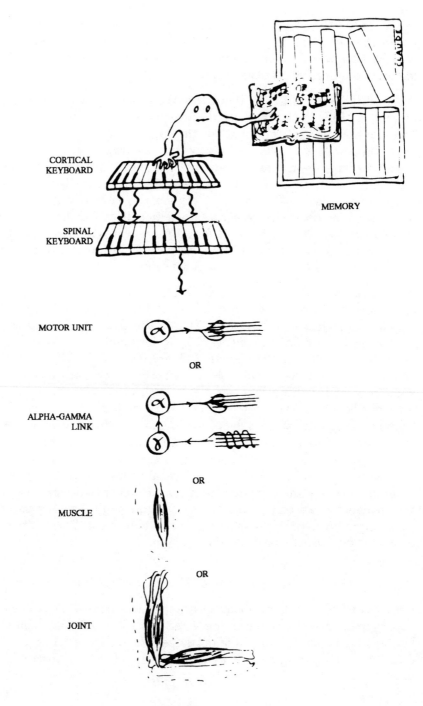

CORTICAL
KEYBOARD

SPINAL
KEYBOARD

MEMORY

MOTOR UNIT

OR

ALPHA-GAMMA
LINK

OR

MUSCLE

OR

JOINT

Figure 1

Michael G. Wade

Figure 2

Imagine that we want to control one of those old-fashioned player pianos. The keys to be played can be regulated as to order and duration of action, and therefore might be said to have two degrees of freedom. The piano roll specifies each of these variables for every key — there is information in the roll that specifies order and duration of the key presses. The device works because the degrees of freedom being controlled (the keys on the piano) equal the degrees of freedom of the thing doing the controlling (the roll, which has holes each of whose location and length can be varied). This is illustrated by Figure 2 which depicts light shining through holes in the roll, which is the "program" song for the piano to play.

But what if the roll had ten commands of a type that directed the piano to "play a happy tune" or "play a C-Major chord?" The piano needs to know which keys to depress for how long and in what order. Obviously, given the rather large number of tunes that might qualify as happy, or the many ways one might play a C major chord, we can see that the number of things controlling is far *less* than the number of things requiring control — a degrees of freedom problem has emerged. In motor skill activity we have a parallel situation, wherein coordinated muscular activity is like making music, with the roll corresponding to an action plan and the keys to the movement parameters. If we assume that motor activity is controlled by some higher executive (the ghost in the machine), in almost every case the degrees of freedom required to control the activity are far greater than the degrees of freedom available in the intelligent executive. This is not an effective style of control.

The traditional view of motor control relies on the intelligent executive, but we have criticized this perspective by noting that one simply cannot keep taking out a loan on the intelligence of this executive every time the control problem increases in complexity! A parsimonious solution to this degrees of freedom problem assumes that the variables — in this instance, the piano keys or the muscles — are not regulated individually. An attractive possibility is that groups of these variables may be partitioned into standard units or, perhaps, small functional subsets. Commands could then be issued to these units, which in turn would take care of the finer details of the act in some stereotyped fashion. For example, the command for a happy song might engage a sub-program within the piano to play "Happy Talk," the sub-program being one specifying the details. In this way, having what might be called "collectives" or "standardized programs" commanded by an executive would permit the piano to play a tune.

This is not an entirely adequate metaphor for coordinated motor activity, because the style of organization that underlies this command formulation is by nature still hierarchical. In other words, the "top down" notion still persists with commands flowing from higher levels down to the muscles, thus, responsibility for control is still entrusted to the executive. The centralization of control assumes that the executive always dominates the variables below it which, in turn, dominate the variables below them, and so on. While hierarchical organization allows for certain savings in the control burden borne by the executive, there is a cost to be paid in other areas. Time does not allow a full account for this but, suffice it to say that coordination cannot be accomplished by means of a controlling executive but must, in some way, emerge out of the natural compatibility between the animal and the environmental context in which the activity goes on. (For a review of this, Michaels and Carello, 1981.) This leads us to think of a style of control that is *coalitional*" or shared rather than executive dominated. Coalitions are distinguished from other styles of organization in that there is not just one component (the animal) that has to be "controlled." Rather, coordination must be defined over three components: an action system, a perceptual system, and

Michael G. Wade

an environmental context in which these two systems function. As mentioned earlier, this is a departure from the traditional viewpoint. What we have then in this view of motor skill expression is a coordinated structure defined as a group of muscles spanning more that one joint, constrained to act as a functional unit. As Kugler and Turvey (1978) have noted:

> "Through biasing or tuning of the spinal cord that arises (in the spinal brain) the individual members of an aggregate of skeletal muscular variables are linked or constrained to act as a functional unit or collective. These are not commands but constraining patterns of facilitation and inhibition of spinal brainstem interneurons."

Let's pause now and briefly review our discussion so far. We have reviewed three basic models that related to skill acquisition in general. First we talked about a closed loop system (Adams, 1971) that incorporated the idea of a memory trace, and a perceptual trace relying primarily on feedback. The drawback to this theory is that it argues only for motor skills represented primarily by slow, relatively simple laboratory tasks.

In response to these and other criticisms, Schmidt (1975) presented his schema theory of motor learning to account for both slow and fast movements, and focused on the concept of a general motor program. Both the closed loop theory and schema idea rely on the computer metaphor, with a higher order executive responsible for the acquisition and control of the skill.

Contemporary theories argue that motor control and coordinated activity cannot be parsimoniously described in this fashion. The central criticism of the computer analogy or the "executive" is captured in the degrees of freedom problem. Recall that I talked about the degrees of freedom problem in terms of an automated piano player with the degrees of freedom on the keyboard side and the degrees of freedom available on the control side. The central point made was that the executive had insufficient degrees of freedom to control all the activities required to program a player piano. I argued that an alternative style of control could be viewed as a coalition rather than a hierarchy. The units of control in this instance are called "coordinated structures." Coordinated structures enforce a style of control effective for a wide range of skilled actions.

Figure 3 depicts a pistol shooter and a drummer, both examples of coordinated, skilled activity. In the case of the pistol shooter, coordination be-

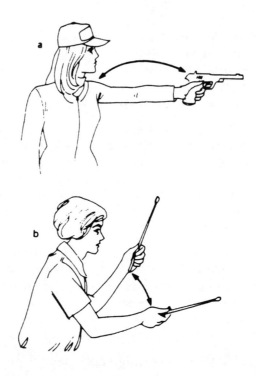

Figure 3

tween movement at the shoulder and movement at the wrist lead to less scatter around the center of the target. For the drummer, the activity is a bilateral rhythmic activity, the same wrist joint is coupled instead with the wrist joint of the opposite limb so that only certain combinations of rhythms are achieved, e.g., a 1-1 or 2-1 beat. The activities of the two wrists are mutually constraining.

Research in Music

Let us now turn to the research that investigates musical skills. As I mentioned earlier, I found few research studies that focused on the acquisition of instrument skills. There is some information on piano playing but little else. There are some interesting ideas asociated with the Suzuki method which might be contrasted with some of the theoretical ideas that I have presented above. Also, there is some preliminary research on inter-limb coordination in the playing of musical instruments. This latter work comes from Esther

Thelen's laboratory at Indiana University, where cello playing has been investigated.

The Thelen group has been studying cello playing in children from a dynamical systems theory perspective; this is part of a research program of Drs. Esther Thelen and Beverly Ulrich on the emergence of skilled behavior in infants. The research sought to find in children evidence of muscle or joint groupings constrained to act as a functional unit. The proposed functional unit has been called a *coordinative structure,* as described above. Data were collected on cello players, both high level performers at Indiana University and novice performers (NP's) — young children between the ages of four and ten years who had been playing the cello for a period ranging from nine months to two years. All of the youngsters were instructed in the Suzuki method (but more on Suzuki later).

The focus of the study was a movement analysis (using a Selspot System) of the elbow and wrist joint and of the lag inherent in these two joints relative to the movement of the bow. Both groups were asked to play loudly and also softly. Remember that there are constraints initially placed on the player of this instrument because of the support configuration of the instrument. The legs and the trunk of the player support the cello and keep it stationary, as does the non-bow arm. The bow arm has to both hold the bow, which is a difficult task, and maintain the bow in a horizontal plane. The first figure illustrates the lag displacement of the elbow and bow in the high level performers.[1]

In Figure 4 the HLP's are playing loudly. Notice the lag between the onset of the elbow movement and the onset of the bow movement — the elbow moves before the bow in all strokes save one. When we look at the movement of the elbow relative to the wrist (lower half of the figure) it is again evident that in all strokes the elbow precedes the wrist. This level of basic organization between elbow and wrist does not change when the loudness of the music is diminished.

While the basic pattern of coordination was consistent for all HLP's, the data were rank-ordered across the subjects, but the order was constant,

---

1   I wish to acknowledge the generosity of Drs. Thelen and Ulrich in allowing me to use their data here.

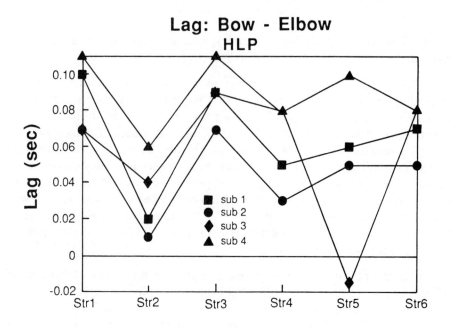

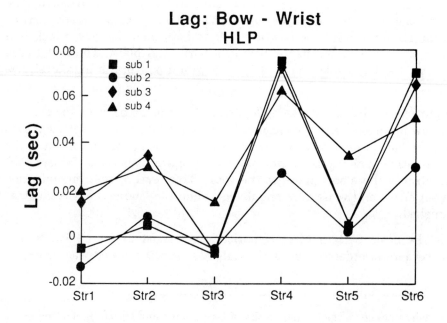

Figure 4

170   Michael G. Wade

showing that the lag variability was consistent among performers and probably influenced by the direction of the bow and the joints involved. The *elbow* showed relatively greater lag on the up bows than on down bows. The *wrist* lagged relatively more on the down bows than the up bows. The lag between the elbow and the wrist was least on the down bow. The position of the bow on the strings also affected the lags.

The emergence of a consistent lag in this situation may represent the attempt to make smooth transitions when changing directions, when bow movement is close to zero velocity. At zero velocity the strings no longer vibrate and the sound is lost. When making directional changes, cellists take advantage of the momentum built in during the stroke and allow the wrist and arm to move in a circular or elliptical motion at the end of the stroke, avoiding the less efficient linear reversal (i.e., coming to a stop and starting again). This causes the arm to move more like a pendulum, with a greater range of motion possible for different joints depending on where the limb is and when the stroke begins.

Let us now look at the novice performers. Figure 5 illustrates the novice performers (NP's) playing loudly. It is obvious from this point that there is considerable disorganization compared with HLP's. Sometimes the elbow moves before the bow, sometimes the bow moves before the elbow. The wrist action (lower half of Figure 5) demonstrates relatively more consistency than the elbow in that it more often moves before the bow, although irregularities are still apparent. Also, there is less differentiation between up bows and down bows.

Figures 6 and 7 illustrate the sequence of action between the wrist and elbow for the HLP's (Fig. 6) and NP's (Fig. 7). There are a large number of reversals of order as well as an absence of organization for the NP's. That the wrist tends to move before the bow more frequently for the NP's than the HLP's may be due to the effect of specific instructions of these children, all of whom were instructed in the Suzuki method. One strategy used to emphasize "unlocking" the shoulder and elbow flexion in the movement is to practice keeping the upper arm stationary while moving just the forearm. The subjects' actions may represent successful and unsuccessful attempts to carry out these instructions. Fluctuations in the organization of joint actions may be inherent in their method of compensating for such problems as over/under bowing. Nevertheless, the NP's were still able to maintain correct timing and directional changes required by this segment of music.

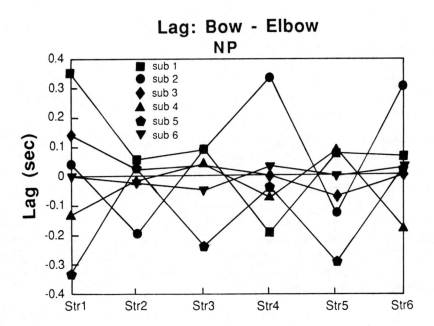

Lag: Bow - Elbow
NP

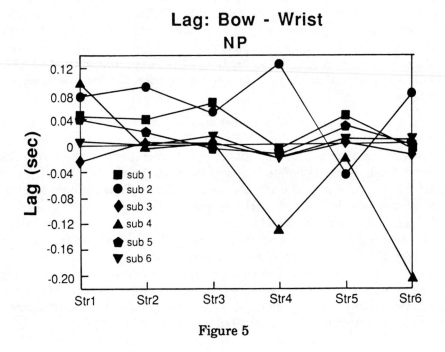

Lag: Bow - Wrist
NP

Figure 5

Michael G. Wade

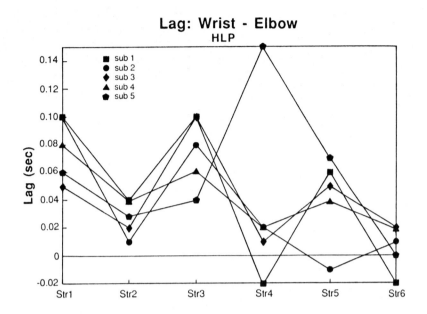

Figure 6

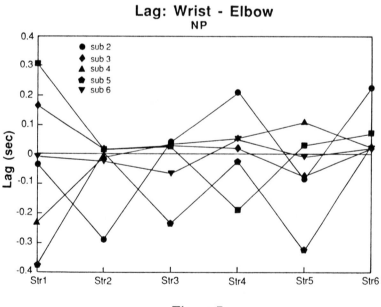

Figure 7

I should emphasize that these studies are preliminary attempts at investigating these kinds of coordinated movements, not only in music but in other motor skills. There are still many questions unanswered. The organization of limb segment movement obviously varies between high level performers and low level performers in this activity, but one cannot be certain that this difference would be found in other bowing situations.

While not an expert musician or music teacher, I suspect that anyone playing any musical instrument has a more difficult task than an athlete performing a complex sports skill, simply because there are two sets of variables operating in music. First, there is the music itself — the notational details of sound for which particular movements must be generated. Second, there is the task of reproducing the music on the instrument from an internal, mental representation. Based on his observation of children's ability to acquire language, Suzuki decided that, rather than present the dual-task problem to the child, it would be more efficient to imitate what appears to happen in bird song development. If the ideas supporting schema theory and generalized motor programs are valid, at least for learning skills such as violin playing, the best approach may be *not* to practice in the early stages of development, or practice only minimally. The idea is that the music (the tune) to be played must first become firmly fixed in auditory memory. Only when the tune is firmly fixed, as it were, "in the head," would the performer be asked to reproduce the music on the instrument. This approach could minimize possible interference effects between an imagined or remembered sound and the musical sounds being recreated on the instrument.

This is the method used by Suzuki. In Japan, parents of newborn babies select a single piece of music and play the recording to the baby each day. The piece of music must be very well played and be of very high fidelity to ensure that the sound in memory is perfect in all respects. Once the first piece of music is played a sufficient number of times, perhaps a second or even a third piece of music is played. It is only in later years, when the infant recognizes the music, that he is given the instrument and taught how to reproduce the sounds that are already accurately stored in its head. Whether or not this is in fact what happens, the Suzuki method has been very successful and is used widely not only in Japan, but in the western world.

The Suzuki method also requires the pupil to participate in several rituals, such as picking up the bow, holding the bow and playing with a variety of shapes that are meant to represent the violin. This strategy might offer

Michael G. Wade

some support for the variability or practice argument proposed by Schmidt (1975) since the pupil becomes familiar with the shape of the violing and the posture appropriate for holding and controlling the violin while it is being played.

You can probably deduce from the research I have reviewed that the study of motor skill acquisition as it relates to the acquisition of instrument skills is not only an intriguing problem, but also one that has received too little attention. It is not easy investigating the dual-task problem of learning to read music from a score and also the making of music on an instrument. There are several issues that make it potentially difficulty (but not impossible) to conduct research in this area.

First, with visual information and auditory information figuring in the majority of skill acquisition contexts, vision is usually the primary source of information. In music, the player often cannot observe the movements of the hand on the strings (I am thinking particularly of the bass and cello) and may rely more heavily on auditory information. This is an important departure from the norm in motor skill learning.

Second, reading music puts the acquisition of the musical instrument skill in a context, in which the individual must transfer into sound what he or she reads. You will recall that one of the main tenets of the Suzuki method is to avoid these two competing influences by ignoring the reading of the music early in development.

Third, the playing position and physical configuration of the play influences the ability to acquire skills and also the ability to produce the correct movements that are regarded as essential if the instrument is to be played correctly.

Fourth, the configuration of the instrument produces different physical positions that the player must adopt to play the instrument. An instrument of different shape and different configuration requires a different anatomical positioning of the limbs.

Fifth, there is the issue of continuous versus discrete activity. In a number of skill contexts, the activity tends to be continuous; whereas, in music the sound appears continuous but often a discrete activity with the player being required to accurately reproduce discrete musical notes in order to produce a particular continuous tune!

Sixth, the playing of a musical instrument may involve the two hands playing in a coordinative (bimanual) fashion, often with the activity of each limb being considerably different. On a stringed instrument, one hand holds and moves the bow while the other presses strings against the fret board. Despite these variations in left-versus-right movement, the limbs must be assumed to be tightly coupled; drum playing is an obvious example. In playing the piano, however, the left hand can be playing one rhythm and the right an entirely different one, and in this case the limbs may, in some way, *not* be coupled.

All of the above issues provide interesting opportunities for further research — not only in the playing of musical instruments *per se*, but in the developmental aspects related to how children acquire instrument skills.

From a theoretical point of view, research in all aspects of motor skills will have to come to grips with the role of cognition in a working theory of motor skill acquisition, and especially with the relationship between cognition and coordinative structures. You will recall that the degrees of freedom problem cannot be resolved by relying entirely on an executive control. Nevertheless, there must be a role for cognition in motor control. LaBerge (1981) has made some attempts to bring about a theoretical marriage between the schema idea and coordinative structures. He points out that relying on the "little person in the head" metaphor can lead to two particularly erroneous notions: first, that the motor area of the cortex is the site of the voluntary selection of movements, and, second, that there is a one-to-one correspondence between impulses selected at the higher levels and the selection of specific muscle movements.

The picture that is emerging is that the connection between cortical activity (or "the executive") and muscle movements in performance skills is physiologically remote. A contemporary view of control and coordination suggests that certain executive commands are sent to the coordinative structures which appear to interpret the commands more as advice (see, for example, Easton, 1972) than as direct commands. It is the coordinative structures that make adjustments to the external forces, e.g., the mechanical features of the movement related to the instrument to be played; the feedback about muscle length and tension; the inertia of a moving finger or a moving arm. In addition, even postural states are accounted for by the establishment of a coordinative structure.

Michael G. Wade

The above conceptualization is speculative; we have yet to provide clear evidence that this model describes what is going on. In addition, cognition must somehow play a role in the execution of motor skills; it seems reasonable that the executive might activate centers in the coordinative structures which, in turn, activate the components of muscle action subject to environmental and limb conditions. LaBerge's idea is that "advice," rather than direct commands, comes from the motor centers in the brain. Thus the schema plays a role as an advice executive rather than that of the traditional "top down" command executive. This is a view shared by Smyth and Wing (1986) who talk about a "shared managerial style of control."

The problem of determining what unit is in control at a given instance is difficult. The key to this question, from a theoretical point of view, is to determine more clearly the nature of cognition. Traditionally, cognition has been regarded as a set of what we might call predicates or rules. This in fact may not be the case, for we must remember that the brain itself is in a chemical bath. The brain reacts to its own chemical environment, and reacts to light and also the influence of gravity. None of these appear to have primacy. Cognition may be a property of the brain as a chemically reactive field, while motor activity is generated in time and space. [2]

The study of musical skills deserves to be a part of the larger effort to explain coordination and control in all mammals. I hope my remarks have provided a brief insight into the interest that movement scientists share with all of you in the making of music.

2. Personal discussion with Peter Kugler, Department of Kinesiology, University of California, Irvine.

References

Adams, J.A., "A closed-loop theory of motor learning," *Journal of Motor Behavior, 3*, 111-150, 1971.

Bernstein, N. *The coordination and regulation of movements,* Oxford: Pergamon Press, 1967.

Easton, T.A., "On the normal use of reflexes," *American Scientist, 58,* 5, 1972.

Kugler, P.N., & Turvey, M.T., "Two metaphors for neural afference and efference," *Behavioral and Brain Sciences, 1,* 1, 1978.

LaBerge, D., "Perceptual and Motor Schemas in the Performance of Musical Pitch," in Symposium on the Application of Psychology to the Teaching of Music, Ann Arbor, MI:Music Educators National Conference, 179-196, 1981.

Michaels, C.F., & Carello, C., *Direct Perception,* Englewood Cliffs, NJ: Prentice-Hall, 1981.

Pew, R.W., "Human perceptual-motor performance," in B.H. Kantowitz (Ed.), *Human information processing: Tutorials in performance and cognition,* Hillsdale, NJ: Erlbaum, 1974.

Schmidt, R.A., "A schema theory of discrete motor skill learning," *Psychological Review, 82,* 225-262, 1975b.

Shapiro, D.C., & Schmidt, R.A., "The schema theory: Recent evidence and developmental implications," in J.A.S. Kelso & J.E. Clark (Eds.), *The development of movement control and coordination,* (pp. 113-150), New York: Wiley, 1982.

Smith, M.N., Wing, A.M., *The Psychology of Human Movement,* New York, NY:Academic Press, 1984.

Timing Mechanisms in Skilled Hand Movements

Hans-Joachim Freund and Harald Hefter
Department of Neurology
University of Düsseldorf

Temporal Properties of Single Rapid Movements

Certain elementary facts should be considered by musicians interested in the empirical and scientific basis of musical skill acquisition. The simplest types of movements that have been studied extensively are rapid, so called ballistic movements. They represent concise components of movement out of the huge continuum of possible performances. Such rapid single movements are called open loop movements because they are terminated before sensory control could modify their further course.

When a subject is asked to move the arm or finger as fast as possible, the recording of muscular contraction producing that movement shows a curve very similar to that elicited if electrical stimulation is applied to the nerve supplying the muscle. The actual time required for the contraction depends on the preponderance of fast or slow contracting fibers of the muscles just as with electrical stimulation, so that the electrical and voluntary contraction times are comparable (Figure 1). The limitation of our fastest voluntary movements is therefore determined mainly by the contractile properties of the muscle fibers. It is presently unknown whether adequate training could alter the contractile properties of hand muscles so that they could become faster.

The next issue to be discussed is how voluntary contractions of this kind are organized by the central nervous system. One invariant principle underlying the performance of rapid single movements is shown in Figure 2. If a subject is asked to make contractions or movements as rapidly as possible, but at different amplitudes, it appears that the time taken to reach peak force remains about the same irrespective of the amplitude of the contraction or of the movement (Freund and Büdingen, 1978). For musical performances this implies that however forcefully a key or a string is pressed, the time to peak will remain unaltered. This represents an inherent and invariant principle of single rapid contractions and movements and reflects a linear increase of

ELECTRICAL STIMULATION   VOLUNTARY CONTRACTION

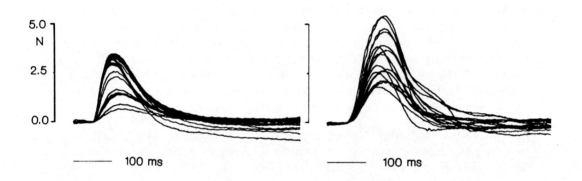

Figure 1

Comparison between electrically evoked (left side) and most rapid voluntary (right side) isometric index finger extensions of different amplitudes. The voluntary contractions have only a slightly longer duration mainly because of the smooth onset due to the asynchronous recruitment according to the size principle.

Hans-Joachim Freund and Harald Hefter

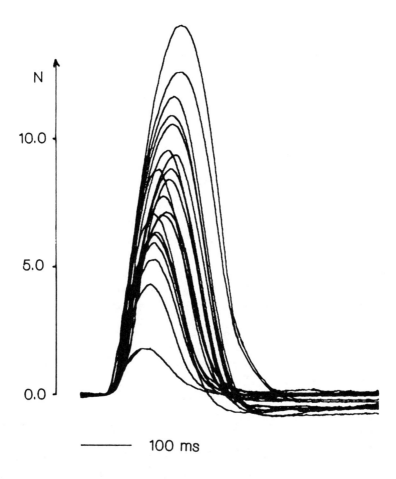

Figure 2

Most rapid voluntary isometric index finger extensions in a 35 year old pianist. Times to peak are nearly amplitude independent over a fairly large range of force amplitudes.

velocity or of the rate of rise of tension with movement or contraction amplitude.

The constant duration is important for the cooperation between different muscles engaged in rapid automatized movement. For example, many muscles are synergistically active if one catches a ball. Some of them produce only small, others large forces. If their time to peak were different, they would have to come into action in a temporal sequence that would depend on amplitude. This would be a much more difficult task than the actual simultaneous activation.

The simple principle of isochrony applies to a wide range of rapid automatized distal contractions and movements as they are performed during musical performances. As discussed below, this isochrony also applies for rapid serial movements. But it does not apply for movements of larger masses in proximal joints where mechanical damping prolongs larger amplitude movements. Isochrony also does not apply for movements that require precise sensory guidance.

The dependence of movement velocity on the precision of the required motor behaviour is defined by Fitts' law (1954): the smaller the target zone for an aimed arm movement, the longer the performance time. In more general terms it turns out that sensory guided motor acts need more time than rapid automatized movements. The latter can be faster because they are largely preprogrammed and require little sensory feedback.

Another factor that influences performance time is task complexity. Sternberg and colleagues (1984) have measured the influence of the number of sequences and of sequence length on typing speed. For that purpose the finger movement for one key stroke was subdivided into five phases: hit, early lift, late lift, early and late hold. All phases except the late lift phase remained unaltered during variations of task complexity. The central processing time affected only the late lift period which therefore was the principal source of increased time of the whole performance.

Serial Movements

Most of our natural motor acts are not single, but instead consist of sequences of alternating movements. This certainly does apply for most musical performances. Serial movements can be conceived as a sequence of single movements or as a group of continuous sinusoids. Such serial movements can be subjected to spectral analysis, so that any regularity, or the major frequency components, of single contractions making up a serial movement will be revealed. A spectral analysis is shown in Figure 3, indicating the preferred frequencies of fast finger taps plotted along the abscissa and amplitude on the ordinate. The consistent performance of one subject is characterized by a sharp peak indicating that this is a preferentially sinusoidal movement performed at a rather stable frequency. In contrast,

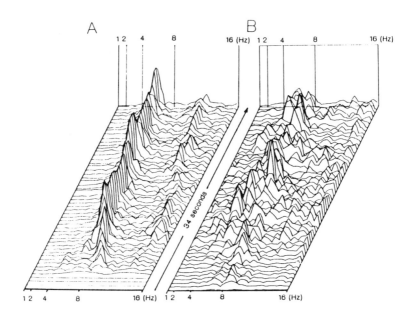

Figure 3

Comparison of the spectral analysis of a regular (A) and an irregular (B) most rapid voluntary alternating index finger movement of two untrained normal subjects. Compared to (A) where only the dominant peak with its harmonics is visible, the record in (B) shows not only a considerable variation of the dominant peak but also many non-harmonic peaks. Consecutive power spectra are shown from bottom to top.

the spectral analysis of a second subject, whose performance was intentionally irregular, shows a shallow profile with a wide scatter over many frequencies.

These displays are suitable for evaluating such aspects of musical performance. The advance of optoelectronic techniques allowing the recording of any movement in a virtually unrestricted way will enable us to disclose the sensorimotor principles underlying musical performance. Such measurement can also determine the frequency of the most rapid serial movements that an individual can produce. The fastest repetitive finger movements on the keyboard lie in the 8 to 12 Hz range (Ream, 1922). Schlapp (1973) measured the vibrato of violinists at around 5 to 6 Hz. Taylor and Birmingham (1948) have reported that a pianist's alternating movements can approximate 16 Hz. This is anecdotal and I have not found anything else to substantiate this notion. Thus, the data scattered through the literature and our own measurements (Freund, 1983) indicate that the upper frequency range for the most rapid alternating serial finger or hand movements lies in the 8 to 12 Hz range. An important limitation of such movements, however, is that those executed at the fastest frequencies can be produced only within a restricted amplitude range.

The Relation Between Rapid Serial Voluntary Movements and Physiological Tremor

Tremor represents an involuntary alternating serial movement. Although some people think that they have no tremor at all, everybody has physiological tremor. Tremor is an inevitable side effect of any movement or contraction. Figure 4 shows a physiological tremor record from the forefinger of a healthy subject. Spectral analysis of this record shows a peak at around 8 Hz in the power spectrum. This frequency is similar to the rhythmic burst rate of neurons in the cat's inferior olive. Lamarre, et. al., (1975) have considered the inferior olive as a possible generator of physiological tremor. One can compare the involuntary alternating serial movement (tremor) with the fastest voluntary alternating movements which a subject can generate.

We have compared individual physiological hand tremor peak frequencies and maximal tapping rates in 30 normal subjects and found that the maximum tapping rate was always just below tremor frequency (Freund, 1983). This implies that the peak frequency of physiological tremor demarcates the upper margin of the range of serial voluntary movements, and that nobody can move faster than he or she trembles. This principle is of interest when one considers children's capacity to produce rapid alternating movements. Children have lower tremor frequencies which become faster with age. Whether maximal tapping rate increases in parallel with tremor rate is an open question. To our knowledge, cross sectional or longitudinal studies on this issue are not available in the literature. Although such information is not available for the correlation between tremor and maximal tapping rates, it is known that children have slower tremor (Marshall, 1961) and tap

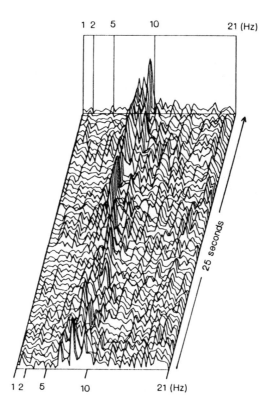

Figure 4

Spectral analysis of physiological tremor. Physiological tremor is characterized by a broad base peak ranging from 7 to 12 Hz with a maximum at 9 to 10 Hz and a considerable variation of tremor amplitude. Consecutive power spectra are shown from bottom to top.

slower. It therefore seems possible that the same close correlation observed in adults exists in children. The simple measurement of tremor peak frequency could then be taken as a measure of a child's motor capacity for the production of rapid movements that are so frequently employed in the execution of musical skills.

Not only musical skills but also many other activities consist of a series of sinusoidal movements. The characteristic speed for such activities, like writing one's signature, is important for the generation of the individual spatial features. If one slows down the characteristic speed, the typical pattern of the signature is lost. Everybody can prove that to himself by imitating one's own signature very slowly. The temporal controls for the production of certain automatized motor behaviors are more strict than those determining the set of muscles that must be used. A signature written on a blackboard is generated by different muscles as a signature written on a piece of paper: the muscles are different, but the geometric pattern produced is the same.

Many learned manual skills like handwriting are performed in a 4 to 6 Hz frequency range. Since such movements are performed isochronously, their performance time remains the same irrespective of their amplitude (Katz, 1935; Viviani and Terzuolo, 1980). The same range of frequencies as recorded for handwriting, pencil shading, typing or erasing applies for speech. When a subject is asked to speak as fast as possible the speaking rate resembles that of the fastest tapping rate. Together with the other above mentioned rapid serial manual skills, the frequencies lie in the 4 to 7 Hz range. Figure 5 illustrates this frequency grouping and its relation to physiological tremor. This schematic graph which is based on recordings from 30 normal subjects reported elsewhere (Kunesch, et. al., 1989) reveals that a broad range of highly overlearned hand skills are performed within a surprisingly narrow frequency range. Although all these movements can be executed deliberately at any possible rate, their self-selected natural performance keeps to a fairly restricted frequency range. This is an interesting contrast to serial movements in music, which obviously must be varied across the frequency range. But it is not known whether even in musical performance there is a preponderance for certain frequencies.

The work of Epstein (1985) has shown that changes in tempos in musical performance change naturally by low order integral ratios. This proved to be the case for widely different types of music in a transcultural study. He advanced a theory that proportional tempo represents a universal principle in music, which infers the existence of a biological mechanism underlying such temporally invariant behavior. An intrinsic cerebral oscillator that generates tremor and attracts alternating movements towards a preferred frequency would be a biological mechanism underlying such temporal invariant behavior. Support for such a view comes from the observation that other involuntary motor activities also behave in the same way: laryngeal recordings from the throats of stutterers show that the involuntary syllable repetitions lie in the 6 to 10 Hz range. The vibrato in wind or string instruments or in singers also lies in the same frequency domain, and almost cer-

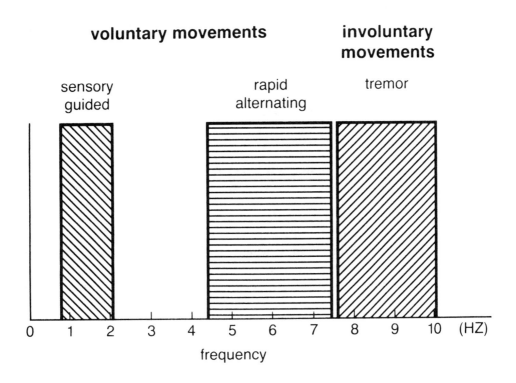

Figure 5

Schematic illustration of the frequency ranges of different types of movement employing different sensory control modes. In addition, the range of frequencies of physiological hand tremor is shown by the right. For further explanation see text.

tainly represents nothing but a natural tremor overlaying sound productions of this kind.

Sensory Control of Hand Movements

Sensory processes must control what we are doing. The visual control of hand movements was examined in a simple experiment we conducted together with Andreas Leist and Bernie Cohen (Leist et al., 1987). Subjects watched their arm while driving a handle faster and faster over thirty degrees. Everybody knows that one can see the hand during such a performance, but if one goes faster the image becomes less sharp. Monitoring of eye and hand position showed that the eye stopped pursuing the moving hand at around 2 Hz, which implies that faster movements are monitored by the fixated eye. Consequently, these are not open loop movements according to older concepts of ballistic movement, but employ a different type of sensory control. The performance is not executed blind; rather, a global sensory control mode is operating that is distinctly different from that mediated by focal (foveal) vision (Julesz, 1985).

The distinction of natural hand and finger movements into two distinct frequency classes as described by Kunesch et al. (1989) and illustrated by Figure 5 corresponds precisely to the earlier distinction between extrinsic and intrinsic hand movements by Elliot and Conolly (1984). On the basis of Napier's (1956) previous classification of a power and precision grip, they proposed to use the term *intrinsic* when the fingers are moved against the palm. *Extrinsic* movements are those of the whole hand or of a prehended object. Intrinsic movements correspond to our low frequency group, where the fingers collect focal sensory information. Extrinsic movements correspond to the high frequency group. The former employ the hand as a sense organ. The latter project internal, mental images into extrapersonal space. The application of this classification to music offers interesting perspectives, in particular with respect to their significance for motor learning. Skillful motor behavior must first be performed slowly to allow for detailed focal sensory control. As more is learned, the larger parts can be predicted until preattentive mechanisms are sufficient to monitor the ongoing activity.

Is There an Internal Clock?

The question of why automatized, extrinsic hand movements are performed near the tremor domain raises the issue whether this could be due to the attractor function of an intrinsic oscillator (Llinas, 1984). Pathological conditions like Parkinson's or cerebellar disease represent experimental models supporting such a view. In these conditions, tremor becomes slower and so does the ability to make rapid alternating movements which is affected to the same extent as tremor. Musicians with such disorders have the problem that they cannot play as fast as they could before. The relation of the performance range of rapid automatized movements to central oscillators and to different types of sensory control may be of major significance for a better understanding of the sensorimotor processes underlying and determining musical skills. A better understanding of the brain mechanisms underlying oscillatory behavior may not only provide a better scientific basis for musical education, but also give us new insights in the dimension of rhythmic structures in music and their relation to biological mechanisms.

References

Elliott, J.M., Conolly, K. J. "A classification of manipulative hand movements," *Developmental Medicine and Child Neurology*, 26:283-296, 1984.

Epstein, D. "Tempo Relations: A Cross-Cultural Study," In: *Music Theory Spectrum*, Vol. 7, "Time and Rhythm in Music," pp. 34-71, 1985.

Fitts, P.M. "The information capacity of the human motor system in controlling the amplitude of movement," *Journal of Experimental Psychology*, 47:381-391, 1954.

Freund, H.-J., Büdingen, H.J. "The relationship between speed and amplitude of the fastest voluntary contractions of human arm muscles," *Brain Research*, 31:1-12, 1978.

Freund, H.-J. "Motor Unit and Muscle Activity in Voluntary Motor Control," *Physiological Reviews*, Vol. 63:387-436, 1983.

Julesz, B. "Adaptation in a peephole; a texton theory of preattentive vision," In: Spillmann, L., Wooten, B.R. (eds.) *Sensory Experience, Adaptation and Perception*, Festschrift für Ivo Kohler, Erlbaum, Hillsdale, NJ, pp. 37-52, 1984.

Katz, D. *Gestaltpsychologie*, Basel, Schwabe, p. 124-129, 1948.

Kunesch, E., Binkofski, F., Freund, H.-J. "Invariant temporal characteristics of manipulative hand movements," Experimental Brain Research, 1989 (In Press).

Lamarre, Y., Joffroy, A.J., Dumont, M., De Montigny, C., Grou, G., and Lind, J.P. "Central mechanisms of tremor in some feline and primate models," *Canadian Journal of Neurological Science*, 2:227-223, 1975.

Leist, A., Freund, H.-J., Cohen, B. (1987) "Comparative characteristics of predictive eye-hand tracking," *Human Neurobiology*, 6:19-26, 1987.

Llinas, R.R. "Possible role of tremor in the organization of the nervous system," In: *Movement Disorders: Tremor*, edited by L.J. Findley and R. Capideo, MacMillan, London, p. 475-477, 1984.

Marshall, J. "The effect of aging upon physiological tremor," *Journal of Neurology and Neurosurgery, Psychiatry*, 24:14-17, 1961.

Napier, J.R. "The prehensile movements of the human hand," *Journal of Bone and Joint Surgery*, 38:902-913, 1956.

Ream, M.J. "The tapping test — measure of motility of the human hand," *Iowa Studies in Psychology*, 8:293-319, 1922.

Schlapp, M. "Observation on a voluntary tremor — violinist's vibrato," *Quarterly Journal of Experimental Physiology*, 58:357-368, 1973.

Sternberg, S., Knoll, R.L., Monsell, S. and Wright, C.E. "Control of rapid action sequences in speech and typing," *Bell Laboratories Technical Communication*, pp. 1-20, 1984.

Taylor, F.V., and Birmingham, H.P. "Studies of tracking behaviour," II. "The acceleration pattern of quick manual corrective responses," *Journal of Experimental Psychology*, 38:783-795, 1948.

Viviani, P., Terzuolo, C. "Space-time invariance in learned motor skills," In: Stelmach, G.E., and Requin, J. (eds.) *Tutorials in motor behavior*, Elsevier, Amsterdam, pp. 523-533, 1980.

Rhythmic Control and Musical Understanding

Max W. Camp
School of Music
University of South Carolina

A large portion of a child's musical experience in the past few decades has centered around the concept of "learn the piece and win the prize!" This has been true to a large extent for both public school music programs and private lessons, especially in the area of piano study. Preparing for musical competitions can be a great incentive for studying music, but many times it fails to provide children with an understanding of how to learn and interpret music well enough to continue music-making independent of a private teacher or a school music program. The most gifted survive, and many others experience excellent musical training, but thousands of other students will stop making music when lessons cease or when participation in the marching band is finished. The reason? Too many students are unable to comprehend "how the music goes," or in some cases to comprehend what the symbols on the page represent. More can and must be done to develop students so that they can function musically long after lessons have ceased.

Developing students musically always has been an enigma. At the beginning of the twentieth century, teachers attempted to hand down the interpretive secrets of the old European masters; students imitated their teachers, who had learned from their teachers, and so on, in a kind of apostolic succession. But this venerable method is limited as a means of developing a child musically, because the underlying principles of musical understanding are neglected. To the extent that this omission occurs, the imitative approach prevents many children from developing their musical potential. Music must be experienced cognitively, emotionally, and physically by the person who is attempting the task of learning and performing it.[1]

No student can hear a teacher's aural image of a musical idea. Nor can physical responses to rhythmic patterns be based on another person's understanding of the rhythmic structure of a piece. The musical education of children must provide experiences which develop their ability to read, listen, understand, and make music *musically*.

Rhythm and Musical Achievement

Music teachers have long recognized that children with a heightened feeling for rhythm tend to learn music easily and to perform successfully; sometimes children seem to feel tempo and rhythm or the pulse-beat in music intuitively. Pulse, used more and more interchangeably with the word *rhythm,* is the rhythmic swing or beat in music that makes us nod our heads and tap our feet. It's the element in music that organizes our listening. It's the aspect of music which makes the notes on the page come alive and makes our bodies want to move to what we hear. Dancers organize their movements to it. Jazz players feel it in their bones. Composers need to have a sense of it because their musical ideas ride upon it.

The pulse-unit of music must be understood, heard, and felt before a tempo can be decided on, because it is also the basic unit which guides the continuity of physical motions at the piano or other instruments. It also provides a framework for understanding phrase shapes, sections, and complete compositions. Remember that music has a hierarchical structure just as language does. A child first learns to read and understand letters or words, then phrases and complete stories. The same *should* be true for music. After separate notational values are understood and heard, the pulse-unit can replace single notes as the "beginning whole," and in turn lead the child gradually to understand and hear phrases, the relationship of phrases and sections and the complete piece. An understanding and feeling for pulse-units is essential for the holistic perception of music symbols on the page, a cognitive and emotional reaction to the symbols, the creation and shape of an aural image, and the organization of the motor skills to produce the image.

My own observations of both children and adults persuade me that there is a strong relationship between success in learning and performing music and the ability to perceive music in metrically-grouped pulse patterns. That means having the ability to perceive pitches in definite strong-weak or weak-strong relationships as they occur within a meter, such as 3/4 or 4/4. For example, note values within a 3/4 meter, as in a waltz, group to form a strong-weak-weak pattern which is delineated by a natural (also referred to as strong) metric accent, occurring on the first beat of the measure. Accent marks that appear on the score, such as ∧ denote a dynamic accent. But the natural accent occurring on a downbeat refers to the relative strength of the downbeat, not necessarily the dynamic loudness of that beat. For instance, listeners may react bodily to a downbeat, and they may hear it coming, even though that downbeat is not dynamically loud. Think of your own heartbeat. We hope it keeps recurring, but we don't want to be jolted every time it happens. As we listen to music, we don't want to be jolted by every downbeat, but we do have a need to sense inwardly when they occur because they help organize our listening. The downbeat signifies the beginning of a new circle of musical motion. As soon as one occurs, the remaining musical activity has a natural pull towards a subsequent beat. This tendency promotes musical continuity throughout a composition.

The grouping of notes into strong-weak patterns is not written out on the score, but is a part of the structure of the music the player must understand. And there lies the problem: if people are not able to sense these groupings intuitively, music instruction must provide them with the basic tools for understanding it. Without the ability to decide how the notes will group into strong and weak beats, the student has no tools for deciding "how the music goes," and will find learning music to be an extremely frustrating experience.

The strong-weak grouping of notes is critical to musical interpretation, because the strong beats serve as the rallying point for many of the important events within a composition: cadences, phrase beginning, melodic decoration, and phrase focal points (the axes of phrase direction, such as points of climax and repose).[2] In addition, the player has to feel where the strong beats occur before syncopation can be executed, since syncopation bounces off the strong beats. So without it, jazz, blues, and an enormous amount of pop music would be eliminated immediately. The same applies to much classical music, because most composers use syncopation. Without recognizing and feeling where the strong beats are, children and adults alike will always play chords of tension as strong beats and chords of repose as weak beats, regardless of where they appear in the measure, thus constantly causing measures to be re-barred.

Obviously, we are confronting questions of motor skill development in this situation, because physical motions are responses to mental commands. How the musician views a score determines the movements required to execute that score. And if a child is to base his psychomotor activity on a metered-pulse organization, he must be able to respond to the music cognitively at a higher level than that given by separate note values.

The child may actually have one set of procedures to learn music and another set to perform it. The child learns the notes and then the teacher shows him how to play them. Having two separate tracks — one to learn by and one to perform by — effectively disconnects that child's musical understanding from his psychomotor development and undermines the development of his or her full musical potential. The teaching of motor skills in music cannot be separated from the system used to develop an understanding of the underlying musical ideas.

Motor skill development is dependent upon sensing and understanding many rhythmic variables. These variables may be grouped basically into two categories: 1) metered rhythms — those inferred by patterns of strong and weak beats; and 2) motivic rhythms — those consisting of various durational patterns that can be seen on the score.[3] These durational patterns may begin or end at any point within the strong-weak grouping of a measure or groups of measures. (Indeed, measures and groups of measures can have a strong-weak relationship analogous to the strong-weak relationship of beats within a measure.)[4] When a child learns to read music, the motivic rhythm can easily dominate the perception of the symbols, because the motivic rhythm is what is written on the page. The metered rhythm may be sensed intuitively, or understood and felt after having studied the interaction of the elements and the musical texture (i.e., the general make-up of the notational patterns and articulation).

The more I observe children who read music in pulse-units as opposed to reading by motive or individual notes, the more I recognize the importance of rhythm and timing in developing children musically. Still, as music teachers, we seem to ignore this basis for success in the natural learners, and more inclined to follow the path of correcting wrong notes, poor fingering and incorrect rhythmic execution. Pointing out errors, although it is necessary, is like treating a disease rather than practicing preventive medicine. I think we would have to spend far less time correcting errors if our teaching took into account the important relationship between rhythmic control with musical understanding.

The Tangibles and Intangibles

There are many tangible and intangible aspects of making music. Seeing a note value or a 3/4 meter signature is very tangible, but deciding on a pulse-unit or tempo is not. Most of the difficult aspects of rhythm are intangible, such as keeping a steady tempo or gauging ritards without distorting the rhythm. Markings like *Lento* or *Allegro* do guide a child, yet the interpretation of these markings — how slow or how fast — has to be understood and felt by the child. Rhythmic nuance or freedom, length of staccato notes, agogic accents, and the correct rhythmic proportions of long notes to short ones all depend upon intangible rhythmic decisions.

We all know teaching the tangibles in music is easier, especially with young piano students at 5:00 o'clock, or worse, at 7:00 o'clock in the evening after a string of bad lessons. At this point a teacher may find it appropriate, and understandably so, to say: "Please learn the notes better for the next lesson, and please *use that metronome!*" It is encouraging that some psychologists, neurologists, and musicians are beginning to delve into that intriguing arena of timing and how it affects musical competence.[5] A recent issue of the *Music Spectrum* devoted an entire issue to "Time and Rhythm in Music.[6] The experimental studies of skilled performances done by Eric Clarke have illustrated that an inner sense of rhythm helps performers communicate in a more aesthetically expressive way.[7] Clarke's studies substantiate two rhythmic concepts concerning musical performance: 1) rhythmic control in musical performance depends upon one's ability to feel pulse within a metered organization; and 2) musical performances are composed of expressive rhythm, sometimes called musical rhythm, as well as exact durational values which transform into more complex groupings.[8] Clarke's studies add support to the idea that all children should be taught a system for learning to read and perform music with rhythm as its guiding influence. Without such guidance, too many children develop a piecemeal approach to music study, and their playing is marked by disorganized physical motions and unorganized sounds.

Model Learners

Upon hearing a very gifted child make music, listeners often comment: "My, what a talent! I just love *watching* her perform because her body moves so perfectly with the music." Although one thinks of a musical performance as being an aural experience, listeners usually describe the experience in both aural and visual terms. "People only half listen to you when you play," says violinist Itzhak Perlman. "The other half is watching." The listening and watching become intertwined. This idea suggests that audiences not only love experiencing a performer's emotional response to the music through the sound, but they also enjoy seeing the performer's body response to the rhythm. In other words, convincing performances suggest a marriage between the performer's emotional and physical responses to the music. When children are able to create the feeling of this rare marriage, we can only marvel at their ability to order musical and psychomotor processes into a rhythmic synthesis or gestalt. Although only a few children are musical prodigies, their system for approaching a musical task can serve as a model for all learners. The most salient feature of the prodigy's process appears to be the ability to *see* and *hear* music symbols in logical rhythmic proportions and tonal relationships without apparent effort. They just *see* it and *do* it. For many others, the trial and error approach dominates. If that is the case, a program for establishing rhythmic accuracy is of major importance from a child's beginning lessons.

Reading Music and Psychomotor Development

Often we find both children and advanced players who display a very natural sense of timing when playing by ear or improvising. But reading from a musical score may not be so easy. It is as though one set of mental and physical switches turns off and another set turns on. How is this possible? Does an individual's sense of rhythm direct mind and body synchronization more easily when the eyes are not involved with reading a score? Do some individuals' auditory systems "shut down" when the eyes become involved? Is it an eye-hand coordination problem? The more I observe the problem, the more the path leads me back to the process whereby an individual sets up patterns of learning to read music as a child. When random patterns of reading dominate the reading process, there is real difficulty acquiring reading skill that is rhythm-based, regardless of any apparent preexisting natural sense of rhythm. The random reader continues to approach a score based on how it looks, not on how it should sound. This leads me to believe that an inner sense of timing is the most crucial aspect of learning to read and make music.

Confronting a notated score obviously changes some students from aural learners to visual learners. With the super-talents, bringing the score into the picture doesn't seem to alter the situation; the rhythmically-organized cognitive processes appear to stimulate the auditory system and to direct the motor activity simultaneously. Bringing the score into the picture should not block the auditory monitoring of what has been produced if the notes were perceived rhythmically from the beginning. Obviously, the ability to create aural images — the pre-hearing of musical ideas — is a skill of fundamental importance to any musician, because you have to know what sounds you want before you can judge the quality of the sounds you actually produce.

Influence of Personality

In students with extremely detail-oriented personalities, there is a common need to click off each note value or chord individually when playing from a score. This is similar to a child's having to line up his or her toys before agreeing to go to bed at night. For some people there is an overpowering obsession to keep items visually organized. Such an individual may check to see that each item is returned to exactly the same spot every time a table is dusted. Another person will label containers on a desk, "gem clips" or "rubber bands" even though the containers are made of clear plastic.

This same kind of personality usually has difficulty both in grouping notational patterns into pulse-units and in grouping the related physical motions. It's like an uncanny need to finish with one vertical structure of pitches before considering another set. The individual may understand intellectually what to do, but is reluctant psychologically to let it happen. The teacher observing this situation can see the frustration in the eyes and face instantly. The mind, wrists, and fingers want so badly to make a clean sweep before beginning anew. The head will make individual responses at the piano, and wrists will make separate pumping motions. Those movements reveal exactly what the mind is thinking. Perhaps there must be a correlation between how someone views the world — holistically, or by separate details — and how that same person views a notated score. Whatever the explanation, young children can adapt to the "grouped-notes" idea and learn to perceive symbols in metered-pulse patterns holistically much more easily than adults.

Another confounding factor is the apparent need to hear a set of pitches longer than is notated on the score. This trait has been observed in a number of students, especially those with perfect pitch. Some individuals may have a terrific sense of pitch, but may need to hear these pitches without any regard for the pulse pattern. Here, there may be a tendency to resolve one set of pitches — say a melody note and a harmony — into the next set of pitches without regard for note values, pulse, meter, or tempo. This may not be a problem when the individual is listening to music produced by someone else. Perhaps when an individual is involved in playing from a score, the visual aspect may subdue the auditory system's monitoring of the music, while in that same individual, responding to music as a listener, the auditory system may be inclined to direct the response. If this is the case, perhaps the motor learning — the body response of large muscles when listening to music — does not transfer easily to the motor activity required of the small muscles needed in making music with an instrument from a notated score.

The Effects of Eurythmics

The eurythmics of Jaques-Dalcroze and other prescribed curricula used for fostering a sense of rhythmic feeling and understanding may not be as effective in developing musical achievement as previously thought. Bodily responses made when listening to music may offer experiences which are helpful in fostering rhythmic feeling, but not necessarily in making music from a score. The question arises: is rhythm mental, aural, psychological, and/or physical? Not only Dalcroze, but James L. Mursell and many others have advocated the teaching of rhythm through clapping, walking, and other movements involving the large muscles. Children usually are receptive to the experience, but many fail to transfer what they have experienced to the reading of music. Some musicians question whether or not there is ever any transfer. Artur Schnabel, the famous pianist, did not approve of the rhythmic clapping and tapping exercises of the Dalcroze School and considered them artificial isolations of the tone element.[9] In any case, there is a growing awareness among teachers that physical approaches help, but are not sufficient alone for teaching rhythmic awareness.

Learning Habits

Children very quickly develop habits, or a system, for doing a task such as reading music. Some of the less desirable habits can be modified if change is approached when the student is young. The older the student is, the more difficult it is to change the approach. Adults bring to a learning situation a mind-set for approaching any task, whether it is reading music, mowing the lawn, or putting the dishes in a dishwasher — one discovers this very quickly upon loading the dishwasher at one's parents' home. Obviously, since the best time to correct bad habits is before they get started, I believe attention needs to be given to providing children at the beginning a model process of learning and performing music. For me, this means stressing the *process* over the learning of specific pieces. At a young age, long term goals can be realized more easily, and well-trained children can continue as adults to learn music able to make their own interpretive decisions.

Children develop reading habits from the beginning stages of formal music lessons. And whatever one did during those early years usually continues to guide the *reading* of new pieces, regardless of how well one performs as an adult. I have tried the experiment on many advanced students in pedagogy classes and the results are similar no matter where they were trained as children. Those whose childhood reading was dominated by aural images, metrically perceived, continue to use this method as they advance. Those whose reading was dominated by the visual aspect of the score, the motivic readers, tend to continue the practice as adults.

When children form poor reading habits in music, learning to play an instrument remains puzzling throughout their lives. If a child's lessons involve more corrections than instructions, the situation becomes intolerable by age twelve and the child drops out. Commenting to the parents, the child says, "I hate music and never want to take another lesson." It's not that he hates music; he is just frustrated with the struggle involved in getting the notes off the page. Rather than automatically applying the label of untalented to children who are frustrated, we should find ways to fill in the missing links for students who have problems, especially rhythmic ones.

The Many Faces of Rhythm

The word "rhythm" means different things to different people. To some, it refers only to note values or the mathematical side of rhythm. To others, rhythm refers to the recurring swing in music as well as to all other aspects of the rhythmic structure. Rhythmic control continues to baffle the music world. Although it is difficult to teach, we certainly know when it is lacking. It's like electricity: we can't see it, but we sure know when it is not there. Musicians continue to go around and around in an effort to define it, but it is still much easier to describe than to define. All during the twentieth century, music teachers and critics have called for the development of it. The famous English piano pedagogue, Tobias Matthay, stated as early as 1913 that no performance could be saved without it.[10] Abby Whiteside, the famous American pedagogue, contends that it is "the most important factor in a musical performance."[11] Sometimes a music score calls for rhythm to be non-relenting. At other times the score suggests that it should be expressive.

Since music generally has been organized metrically by composers, the study of the metrical organization of musical ideas, as they unfold at higher structural levels, is the most obvious and practical way to foster learning, interpretation, and performance.[12] There are many reasons for this. "All element-processes are rhythmic."[13] A musician cannot judge the relationships and proportions in music without understanding or hearing rhythmic grouping. And a musician's interpretation of music depends upon the "sensitivity to an awareness of rhythmic structure."[14]

By becoming aware of the relationship between the organization of music and the perceiving, learning, and performing of it, one understands how to develop a child musically. As a child grows up to play more advanced music, he or she will need to comprehend rhythmic and metric analysis because doing so is vital to understanding the phrasing and articulation in music.[15] Our approach to helping children develop a system for learning and performing music must be one that will carry them throughout their musical lifetime, because the learning and performing of music is not different at the more advanced levels; it is only more complex.[16]

Footnotes

1. Max W. Camp. *Developing Piano Performance,* Chapel Hill: Hinshaw Music, p.1, 1981.

2. William Christ, et al. Materials and Structure of Music I, Englewood Cliffs: Prentice-Hall, Inc., 62-64; 1966. See also, Wallace Berry, *Form in Music*, Englewood Cliffs: Prentice-Hall, Inc., p. 15, 1966.

3. Jonathan D. Ensminger. "An Approach for Understanding The Rhythmic Structure of Piano Compositions," Unpublished Doctoral dissertation, University of South Carolina, p.2, 1986.

4. Wallace Berry. *Form in Music*, Englewood Cliffs: Prentice-Hall, Inc,. p. 116, 1966.

5. Frank R. Wilson. *Tone Deaf and All Thumbs?*, New York: Viking Penguin, p. 116, 1986.

6. Music Theory Spectrum. *Journal of the Society for Music Theory* 7, (1985).

7. Eric Clarke. "Some Aspects of Rhythm and Expression in Performances of Erik Satie's Gnossienne No. 5," *Music Perception* 2, Spring, pp. 299, 312, 324, 1985.

8. Clarke. pp. 299-328; see also L.H. Shaffer. "Performances of Chopin, Bach, and Bartok: Studies in Motor Programming," *Cognitive Psychology* 13 pp. 326-376, 1981.

9. Konrad Wolff. *The Teaching of Artur Schnabel*, New York: Praeger, p. 173, 1971.

10. Tobias Matthay. *Musical Interpretation*, London: Joseph Williams, rpt. Westport, CT: Greenwood, 1970, pp. 31-33, 1913.

11. Abby Whiteside. *Mastering the Chopin Etudes and Other Essays*, Joseph Prostakoff and Sophia Rosoff, eds. New York: Scribners, p.4, 1969.

12. Max W. Camp. *Developing Piano Performance*, Chapel Hill: Hinshaw Music, p. 66, 1981.

13. Wallace Berry. *Structural Functions in Music*, Englewood Cliffs: Prentice-Hall, Inc., p. 301, 1976.

14. Grosvenor W. Cooper and Leonard B. Meyer. *The Rhythmic Structure of Music,* Chicago: The University of Chicago Press, p. 1, 1960.

15. Berry. p. 301.

16. Camp. p. 2

The Role of a Motor Grammar in Musical Performance

John Baily
Department of Music
Columbia University

Introduction

The way the human body is organized to move is a crucial element in the structure of music, and is one of the ways in which music may be said to be rooted in the human body. A musical instrument is a type of transducer, converting patterns of body movement into patterns of sound. There is a precise isomorphism between music structure and movement structure: every nuance in the micro-structure of the sound pattern reflects a subtle adjustment of the motor pattern. The interaction between the human body, with its intrinsic modes of operation, and the morphology of the instrument may shape the structure of music in various ways (Baily 1977, 1985).

If we compare different styles of playing an instrument, we find that they are characterized by particular patterns of movement. For example, the violin, one of the most widely disseminated standard instruments, is used for a great variety of musics, such as Western, Middle Eastern and Indian art musics and a range of folk fiddling styles. The characteristic movements associated with each musical style constitute the *motor structure* of that style. Some of the differences between violin/fiddle styles arise from the way the instrument and the bow are held, which forms the basis on which the motor structure develops. Intuitively, one might expect the motor structure to embody a set of rules which constitute some form of motor grammar. This determines the way movements are put together, as simultaneous combinations and as movement sequences, and which can generate novel sequences of movement, and hence of music. As you might guess, although motor grammars may be easy to talk about as abstract entities, they are not so easy to pin down in practice. However, in my research on the movement-music issue in playing various types of plucked lute in Afghanistan, I came across an interesting example of a simple motor grammar, and it is this that I want to speak about today.

The Afghan Rubāb And Its Music

The instrument in question is the Afghan *rubāb*, which is a waisted short-necked plucked lute with three main strings and sets of drone and sympathetic strings.

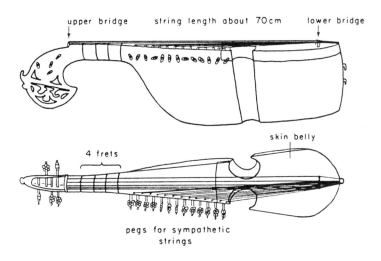

Figure 1. The Afghan *rubāb*

The instrument is played with a small wooden or horn plectrum (*shāhbāz*) held between the thumb and forefinger. A small but significant morphological feature of the *rubāb* is the way the shortest sympathetic string is raised by a small protuberance on the bridge, as shown in Figure 2. This allows it to serve as a high drone, which is struck in alternation with the main strings in complex right hand patterns.

Rubāb music is characterized by a sophisticated right hand technique which exploits the possibilities of rhythmic variation. This is shown very well in the example I have elected to discuss, which is the middle section from a genre of Afghan instrumental art music. The section is called an *āstāi*, in which the *rubāb* plays a fixed composition with tabla drum accompaniment in *Tintāl*, a rhythmic cycle of sixteen units, each unit being called a *matra*. In this particular example the *āstāi* composition is played through some twenty-three times with a variety of rhythmic patterns. There are also

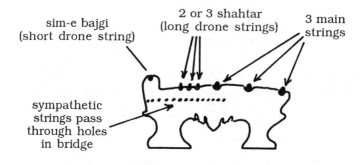

Figure 2. Bridge of the *rubāb*

several interpolations of a second composition, the *antara*, and of a simple scalar pattern called *paliteh*, but these need not concern us here.

The basic melody of the *āstāi* composition is shown in Figure 3. Transcribed in "E", the scale used corresponds to the western Phrygian mode. The last note of the basic melody has an optional partner an octave below.

Figure 3. Basic melody of the *āstāi*

The composition is an abstract melodic outline of sixteen *matra*s in length which can be realized in many ways using different patterns of right hand strokes. The first beat (called *gor*) of the cycle is the point of rhythmic resolution. The first two cycles of the *āstāi* are shown in Figure 4.

Figure 5 shows the right hand patterns played in the twenty-three cycles of the *āstāi*, arranged in six "episodes."

Those cycles labeled "simple" are played somewhat as in Figure 4, whereas most of the patterns consist of four strokes per *matra*, or in cycles 14-19 of three strokes per *matra*. Changes from one pattern to another tend to occur at the start of a cycle. Downstrokes are labeled ∨, upstrokes ∧, and strokes

Figure 4. First two cycles of the _astai_

on the upper drone strings as ˅ and ˄. The notation is deliberately simple and does not show certain small but important audible differences between the various patterns; it is a type of action notation that seeks to represent the rhythmic movements of the right hand. Patterns which use strokes on the upper drone string would seem to lead to "auditory streaming" (McAdams and Bregman, 1979), the strokes on the high drone being heard as an independent rhythmic pattern.

(The audio example was then played, being the _āstāi_ section of a _naghmeh-ye Kashāl_ in _Rāg Bairami_ played by Mohammad Rahim Khushnawaz of Herat in 1974, and published by Baily 1987.)

It should be evident from the transcription that the rhythmic variations are "episodic." In the course of each episode there is a gradual increase in "rhythmic tension" which finally resolved with a rhythmic cadence onto the first (_gor_) beat of a _Tintāl_ cycle. Two main components of the build-up of rhythmic tension can be identified, though they are not both necessarily present in every episode:

The Role of a Motor Grammar in Musical Performance   205

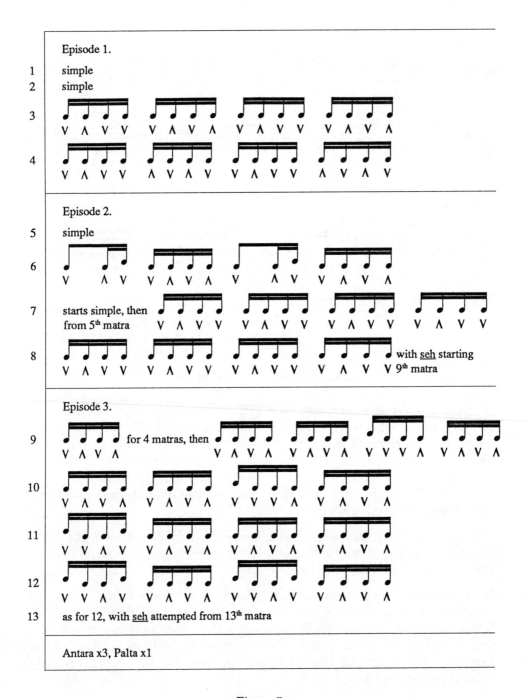

Figure 5

Rhythmic patterns used for playing the $\bar{a}st\bar{a}i$. (Continued on next page.)

John Baily

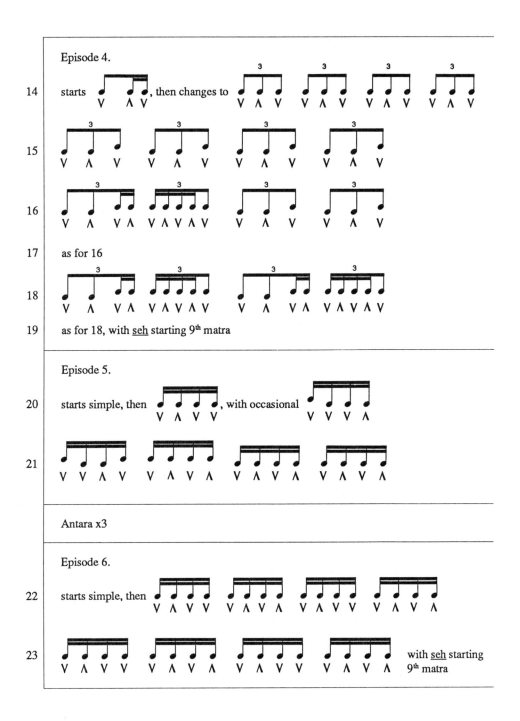

1. an increase in tempo, evident during the course of each of the six episodes;
2. an increase in the "density" of high drone strokes, shown in Episodes 3, 5 and especially in Episode 4, with its fast tremolo on the high drone string.

A third way of increasing rhythmic tension is through the stressing of unaccented beats, as in Cycle 4.

The end of an episode is marked in several ways:

1. by the use of the rhythmic device called the *seh*, "three," a rhythmic pattern repeated three times, the end of the third repetition coinciding with the *gor* beat of the next cycle;
2. by a return to a simple statement of the theme;
3. by a drop to a slower tempo.

Right Hand Stroke Patterns

The variety of rhythmic patterns for playing the *rubāb* arise from differences in the properties of the strong downstroke ∨ and the weak upstroke ∧ of the right hand holding the plectrum. These differences arise from the mechanics of the movements themselves. The player holds the plectrum between the first finger and the thumb, the other fingers are flexed and tucked into the palm. The wrist is flexed at an angle of 60-90 degrees relative to the forearm. The forearm rests near the bottom of the body of the instrument to provide support for the hand. Movement of the plectrum is brought about by rotation of the wrist. The main stroke is not only downward but also inward toward the belly of the instrument. The downstroke is physically more forceful than the upstroke, and the hand also hits onto the skin belly, adding a percussive component to the sound of the stroke. The downstroke is more intense than the upstroke and results in a wider spectrum of partials being evoked from the sympathetic strings. There are also small differences in timing because the upstroke tends to be slightly delayed after a downstroke. A specific stroke sequence therefore produces a particular rhythmic pattern, and there are clearly audible differences between patterns such as:

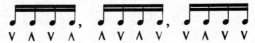

depending on the temporal distribution of the stressed downstrokes.

John Baily

The rhythmic patterns shown in Figure 5 can be generated from a number of rules about possible sequences of strokes, which constitute part of the generative grammar for playing the *āstāi*. Some of the basic rules are listed in Table 1.

Rule 1.   ∨ is the dominant stroke

Rule 2.   ∧ occurs only in association with ∨

Rule 3.   ∧∧ is an impossible combination

Rule 4.   The maximum number of ∨'s in a row is 3

Rule 5.   When two ∨'s follow a ∧ , the first ∨ can become ˅ on the upper drone string.

Rule 6.   4 matras shall be the longest patterned unit

Table 1
Generative rules for *rubāb* playing

These rules can generate various one *matra* units, such as ∨∧∨∧ ∧∨∧∨ and ∨∧∨∨ which can then be combined in two *matra* units such as ∨∧∨∨ ∨∧∨∧ and ∨∧∨∨ ∧∨∧∨. The ∨∧∨∨ unit is the key pattern for generating many other patterns, especially when Rule 5 is used to give transformations such as ∨∧˅∧, ∧˅∨∨, ˅∨∨∧ and ∨∨∧˅, and these can be combined with other units. Not all combinations are possible: for example, ∧˅∨∨ ∨∧∨∧ would contravene Rule 4.

Most of the stroke patterns used in this example can be generated from rules of the kind discussed above. A few would require certain extra rules, for example to generate in cycle 21 the following pattern.

V V ∧ V   ∧ V ∧ V   V ∧ V ∧   V ∧ V ∧

A further principle which may be used in the generation of stroke patterns is "re-phasing" of the stroke pattern. Take the pattern ˅∨∧˅ ∨∧∨∧ adopted in cycles 12 and 13, which is one of the commonest patterns using the high drone. By starting the sequence on each of its eight strokes in turn, eight stroke patterns can in theory be generated, as shown in Table 2, i.e., the same sequence of hand movements starting at eight different places.

I have not attempted to construct a formal grammar (in the sense of a complete set of rules which could be tested by computer simulation), but even without doing that one sees an interesting problem ahead. The grammar generates far more patterns than are actually used by *rubāb* players. For example, of the eight related sequences shown in Table 2, only pattern 1 is at all common. Why this one and not the other seven?

1	V̌VΛV	VΛVΛ
2	ΛV̌VΛ	V̌VΛV
3	VΛV̌V	ΛV̌VΛ
4	ΛVΛV̌	VΛV̌V̌
5	VΛVΛ	V̌VΛV̌
6	V̌VΛV	ΛV̌VΛ
7	ΛV̌VΛ	VΛV̌V
8	VΛV̌V	ΛVΛV̌

Table 2

Right hand stroke patterns generated by rephasing of
stroke cycle.

One must not confuse art and physiology, and there are no doubt purely aesthetic criteria operating in the making of this selection, but certain human constraints can also be suggested. Some patterns pose problems of motor technique. For example, stroke patterns that contain an upstroke ∧ at the beginning of a *matra* are difficult to perform because the melody may require a change of string between a ∨ and the succeeding ∧, a difficult movement to coordinate. Changing strings is more readily achieved when the change precedes a downstroke, that is, when the hand's starting position

John Baily

is above the strings and all that is required is a small change in the angle of the downstroke to strike the appropriate string. Problems arise when the change of string precedes an upstroke, which, according to the principles by which stroke patterns are organized, will occur only after a downstroke. Now the plectrum has to be moved from below one string to below the next string to reach the starting position for the upstroke; a change of hand posture has now been inserted between ∨ and ∧ (see Baily 1985:255). This consideration would tend to eliminate all but patterns 1 and 5 in Table 2. Some patterns may be difficult to organize as auditory gestalts, such as patterns 6, 7 and 8, which break down into 3 2 3 groupings. In fact, only patterns 1 and 5 in Table 2 satisfy both criteria, yet pattern 1 is common and pattern 5 is rare. This is possibly because the 3 3 2 grouping of pattern 1 is more readily organized than the 2 3 3 grouping of pattern 5. Further research is required in analyzing these patterns.

The patterns generated from the grammar are not therefore equally available, some are more compatible with the human sensorimotor system than others, and they are the ones that probably lie at the core of the repertory of patterns actually used by *rubāb* players. Those that are difficult to use, however, are the domain of the virtuoso, who may for example, deliberately select patterns which begin a *matra* with ∧ in developing an episode. In the art of playing *āstāi*, varying degrees of perceptual confusion may be engendered by using units which tend to group themselves out of phase with the metrical framework of the composition. It is a play on rhythmic ambiguity, an effect enhanced by the use of the high drone to create two perceptual streams with different rhythmic patterns, and by shifting the melody about in relation to the abstract melodic outline. The cyclic variations present a shift between stability and confusion, and conform to the principles of "simultaneous deviation" set out by Meyer (1956:234-244).

The Role of the Motor Grammar

The type of improvisation found for playing *āstāi* on the *rūbāb* may be described as rhythmic variation according to rule. A motor grammar has been described which generates rhythmic units one, two or four *matras* in length. The structure of these units arises in part from the physical characteristics of the movements used to pluck the strings. In playing the *āstāi* the musician subjects the composition to a succession of treatments. Performance is organized through the sequential retrieval of motor programs which together constitute a vocabulary of patterns. He makes choices between already overlearned patterns to create the structure of the episode, with its gathering rhythmic tension and perceptual confusion. Sometimes, no doubt, a new rhythmic pattern is generated from the motor grammar, which can then be elaborated in the development of an episode. This would seem to correspond to what Pressing (1984: 350) terms "the development of seeds."

The grammar generates a large number of seemingly equivalent units but these are not equally easy to control; there is a hierarchy amongst them. There are difficulties with making certain movements, and in maintaining certain rhythmic patterns, which tend to reorganise in different gestalts and disrupt performance. These are matters which require further investigation.

This brings us finally to the conscious level of control. Here are conscious choices, the selection of the next pattern and bringing it in at the right point, etc. How does the musician identify these patterns in the act of performance? There is a vocabulary for labeling such patterns in speech. Essentially these describe aspects of the movements of the right hand, which suggests that in this case the musician may be thinking primarily in terms of movements rather than sound patterns. For the musician it is a question of "What do I *do* now?", not "What's the next sound pattern I should produce?" It is a form of creativity in movement, a "dance of the hand." The spatio-motor mode of musical performance can be just as "creative" as the auditory mode. Creativity in music may often consist of deliberately finding new ways to move on the instrument, which will then be assessed, and further creative acts guided by the aesthetic evaluation of the resultant novel sonic patterns (see Baily 1985:257). The motor grammar may form an important element in this kind of musical thought.

References

Baily, John. "Movement patterns in playing the Herati *dutār*," in John Blacking (ed.) *The Anthropology of the Body*, London: Academic Press, 275-330, 1977.

Baily, John. "A system of modes used in the urban music of Afghanistan," *Ethnomusicology* XXV(1):1-39, 1981.

Baily, John. "Music structure and human movement," in Peter Howell, Ian Cross and Robert West, (eds.), *Musical Structure and Cognition*, Academic Press, London: 237-258, 1985

Baily, John. "Principes d'improvisation dans le jeu du *rubāb* d'Afghanistan," in Bernard Lortat-Jacob (ed.) *L'Improvisation dans les musiques de tradition orale*, Paris: SELAF, 1987.

McAdams, Stephen and Bregman, Albert. "Hearing Musical Streams," *Computer Music Journal*, 3(4):26-44, 1979.

Meyer, Leonard B. *Emotion and Meaning in Music*, Chicago: University of Chicago Press, 1956.

Pressing, Jeff. "Cognitive processes in improvisation," in Crozier, W. Ray, and Chapman, Antony J. (eds.), *Cognitive Processes in the Perception of Art*, Amsterdam: Elsevier, 345-63, 1984.

Acknowledgments

This research was supported by a post-doctoral research grant from the Social Science Research Council to the author when a research fellow in the Department of Social Anthropology, The Queen's University of Belfast, 1975-1978. The present paper is an adaptation of Baily (1987), which was written while the author was a visiting research fellow at the Laboratory for Experimental Psychology, Sussex University, 1983-84. My thanks to Dr. James Kippen of QUB for suggested improvements to my original transcriptions.

The Development of Musical Performance Skills in Children

Jack A. Taylor
Center for Music Research
Florida State University
Tallahassee, Florida

In my dual role as a music perception/cognition researcher and computer person, I'm going to talk about music performance, review some relevant research about children, and describe our proposed computer applications at the Center for Music Research at Florida State University. But first, allow me to discuss briefly a perspective I have on music psychology research.

We know that when researching music we must deal with a unique integration of art and science. In earlier times, the study of musical behaviors and ideas was considered a sacrilege; music is, after all, a feelingful art form, an ideal conveyer of emotional and other "nonscientific" phenomena. Music was not presumed to be, nor was it thought it could be, scientifically examined. Today, however, we know much more about the physical structure of music. We realize that while a few individuals seem to be endowed with special musical "gifts," the vast majority, if they want to learn to sing or play an instrument, must deal with music as they would any other endeavor, i.e., they have to build up skills and concepts, progressing from very simple tasks to more highly coordinated ones. Being able to identify these skills and concepts and manipulate them in research situations has led to the development of a new field of study, music psychology.

Music psychology is not, at present, at a very advanced stage; in fact, I see it as rather primitive compared to what it may eventually grow into. There is, of course, good research being done. What bothers me about much of the music research I have looked at is its focus on designs that all too often are amusical. It seems that researchers could more adequately define the specific musical problem area, then follow through with a series of planned studies that thoroughly address the questions posed. Often, single research projects are undertaken with no thought about their connection(s) to more general music problems or to the experimental research that preceded or follows from current investigation. Nonmusical research refers to projects that seem disconnected from "real" music; for example, psychoacoustic studies that deal with the perception of isolated sounds. While this kind of research provides fundamental insight into sound *per se*, it doesn't give us much direction toward understanding how people deal with music.

A solution to these problems is to step back and look at what people do when engaged in musical activities. Their activities can be categorized: within these categories of activity are found the materials for music research. We are trying to do this at the Center for Musical Research. It turns out to be a nontrivial task to break down broad categories of music activity into their many dimensions — and I won't attempt to describe our progress here. But at least we have identified the broad categories: composing, listening, performing, verbalizing, conceptualizing, and the extramusical aspects of music. The first three categories are fairly obvious, but perhaps the last three are not. My colleague at the Center, Dr. Clifford Madsen, has defined them well (Madsen, 1987). Verbalizing is both talking and writing about music. Talking ranges from simply discussing music to teaching music. Conceptualizing music, on the other hand, means that one thinks about music in the sense of analyzing it, criticizing it, choosing alternatives, and so forth. This is something that a music theorist might do (of course, conceptualizing music also is seen in the categories of composing, performing, and listening). Aesthetic appreciation is also a part of conceptualizing, but thus far has escaped an operational definition. That being the case, it does not, for the time being, lend itself to rigorous research protocols. Madsen (1987) proposes that, "Perhaps this 'mystical aesthetic experience' represents the composite emotional and intellectual responsiveness to music which is reinforced through time and is always defined as good." Finally, there are extramusical aspects: dance music, music used in therapy, background music, cocktail music, industrial music, and so on.

At the present time, we have decided to focus our major research efforts on music therapy, music listening, and music performance. We are making a great effort to research these areas systematically and musically; that is, our research projects are designed in what we believe are logical series that deal with real musical problems.

Music Performance

Singing or playing a musical instrument is a task that involves the interactions of refined cognitive and physical skills. Physically, what musicians do is much like athletics, except that the movements required in music performance usually are much smaller than those in sports activities. Furthermore, the combinations of movement, or patterns of movement, are much more refined in music than in sport. Also, whereas the product of sports activity is easily measured or judged in terms of speed, distance, trajectory, etc., the product of a musical event — the performance itself — is not so easy to measure.

Let's look at the perceptual, cognitive, and biomechanical aspects of musical performance — and please, understand that no one really understands these processes. What I'm going to describe remains yet to be established empirically. First, the musician must read music, which really means that s/he must match visual perceptions of the musical symbols to their motor correlates. But before any matching can happen, the musician needs to know how to interpret and use musical notation. Music notation is a code for concepts that are translated into biomechanical processes. With it, one represents the three basic dimensions of music: the actual tones to play, their durations, and their intensity or loudness. Music notation also is a code for other musical considerations such as, for example, tempo, where to place the bow on the string, articulations, and how to phrase groups of notes.

When the musician has developed even an elementary facility with the code, s/he is ready to connect it to motor processes. The performer now has mental schema that are sufficiently robust to allow for connections with basic movement processes that already exist in neural memory; these connections, then, make possible a reasonable approximation of the correct tone or pattern of tones. We can hypothesize that a crude motor schema is organized and tentatively stored in the nervous system, one that is an obvious consequence of its initiating mental schema, which itself was born from a decoding of musical notation. This motor schema probably becomes a part of a growing motor memory, one that is more or less unique to a particular instrument or voice and with roots in more basic motor processes.

With most children, we would have to say that their performance skills are not well developed. A beginner must build up and refine motor schema through practice. Not only must the schema become refined, but many more must be created and added to motor memory. Performers are called upon to play many kinds of music, which means that a huge number of motor schema must exist in memory. These crude schema and their movement responses are refined through feedback — the purpose of practice. Feedback is received from four sensory sources: aural, visual, tactile, and proprioceptive. Since the product of performance is rendition of the music itself, we know that aural discriminations of the sound serve to adjust both mental and motor schema. After playing a note, or a pattern of notes, the performer adjusts the mechanics of the body parts in ways which will result in a more accurate rendering of the desired sound. For example, it may happen that after playing a four-note chord, a pianist might decide that the four notes were not balanced; that is, they did not sound at equal intensity. Having received this aural feedback, the pianist now can achieve balance by adjusting the striking force of one or more fingers in a second playing of this same chord. It must be emphasized that to a large extent, musical practice is trial and error — although as one becomes more skilled fewer errors occur. At any rate, it seems clear that correct, repetitive practice refines motor schema, thus improving performance.

Visual feedback, on the other hand, is not very useful for performers who cannot see their fingers and hands on the keys of an instrument; but obviously, it's extremely useful for the keyboard player, the percussionist, guitarist, and many others. For those who can't see their fingers, tactile and proprioceptive feedback becomes very important. This is the pressure one feels from striking or moving keys on an instrument or, in the case of a singer, feeling the vibration of the vocal folds in the throat. Proprioceptive feedback is what allows people to sense where in space the muscular and skeletal body parts involved in music performance are. Tactile and proprioceptive feedback can be very useful to the musician, particularly when considered in conjunction with aural feedback. For example, after hearing the four-note chord and noticing its imbalance, the pianist might conclude that "I am striking the keys too hard with the 3rd and 5th fingers of my right hand."

Let's assume that the performer now has become quite skilled and can perform a wide range of musical literature with almost no errors and with obvious musicianship. Is it reasonable to think that the perception of music notation must pass through mental schema, which I have described as a conscious process, before moving on to motor schema? Since at the level of a skilled performer music can become very complicated, requiring almost instantaneous reaction to notation, it appears almost certain that perceptions, the mental and motor schema I just described, either become faster and faster or that something else in these stages is shortened or deleted. After all, the reader of musical notation has not only to process the current notations, but must also look ahead in order to keep the music flowing.

I'm afraid we don't know very much about what happens to the processing of musical information in the skilled performer. It may be that the mental schema disappear. That is, the perceptions of musical notations may lock directly onto motor schema, which in turn immediately trigger the appropriate movements. In other words, the performer's very large repertoire of motor schema may become "automated," allowing the player to focus on reading ahead and experimenting with subtle expressions. Concert pianists, for example, don't think very much about the mechanics of playing, concentrating instead on expression, as when they transmit a feeling or "sense of the music" to their fingers through very subtle changes in finger forces and timings.

I should mention two other matters related to this discussion: playing from memory and its counterpart, sight reading. Time doesn't permit a complete discussion, but I do want to point out that playing from memory, while eliminating the task of visually perceiving music, still means that music must be read or "perceived" from an internal memory. This type of perception may be very different from overt visual perception in that the emphasis may be more on retrieving and decoding the serial events of music from a special memory. Because it is essentially a test of the quality and quantity of the performer's motor schema memory, sight reading is an especially interesting phenomenon. If the performer can sight read easily, it probably means that s/he has a good motor memory. At least one research project (with pianists) has shown a strong relationship between good sight reading and good performance (Trice, Taylor, and Pembrook, 1987).

Research and Children

Now let me turn to children and musical performance. Understanding how children develop performance skills is not only important if we want more effectively to help them learn to play an instrument or sing, but it is also important to our research of the basic mental and motor processes I've previously described. Because adults are physically and psychologically more or less fully developed, it may be difficult to detect in them various levels of performance phenomena — even if we observe adults who are just beginning to learn to play an instrument. Children, on the other hand, are naive in terms of experience and have undeveloped or incompletely developed motor skills. It would seem to me that if we researched the growth of their performance skills together with their physical and psychological development, we would be more likely to identify important elements of musical skill development.

Let me explain some of our approach to this type of research at the Center for Music Research, adding that we are just now beginning to do research with children. Personally, I've been an admirer of Jean Piaget, but recently have become somewhat disenchanted with the structures of his four stages of cognitive development. As you know, Piaget described (1952) four stages of skill behavior: sensorimotor (from birth to two years); pre-operational (from two to seven years); concrete operations (from seven to eleven years); and formal operations (from eleven to about eighteen years). Piaget emphasized changes in reasoning strategies across the four stages. However, I would suggest that these changes may not be applicable to the development of music performance skills. If you have had experience giving music lessons to children, you may have observed that the underlying reasoning processes that children use in acquiring music performance skills are the same, regardless of age. In other words, Piaget's four stages may not be discrete stages, since learning to sing or to play an instrument is regulated across age by the commonalities of problem solving, imitation, and exploration (Case, 1985).

There is also some music research that has been aimed at relating Piaget's nonmusical tasks to musical tasks (conservation has been a favorite topic), with the hypothesis that musical and nonmusical skills develop at the same time and the same rate. Early research showed some positive evidence for this; but more recently researchers have discovered that some performance skills don't develop in parallel with nonmusical skills, and others don't develop at the same rate (Nelson, 1987a). For example, motor skills begin to fully develop after visual and auditory skills have become reasonably well established. There is also evidence that auditory and visual conservation in music develop at different rates. Thus, if Piaget meant that all or most skills develop in parallel and at the same rate, it seems unlikely that this notion can be applied to music performance.

I think it is now becoming apparent that the development of musical skills needs to be studied as a unique field of inquiry. That is to say, it may be fine to look at nonmusic theories for guidance, but we should not assume that they are adequate models for explaining musical skill development. It is only recently that music researchers have undertaken true musical research with children, particularly in regard to observing their development of skills related to musical performance. Unfortunately, many of these studies do not look at skill development in real musical contexts; instead, they study skill development in relation to isolated aspects of music and sound. Also, these studies rarely relate skill development to other elements of music performance; nor is there solid follow-up research.

Nevertheless, some good research does exist, the results of which are very useful to our work at the Center. There is research which suggests a possible relationship between music listening ability and visual/spatial ability (Nelson, 1987b). Music listening ability means that one can comprehend acoustic figures and spatial ability means that one can comprehend visual figures (Karma, 1983). In addition, spatial ability is strongly related to composition and improvising skills. Skills in spatial and music ability appear to increase at a fairly steady rate among children from six to twelve years of age, while music listening skills seem to start at a later age.

At the Center, we are interested in the ways that motor skills develop. Research seems to support what one might already suspect; motor skills improve gradually with increasing age (ages tested were from three to ten years), and children, particularly during primary school years, can better synchronize movement to music if the music's tempo is adjusted to the child's "personal beat" — which the child can indicate by patting hands on the knees at a comfortable speed. Proprioceptive feedback becomes important when a child becomes more proficient in playing an instrument. Being able to see what one is doing while playing is necessary in the early stages of musical performance. More advanced children don't have to see their arms, fingers, or other body parts because they receive fairly complete proprioceptive feedback from their muscles and joints (Hedden, 1987). One might also suspect that skill practice in one area of music could transfer to another area. This seems to be the case with young children. Systematic use of vocal training in instrumental rehearsals, for example, has been shown to improve instrumental performance and intonation accuracy. Interestingly, even mental practice of the music, that is, playing the music without activating the keys on the instrument or blowing into the mouthpiece, raises the performance level — but only when interspersed with actual practice.

One interesting way to test motor skill behavior in children is to ask them to tap. Tapping skill is a good indicator of finger speed and synchronization, clearly essential to music performance. Tapping research, in both music and nonmusic settings, is of two types: rhythmic and nonrhythmic (Grieshaber, 1987). Nonrhythmic tapping simply requires the child to tap as fast as possible, given the conditions of the experiment. Not surprisingly, children tap faster and smoother as they get older, ranging from 2.2 taps per second for preschoolers to 7.3 taps per second for 10th graders. Of course, hand dominance plays a role, the dominant hand tapping faster (hand dominance becomes established when the child is five to seven years old). The ability to

Jack A. Taylor

alternate tapping from hand to hand seems to be established by the time the child is five years old. As a matter of fact, children at this age can do this faster than tapping both hands simultaneously.

Rhythmic tapping may be even more relevant to music performance. Again, there are two types: tapping in synchrony and tapping in imitation. Synchronous tapping requires children to tap along with a series of notes that are either evenly spaced or rhythmically grouped. It seems to be a task that children can do quite well by the 3rd grade. However, younger children (preschoolers) tap more accurately when the tempo is faster, i.e., in the range of 120-186 taps per minute.

Imitative tapping is really more a test of memory than of motor skills, because it requires children to listen to a rhythmic pattern and remember it. Nevertheless, it can lead to insights about the sense of rhythm, which is important to the study of music performance. Research shows that the ability to imitate rhythmic figures correctly increases with age, but it still remains still to be determined if children reach a plateau at the 3rd grade as some research suggests, or if imitative tapping continues to improve. Tempo is probably a factor, as is the complexity of the tapping task, but there is insufficient evidence to make positive statements at this time. Children do have a tendency to tap faster than the rhythmic stimulus, and also to accelerate the tempo. These deviations, however, stabilize after a short period of practice. Interestingly, children make many more tapping errors in compound than in simple meters. This seems also to be true in adults across other kinds of memory tasks as well, and may be a matter of density, i.e., the greater number of taps available in compound meters.

In all the research I've described, there seems to be little difference in performance as a function of gender. With few exceptions, boys and girls generally perform equally well.

Computer Applications

At the Center, we hope to build on the research I've just described; but we want to do this directly in the context of musical performance. We intend to measure subjects in several ways while they play at the keyboard (later we'll use other instruments). We believe it is possible to do this with the help of our considerable computing power. Currently we are developing computer systems that will help us to examine the perceptual processes of music reading and the development and refinement of motor schema from those precepts.

Let me briefly describe the computer systems. We have two digital tachisto-scopes, that is, a pair of shutters that will control the presentation time of two 35 mm slide projectors. They will let us present music notations to children at rates from 5 milliseconds to any number of seconds. This means that we can control the duration of the perceptual field. How correctly a child plays the presented notations, and how long it takes the child to respond, are variables that we can measure and compare, no matter how many responses and how short the timings. Given a sufficient number of carefully designed experiments, we should be able to determine what children see in the music notations and, maybe, how they encode their per-ceptions.

Another interesting system we've developed, one that will measure both motor and conceptual skills as the child performs, is a piano keyboard con-nected to an Atari 1040 ST computer. The Atari and the keyboard are reasonably portable, allowing us to take them to the child's school or home. The system works like this. While the child plays, the computer measures key strikes by first identifying the keys pressed and then calculating the speed of each key travel (down and up), the resting time at the bottom of the key travel, and the time between each key strike. Without going into detail, this makes it possible to measure the force of a key strike, the duration of each key strike, and the time taken between key strikes. The computer col-lects all the data, sorts them, and formats them into a table easily under-stood by the researcher. In this way, it becomes possible to calculate all specified parameters of a performance, e.g., the actual note played, its dynamic, and its articulation.

Another project is our motion study of a child's performance. We intend to do analyses of performance biomechanics by recording arm, finger, and wrist motions on film. There are a number of ways this can be done. At the Cen-ter, researcher Victoria MacArthur has chosen to attach reflective dots to selected locations on the performer's arms, hands and fingers. She then videotapes the performance, obtaining precise angles, displacements, and velocities of the movement of these extremities. For every frame of the videotape, she enters into the computer the reflective dots as X-Y coor-dinates, thereby generating a huge amount of data (the standard video camera records 30 frames per second). By this technique, Dr. MacArthur has collected and stored data that provides us with a very accurate biomechanical picture of the child's performance. These data can be manipulated mathematically or played back as motion on a computer screen. The computer can also superimpose several pictures so that comparisons of various children's performances, or comparisons of different times in one child's performance, are possible. Eventually we would like to synchronize biological measurements with motion analyses.

As you can imagine, the research potential for the three computer configurations just described seems quite large, including implications for music education, music medicine, and music therapy. It is also possible that these technologies, imaginatively configured, may lead to the development of a complete measurement system of musical performance. Clearly, it is our hope to be able to study music performance comprehensively. We see computers as enormously effective tools for the exploration of interactions between humans and their musical instruments. Our system is presently 50% complete; and even when completed, we expect to encounter unanticipated problems and limitations, many of which we hope will be solvable. On the other hand, there's always the possibility that these measurements, no matter how precise, may not tell us much about music performance. We must be ready for that possibility.

References

Case, R. *Intellectual development: Birth to adulthood*, Orlando: Academic Press, 1985.

Grieshaber, K. "Children's rhythmic tapping: A critical review of the research," *Bulletin for the Council for Research in Music Education*, 90:73-81, 1987.

Hedden, S. "Recent research pertaining to psychomotor skills in music," *Bulletin for The Council for Research in Music Education*, 90:25-29, 1987.

Karma, K. "Selecting students to music instruction," *Bulletin for the Council for Research in Music Education*, 75:23-32, 1983.

Madsen, C. "Research in music: Science or art?" *Design for Arts in Education* 88(5):10-14, 1987.

Nelson, D. "An interpretation of the Piagetian model in light of the theories of Case," *Bulletin for the Council for Research in Music Education*, 92:23-34, 1987a.

Nelson, D. "Children's age related intellectual strategies for dealing with musical and spatial analogical tasks," Unpublished paper, 17 pp, 1987b.

Piaget, J. *The origins of intelligence in children,* New York: International Universities Press, 1952.

Trice, P., Taylor, J., & Pembrook, R. "The effect of performance complexity and timed exposures to music notation on looking ahead while sight-reading melodies at the piano," Unpublished paper, 23 pp, 1987.

Jack A. Taylor

Section IV

Teaching the Child with Special Educational Needs

The Paradox of the Gifted/Impaired Child

Martha B. Denckla
National Institutes of Health[1]
Bethesda

I would like to give you a brief review of the brain map with respect to music, especially as it relates to other forms of non-verbal perception. Then, and I will be very theoretical, I want to give you a definition of dyslexia. We will see that dyslexia is thought to be understandable based on a difference in the way the dyslexic's brain is put together, and this will permit us to consider specifically how this difference would affect the musical development of a child. Later I will talk a little bit about autism.

I can't imagine that anyone in this audience hasn't heard that the left side of the brain is more committed than the right side to what is known as analytical processing. You may not be aware, however, that both visual and auditory functions are subserved by *both* sides of the brain — it is complete nonsense to say that the left side of the brain is auditory and the right is visual. Visuo- and auro-spatial kinds of abilities are strongly represented on the right side of the brain — *holistic, Gestalt, configurational, simultaneous* — all of those words apply more to the processing capabilities of the right posterior area.

I also want to mention the cerebellum to you, because I will show you that this is the part of the brain where something is wrong in a good number of autistic people. The startling thing is that the brain in autistic people is perfect above the cerebellum, in the hemispheres, unlike the situation in dyslexic people, whose hemispheres show a tissue imbalance.

You've already heard that there is really no consensus on the cerebral organization of musical abilities. But this must certainly stem from our failure to understand the complexity, as well as the individual and cultural variations, of the organization of musical abilities. The right side of the brain is *not* bigger than the left in musically gifted people; if anything, there is an *imbalance* of tissue, rather than a simple left-right size discrepancy.

---

1   Dr. Denckla is currently at the Kennedy Institute, Baltimore, Maryland.

Exceptional musical memory is unusually prevalent in symphonic musicians, but is also found in those autistics who are musical *idiots savants*. One can have a very narrowly channeled neurologic endowment permitting a sort of excellence in a particular skill, and for some autistic children this endowment is in music. Unfortunately, prodigious or exceptional musical memory, or even perfect pitch as you all know, hardly makes one a gifted musician.

I think we must concede that the truly gifted musician depends on a broader, and indeed, a superior *bilateral* endowment. As a matter of fact, I would submit that music and mathematics are very similar in that both are *par excellence* — when performed well — duets between the two sides of the brain. Speaking is far more lateralized than anything in musical expression is, and nevertheless it remains dependent on contributions from both sides of the brain.

Having said this, I want to emphasize the existence of differential contributions from the two sides. The complexity of the arrangement is apparent from a review of the literature on dichotic listening. As you heard earlier this week, this research involves presenting two sets of stimuli simultaneously to the left and right ear, producing what we call an *ear effect*. To explain, earphones are provided to the listener, and then dissimilar sound stimuli are delivered independently to each ear. These can be words, they can be environmental noises, they can be pitch sequences, pitch and rhythm variables, or chords. The object is to have people describe what they've heard when stimuli reaching the right and the left ears compete with each other. Their responses tell you if they are better at detecting the stimuli going to the right or to the left ear. By the way, there do seem to be real differences between trained and untrained listeners: in general, the more musically trained person, the one who has usually acquired a symbolic notation system, will tend to shift to a right ear — hence *left brain* — effect on musical tasks. Musically naive subjects, when presented with melodies, that is, temporal patterns which can be described by the up and down pitch contour, will tend to have a *left* ear — hence, right brain — effect.

Another approach described in recent literature involves a *dihaptic* task, in which people palpate things in both hands. The test was developed by Sandra Whittleson, who argued that dyslexic children have what amounts to two right hemispheres and no left hemisphere, because they seemed to be so much better with the right hand when asked to palpate stimuli in order to choose between them. Success in this test seemed to be developmentally correlated with being a male, musically trained person. That is, if you were male *and* trained as a musician, you shifted your hand effect from left to right at puberty. But musically untrained males and females — pre-and post-pubertal — did not show this shift. So there are differences even among what we call normal people.

This reminds me that yesterday, when I was leaving a convention on autism, a friend of mine said, "Remember, everyone has at least two diagnoses: one, you're human, and two, you are either male or female." We were discussing what is meant by a "diagnosis" as opposed to simply a description of somebody. In any case, while the *ear effect* literature is intriguing, it doesn't really help us much as we look at this musical map.

Next I want to give you a general picture of the role of the right hemisphere, which, when we communicate verbally, is actually complementary in the synthesis of linguistic, cognitive and affective behaviors. One of the things I hope to sell you is the parallel between music, in which there is a duet between the right and left sides of the brain, and language, involving a similar interhemispheric duet that must be going on for me to speak with you. If I were to speak to you as some of my autistic patients do, in a completely flat and expressionless manner, you would all leave very rapidly, because if I had no prosody — prosody being the melody of speech — you would just be bored stiff. In fact, if you think about it, the reason you like some speakers and you *don't* like others is just as much because of prosody as it is because of what they're saying to you. People sometimes say wonderful informational things in an utterly boring way.

So, in brief, the right side of the brain has neocortical areas for the perception and decoding of affective behaviors, while comparable areas on the left are for linguistic and serial, *analytic* kinds of behaviors. Even in speech, prosody and pragmatics are more a property of the right side of the brain. Phonology and syntax, or the sequence — the specific speech sounds and the seriation of them — is more in the domain of the left hemisphere. Then of course, there are the limbic areas, modulating experiential aspects of emotional and mental phenomena. I will come back to this issue even more when we talk about the autistic people.

Among the many structures beneath the cortex are some that function as energizers. I've already mentioned the cerebellum; there are also limbic areas that put in the *ergs*, stimulating all the activities of the cerebral cortex, and there are interhemispheric influences carried via callosal connections.

We also have on the right side neocortical *motor* areas, controlling affective language and behavior and of, course, limb movements on the other side of the body. Whenever I try to explain the two motor systems in the brain and why they depend on programming from all these different sources, I always ask people to think of a string instrument player and the distribution of motor behaviors between the left and the right hand. The different performances of the two hands fit quite well with the kind of information drive of the motor system coming from the two sides.

Of course, you only have one mouth, so you have only one outflow, but the control of the affective components of language comes out of the right hemisphere. Of course your left hand is still getting certain kinds of affective information, even when the fingers are ostensibly moving in a very sequential manner; in other words, even the left hand of the string player is getting information from both sides of the brain. What I want to get across is that there is a bilateral supply of information for the mouth, which is a midline structure, and also for the limbs on either side of the body, all of which is provided simultaneously. The bow arm is doing things that are programmed both by the right and the left hemisphere, and so are the fingers on the fingering board of this string instrument.

To sum up this point, the right hemisphere has a dominant role in encoding and decoding nonlinguistic and affective components of communication, and I would submit to you that that has a great deal to do with music — nonlinguistic and affective.

The right hemisphere imparts a more negative emotional valence to experience. That's an interesting thing, too. There's a greater tendency to pick up on what is negative in the environment if you have an imbalance towards the right hemisphere. The right hemisphere contains mechanisms for attending to both sides of space, it has an orienting ability, and is better at visuo-spatial skills. I would add here that it's also better for auro-spatial skills. The right hemisphere is better at the part of music that is *configurational, simultaneous, holistic and Gestalt*. (Neurology is much more preoccupied with these visuo-spatial things because they're a traditional part of the testing repertory.)

So, the right hemisphere has very essential contributions to make. I would say, in terms of the necessary and sufficient relationships, that I don't think a person can be a good musician without a normally *functioning* right hemisphere.

At this point we're in a position to consider what happens to musicians when they have impairments. I'm sure all of you have read medical case histories of famous musicians — I remember hearing a few years ago a paper presented to the American Academy of Neurology describing Ravel after his stroke. The example they provided representing his post-stroke music was *Bolero*, which has always struck me as very boring. As a neurologist, however, I suspect he may have done something quite interesting here: namely, substitute timbral and instrumental novelty for the inventiveness in melodic or harmonic structure that he could no longer manage because of the stroke. The presenter of the paper was suggesting that Ravel's *Bolero* is an example of a superbly trained musician forced to revert to the utilization of a preponderantly right hemisphere endowment. So perhaps we should add to our list of right hemisphere musical endowments the ability to appreciate different timbres of the instruments.

Recently, I brought a number of children to a very high-tech friend of mine in Boston, Dr. Frank Duffy, to study electrical brain activity with an ordinary EEG. After doing the usual recording, he prepared a map showing the areas of maximal difference between two groups of children. The study suggests that dyslexic and nondyslexic boys differ physiologically in different areas of the brain under different testing conditions.

Physiologic studies on dyslexics have produced some surprises. For example, we may see in just a simple EEG of a boy listening to music and listening to speech that the alpha wave activity (which is correlated with the relaxation response) is greatly *reduced* when he is listening to music. When this happens, we would be inclined to say that music has activated this brain much more than speech.

In contrast, a study of one dyslexic child showed very little difference in the two conditions (listening to music and listening to speech). In this dyslexic child, who did not appear any different from his age-matched control on the standard EEG recording, what was striking — to us at any rate — was a rather *invariant* pattern in the location of areas of maximal difference.

This is the puzzle with dyslexic children: as you get into more refined tests, you find peculiar failures of their brains to activate in a way comparable to their age-matched controls. For example, you can do a regional blood flow study, using inhaled Xenon to track maximal blood flow. This has been done during a test called Line Orientation, a difficult visuo-spatial task. Here, the main difference between dyslexics and controls (and these are twenty-one to thirty-year-olds, not children) was that in the controls there was a greater degree of *frontal* activation. In the dyslexics, although there was frontal activation, it wasn't as much as in the controls. There was little difference between the two groups in the right hemisphere findings.

By the way, they *performed* equally well, as did all the dyslexics who were doing the tasks during the EEG. For example, even though one child looks very different inside his brain, he was not discernibly doing any differently except on one task that required learning words to go with pictures. So performance differences may or may not occur when, inside the brain, something's different in the brain reactivity to the stimuli. That's part of the puzzle of dyslexia.

Let me define dyslexia for you. First of all, dyslexia means trouble with words — it does *not* mean trouble with reading. The trouble with reading is the main reason why the people come to your attention. But dyslexia means *trouble with words* and it means, in general, that although you speak and you've learned your language in a naturalistic setting, you really do have certain difficulties with language. These manifest themselves as difficulties with pronunciation sometimes, with spelling frequently, with word order in sentences, and with learning the irregularities of the person's native language. For example, there is my son (the middle one who is quite a gifted musician — that is, if you like rock music, he's gifted). Until he was over ten he used to say, "I *tooked* the last piece of chicken," and "I *breaked* the toy." He sounded like a time-traveler from Elizabethan days. He lived in a house in which people said I *break*, I *broke*, I *take*, I *took*. He could not pick up naturalistically the accidentals, as we would say in music, of the irregular past tenses. That is the kind of subtlety not often picked up by people who are not professionally trained, but it's the kind of problem that we see in dyslexic children.

There is a growing body of evidence confirming that the chief function affected in dyslexia has to do with subdomains of language, not *all* of language. Dyslexics certainly can speak well enough to get along in life. In fact, living in Bethesda, I often see diplomats' kids who are dyslexic; they learn English in the street, not in the school. They learn other languages, too. They make the same kinds of mistakes in the other languages, but they can be understood. The semantics, the meaning of language, a useful vocabulary, a reasonable degree of articulation so folks know what you are saying — these major aspects of language are available to dyslexics, but they often miss the real refinements and subtleties of language.

Martha B. Denckla

There is almost no evidence for any visual perceptual problem in dyslexia and I want to emphasize that because Frank Wilson sent me an article from a music teacher's magazine in which the author was describing the perceptual problems in learning disabilities. There are *other* learning disabilities, not dyslexia, in which one finds perceptual problems, but dyslexic children do not have what any respectable psychologist or neurologist would call perceptual problems. They have problems with certain kinds of discreet memories for phonology and sequence "incidentals of language" and they have trouble when they get into reading, because although they can make speech sound discriminations, they are very unstable in memory — the connections just don't seem to stick.

What I now want to tell you about are the changes described in the brains of young dyslexics who have died in accidents. Compared to normals, there is an anatomical difference, and I want to emphasize the word *difference*, because I don't like the model of disease or damage for dyslexia. The brains of dyslexic persons, when examined after an untimely demise, show a characteristic structural feature in the relationship of the right to the left, mostly in the direction of symmetry. They basically have big, fat, symmetrical brains.

There is no lesser amount of brain tissue in any dyslexic brain thus far examined. They do not have a shrunken or small left planum temporale. Nor do they have an inordinately large right hemisphere. They have large everything. They have generally big brains with a preservation of what may be an earlier embryonic stage of symmetry between the two sides.

It is thought also that some of the migration defects that are seen, in which some of the nerve cells don't get to the right places, may be related to an underlying *failure of cell death*. This is a very bizarre concept, but I have to assure you that one of the ways that the brain is sculpted during development is by pruning. It's almost like mini-Darwinian evolution. During fetal development the brain overproduces neurons, and overproduces connections, which we call synapses. Then a series of processes which we are only dimly beginning to understand leads to the pruning. Interestingly, experience may be one of those processes.

It has been proposed that even intrauterine reception of vibrations and sounds are among the many influences that may have to do with the pruning of the nervous system. Certainly one thing that has to do with it is hormone levels, and one reason why there seem to be four times as many male as female dyslexics is that testosterone, the male hormone which is present in male fetuses, is known to increase the survival of nerve cells. So the present hypothesis about dyslexia (and this may change by next year) is that the right side of the brain keeps too many cells. The right side of the brain then has an advantage in the competitive race, not only for survival of its own side, but for influence over target cells on the other side. This process confers a lion's share of connectivity to the cells from the right side of the brain.

Even so, the left side does not end up shrunken. It develops later than the right, but it still develops. However, its developmental pattern is now influenced by the increased survival of cells on the right side, with the result that you seem to get a rather large, hypercellular brain. There are too many nerve cells, and a left-right equality, and somehow having equality leads to a difference in the way in which function develops. We still don't quite understand that part of it, but these people do *not* have any holes in the head. They don't have any damage. They don't have any missing pieces. They have some very subtle resculpturing of the brain, period.

In living persons we have been able to see this with computerized tomography (which is almost obsolete now) and we have also seen with magnetic resonance imaging that these are more symmetrical brains. The next step with magnetic resonance imaging will be to try to get a look at the planum temporale, which we think is particularly involved in language. With luck we will get the angles, the photographic cuts, which will allow us to see what the balance or imbalance is between these two sides in living dyslexic persons

We know from a behavioral point of view that dyslexic children are late bloomers. We don't know exactly why this is so, but they seem to go through all of their first ten years of life with a sort of locked-in syndrome. This just means that the strengths that are mainly subsumed under the left hemisphere repertory are not coming out. Somehow, the balance between the two sides of the brain is not established until the events of puberty, when things start happening in both the corpus callosum and the frontal lobes. Unfortunately, there isn't time to discuss the frontal lobes, which provide a kind of the piloting function for the whole brain. Even when the dyslexic is given a difficult task, and is able to do it, he doesn't seem to be juicing up the piloting centers in the front of the brain as much as the controls do — that's one of the things that's puzzling to us. But by the second decade of life they are

Martha B. Denckla

able to do a lot of things with left hemisphere output that they were not able to do during the first decade.

Many of these kids, therefore, are going to have terrible trouble with the usual curriculum of music; introduction of a symbolic notation, introduction of seriation, introduction of labels for things and specific names for things, all create real difficulties for them in the first decade of life. Dr. Frank Wood at Bowman Gray is doing a study of about 600 dyslexic men who were seen in a famous Orton dyslexia therapy program when they were children. He tells me an extraordinary number of them are what he calls untutored, naturalistic musicians — you know, mountain fiddlers or jazz piano players who can't read a note of music. He commented that it was better to be from a rural setting if you were dyslexic because then people would leave you alone and allow you to be a naturalistic musician. He uses that terminology much as I use the phrase naturalistic learner of language to describe the dyslexic's spoken language capabilities.

Once again, what I'm trying to say to you about the dyslexic is he's got a *different* brain, not necessarily an abnormal brain. As a matter of fact, Dr. Norman Geschwind, with whom I trained, had speculated that the mechanisms for sculpturing different brains are actually a critical part of our legacy as human beings. Being as social as we are, and as interdependent, teleologically speaking we need to produce a very diverse population of human beings. We have all sorts of situations to adapt to and so we need different kinds of brains in the population. It wouldn't be good for our own survival to have everybody come out at birth with exactly the same kind of brain. So he speculated that there is a "program for randomness" or for diversity that operates in human brain development to ensure that there will always be some among us able to confront the stresses we may as a group encounter. That's a very appealing idea.

For me, this concept fits with the fact that by and large dyslexic boys (they are mostly boys, that's why I emphasize it), as they reach that eleventh year inflection point, will suddenly blossom. They will suddenly come out with a whole range of skills.

Even as young children, one of the things about them that is very striking is high emotional sensitivity, high musical sensitivity and high sensitivity to environmental noise. This sensitivity causes them to be called distractible, or in some cases misdiagnosed as having attention problems, when actually they are going to be the first to warn you if the boiler in the elementary school is about to blow up. They are gifted and their gifts often get them into trouble. For my money, though, if the boiler is about to explode, we should be very grateful if there is someone with us who will tell us that something funny is going on — a noise in the basement — and we should pay attention.

Since they are extraordinarily sensitive to emotional stimuli, a teacher who doesn't like them can destroy the entire learning operation. They are not able to tune out the "vibes" others are giving them; they are very tuned in. They come across as very manly and very well put together, but they are, in a sense, hypersensitive little boys and you don't often suspect this.

You may remember that I said the right hemisphere is very sensitive to negatives. This is probably a survival mechanism, because the right hemisphere is responsible for orientation. However, this tendency may create a propensity for depression; these are realists, these little boys, and reality *is* kind of depressing. It is possible that this has some relevance to their school failure, and it would have relevance to how you deal with them.

By the way, there is a very charming experiment that's been done on right and left hemisphere orientation with newborns, using just a single EEG electrode on both sides. They put a drop of sugar water on the baby's tongue and they get a sort of "ah, okay, that's *nice*" little blip over both sides of the brain. But when they use quinine, they get an enormous right hemisphere spike, showing that right from birth, the right side of the brain is telling you the "no-no's" and the "uh-oh's" and telling you to back off from things that are going to threaten you. So this enormous emotional sensitivity, especially to the negative, is one of their blessings and curses. It is not entirely a blessing to be born with a propensity to be a realist.

Musical development is often completely neglected or missed in any formal instructional setting with these children, and the stories they tell you about having suddenly discovered, quite by accident, that they *could* do something musically, fiddling around with somebody else's synthesizer, fooling around with their older brother's guitar, are really poignant, because so often they have been failures and dropouts in both school and individualized music settings.

And this brings me to an important practical issue: if these kids have a natural propensity for music, what is it that prevents them from achieving more? Why are they usually better off staying away from tutors and institutions?

Let me get at this paradox telling you about myself, because I am a mirror image dyslexic. I have exactly the opposite trouble of what most dyslexics have, although it came out in a similar way. I have trouble reading music, which profoundly influenced me not to become a musician. I just would freeze if anyone gave me a new piece of music at an audition. My mother was a very good amateur pianist who in her moments of theatricality would storm around the house saying, "If I hadn't married your father, then I would have been a pianist." She was the kind of person musicians, especially singers, would want to have in their confidence. They could say to her, "Take it up a third, Becky" and she could do it like breathing. She also spoke eight languages. She was super at all aspects of music.

When I was about three everybody thought I had a very good "ear," but also a good connection from ear to vocal chords, because I could sing anything. Take me to a broadway show, and I would come home and sing the entire score. So, of course, if you're talented, you are supposed to start your music. My mother sat me down at the piano and started to teach me. I couldn't make any sense out of reading the notes. The spatial arrangement of those lines and spaces and the piano was opaque to me.

Incidentally, I have a pervasive difficulty with map reading. I get lost in a paper bag. As I stand here I am terrified that I may not be able to start back to the hotel without getting lost. I also got my lowest grades in math. If I got a B it was a *blood, sweat and tears* B. When I was freshman in college I took beginning German and first year calculus. I spent 15 minutes a day on beginning German and I got an A. I spent 2 hours a day on calculus to get the B. The way you overcome a learning disability is that you kill yourself.

So with reading music, the way I did learn so much is that I named the notes. I have in my head a little library of what the interval corresponding to the name "A to C" or "C# to F" sounds like. That's all in my head as a little dictionary. But it takes a long time to read that way and it is very inefficient. My mother accused me of deliberately trying to withhold from the her the pleasure of my being a good musician. It became an emotional issue between the mother and the child. My mother said, "You're obviously so musical." I was musical, yes, but I was missing a piece.

I had a disability in the mapping function part of reading musical notation. I had no trouble with the names. I never had trouble taking theory, because theory was names of things and theoretical construct. This strength haunted me. I switched from piano to cello, thinking that maybe if I didn't have to deal with chords it would be better. I was still bad at sight reading. I switched from cello to singing. That was better, but I never have been able to overcome what I think was by then an emotional block. If you have a problem and people not only don't recognize it but accuse you of either stupidity or moral turpitude, and nobody recognizes that you can be musical even with a piece missing, then it becomes a bona fide psychiatric problem.

For dyslexics, the problem is sort of the opposite of mine. The map is great for them. They would prefer an invariant map, dealing only with up and down, so that they wouldn't be forced to remember how things are organized left to right, but they have a very good sense of mapping.

The dyslexic who's having trouble with music lessons tells me everything would be fine if only the teacher would stop telling him or asking what the thing is called. "They should stop asking me 'Is it an A?; is it a B?'" Just give this kid the instrument, give him the map (the music) and keep pointing to how they correspond to each other. If you want to put a dot somewhere on the piano at a reference point and the same thing on the map, fine, but the big thing to avoid with a dyslexic is talking. They do not have any difficulty recognizing the symbolism with which music maps onto their instrument or their voice. That is not their problem. But you impede them by talking to them about it; even solfege — anything where you have an assigned nomenclature.

Let me review for you. Every piece of research that has been done on dyslexia shows that these people have their deficits on tasks of *naming*, tasks where they have to deal analytically with speech sounds, where they have to segment words into syllables, make rhymes for speech sounds. If you ask them to give a family of rhymes for something, they just stare at you. They have no idea how to get those speech sounds out of their brain without a meaning attached to them, and a lot of the words we use in music will not be easy for them to attach any meaning to for years and years.

If you're trying to teach them music it's much better for you to pretend they don't speak your language. Make believe they're from another country and you don't know what the notes are called in their language. You would both be able to use the musical map, by just pointing to the notes and pointing to places on the instrument. That is the best fundamental strategy.

I think you will definitely find that they also have trouble with fractions in school, and this problem will give them trouble in the formal representation of rhythm. We do deal with fractions rather early in music, even earlier than

Martha B. Denckla

in school curriculum, and fractions happen to be very difficult for dyslexic children because they present a very complicated syntax to work with. All those little lines and symbols tell you the invariant order of an operation, which is the essence of syntax/grammar.

So you would be much better off going directly to the auditory experience: what the different note qualities are and the actual time durations, beating it out and having them beat it out. You'll never get anywhere with this kind of child dealing with music as if it were school mathematics. As you know, music is full of spatial relationships — they are *auditory* and *visual* spatial. These kids are good with both kinds, but when you try to funnel concepts to them through any kind of symbolic system, you are going to run into trouble.

In the short time remaining, I would like to tell you briefly about the most recent work on autism. Autism is characterized by a profound failure to develop social relationships, a profound failure to develop normal communication. Although they may speak, autistic children lack prosody and they lack what we call pragmatics, which means what to say to whom, when and where. They have a restricted, nonexploratory, rather robotic repertory of interests. The modern concept of autism is that the problem is either in the limbic system or, as a magnetic resonance image demonstrates, in the cerebellum. What we are finding in many, many autistic persons is a lack of certain parts of the cerebellum, which we think helps explain the failed activation of the brain. The MRI shows you in a living person the missing cerebellar vermis: lobules six and seven, specifically, seem to be abnormal in autism.

The main thing to understand about autism is that it is an underactivation disorder. The cerebral cortex in all autopsies, all magnetic resonance images and all the other usual measurements is normal. The thinking brain, the brain that has all these fancy perceptual motor capabilities, is normal. The problem is that something is wrong in the basement. It's as though somebody went downstairs right now and took away all the power coming into this building complex. No matter how beautiful the fixtures and every thing else in this amphitheater is, we would be in the dark.

We don't quite know why autism is so disabling in the social domain except that the social domain may be a lot more complex than we have thought heretofore. That is, forming relationships with others may not be as "instinctive" as we all assume it to be, or that it just comes along without any energizing. Apparently the energizing source is the cerebellum and/or limbic system, both of which are abnormal in autism.

The Paradox of the Gifted/Impaired Child   239

What's significant musically is that many autistic children of the higher functioning type learn exactly the opposite of what I said about dyslexics. They learn to play instruments mechanically. They play with all the symbolic notation and the correct counting and the correct wiggling of their fingers, but as one teacher put it to me recently, "Why does she never put any emotion into it?" I said, "She doesn't *have* emotion to put into it". That's the terrible thing — that they have a very limited reservoir of what you would call emotion or expressivity. I think that we need to give them this opportunity, though, because often it's something that they can do "well," and in contrast to the dyslexic children, who tend not to be discovered until the second decade, these kids, during their elementary school years, may do music well and it may be the only thing for which they get any kind of positive reinforcement.

I have a taped musical example of one autistic man, and I would like to play one little selection. This is a twenty-six-year-old man who does virtually nothing else. [Musical example] Notice the little pauses between each repetition. Now, I'm just curious, what age would you think that person was had I played it without telling you the background? Eight or nine years; anyhow, long before formal operations.

This man, though, is very interesting because he is so hypoactive that he's like a Parkinsonian. He will come home from the sheltered workshop, sit in the living room, it will become dusk, and he will not turn on the lights. He will just sit there, sit there, sit there. His mother will come home and she will turn on the light over the piano, and *then* he will get up out of his chair and be drawn to the piano and will sit and play for hours. But he will never himself stand up, turn on the lights, or walk towards the piano. That gives you the flavor of what we're finding as autistic children grow up. They get locked into a hypoactive state. But for those who can perform the mechanical operations, playing becomes the one thing they can do and, to the extent that we are able to tell, can enjoy.

Childhood Sequential Development of Rhythm, Melody and Pitch

Dale B. Taylor
Director of Music Therapy Studies
University of Wisconsin-Eau Claire

It is the quality of one's ability to process sensory information and to produce independently a unique and appropriate response that distinguishes human intelligence. Investigators have sought to describe the development of cognitive skills associated with specific behaviors and to correlate them with developmental stages as described by Piaget and others. It is important to note, however, as we investigate sequential development of musical skill and its relationship to Piagetian developmental stages, that Piaget sought to describe acquisition of cognitive structures in a predictable sequence due to biological maturation and not to describe the content of consciousness or sequential learning ability for any specific areas of knowledge. Therefore, any relationships described between musical skills and developmental stages represent the approximate age ranges at which the child acquires the prerequisite cognitive structures and systems of symbolic organization necessary for performing those skills. It still remains that the material to which those structures and systems will be applied must come from experience.

The purpose of the paper is to investigate the relationship between development of several musical skills and the acquisition of selected cognitive abilities during each of the four main developmental stages described by Piaget. These findings are then used along with recent information on human brain function to describe a model in which a controlled increase in musical complexity is used to enhance cognitive development in the education of handicapped children.

Stage Theory and Music Skill Development

Piaget's theory of developmental stages asserts that "the mind of the child is qualitatively different at various stages throughout its development,"[35] and that cognitive development occurs in an invariant sequence. The very essence of intelligence is, in Piaget's view, the development of cognitive structures through maturation and growth as well as through physical and social experience. The following studies describe attempts to correlate the development of specific musical skills with age and cognitive structures indicative of the four main Piagetian stages: sensorimotor (0-2 years), preoperations (2-7 years), concrete operations (7-11 years), and formal operations (11+ years).

Much of the research on musical development has been focused on attempts to ascertain how the child's transition from preoperational logic to the stage of concrete operations is manifested in musical capabilities. Closer examination of these two stages reveals that at the preoperational level, a child does not exhibit role-taking capability, shows centration tendencies, and seeks cause-and-effect relationships. Because children typically do not perform reversible mental operations on an altered stimulus, they lack the capability for mental conservation under transformations of the stimulus. Their logic system is governed by intuitive reasoning. Upon acquisition of operational logic, thought becomes independent of perception, decentering appears in the child's perception of unified wholes, play becomes separate from reality, and reversibility appears, providing the basis for conservation of volume, length, and time. Conservation is therefore the mental capacity most studied by experimenters in developmental musicology.[42]

Sensorimotor Stage

Farnsworth[10] reports that a child is capable of responding to sudden loud noises 30 days prior to birth. When sensorimotor development becomes directly observable at birth, children show "considerable sensitivity" to tone. By the eighth day, they will usually stop feeding at the sound of a gong. In studies by Chang and Trehub,[6] and by Melson and McCall,[23] 5-month-old babies showed dishabituation of heart rate in the form of deceleration in response to temporal position changes of all notes of a melodic pattern. Transposition of the intact melody up or down a minor third did not produce dishabituation. Kinney and Kagan[20] tested 7-month-olds and found heart rate dishabituation in response to alterations in both melodic contour and rhythmic pattern. Further indication of receptive musical capacity in infants was reported by Simons,[37] who found that reactions to rhythm are stronger than reactions to melody between the ages of 9 and 31 months.

While there are very little data showing expressive musical behavior during the sensorimotor stage, at least one study[19] has demonstrated that babies under 6 months of age can be taught to match pitch by singing back the pitch sung to them. In the second year, children begin to recognize specific melodies as having meaning in the environment and to repeat certain songs and phrases with replicable contour and coherent rhythm, but with varying pitch and interval relationships.[9]

Preoperational Stage

The stage of preoperations (age two to seven years) is characterized by a wide variety of both receptive and expressive musical behaviors. Suzuki, the well-known Japanese violin teacher, used decreased size violins to teach children as young as two and a half years old to match both pitch and rhythm with practice.[10] Gardner, et al[13] found that one and three-year-olds could reproduce vocally the contour of isolated phrases, and four-year-olds kept stable scale patterns within each phrase. The descending minor third appears during the fourth year in the musical vocalizations of children of all cultures.[29] Five-year-old children have been found to be able to maintain tonality throughout a song and reproduce easily recognizable versions of a model,[13] distinguish near from far keys unless many notes overlap,[1] and show measurable ability in rhythmic conservation, although with some difficulty.[42] Such findings have prompted Dowling[9] to conclude that five years of age may be used as an approximate guideline for the appearance of stable tonal structure.

Rider[31] found that the approximate normal age for acquisition of conservation of rhythm is 6.1 years, and that this appears first in an invariant sequence of acquisition of conservation of area (non-musical) 7.6 years, volume (non-musical) 8.1 years, and tempo at 8.3 years. The five and six-year-old age group is characterized by direct intuition of duration, seriation, and conservation of velocity.[18] Identification of alterations in pitch becomes predictable with six and seven-year-olds.[9] Seven-years-olds noticed sudden key changes in the middle of familiar tunes, while eight-year-olds could distinguish changes from major to minor.[1]

Concrete Operations

The transition from preoperations to the stage of concrete operations (age seven to eleven years) is reflected by improvement in ability to imitate tonal and rhythmic patterns, [25,26] to perceive durational changes,[42] and to exhibit conservation skills on rhythmic patterns under deformation of melody[42] and on rhythmic inversion and pitch transposition of melody tasks.[15] Conservation of auditory number and tempo have also been demonstrated.[32]

Full acquisition of concrete operations has been found to provide the cognitive structures needed for conservation of melody and rhythm. It appears that the number of years of private music lessons has very little effect on the refinement of these skills.[39] Conservation of rhythm appears at seven to eight years of age due to the ability to differentiate between succession in space and succession in time.[18] Successful meter conservation is exhibited and is positively related to success on Piagetian tasks involving conservation of other physical properties, is resistant to training at the preoperational level,[36] exhibits a plateau in improvement at about age nine, and precedes conservation of rhythm, in the developmental sequence.[35] One study of five, nine and thirteen-year-olds found that improvement in melodic conservation preceded improved conservation of meter.[27]

Tonal memory, which has been found to improve with age during the developmental period, is essential to the perception, cognition, and conservation of melodic phrases. Research has that found that the greatest improvement in tonal memory occurs between ages eight and nine. The increase in skill continues at a declining rate of improvement until a leveling off occurs at about age fourteen.[43] Melodic perception is also dependent upon pitch discrimination. It has been suggested that the period from six to nine years of age is critical for development of perceptual pitch discrimination.[43]

In tests of conservation of velocity, immediate seriation, and double seriation, children of ages seven through nine years showed their earliest success.[18]

Formal Operations

Very few studies have been completed which test cognitive structures appearing in the stage of formal operations in Piaget's stage theory. One such report tested eight, ten, and twelve-year olds on their ability to order resonator bells according to a given melodic contour and to explain and reproduce permutations of the original melody. Only the twelve-year-old subjects accepted as valid and reproduced all inversions, retrograde and retrograde inversions. The researcher concluded that the older children were able to use the formal operation identified by Piaget as "reciprocity."[22]

The above review seems to indicate that music conservation abilities do appear to improve with age as Piagetian stage theory would predict. In addition, certain consistencies in the order of skill acquisition have been identified. For example, conservation of tonal patterns seems to appear before rhythmic pattern conservation,[15] and rhythmic perception develops before tonal discrimination.[29] Changes in instrumentation, harmony and tempo are recognized earlier than those of rhythm, mode, and contour.[15]

Musical Enhancement of Cognitive Development

In the remainder of this paper, a model will be set forth to provide a basis for using musical activities to maximize use of cognitive structures in the education of children with special needs. The effectiveness of the model in accomplishing this goal will depend in part upon the teacher or therapist's understanding of the effects of training on sequential development of music skills, and the use of appropriate assessment tools to determine levels of cognitive functioning in children. An understanding of theories concerning ways in which the brain processes musical information may also be helpful in deciding the most effective musical learning tasks for children whose development reflects various levels of maturation.

The teaching-learning model itself begins with musical tasks in which the handicapped pupil can achieve immediate success and enjoyment. Gradually, the complexity of rhythmic, melodic, harmonic, dynamic and other musical elements of those same tasks can be increased to both challenge and motivate the child to use more and more of his or her developing potential. New cognitive schemes and levels of aesthetic sensitivity will be identified and utilized within the framework of musical participation as the child becomes capable of functioning at each succeeding developmental stage.

Progressing through the sequence of stages of cognitive development is afforded by changes in the brain due to maturation and experience. Uniquely human behavior, such as complex speech and aesthetic expression, are also possible because of the immense complex of neuronal pathways in the human brain. Even children with emotional, physical, perceptual and other developmental disabilities most often have normal brain capacity in the area of musical behavior. In efforts to relate musical behavior to biological changes in the developing human brain, some attempts have been made to propose a simplistic neurophysiological explanation for the superior musical ability exhibited by some individuals. One such attempt proposed that a relatively large planum temporale in the right hemisphere could be an indicator of inborn ability in music.[34] In the absence of statistical confirmation of this hypothesis, most researchers have sought other correlates between music and human brain function.

In attempting to determine the value of music to the brain during learning experiences, direct observation of the effects of music on the brains of children has been made through study of alpha rhythm production in brain waves during music.[12] Alpha waves are interpreted as signifying relaxation or attention directed inward. Results showed significantly higher alpha production during silence than during music. This could be interpreted to mean that the children became more alert and attentive to external stimuli during music, a condition which is essential to effective application of the music-cognitive development model with handicapped children. In another study, college students scored significantly higher on a test of focused attention after listening to five minutes of "sedative" music than after listening to "stimulative" music. Percent of time spent producing alpha brain waves showed a statistically significant (.01) positive correlation (r=.4301) with test scores.[4]

Just as the study of aphasia resulted in identification of language centers in the brain, clinical examinations of patients suffering from amusia have assisted in determining cerebral locations for musical functions and their connections.[41] Because nonverbal auditory task performance has been found to be impaired in patients with lesions in the right hemisphere, it has been suggested that the mechanisms for musical perception are located in the temporal lobe of the right hemisphere.[33] Other results have shown that analytical processing in musical perception is handled primarily by the left hemisphere,[2] the same side in which speech centers are located. Because patients with many forms of aphasia do not lose singing and other musical abilities, it has been suggested that specific musical activities could be used to assist in the rehabilitation of persons whose speech centers have been damaged.[38] A technique known as Melodic Intonation Therapy has been shown to effect significant gains in the verbal behavior of children with apraxic language delay, an impairment that is frequently associated with development aphasia.[21]

Similar to the way in which the processing of music may assist the brain in regaining language abilities, such processing also may be helpful in developing other cognitive capabilities, e.g., seriation, a cognitive procedure identified by Piaget that normally begins to be used during the stage of pre-operations.[29] The practice of seriation skill using such familiar songs as *The Farmer in the Dell, The Twelve Days of Christmas* and *She'll Be Coming Round the Mountain* may aid development of seriation as a cognitive ability in areas of the brain that are responsible for analytical, language, association, memory, holistic, motor, auditory, visual, and musical behaviors.

Such generalized and diverse benefits are made possible by the capacity of the brain itself for sharing information with all of its portions. In the normal, healthy brain, the 200 million fibers of the corpus collosum provide interhemispheric communication at the rate of four billion impulses per second.[16] Information may be transferred immediately to provide global integrated access and processing throughout the brain. Pribram[39] has even proposed a holographic model of brain functioning in which all parts of a stimulus image are sent simultaneously to all parts of the brain for manipulation, response, and memory storage.

Two of the 15 tasks included in the Musical-Perception Assessment of Cognitive Development focus on tempo and duration.[32] Although the instrument was originally tested using normal children in an elementary school, it has subsequently been supported as a valid instrument for measuring musical perception tasks and for assessing cognitive development in mentally retarded students.[17] It has also been suggested that the tasks could be incorporated directly into musical activities for the purpose of improving cognitive skills[32] such as ability to use seriation in processing information.

An earlier study of conservation utilized a group of forty developmentally disabled children to develop a cognitive assessment tool using music. The average chronological age was 9.5, and the average mental age was 8.1 years. Disabilities included visual impairments, orthopedic handicaps, borderline mental retardation and learning disabilities. The children were tested on conservation of area, continuous volume, rhythm, and tempo. Pairing of the four tasks yielded six paired comparisons using the phi coefficient and the chi-square conversion. A significant relationship was found between aural conservations of rhythm and tempo and visual conservations of area and volume. [31] These results were characterized as empirical evidence that the aural tasks may be substituted for the visual tasks in assessing cognitive development in visually handicapped children since both aural and visual conservation abilities occur in an invariant sequence.

The Musical Enhancement of Cognitive Development model being proposed is not intended to offer a scheme for accelerating development of musical capacity in handicapped or nonhandicapped children beyond that which they are capable of at any given stage of cognitive development, or beyond the limits of their various abilities or disabilities. Although Suzuki has demonstrated the ability of very young children to match pitch and rhythm through training and practice'[10] many studies show that acquisition of music skills prior to their normal stage of development is resistant to training.[36, 9, 39] For example, although first graders made a 20% improvement after training in recognition of changes in melodic contour using different pitches, training had little effect on their ability to identify melodies with the same pitches but placed in a different order. The second task required conservation of temporal order of an auditory series of stimuli. Third graders, however, improved dramatically form 65% to 80% correct after training.[9]

Children five years old showed no consistent ability to recognize tonal or atonal 3-note sequences, while six to ten-year-olds improved greatly on recognition of tonal passages. At twelve or thirteen years of age, atonal accuracy caught up. Similar results were achieved for 4- and 6-note passages. It was suggested that a test could be constructed to measure internalization of culture-bound scale structure.

A study was done to investigate the effects of music training on number conservation in a visual task and on conservation of a tonal pattern. It was concluded that the training did aid development of conservation for the musical task, but did not transfer to the visual task.[40]

In a study designed to investigate the relationship between conceptual understanding and aesthetic sophistication, children were tested who were between the ages of three and sixteen and a half. Correlations were sought between performance on an aesthetic responsiveness task and age, conservation of rhythm, and years of violin study. Among the numerous correlations reported was a substantially higher correlation between age and rhythmic conservation ($r=.60$) than between years of violin study and rhythmic conservation ($r=.09$).[24] These findings provide further support for maturation over training as a determiner of acquisition of cognitive ability. Extremely low correlations (below plus or minus .1) were also obtained between years of violin study and all four sections of the author-designed task of aesthetic responsiveness. The low correlation between training and rhythmic conservation illustrates the need for teachers to separate training in musical skills from training aimed at enhancement of cognitive abilities through musical tasks. It showed that training on a musical instrument did not provide training in conservation of musical elements independent of development stage.

There is evidence that at the proper time in a child's development, training may improve conservation of rhythmic pattern,[11] and conservation of tonal pattern[11] or melody.[5] In the latter study, training in conservation of melody also resulted in improved performances on Piagetian visual conservation tasks in mass, weight, and number. These authors concluded that musical conservation can be improved with training, and that because both musical and non-musical types of conservation appear to utilize the same cognitive structures, effective training in one may result in improved performance in the other.

It is important for educators to realize the interdependence of cognitive development and perceptual experience as children progress through stages. Simply acquiring a certain cognitive structure does not ensure the child's ability to perfect use of that structure in all situations. For example, it may be inferred from Piaget's stage theory that development of conservation is an entirely natural phenomenon.[11] However, music educators cannot afford to leave such development up to nature. Especially in trying to teach music and other skills and abilities to developmentally handicapped children, specific learning experiences must be administered to motivate the students to practice and improve conservation techniques with various perceptual strategies.

Educators must "serve as disequilibrators of students."[7] Only then will training schemes lead to more effective use of cognitive structures. Continued stimulation at levels which the student has already mastered may lead to boredom and apathy, and progress may be slowed. Similarly, teacher demands for performance too far above present levels may result in emotional distress and withdrawal.[8] Instead of searching for an optimal level of mismatch, educators should begin with tasks at which the student can gain immediate success, such as previously learned music skills, and gradually increase the complexity of rhythmic, melodic, harmonic or other musical characteristics appropriate to assessed cognitive capability. For example, recognizing, singing, or playing a 4-note melody involving only two separate tones (pitches) may be expanded by adding tones, notes, repetition, rhythmic variation, words, accompaniment, phrases, harmony, timbre options, and dynamics. As the child becomes comfortable with each addition, another element may be added to renew short-term disequilibration and foster new efforts toward accommodation.[8]

As the child masters each new level of complexity in the musical tasks administered by the teacher, a new level of aesthetic sensitivity will be achieved along with improved ability to use available cognitive schemes. Concerning man's aesthetic behavior, Gaston has stated: "As his aesthetic sensitivity develops, he must elaborate and make more complex his sensory and motor behavior."[14] It is important, therefore, to provide increasing complexity in the musical experiences of each child while allowing that child to progress at his own pace through the necessary sequence of developmental stages.

References

1. Bartlett, J. C. and Dowling, W.J. "The recognition of transposed melodies: A Key-distance effect in developmental perspective," *Journal of Experimental Psychology: Human Perception and Performance,* 6:501-515, 1980.

2. Bever, J.G. and Chiarello, R.J. "Cerebral dominance in musicians and nonmusicians," *Science,* 185:535, 1974.

3. Boardman, E. "An investigation of the effect of preschool training on the development of vocal accuracy in young children," Doctoral Dissertation, University of Illinois, 1964. In Zimmerman, M.P. *Musical Characteristics of Children,* Music Educators National Conference, 1971.

4. Borling, J.E. "The effects of sedative music on alpha rhythms and focused attention in high-creative and low-creative subjects," *Journal of Music Therapy,* 18:101-197, 1981.

5. Botvin. G. "Acquiring conservation of melody and cross-modal transfer through successive approximation, *Journal of Research in Music Education,* 22:226-233, 1974.

6. Chang, H.W. and Trehub, S. "Auditory processing of relational information by young infants," *Journal of Experimental Child Psychology,* 24: 324-331, 1977.

7. Cowan, P.A. *Piaget, With Feeling.* New York: Holt, Rinehart and Winston, p. 34, 1978.

8. Cowan, op.cit.

9. Dowlig, W.J. "Melodic information processing and its development, In Deutsch, D. (ed), *The Psychology of Music,* New York: Academic Press, Inc., 1982.

10. Farnsworth, P.R. *The Social Psychology of Music,* Ames, Iowa: The Iowa State University Press, 1969.

11. Foley, E. "Effects of training in conservation of tonal and rhythmic patterns of second-grade children," *Journal of Research in Music Education*, 23:240-248, 1975.

12. Furman, C.E. "The effect of musical stimuli on the brainwave production of children," *Journal of Music Therapy*, 15:108-117, 1978.

13. Gardner, H., Davidson, L. and McKernon, P. "The acquisition of song: A developmental approach," *Documentary Report of the Ann Arbor Symposium*, Reston, Virginia, Music Educators National Conference, 1981.

14. Gaston, E.T., *Music in Therapy*, New York: Macmillan & Co., p. 21, 1968.

15. Hargreaves, D.J. Castell, K.C. & Crowther, R.D. "The effects of stimulus familiarity on conservation-type responses to tone sequences: A cross-cultural study," *Journal of Research in Music Education*, 34:88-100, 1986.

16. Hodges, D.A. "Neurophysiology and musical behavior," In Hodges, D.A. (ed), *Handbook of Music Psychology*, Lawrence, Kansas: The National Association for Music Therapy, Inc. pp. 43-62, 1980.

17. Jones, R.E. "Assessing developmental levels of mentally retarded students with the Musical-Perception Assessment of Cognitive Development," *Journal of Music Therapy*, 23:166-173, 1986.

18. Jones, R.L. "The development of the child's conception of meter in music, *Journal of Research in Music Education, 24:142-154, 1976.*

19. Kessen, W., Levine, J., Wendrich, K., "The imitation of pitch in infants," *Infant Behavior and Development*, 2:93-99, 1979

20. Kinney, D.K. and Kagan, J. "Infant attention to auditory discrepancy," *Child development*, 47:155-164, 1976.

21. Krauss, T. & Galloway, H. "Melodic intonation therapy with language delayed apraxic children," *Journal of Music Therapy*, 19:102-113, 1982.

22. Larsen, R.L. "Levels of conceptual development in melodic permutation concepts based on Piaget's theory," *Journal of Research in Music Education*, 21:256-273, 1973.

23. Melson, M.H. and McCall, R.B. "Attentional responses of five-month old girls to discrepant auditory stimuli," *Child Development*, 41:1159-1171, 1970.

24. Nelson, D.J. "Trends in the aesthetic responses of children to the musical experience," *Journal of Research in Music Education*, 33:193-203, 1985.

25. Petzold, R.G. "The development of auditory perception of musical sounds by children in the first six grades," *Journal of Research in Music Education*, 11:21-43, 1963.

26. Petzold, R.G. "Auditory perception in children," *Journal of Research in Music Education*, 17:82-87, 1969.

27. Pflederer, M. and Sechrest, L. "Conservation-type responses of children to musical stimuli, *Bulletin of the Council for Research in Music Education*, 13:19-36, 1968.

28. Piaget, J. 1936) *The Origins of Intelligence in Children*, New York: Norton, 1963.

29. Radocy, R.E. and Boyle, J.D. *Psychological Foundations of Musical Behavior*, Springfield, Illinois: Charles C. Thomas, 1979.

30. Pribram, K.M. *Languages of the Brain*, Englewood Cliffs: Prentice-Hall, 1971.

31. Rider, M.S. "The relationship between auditory and visual perception on tasks employing Piaget's concept of conservation," *Journal of Music Therapy*, 14:126-138, 1977.

32. Rider, M.S. "The assessment of cognitive functioning level through musical perception," *Journal of Music Therapy*, 18:110-119, 1981.

33. Roederer, J.G. *Introduction to the Physics and Psychophysics of Music*, New York: Springer-Verlag, 1975.

34. Scheid, P. and Eccles, J. "Music and speech: Artistic function of the human brain," *Psychology of Music*, 1:21-35, 1975.

35. Serafine, M.L. "Piagetian research in music," *Bulletin of the Council for Research in Music Education*, 62:1-21, 1980.

36. Serafine, M.L. "A measure of meter conservation in music, based on Piaget's theory," Unpublished doctoral dissertation, University of Florida, 1975.

37. Simons, G.M. "Comparisons of incipient music responses among very young twins and singletons," *Journal of Research in Music Education*, 12:212-226, 1964.

38. Taylor, D.B. "The theoretical basis for the use of music therapy with aphasic patients," In Pratt, R.(ed) *The Fourth International Symposium on Music,* New York: University Press of America, pp. 165-169, 1987.

39. Thorn, B.A. "An investigation of Piaget's conservation theory and its implications for teaching and developing melodic and rhythmic concepts," Unpublished doctoral dissertation, University of Oklahoma, 1973.

40. Tracey, C. "The effects of training through music on number conservation," Unpublished research report, State University of New York at Buffalo, 1982.

41. Verdeau-Pailles, J. "Music and the body," In Pratt, R. (3d) *The Fourth International Symposium on Music,* New York: University Press of America, pp. 37-48, 1987.

42. Wyllie, L.L. "Further study of Piaget's principle of conservation in the responses of children to musical tasks," Unpublished Master's thesis, University of Kansas, 1976.

43. Zimmerman, M. Musical Characteristics of Children, Washington D.C: Music Educators National Conference, 1971.

44. Zimmerman, M. & Sechrest, L., "Brief focused instruction and musical concepts," *Journal of Research in Music Education,* 18:25-36, 1970.

Music Therapy with a Child Having Motor Delay and Elective Mutism

A Case Report

Chava Sekeles
The David Yellin Teachers College
Jerusalem, Israel

This paper will present a developmental approach in music therapy, based on the following assumptions:

A. stages of biological development and mental development are closely related;

B. the control of movement and posture, through which important aspects of development manifest themselves, is inherent in both the art of music and the normal growth of the human infant;

C. music is a medium which, due to its inherent nature, activates several systems in the human organism: sensory,[1] motor,[2] vocal, emotional and cognitive;

D. therefore, music as an art complex, or even separate sound components, has the potential of affecting all these systems, either positively or negatively.

Following the developmental approach we first examine through music the present state of the child from different aspects,[3] then work out a therapeutic program.

The following case analysis demonstrates the way music may have positively affected a child who suffered from both neurological and emotional problems.

Alon: Medical and psychological background

Alon[4] was born at term in January, 1979. He was bottle-fed and preferred semi-liquid food until the age of six years. During his first three years he suffered from recurrent upper respiratory infections and showed difficulties in breathing, nursing and eating. The parents, who were mainly concerned with Alon's physical condition, paid no attention to the slow development of motor skills, nor to the fact that he used speech at home only.

At the age of three and a half, Alon underwent tonsillectomy and adenoidectomy. Upon awaking from anesthesia he rejected any verbal or other contact with his parents. This kind of rejection continued for several years.

In kindergarten Alon remained passive and did not use verbal communication.

At the age of four he was referred to a Child Mental Health Clinic and was diagnosed as suffering from Elective Mutism.[5] EEG examination showed no pathology; a developmental examination could not be properly carried out because of his refusal to cooperate. The decision to refer him to music therapy was made for the following reasons:

A. he did not cooperate in conventional play therapy;

B. in Alon's family, music was highly valued, and thus there was a natural inclination to accept such treatment;

C. in the Child Mental Health Clinic, music was accepted as a pre-verbal medium capable of circumventing speech.

After observing the child at home, the following rule was laid down: "In the music room it is forbidden to *talk*; here we make music." The rule was set for the child with the assumption that his mutism should be viewed as a symptom; de-emphasizing speech might decrease the pressure placed on Alon to speak. At the same time, music supplied a much needed means of expression which Alon was desperately seeking. Indeed, as a result of the above-mentioned rule, Alon showed his ability to verbally communicate from the very first moment he entered the music therapy room. (See Figure 1.) Consequently, later in the process the rule could be canceled and attention could be directed to the underlying origins of the problems. However, after one month, and on the basis of the above-mentioned observation, we hypothesized that Alon's condition was a result of a combination of three interrelated factors:

A. a basic neurological deficiency from birth that affected motor development, most probably minimal brain dysfunction (MBD) as was diagnosed later on by a neurologist;

B. general and continuous upper respiratory infection from early childhood which had a deleterious effect particularly on the functioning of those parts of the body connected with the oral phase;

C. these problems erupted in the form of severe emotional disturbances, subsequent to the trauma of surgery.

Figure 1

First month observations and evaluation[6] (May, 1983)

Vocal Development	Motor Development
1. Able to talk, does so only at home and during music treatment	1. General hypotonia
	2. Cannot jump with both feet or either foot
2. Emphasizes musical characteristics of speech rather than the verbal content	3. Cannot skip
	4. Normal but slow crawling
3. No correspondence between the verbal content and the musical characteristics of speech	5. Difficulty in alternate left-right drumming
	6. Difficulty in maintaining steady beat-unit while drumming
4. Is able to utter all syllables	7. Not able to cross mid-line in play
	8. Poor eye-hand coordination
	9. Poor imitation of rhythmical patterns
Recorded Example Played	10. Pincer grasp inadequate
	11. General dependence in activities of daily living

Therapeutic Considerations: 1st Stage

During infancy, Alon experienced respiratory distress and pain while nursing:

> "Organic feeding disorders become the basis for the non-organic types. Neurotic disturbances arise more easily where loss of pleasure in the function of eating has prepared the ground for them." (A. Freud, 1946. p. 131).

Concerning consequences in the mother-child interaction one might evoke Anna Freud's suggestion that rejection of nourishment represents to the mother her own rejection. In the case under discussion, in addition to that, slow motor development during the oral stage severely limited early mobility which might have interfered with the process of establishing "object permanency."[7] Due to his poor health Alon frequently stayed in bed, became isolated and could not develop stable emotional relationships with other children. Unfortunately, surgery added desperation and anxiety to the pathological development. Rather than experiencing the three hospitalization stages of *protest, desperation* and *denial* — observed by Robertson (1957), Bowlby 1960 and others — Alon probably remained fixated in the protest stage. This might well have found its extreme expression in Elective Mutism. In the light of these considerations, I decided to first establish with Alon a sense of confidence by diminishing pressure to speak and by creating a comfortable atmosphere through music. At the same time I encouraged Alon to produce different kinds of sound in order to experience oral and respiratory gratification through the pleasurable aspects of music.

Music Therapy: 1st Stage

May, 1983 - September, 1984)

During these 14 months of treatment Alon progressed slowly, gaining more self-confidence. In this period he used verbal communication at home and during the music therapy sessions. He still was not communicating in the special-education kindergarten.

In September, 1984 his father had to remain abroad for several months, which resulted in severe regression. Alon was overloaded with unexpressed anxiety and anger.

[2nd recorded example — September, 1984]

In this recorded example one can hear how the child is being encouraged to "shout his anger away." He does so especially when assisted by the guitar, or by hitting the drum while the therapist is supporting with the piano.

[3rd recorded example — September, 1984]

However, Alon's condition became more severe. He became subdued, shutting himself off and withdrawing from his usual level of functioning even at home and in music therapy. In the next example he reacts merely with spitting and hawking.

[4th recorded example — November, 1984]

Therapeutic Considerations: 2nd Stage

The music I used until this stage of regression was mainly of the relaxing type, allowing the child a comfortable atmosphere and easy initiation. By using such music I actually continued the language that Alon was versed in at home — so much so that on several occasions the child told me that he despised the "sweet music" and the violin, which was clearly associated with one of his parents. In addition, the effort to create a relaxed situation prevented me from dealing with Alon's hypotonia and apraxia, a problem which was not yet treated properly at the kindergarten.

As a result I decided to change my approach by first treating Alon's hypotonia and then proceeding with his psychological problems. From this moment on the music therapy session assumed the following form: (See Figure 2.)

From this time on, and for a period of about 28 months Alon continued to produce spontaneous, imaginary fantasies using means of expression in a remarkably symbolic and suggestive manner. Interestingly, the stages through which he passed during this period seemed to reflect the normal transition through the oral, anal and oedipal stages of development.

"Oral Stage" in therapy - In the Jungle

(March, 1985 - July, 1986)

Alon conceived of the studio as a jungle. He who usually was extremely anxious about aggression from both outside and within turned himself by

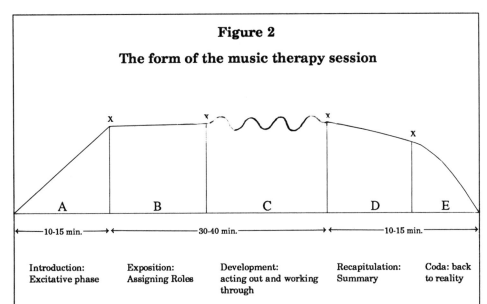

Figure 2

The form of the music therapy session

Introduction: Excitative phase	Exposition: Assigning Roles	Development: acting out and working through	Recapitulation: Summary	Coda: back to reality

A. **Introduction**: in which the child reacted with movement to excitative music taken mainly from ecstatic rituals of non-literate societies.[8] His vigorous activity evoked vestibular stimulation[9] and consequently elevation of muscle tone. At the same time it permitted recourse to chaotic behavior. After several weeks the spontaneous locomotion became more organized and structured, allowing the therapist more guidance.

B. **Exposition**: in which the child planned the content of the session (the content of his fantasies and magic thinking); arranged the musical instruments for his use, and assigned roles.

C. **Development**: in which Alon acted out his fantasies, used verbal and musical means of expression while the therapist helped in the elaboration and working through of his problems.

D. **Recapitulaton**: in which major events were summarized by the child and the therapist.

E. **Coda**: to conclude the session and help return from fantasy to reality.

Figure 3

Alon's Stages of Development from March, 1985 to June, 1987

Months	Developmental Stage	Fantasies	Settings
March, 1985 - July, 1986 16 months age: 6-7½	"ORAL"	"I am a bad and dangerous animal." (tiger, snake). Father=lion. Fantasies of aggression and ravaging. Magic separation between bad and good.	The Jungle Inside a tiger cave
July, 1986 - Sept. 1986 3 months age: 7½ on	"ANAL"	"I am a singer and a musician. I master the outside world by singing."	A studio
July, 1986 - June, 1987 10/11 months age: about 8-8½	"OEDIPAL"	"I am a prince." Fantasies of marriage, war, death and victory	A palace A castle

magic into a "bad" animal. (Odier, 1948). By becoming a devouring and destroying beast of prey he was able to express aggression without guilt. Again, I should re-emphasize the role of the excitative music and its intense stimulation which not only influenced muscle tone and enabled better loco-motion but also released inhibitions and unblocked the child's speech:

[5th recorded example — March, 1985]

> "I am the tiger. I am the baddest animal. I'll put all the good animals in the mouth of the animal who'll eat them up. It'll be breakfast. They are not sweet animals, they are dumb animals."

Listening to this recording one can hear the way Alon emphasizes his words by drumming in steady rhythmical patterns. By using these patterns Alon appears to build a kind of protective framework around himself. At the end of this session he was able to cooperate again with an organized "sweet" (according to his own description) jungle song:

[6th recorded example — March 1985]

With this jungle song, Alon permitted himself to bridge between the period of mutism and regression and the period of aggressive expression.

After several sessions Alon agreed to cooperate with another child. The child played the role of a frightened bird and Alon was the dangerous tiger. At a certain point he picked up a doll and treated it aggressively:

[7th recorded example — April, 1985]

> **Alon**: "What! Speak to me! Speak to me! What are you, a baby?"
>
> **The doll**: "I cannot speak."
>
> **Alon**: "Speak up!"
>
> **The doll**: "I cannot speak."
>
> **Alon**: "You want the 'baddies' will hit you?"

He pulls out the doll's hair and throws it down, reinforcing his speech with a cymbal:

> **Alon**: "Go to sleep! (3 times). You want your mother to get angry at you?... Take a stinking blanket. Think that this is Mommy! Think! On the head...They will think it's a monster in you...The lions and the drums are playing and the baby cannot fall asleep."

Notice that Alon picked the object most similar to a human figure. He had turned the doll into a symbol of himself while he himself played the role of the mother. The doll, like himself, is passive, unable to protect itself, hypotonic and thus an ideal target for discharging aggression. For the first time in his life, Alon dominated and directed the situation. He assigned roles, wrote the script and chose the musical instruments. My role as therapist was to set protective limits, play the roles assigned by the child, mirror his emotional state and supply a concluding cadence to each session. Approximately after a year, "anal" material emerged. Still, for 16 months the music therapy room remained a jungle.

"Anal Stage" in therapy — In the Recording Studio

(July, 1986 - September, 1986)

The music room was transformed by magic into a recording studio. In a comment from this stage Alon said:

[8th recorded example — July, 1986]

> **Alon**: "This studio is a new strong studio, a very beautiful studio. The other was a little bit very old. What a stink it had! Until we started the music, skunks kept coming through the door... We had to light two spotlights on the drums."
>
> **Therapist**: "Do you feel safe in this studio?"
>
> **Alon**: "It is good to live here. It is forbidden to leave. We even locked the door...Outside there are skunks who'll fart everything up...Everything is O.K. We have to be in the studio, this is our home."

In this stage, the functions of organization and control took precedence. It should be recalled that during the oral process Alon acted as a ravenous "bad animal," emphasizing it with aggressive drumming. On other occasions he used to choose from among many musical selections such as the *Symphony* of Luciano Berio or John Cage's *Solo No. 1*, describing it as "the music of the baddies." In contrast, during the anal process, he turned himself by magic into a singer and assigned me the role of the recording technician:

[9th recorded example — September, 1986]

In this example, we can hear Alon singing and accompanying himself at the same time with different musical instruments. This occurred when he no longer needed the image of the strong aggressive tiger in the jungle. He already was sufficiently strong in his own right to be a singer. Music, which until then had served to reinforce emotions, became an end in itself and therefore took on organized content as well as melodic and dynamic variety. Alon sensed that he could control the situation without aggressive violence.

Gradually, he expanded the area of his control from the recording studio to other areas of fantasy, such as illness, hospitals and death. Memories from his first three years of childhood emerged very clearly and were worked through by means of repetitive re-enactment. The child allowed himself to experience all kinds of imaginative medical catastrophes and looked for means of mastering them. Situations which previously caused severe anxiety already could be controlled. The form of the session remained the same, but the excitative phase diminished from 15 minutes to 5 minutes.[10]

"Oedipal Stage" in therapy — In the Palace

(September, 1986 - June 1987)

After about 3 months, oedipal content appeared in Alon's fantasies. The recording studio became a palace or a castle. The fantasies centered around the royal family: the king, the queen and the little prince. Alon was often agitated by the content of his own imagination, to which he responded by cursing himself harshly.

[10th recorded example — October, 1986]

> **Alon**: "You are a dumbo, a son-of-a-bitch. You are stupid. You are 'ostimuck.' You're nothing. You should be hit. Weak, don't exercise. Do not go to the doctor. Drop dead! You'll never move."

Suddenly he turned to me and said:

> "And don't you dare sing that stupid song. You hear? I can't stand this song. It's stuck on to me. Yeah! Get rid of this song."

> **Therapist**: "Maybe you already got rid of it, when you sang it."

> **Alon**: "It is stuck on to me. It got inside me. Get it out of me!"

By singing, accompanying myself on the piano, I "exorcised" the song from Alon. He shouted: "It's gone out. (4 times) Hurry! Has it gone out?"

> **Therapist**: "Yes, it has."

> **Alon**: "So keep singing in case some of it is left."

I sang again, using his own key words. The child calmed down.

In this episode, Alon requested direct assistance from the therapist for the first time. Likewise, it was not the tiger or the singer, but himself, who was in distress. The demon which possessed him was symbolized by a song and a song in turn exorcised it, the way that "like acts on like" in pre-logical thinking.

For the last ten months Alon fantasized out rituals of marriage, birth and death:

[11th recorded example — June, 1987]

> "There was a king, a queen and a prince. They lived in a palace. At night cruel knights kidnaped the prince and turned him into a weak, dumb boy. Then they regretted it and brought him back to his bed. Instead they killed the king, his father. The queen and the prince disappeared to another place, to another country."

We have heard here two versions of the song: the first one, in which a melodic line developed, is unaccompanied; the second is accompanied by the piano according to the child's wish.

Summary

Through a case analysis I have attempted to show a developmental approach in music therapy. The problems of the child presented were caused by a combination of neurological and psychological difficulties (MBD and Elective Mutism). It was not efficient to treat one problem in isolation from the other. Without dealing with Alon's physiological condition it would have been impossible to improve his mental state. From a technical point of view, we began each session with excitative musical stimulation, the purpose of which was to encourage spontaneous movement and increase elevation of muscle tone, thus improving body alertness. Flow of movement and control of posture are inherent to both music and child development. It is therefore natural to use music in order to stimulate and control movement and posture. After a period in which Alon reacted spontaneously to music, a phase of guided movements to improve motor-planning (praxis) began. This role was given a year ago to a developmental-occupational therapist allowing the music therapist to deal mainly with Alon's emotional state. Since January 1987, Alon has been communicating verbally in all social situations, with both children and with adults. From a psychological point of view, ecstatic music reduced inhibitions and cognitive control. Thus, Alon dared to bring up those disruptive contents which previously had sealed his lips.

Notes

1. That is: senses (auditory, visual, vestibular) and sensations (tactile, proprioceptive).

2. Locomotion as a reaction to sound and/or while playing a musical instrument.

3. According to the Observation and Evaluation form developed at the music therapy program. David Yellin Teachers College, Jerusalem, 1982, 1987.

4. The name of the patient presented has been changed. The dialogues were translated from the original Hebrew.

5. "The essential feature (in Elective Mutism) is continuous refusal to speak in almost all social situations, including in school, despite ability to comprehend spoken language and to speak." (DSM-III, 1980, p. 62).

6. The observations were partly made at the child's home and partly during music therapy sessions.

7. The attainment of "object permanency" in 8-10 month old infants is important to both the development of sensory-motor intelligence as well as to the establishing of basic trust and self-confidence.

8. The principles of which were described in "Music in Healing Rituals of Non-Literate Societies," (Sekeles, 1979, chap. 4).

9. The importance of vestibular activity and postural control in mental and emotional health is widely discussed by Kohen-Raz (1986).

10. What happened to Alon is very similar to the inducing of trance in healing rituals of ecstatic nature, such as those of the Hamadsha group in Morocco (Carpanzano, 1973). After having enough practice, the participants might enter the state of ecstasy within a few minutes of musical stimulation and dances.

Recorded examples (Alon's improvisations)

A fragment from the 1st recorded example, imitations of syllables, May 1983

Singing & guitar

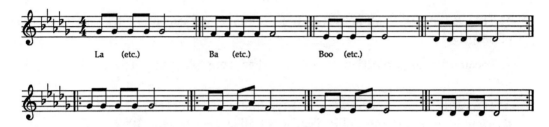

La (etc.)   Ba (etc.)   Boo (etc.)

Organizing his anger in steady rhythmical pattern, 3rd example, September 1984

Drum & piano

Emphasizing his words ("I am a tiger...") with musical instruments, 5th example, March 1985

Rattle   Gong   Drum

The ape in the jungle, 6th example, March 1985

Therapist

I   II   V   I   V/VI   VI   V/V   V7

Child

I   VI   II   V   I

"I am a singer." Singing and accompanying himself at the same time,
9th example, September 1986.

zanza   xylophone   gong   drum

Melodic line

Alon cursing himself harshly, 10th example, October 1986

Melodic line

Melody of "exorcism"
Chromatic accompaniment, piano

References

Bowlby, John. "Separation anxiety," *The International Journal of Psychoanalysis*, Vol. XLI:89-113, 1960.

Carpanzano, Vincenzo. *The Hamadsha, A Study in Moroccan Ethno-psychiatry*, Berkeley: University of California Press, 1973.

American Psychiatric Association. *Diagnostic and Statistical Manual of Mental Disorders-III*, Washington, D.C. APA, 1980.

Freud, Anna. "The Psychoanalytic Study of Infantile Feeding Disturbances," *Psychoanalytic Study of the Child*, Univ. Press, New York, Vol II: 113-119, 1946.

Kohen-Raz, Reuven. *Learning Disabilities and Postural Control*, London: Freund Publishing House, 1986.

Odier, C. Anxiety and Magic Thinking., New York: International University Press, 1956.

Robertson, James. *Young Children in Hospital.*, London: Tavistock Publishing, 1957.

Sekeles, Chava. *Music in Healing Rituals of Non-Literate Societies* (MA Thesis), Hebrew University, Jerusalem, 1979.

Section V

Teaching the Gifted Child

Psychological Issues Encountered in Gifted Children and Adolescents

Gary S. Gelber, M.D.
University of California, San Francisco

What is your image of a child prodigy? Is he or she equipped with a golden halo or perhaps with a whitish blue electrical current zapping back and forth between intense, riveting eyes? Descriptions of prodigies are familiar to us from our knowledge of Mozart or, for example, pianist Arthur Rubinstein. When Rubinstein was three years old, his parents bought a piano so that his older siblings could take lessons:

> "The drawing room became my paradise....Half in fun... I learned to know the keys by their names and with my back to the piano I would call the notes of any chord, even the most dissonant one. From then on it became mere 'child's play' to master the intricacies of the keyboard, and I was soon able to play first with one hand, later with both, any tune that caught my ear.... All this...could not fail to impress my family — none of whom, ...including grandparents, uncles, aunts, had the slightest musical gift... By the time I was three and half years old my fixation was so obvious that my family decided to do something about this talent of mine."[*]

Have you ever wondered what very accomplished musicians were like when they were children? Were they isolated prodigies, working away on their own? I think that our speakers this afternoon will give us a chance to glimpse what gifted musicians are like during childhood, and we will see what some of their needs are.

Although many gifted children may be socially isolated, I am struck by how much environmental support is actually necessary to produce exceptional performers. At the age at which piano and string instruction should begin, the child usually needs to be held to a routine by a parent, and encouraged and praised by parents. The young child of five will not apply this discipline

---

[*] Rubinstein, Arthur, *My Young Years*, New York: Alfred A. Knopf, 1973

to himself naturally. Parental involvement is so important that we could speak not just of the child prodigy, but of the child-parent unit. And the teachers, of course, form a part of the unit.

Much is demanded of the parent who needs to keep up with the child's expanding horizons. The parent is both a talent scout who not only finds the right teachers, but also a chauffeur. The parent and the teacher may apply pressure if the child does not want to cooperate in what the adults expect of him. Such patterns of deep parental involvement can also be observed in some households having children who are highly gifted in areas other than music.

What are some of the possible negative aspects of parental involvement? To begin with, the parents have often labeled their very talented child as "special." Granted, it is important for children to feel that they are special to their parents. But, as Dr. Sosniak shows in her studies, the future piano virtuoso may be a favored child who does not have to do ordinary tasks because of his need to focus on practicing. Having permission to escape from chores that other siblings must do can lead the child to feel entitled — entitled to getting his way. For the child thus privileged, frustrations can lead to tantrum-like behavior in adulthood.

The isolation of the practice studio also contributes to the future artist's risk of heightened egocentricity. An intense musical practice schedule leads to less interpersonal practice in negotiating, compromising and giving. This reminds me of Victor Borge's remark: "Ah, Mozart — he was happily married. But his wife wasn't!"

An antidote to entitlement and egocentricity normally develops during adolescence. This antidote is altruism. The burgeoning of altruism, which is so important to our interpersonal relationships, can be thwarted in some musicians. Instead of going through the interpersonal work required to develop altruism, the teen-age musician may elaborate a subconscious substitute for real altruism with a fantasy of giving to others through his music. In doing this, the young musician substitutes intense musical expressiveness, and stage portrayal of emotions, for the more personally taxing altruism and giving that are normally involved in real relationships with others.

For gifted musicians, there is often considerable confirmation of their musical specialness, confirmation by those who appreciate and laud these talents. For example, there may be that wonderful beam of love in the adoring parent's eye. There may be experiences with enthusiastic, adoring audiences. There can even be an identification with royalty — which is not as strange as it may sound. If we think back to what we read and heard about musicians as we were developing as young musicians, we sometimes learned that our composer heroes were under the patronage of the royalty. Classical music was often identified with royalty and people of the highest social rank.

Great recognition at a relatively young age may mean to gifted children that they are special people, not just special as artists or musicians, but special as people, as exceptions to usual expectations, and therefore worthy of special treatment — worthy of treatment as prima donnas. But the teen-age years can be tortured and lonely for the highly gifted individual. The adolescent, feeling rebuffed and alienated from his peers, may withdraw. The four walls of his practice room enclose a kingdom of refuge and narcissistic rewards, where the emotions of music are a welcome substitute for the real life pain of the high school scene.

The last problem I will mention is that the gifted child may sense the parents' need for him or her to succeed. Children may subconsciously realize that if they do not produce in the manner in which their parents want them to, they will lose some aspect of their parent's love. Consequently, the child may feel obliged to help its parent, realizing just how important it is to the parent for him or her to succeed. In this sense, then, the child functions as a sort of therapist to the parent, an emotional splint for the parent's self-esteem. In fact, all of us who work with gifted children need to avoid this pitfall. Our own self-esteem, our ambition and our vicarious participation in the gifted child's progress may contribute to our not appreciating or recognizing the child as a unique young person. Instead, we may run the risk at times of focusing only on what the child can accomplish.

To counterbalance these possibilities, there need to be strong influences from the parents and/or the environment to overcome the entitlement which musical stardom can encourage. Parents may need to make more than the usual efforts during childhood to find other gifted children who can serve as friends or acquaintances. Certain situations also help to counteract an excessive degree of egocentrism; for example, ensemble and chamber music training promote sharing and cooperation. Music teachers and educators, because of the very close ties that they can develop with music students, are sometimes in a favorable position to try to help their students. And of course there is also that great impetus to maturation and growth: falling in love, which may enhance a person's ability to give.

From Tyro to Virtuoso:
A Long-term Commitment to Learning

Lauren A. Sosniak
College of Education
University of Illinois at Chicago

Imagine, if you will, a group of young adults whose skill at a piano keyboard has earned them the highest honors available from the music community. Certainly these outstanding pianists were not born so accomplished. How then did they get to be such fine musicians? What follows is a story of the transformation from tyro to virtuoso. It is a story, too, of a long-term commitment — to the piano, to music-making, and to the process of learning. It holds lessons, I hope, not only for the development of musical talent, but also for the process of successful learning of many sorts.

More specifically, this is a story of the experiences of twenty-one concert pianists who shared their educational histories so that we might better understand the development of talent. The data that provide the foundation for this story are drawn from the *Development of Talent Research Project* (Bloom, 1985). The subjects for that larger study were groups of individuals who, though relatively young, had realized international levels of achievement in one of six fields: concert piano, sculpture, Olympic swimming, tennis, research mathematics and research neurology (two artistic disciplines, two psychomotor activities and two academic fields).

The focus of the *Development of Talent Research Project* was on the role(s) of the home, teachers, schools and other educational and experiential factors in discovering, developing and encouraging such high levels of competence. The study was concerned with questions like: How did an individual begin his or her involvement with a field? How did he or she work at the activity — how were time, materials and other resources used? What roles did family and teachers play in the learning process? How were interest and involvement maintained? How did activities and experiences change as the learner gained skill and understanding? The plan was to search for regularities and recurrent patterns in the education histories of groups of successful learners, consistencies that might shed light on how unusually successful learning is achieved.

The project explored the lives of more than 100 talented individuals in all, approximately 20 in each field. Retrospective, semi-structured, face-to-face interviews were conducted with the individuals who met criteria of outstanding achievement set by experts in their respective fields. Parents of many of the individuals were also interviewed, by telephone, for corroborative and supplementary information.

The Choice of Concert Pianists

Concert pianists were the first group of unusually successful learners studied as part of the Development of Talent Project. The decision to study concert pianists as one of our artistic fields, rather than, say, violinists or clarinetists, was made after considerable discussion with musicians and music teachers. Our informants pointed out not only that learning to play the piano was a fundamental part of much music education, but also that learning to play the piano placed fewer physical requirements on individuals than did many other instruments. A youngster did not have to be as physically well-coordinated to play the piano as would be necessary to play the violin, for example. Further, if a youngster learned which key to strike on a piano, the instrument itself would make the proper sound; a beginner does not have to count on his or her own ability to construct a particular note. These, then, were among the reasons for selecting concert piano performance as one of the artistic fields to be studied.

The selection of the particular pianists to be studied also depended heavily on the advice of music informants. For the purposes of research, we knew we needed to interview approximately two dozen people in each of the fields we were studying. We knew also that we needed to interview people who were relatively young — both so that they would be able to recall their early years of learning and so that we might have the opportunity to interview their parents as well for supplementary and corroborative information. Further, we believed it was important to limit our work to individuals raised in the United States — to avoid confounding our findings with cultural differences. Finally, and perhaps most importantly, we believed it was essential that the particular people we interviewed in each field represent what experts in the field consider to be the highest levels of talent.

For each of the fields we studied, then, we asked informants to help us set the criteria for defining outstanding achievement. They reported to us the evidence they would use to identify relatively young individuals who had reached an extremely high level of achievement. We used the evidence they suggested to identify the talented individuals we should interview.

Our music informants strongly suggested, for example, that we not use as one of our criteria engagements with major symphony orchestras. Their concern with this criteria was twofold. First, they said the decision about who should play with a major symphony orchestra often was made by a single individual, rather than by a group of musicians. Second, they were concerned that these decisions too often were political decisions. Instead, our music informants pointed us toward international competitions they believed were most important at that time for identifying exceptionally accomplished pianists. Pianists who were finalists in these competitions were rated highly by a group of musicians, and typically, by pianists who were themselves recognized for their expertise. The competitions that our informants agreed were, at that time, the most highly rated by pianists themselves were: The Chopin International Piano Competition in Warsaw, The Leventritt Foundation International Competition, the Leeds International Pianoforte Competition, The Queen Elisabeth of Belgium Competition, The Tchaikovsky International Competition, and the Van Cliburn International Quadrennial Piano Competition.

The Concert Pianists Interviewed

Twenty-four musicians met the criteria we set to be included in the study. They were finalists in one or more of the competitions noted above, were under the age of forty, and were raised in the United States. Of the twenty-four pianists who met the criteria, we were able to interview twenty-one. Two who lived in Europe at the time could not join the project because they were too far away to interview. One other pianist never responded to our numerous attempts to contact him. Subsequently, we were also able to interview parents of sixteen of the musicians.

Of the twenty-one concert pianists we interviewed, sixteen are male. All are Caucasian. Six are only children; the other fifteen were equally likely to be the oldest, youngest or a middle child. At the time of our interviews they ranged in age from twenty four-thirty nine. All but two were between twenty seven and thirty seven. We think of them as representing one decade of talented musicians. Of course they are not the only exceptional pianists in their age group; each of the musicians in our sample is, however, undeniably accomplished.

Lauren A. Sosniak

Developing Musical Talent

Three findings stand out from our interviews with the pianists and their parents. These findings and some of the implication that follow from them, are the subject of this presentation. In their most abbreviated form the findings can be summarized like this:

1. talent development takes a long time;

2. the process is essentially one of qualitative change. It involves a continual and perhaps systematic reorientation and transformation — both of an individual and of the activity of learning;

3. talent development involves many people working for the achievement of just one.

A Long-term Commitment

The pianists worked for an average of 17 years from their first formal lessons to their international recognition. The fastest "made it" in 12 years; the slowest took 25. (In our study of Olympic swimmers we found that it took the men and women about 15 years to reach the Olympics from the time they began swimming just for fun, during the summer, in a nearby lake or pool).

The mere fact that it takes a long time to develop talent is hardly surprising. What struck us was that during much of the period of time the pianists spent developing their abilities, it would have been impossible to predict the pianists' (or swimmers') eventual accomplishments. With a few exceptions, the pianists did not show unusual promise at an early age. The pianists were not child prodigies, as the stereotype of musical development would have us expect. Nor did they exude obvious signs of greatness just waiting for development. The pianists, and their counterparts in the other fields we studied, worked for many years before their talents were obvious and before they were accorded the special treatment by teachers that had earlier gone to others who were perceived to have more potential.

The pianists began taking lessons by the age of six, on the average, and playing in small recitals organized by their neighborhood teachers within a year or so. Seven years later, by the time they were thirteen or fourteen, most were playing in local competitions, or for judges at yearly music adjudications. Even after seven years of study and practice, the young pianists did not always win those events. In fact some of the pianists reported that even after seven years of work at music-making they were still losing competitions far more often than doing well (the swimmers, by the way, spent an average of eight years swimming in national competitions before they began to place — that is, to come in first, second or third — in those events).

Instead of finding that the pianists were discovered, and then helped to develop, we found much the reverse. The youngsters spent several years developing musical ability — listening to music, taking lessons, practicing daily — before they were "discovered" as the most musical in their family or in their neighborhood. This discovery, by a parent or teacher, typically led to increased opportunities for further musical development. Then, after several more years of work at an increasingly more sophisticated level, the youngsters were *re*discovered, and so on (Sosniak, 1985a).

The pianists not only spent many years learning their craft, they did so for a considerable amount of time without any clear idea of where they were headed. There was no intention, at the start, to take piano lessons so that one might eventually become a concert pianist. Two parents provide succinct demonstrations of this:

> "Now that I think back, I think I would have started him with a better teacher — at a conservatory — if I had known he was going to become [a concert pianist]...At that time, I didn't think it was important."

> "I just thought this is a nice thing for someone, to have music as well as other things, so I know I never planned this or pushed for it. Never in my wildest dreams did I think he'd be a concert pianist...I thought he'd be something like a physicist or an engineer."

The pianists' experiences were not at all like the stereotype of musical achievement delivered by popular films or fiction. There, our pianists would have shown extraordinary abilities at a very early age and their parents would have dreamed of their success from the start. As youngsters they would have been performing with major symphony orchestras and giving recitals. Instead, we found outstanding musicians who learned to be so over a long period of time. Musical experiences and expectations were integrated gradually into the pianists' (and parents') lives. Exactly what was to be learned, and where it would lead, were decisions made and remade many times in the process of an educative experience.

Qualitative Change

Why did the pianists stick with music-making for as long as they did, even without clear success or a long-term goal? As educators, how can we keep students engaged in fields of study long enough for them to become skilled at and knowledgeable about whatever it is that we want them to learn? How can we keep students engaged even as the tasks become more difficult, even as their lives become more complex and filled with competing interests, and again, even when the students are not always successful at what they are doing?

Part of the answer, I think, will require a better understanding of the qualitative shifts over time in a successful learner's experiences and behaviors. It is obvious from the pianists' histories that change over time in the process of learning was much more than getting smarter or more skilled at the keyboard (Sosniak, 1987), much more than working intensely at more difficult tasks. "To be educated," R.S. Peters (1967) reminds us, "is not to have arrived; it is to travel with a different view." The pianists progressively adopted different views of who they were, what music-making was about, and how music fit in their lives.

There seem to have been three distinct periods of learning, reminiscent of Whitehead's (1929) writings on the rhythm of education and stages of romance, precision and generalization. These three broad, empirically derived phases are revealed in the pianists' and parents' talk about changes in behaviors, perceptions and experiences. They can be identified by looking at the learner's relationship with the piano and the world of music; parents and teachers roles in the process; and motivators, rewards, and symbols of success.

The discussion that follows will provide a brief overview of these phases. Rough edges will be smoothed over, and the subtlety will be lost. Of course, there are many places in the pianists' reports where things did not work exactly as I'm going to describe. Those actually turned out to be quite helpful in our analyses, because the corrections that took place in the pianists' experiences made it easier for us to see the patterns (Sosniak, 1985b).

The First Phase of Learning — The Early Years

The earliest years of learning were playful and filled with immediate rewards. At home, at first, youngsters spent time "tinkering around" at the piano, "tapping out melodies for fun." One pianist recalled "plunking on the keys as much with the palms of my hands as with my fingers, and then running to mother and saying 'was that a nice song?' and then going back and doing it some more."

Listening to music was a natural part of life in most of the pianists' homes. Parents of two of the twenty-one pianists were professional musicians themselves (neither of these was a pianist). Parents of the rest of the pianists represented the entire range of possible associations with music. A few were music lovers who, as amateurs, enjoyed playing an instrument; a few were musically indifferent and unknowledgeable (at least when their children were young). Most liked music well enough, although they were not musical themselves (Sosniak, 1985c). Typically, they enjoyed listening to music on the radio or on records, and, like parents of most children, they believed some music education for their children was "a good thing," (*Music U.S.A.* 1974).

The youngsters were encouraged to play with an instrument if one was available, to sing songs and pick out tunes, and listen to the radio and records. Some parents bought children's records. Some, the few who could play an instrument themselves, sometimes played duets with their children. Parental involvement at this stage shouldn't be overemphasized; still, it is important to keep in mind that music — at least listening to music — was a natural part of life to a greater or lesser extent in the pianists' homes. Music was something "good," "nice," an amusement for the parents and child, an interest for them to share.

Initial music instruction also typically was playful, enticing and encouraging. First teachers were said to be "really great with young kids," "very kindly, very nice," and "enormously patient and not very pushy." First teachers were typically not very good musicians themselves; rather, they tended to be "the local teacher," "a neighborhood teacher," someone nearby and maybe even "a friend of the family."

Lessons with first teachers reportedly were "fun" experiences. "It was an event." "I looked forward to them." Instruction was informal, personal, and filled with immediate rewards. The teacher was likely to "indicate when a

　　　　　Lauren A. Sosniak

piece was finished by putting a star at the top of the page." One pianist told an especially memorable tale about a first teacher: "She carried a big bag of Hershey bars and gold stars for the music, and I was crazy about this lady. All I had to do was play the right notes in the right rhythm and I got a Hershey bar."

For the most part, both the students and teachers seemed unconcerned with objective measures of achievement. The first period of instruction emphasized engaging in lots of musical activity, and exploring possibilities. ("Doesn't that note just feel so good that you'd just want to hold it a little longer?" a teacher might ask.) The students responded to the warmth and enthusiasm of their teachers, and got involved with the piano and music-making.

The Second Phase — The Middle Years

Isaac Stern noted the following about musical development in a *New York Times Magazine* article:

> "Somewhere along the line, the child must become possessed by music, by the sudden desire to play, to excel. It can happen at any time between the ages of 10 or 14. Suddenly the child begins to sense something happening and he really begins to work, and in retrospect the first five or six years seem like *kinderspiel*, fooling around." (Winn, 1979).

So it was, more or less, for the twenty-one concert pianists we interviewed. The age was not necessarily the same, but the experience was very much shared.

The dominant theme of the middle years of the pianists' development, which typically began when the pianists were between the ages of ten and thirteen, was one of precision.

> "I would take more care with how I prepared things. Do it right from the very beginning. Learn it slowly, put in the right fingering. Just do things with care."

This period was marked by a tremendous amount of time spent on details. The pianists did the same thing over and over, now consciously making slight variations each time. They were busy looking for flaws in their own playing as well as in the music-making of great performers.

In the second phase of learning, instruction became more rational and less informal and personal than it had been earlier. Technical skills and vocabulary were the core of lessons. The rules and logic of music-making were dealt with in a very disciplined and systematic way.

Sometime during or immediately before this period the pianists typically moved from working with "nice" teachers who were conveniently located to working with teachers who were recognized in the local community at least for being more musically sophisticated. Lessons changed dramatically.

> "[They] were very long. Very, very detailed. Always working on the shape of my hand and all these little tiny things. She had me phrase things. Had me do things over and over to make them as beautiful as possible. With great attention to detail."

Most of the pianists learned technique by working through the music they were assigned. Each new and more difficult piece was approached as a new problem. The pianists worked on a piece of music for as many as eight or ten lessons, going over it note by note, phrase by phrase, "until I got it right."

And, underlying technical mastery, a new musical dimension was gradually made available to the pianists. One pianist explained it this way:

> "We talked about when this composer lived, and what kinds of things were going on — cultural attachments and the like in the other arts; what this represented, what this went along with, or what was parallel to this. Significance on the very spiritual level. Very detailed. Very intense. Talking about all kinds of things."

Still another reported:

> "[My teacher] continually stressed that there was something behind the notes or underneath the notes that one must respect. That there's something bigger than respect for just the literal facts on the page and that's the heart of the matter, what the music has to say, the content."

Objective measures of achievement — the results of adjudications and competitions — provided both a personal sense of accomplishment and a means of planning subsequent instruction. Knowledgeable criticism from teachers and juries of musicians at adjudications and competitions became as rewarding as applause and adulation had been earlier. The personal bond between teachers and students shifted from one of love to one of respect.

The student/teacher relationship was carried well beyond the once-a-week lessons. The teachers encouraged, enticed and prodded the students to take part in public musical activities. They told students about competitions and adjudications, spent extra hours helping the students prepare for these events, and sometimes went so far as to drive the students several hundred miles to take part in these activities. The teachers arranged recitals, special summer camp opportunities, and meetings and auditions with important musicians — all experiences important for learning and becoming part of the world of music.

Parents began to consider what activities they could allow their child to engage in without the possibility of harming his or her music-making. They thought also about how much of an investment they could allow their child or themselves to make in music without harming the child's larger development. Their actions, both consciously decided upon and spontaneous, generally were strongly supportive of musical development.

Parents began making large sacrifices of time and money to get the child a better teacher, buy a better piano, and travel to competitions. They rearranged life in their homes to accommodate their children's musical activities. Parents and children willingly began to sacrifice all other extra-curricular activities, and sometimes to sacrifice a general education as well, to concentrate on piano practicing.

Over a period of four to six years the pianists developed skills, a sense of competence, and an identity as musicians, although they were still just good amateur pianists. These changes took place gradually. Toward the end of these middle years of learning there was an inkling in the hearts and minds of most of the pianists that they were aiming toward concert soloist status. Earlier, such an idea would have been unthinkable for most. For nearly a dozen years, then, the pianists had been working for the moment, and the moment following that one, not for a dream about years down the road.

The Third Phase — The Later Years

The third phase of learning typically began when the pianists were between the ages of sixteen and twenty. The emphasis shifted from disciplined mastery of specific skills, to a broader and more personal understanding of and commitments to making music. The question that all the pianists and their teachers faced was: Given all the students knew, could they go beyond that knowledge to understand, appreciate, and finally bring something of themselves to the experience?

According to more than one master teacher, youngsters sometimes "sound remarkable...and suddenly they stop dead and they go absolutely no further."

Another reported:

> "Often, even after teaching a young person quite a number of years, and they play very well, you suddenly find a ceiling when they have to do something by themselves. There's sometimes a lack of imagination, or a lack of intellectual grasp."

Some students are simply great imitators. One teacher commented:

> "That's fine, if it's a stimulant [to creativity], but not if it remains as a product.... We all learn by imitation of a sort. But we have [to have] a way of making it our own."

During the third phase of learning the pianists typically worked with master teachers — teachers who were among the most respected faculty at professional schools of music, and who were, or had been renowned concert pianists themselves. Some of these teachers more than lived up to reputations for being abrasive, but a close personal bond between student and teacher was no longer an especially important part of instruction. One pianist described the experience shared by most this way:

> "He was an impossible task master. It was incredible. He would just intimidate you out of your mind. He would sit there.... You played a concert, you didn't play a lesson. You walked in prepared to play a performance... You would get torn apart for an hour."

The pianists remember terror before lessons or tears afterwards. But they also remember the esteem they felt for their teacher, which was often enough to carry them through some very trying months as they acclimated themselves to this new way of working. The pianists spoke with awe about the opportunity to study with such outstanding musicians. "The idea that this man was willing to teach me, to give me his time, overwhelmed me." "What she said to me was like the voice of God."

The shared task between student and teacher in the third phase of learning was to respect and appreciate the music and music making. The pianists were taught to see "the hills and valleys" of different pieces and styles of music. They learned how and when to sacrifice some of the technical details that had been so important earlier, in order to convey meanings or feelings that they believed were essential to the music.

Let two pianists summarize for themselves the third period of instruction, with a master teacher.

> "He didn't teach you how to play the piano, he teaches you...integrity, devotion, and a complete dedication to music-making."

> "He made me think and he made me experience and he made me understand that you have to find your own way. You have to know what's right [and] what's wrong, but the possibilities and tonal color are absolutely endless."

With the help of master teachers, the pianists began to identify and develop personal musical styles. They began finding and solving their own problems, and satisfying themselves rather than their teachers. Eventually, as one explained, "you reach the point where you must become your own critic. You know when you have [given a solid performance] and you know when you haven't."

As a rule, the pianists took one lesson a week for the length of their musical education. Although the amount of instruction remained essentially the same, even as their commitment to music grew, and even when it became obvious that they were planning careers as musicians, the nature of instruction changed dramatically. Much the same can be said about practice time, or playing in recitals. In these two instances there were, of course, changes in the amount of time devoted to each as the pianists became more skilled and more invested in music-making. Still, the changes in amount did not begin to compare to the changes in kind — the qualitative differences in the experiences over time.

Reviewing the pianists' experience with instruction, practice, and performance, we find major changes over time in the pianists' perceptions of musical activities, in their ways of working at music-making, and in their reasons for their continued efforts. The piano shifted from being a toy to being a tool. The pianists' interests were at first in "playing around," later in mastery of the machine, and still later in making music. What seemed like a game at first became hard work; later still it became what one aspired to do for a living; eventually it defined who one was. The pianists reported growing into the perception of themselves as pianists, and then outgrowing even that as they learned to think of themselves as musicians. They were transformed and reoriented and their experiences were reinterpreted again and again as they learned to be as good as they are today.

Talent Development as a Group Effort

The pianists' transformations were matched, typically, by their parents. In the beginning, the parents valued music and music-making, although their valuing was neither very intense nor very focused. Music lessons simply were a "good thing" for all children, theirs included. One mother explained why she gave her children music lessons this way: "Because I liked music. Because I felt the kids needed it. I sent them to church for the same reason. I wanted them to have the experience." The haziness of the parents' investment in music-making is further reflected in the fact that most of the pianists began lessons with a neighborhood teacher, the man or woman down the street, someone their parents knew about without having to find out about.

But as I've illustrated to some small extent, the parents — as well as teachers and other people sometimes involved in a pianists' development — involved themselves wholeheartedly in the pianists' education. Over time, it seems they created an interdependent and self-sustaining system of mutual encouragement and support. They alternately eased and prodded one another to make bigger commitments and to become more involved, as seemed good or necessary at the moment. Parents especially were willing to change their lives dramatically in response to what was taking place in the process of their child's development. They not only gave more money and time than they expected, but they learned an enormous amount about music and music-making in the process of helping their children learn.

No one had any idea what they were getting involved in at the start; no idea how long it would take, no idea where it would lead. In fact, I would argue now that if the pianists and parents had striven for huge successes from the start, they probably would have been less successful than they were. It seems that the parents' and teachers' spontaneous responses of approval and delight for the youngsters' work were all the more meaningful because they were unstudied. The pianists and parents were truly proud of each small accomplishment, and with each came the glimmer of something more to be learned, of further possibilities. Because aspirations and expectations of concert soloist status grew with the development of skills and understandings, rather than the far off goal serving as a stimulus for their development, there was never so much to be done that the task would seem overwhelming.

Musical experiences and expectations were integrated gradually into the pianists' (and parents') lives. The pianists learned to work toward more difficult and distant goals as they learned to care about achieving those goals. Their day-after-day perseverance developed as music-making became an increasingly more vital and valued part of their lives. Parents learned to make an increasing commitment to their child's musical development as that development unfolded. In this way, decisions concerning increasing commitments of time, money and emotional energy were generally not thought of as sacrifices, as many people might interpret them, but rather as responses to the further possibilities being presented.

Implications for Teaching and Learning

There are, of course, a myriad of implications that might be drawn from the findings of our study. I'm going to address just a few that I believe are most important for the development of talent. Much of what I will talk about here relates to the long-term nature of unusually successful learning. That issue obviously is important because it was essential to the experiences of the pianists and all the other talented individuals we interviewed. It is also important because it seems that educators and the population at large seem to pay it little attention.

In fact, one of the most common practices in recent years has been to try to predict as soon as possible which children are especially likely to be successful or unsuccessful at a particular activity — so that we might alter their educational experiences accordingly. This approach to education is clearly incompatible with our findings from the study of the development of talent. The approach is incompatible for at least two reasons. First, our findings suggest that it would have been risky business indeed to forsake youngsters who did not initially show considerable potential. As best we can tell, it would have been impossible, when the pianists were young, to predict their eventual successes. Second, had the pianists (and their parents) aimed for such high levels of development at the start, it is unlikely, given our findings, that they would have been as successful.

There are good reasons, I believe, why we did not find many prodigies in our study (why young children who "demonstrate exceptional talent" are not likely to end up as extremely accomplished adults), and why the characteristics of exceptionally accomplished adults are not likely to be critical for the youngsters who will eventually demonstrate exceptional talent. The quantitative transformation we found in the process of unusually successful learning — the different views the pianists traveled with as they became educated about music-making — help explain this situation. So, too, does the gradual development of commitment — on the part of the learners and their parents — and the importance of this growing and changing motivation for the pianist's eventual successes.

It was important for our pianists to develop a deep interest in and involvement with music-making before they were expected to do the work required for mastering the technical skills of the art. It was important also for the pianists in our study that they could appreciate small signs of growth, and that their parents and teachers could do the same. It was important, further, that the pianists in our study were willing to take chances — to work at skills and understandings that were beyond their grasp at the moment — without becoming overwhelmed or discouraged by lack of immediate success. "Prodigies" are unlikely to have these sorts of experiences.

The question that the findings of our study raise for me is not the traditional one: how we might better identify talented youngsters at an earlier age. It is, instead, the question of how we might help teachers and parents believe in the potential of all children and work for however long, in whatever ways are necessary and appropriate, to help all youngsters succeed at things that are important to us.

To that end, it seems especially important that we take seriously the long-term nature of successful learning. Our current methods of instruction may be quite inappropriate for the long-term development of talent. We have a tendency, it seems, to emphasize momentary attentiveness, the acquisition of quickly acquired and simplistic skills, and immediate success. Are we overemphasizing the very short-term educational experience at the cost of long-term educational growth? Where is there room in our current education programs for playfulness with some subject matter? Where is there room in our current education programs for making some subject matter a vital and valued part of a learner's experiences? Where is there encouragement for students to persist at increasingly more difficult tasks for however long it takes to master those tasks? Where is there encouragement for students to appreciate and learn from less-than-successful experiences?

Perhaps the most problematic implication from our study of the development of talent relates to the fact that unusually successful learning seems to be a group effort. The talented individuals we studied got a lot of help — sometimes from parents, sometimes from teachers, sometimes from other family or family friends. For a good number of years they worked with or had close personal contact with people they felt were "very sincere... very interested in seeing me develop," with people they felt really believed in them, with people from whom they "got the feeling it was worth trying," people who were "openly encouraging...no question about that."

Is it reasonable to assume that the interdependent and self-sustaining system of mutual encouragement and support that we found is necessary for most successful learning? If so, how could most students have such experiences? How might teachers and schools reach out to their communities to make such experiences possible for their students? How might parents be drawn into the work teachers do with students to assure that the value of student learning will be a pervasive and persistent part of the students' lives?

The development of talent is of profound importance for our society, and for all societies. The findings from the Development of Talent Research Project suggest that such unusually successful learning may be within reach of a large portion of our population, if we can learn to orchestrate environments supportive of learning over the long term.

References

Bloom, B.S. (Ed.) *Developing Talent in Young People*, New York: Ballantine Books, 1985.

Music, U.S.A: Reviews of the Music Industry and Amateur Participation, American Music Conference, 1974.

Sosniak, L.A. "A Long-Term Commitment to Learning," in Bloom, B., (Ed.) *Developing Talent in Young People*, p. 477-506, 1985(a).

Sosniak, L.A. "Phases of Learning," in Bloom, B., (Ed.), *Developing Talent in Young People*, pp. 409-438, 1985(b).

Sosniak, L.A. "Learning to be a Concert Pianist," in Bloom, B., (Ed.), *Developing Talent in Young People,* pp. 19-67, 1985(c).

Sosniak, L.A, "The Nature of Change in Successful Learning," Teachers College Record, Vol. 88, No. 1, Summer, pp. 519-535, 1987.

Peters, R.S. *Ethics and Education*, London: George Allen and Unwin, Ltd., p.8., 1967.

Whitehead, A.N. *The Aims of Education*, New York: Macmillan, chapters 2 and 3, 1929.

Winn, Marie. "The Pleasure and Perils of Being a Child Prodigy," *The New York Times Magazine*, December 23, 1979.

The Mind Behind the Musical Ear[1]

Jeanne Bamberger
Department of Music
Massachusetts Institute of Technology

I want to talk about children who early in life are identified as extraordinarily gifted musically, but who after mid-adolescence seem to disappear from the musical scene. As far as I know, no one has taken such a group of young performers, followed their careers for several years, and tried to understand what happened to them as they grew up. No one, for example, has gone to Juilliard, identified the extraordinarily talented students in, say, a particular five-year period, and followed their development into early maturity. Some, probably a minority, went on to solo or ensemble careers as performers. But what happened to the rest, to the majority?

Once I became interested in this question, stories began to accumulate. One, told by a colleague of mine in a certain tone of sadness, almost embarrassment, was that as a child he was a pianist of "great promise." Even though many of you will recognize his name as a distinguished scientist, he still feels as if he failed to realize his promise and potential. There is a similar story about a microbiologist. Another is about a person who was described as the best violinist among his group of students at Juilliard, who now leads an anonymous life somewhere as a free-lance musician.

The stories are many, and they are full of pathos. The question remains, how can we learn more about the developmental course of these youngsters? It seemed to me if we could get a better understanding of what these talented young musicians know how to do so well, maybe that would shed some light on what happens later on. It was my hunch that, in addition to the many obvious emotional, social, cultural, and career issues that descend on adolescents, there are particular *cognitive* issues that also come into play. In particular, I had the hunch that there was a kind of cognitive disequilibrium that occurred during mid-adolescence. It seemed that getting

---

1   Portions of this talk have appeared in a chapter titled: "Cognitive Aspects of Development in Musically Gifted Children" in *Conceptions of Giftedness*, Robert Sternberg and Janet Davidson (Eds.), Cambridge University Press, 1987.

through this disequilibrium required a real transformation in the ways these young people were making sense of their musical world. This, it seemed, was related to the kinds of issues that cognitive psychologists talk about when they refer to development as a reorganization of the most intimate, the most intuitive mental structures by which we make sense of the world around us. Issues like "same and different," "more or less," or what, indeed, do we take to be an "element"; and perhaps most important, how do we construct *boundaries* so as to segment our incoming sensory phenomena. Maybe this sounds philosophical, even metaphysical. I intend, however, for it to be very concrete. This process of reorganization is an experience I think everyone has at those moments when we actually come to see or hear in a new way.

Thomas Kuhn suggested to me one day that we continuously have to "reprogram our sensory perception." Let me give you a straightforward example. One of my interests is working with teachers and children in a place I have created in a public school in Cambridge, Massachusetts. It is called the "Laboratory for Making Things." One afternoon we asked the children to make a pattern with crayons on paper which used three colors and in which the pattern repeated three times. One little boy, as he worked, was saying to himself, "Blue, red, blue, green; blue, red, blue, green;..." Looking at his pattern (see Figure 1), how many different ways can *you* chunk it? As you look at it, new patterns emerge, just as they did for the child. He was very excited to discover that, as he began to examine his drawing, new patterns began to pop out; for instance, his original linear repetitions became diagonals of blue, green, and red, a "cross" with a contrasting square in the middle, repetitions at varying levels of structure, and so forth. The point is that this little universe can be chunked many different ways; and that's what I mean by restructuring or reorganizing our sensory perceptions.

Let me give you another example. I'm going to go over to the piano and play the beginning of a Beethoven minuet. I want you to listen to it, and then clap the repeated pattern which is in the right hand. (Excerpt is performed.) OK, clap it; just the pattern, not its repetitions. Right! It's long-short-long, dotted eighth-note, sixteenth-note, quarter-note). Now, I want you to listen just to the left hand and clap the pattern you hear there. What did you find out? It's the same pattern! Did you hear them as the same the first time I played? No? Why not? If we look at the right hand and left hand notations, we see they obviously have the same durations. They *look* the same; why don't they don't sound the same?

Jeanne Bamberger

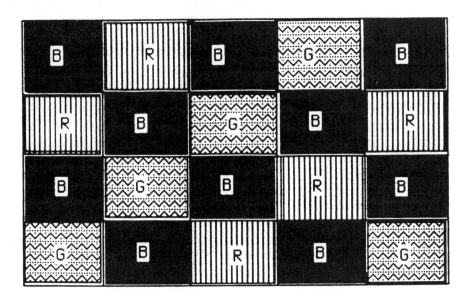

Figure 1

How many ways can you "chunk" it?

Here we have a problem of same and different. Why do they sound so different? Maybe it's because one is in a higher register and the other in a lower register; or maybe the order of pitches is different. There is, however, a critical reason why they sound different: the right hand pattern goes *to* the accent and the left hand pattern goes *from* the accent. Now, an accent is something that is generated by the music itself. That is to say, it's not something you start with *before* the music begins — by tapping your foot or clapping your hands. An accent, or a grouping of beats, is generated in the moment, as you play the music. In our example, the first figure *generates* an accent, going *to* it; the second figure begins on that accent. Although notated they may look identical, they are heard as different. So it's just as important to hear them as *different* as to hear them as the *same*. That's what I mean by restructuring one's sense of an entity, of defining what's the same and what's different. We seem to spend a great deal of time trying to get our students to hear those two rhythms as the same. Then, when they are played the same, we tell them they are playing unmusically!

I would like now to speak about some of my work with musically gifted children. It seemed important, first, to gain some insight into the nature of musical knowledge that serves these young performers so well. Only then, it seemed to me, would we be able to consider the nature of the transitions and transformations that might occur later on in adolescence. This assumes, of course, that one can meaningfully look at and talk about "musical knowledge" — the mind behind that effortless and prodigious "musical ear." But that assumption is hardly shared by all. In particular, it seems that those involved most intimately with musically gifted children, their teachers, often do not share the notion that a kind of "knowledge" may be contributing to their extraordinary performance abilities. One teacher, for example, to whom I went in order to get help in gaining a better understanding of such knowledge, said, "You're wasting your time. The mind isn't involved at all. For these children, making music goes directly from the ear to the fingers." This is not an isolated view, and to articulate it is important because it reflects one side of a division that I've sensed at this conference — a split between, on the one hand, those who hold a view that "musicality" is mostly an "intuitive feel," a "good ear" — similar to the view of the teacher I just quoted; and, on the other hand, those who hold the view that the mind *is* involved in quite particular ways and thus needs to be helped to develop appropriately. The problem is not to take sides for one or the other view, but rather to seek ways of getting these two kinds of "knowing" together.

To explore the kinds of knowledge that gifted young performers may be making use of in their prodigious performances, I arranged to observe a group of children who were participants in the Young Performers Program at the Longy School of Music in Cambridge, Massachusetts. This program accepts children between the ages of seven and twelve on the recommendation of their teacher, together with an audition. The children attend school for the entire day on Saturdays. Their activities include private instrumental lessons, chamber music coaching sessions, theory classes, master classes, and performance. In other words, they become absorbed in a wide range of musical activities which I was able to observe for almost a year. Looking back on this year from an anthropological point of view, it became clear that in my observations I was trying to understand a culture. This group of talented youngsters was, after all, a small community, and I was its observer.

At first, the results of my observations were rather unexpected, though after the fact they seemed obvious to me and the teachers. Let me first summarize some of my findings and then explain what really happened. First, I was struck by the fact that these talented young musicians seemed to have an unusual capacity for making *multiple representations*, for developing multiple schema, of the varying creative and recreative dimensions of a particular piece of music. That is, they could see and hear the music in many different ways. At the same time, these multiple dimensions were not fragmented or in any way separate from each other. Rather, they were a single whole, the result of a dynamic reciprocity among the relations that together give a unique coherence to a single musical moment or to an entire composition.

I think that what happens in adolescence is that this well functioning and reciprocally related network begins to fragment. It separates into dimensions which are differentiated, and which then have to be recoordinated. Adolescents have a critical need to reflect on what they are doing; they ask "How did I do that? what do I know how to do? why am I playing the music this way instead of that?" It's my strong opinion that we don't prepare children to think about, let alone cope with, such questions. These young musicians are so very talented that teachers are reluctant to "tamper" with them. It is almost as if they were encouraged not to think; as if thinking would impede doing. My position is that one should not hesitate to encourage children to experiment, to puzzle, and to question. It seems to me that those who successfully passed through this critical adolescent period are not afraid of these questions; they learn from them.

During my period of observation at the Longy School, I noticed that as the teachers taught they constantly shifted from one "field of attention" to another. In this way, they began to develop in the children a repertory of multiple representations which were never named or made to appear separate from one another. The representations are aggregated, well functioning gestalts. Let me give you an example of what I mean. During a lesson, a Longy teacher said to a student, "You have the same figure repeated three times here." The teacher was obviously talking about the *structure* of the piece, the return of motivic material at various moments in the unfolding of the piece. He continued by pointing out that, as written, the repetitions were visually unnoticeable (while this may strike the reader as confusing, notations of this sort often occur in music). Here, the teacher was referring to the "notation domain." The printed score is, after all, a very different representation of music than the one you have in your ear or your fingers.

But I think the most powerful representation, or inner schema, these young musicians have is related to the way they move with their hands, mouths, and bodies on the geography of their instruments. They have "smart" fingers. For instance, in a composition by Bach, a figure will not look the same at each repetition because of bar lines. In performance, however, the repetitions may feel the same. During the previously mentioned lesson, the teacher helped the student to realize this by saying, "Use the same bowing; then you'll *feel* that they are the same." In that moment the teacher shifted the student's attention to the "instrument domain." Thus, the teacher moved with the student from musical structure, to the notational domain, and to the instrument's kinesthetic domain, all within the context of the repeated passage. Later, when the music reached the point of recapitulation, the teacher said, "And now we come once more to the beginning. It's like a memory — vague. Play it softly." Again we see the process of shifting from one field of attention to another, something we all do quite naturally, usually without a sense of awareness.

Again, I think it's important to note that these coordinated structures are not separate in the children's experience. Yet, toward adolescence the structures begin to fragment as the children begin to reflect and differentiate among them. Then a new problem arises, that of coordinating the varying fields of attention so as to recreate a coherent whole.

While at Longy, I also did a bit of experimentation replicating earlier work I'd done with varying subjects: the musically gifted, the not-so-musical, people from different cultures, adults and children. In this case, I asked *musically trained* subjects to construct "Twinkle, Twinkle, Little Star" using Montessori bells. The bells all look alike; you can't tell them apart except by playing them. Adult musicians and children over the age of eleven or twelve, when confronted with this task ask: "Can I put them in order?" The order they seek is a felt path, a familiar kinesthetic pattern where they know where everything is. For most of the subjects who read music, "in order" means arranging the bells by pitch, from low to high, from left to right, in a scale pattern. All subjects create a bell-path (the arrangement of bells on the table), an action-path (the physical movement necessary to play each bell), and a tune-path (the sequence of pitches in the tune). Musically trained subjects construct what I call a formal bell-path (the pitches ordered from low to

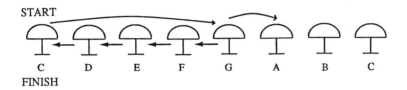

Figure 2

Formal bell-path and action-path

high), but their action-path in playing the tune must skip around on it so as to comply with the "fixed reference" scale. (Figure 2)

The preceding seems to be normal, typical, and expected. It is not, however, what all people do, especially those who have *not* had musical training. Surprisingly, their strategy is quite different — and very appropriate. *They place the bells in the order they appear in the tune.* First they play through all the bells, selecting what we would call the tonic, or in this case, the first note of the tune. They then test the remaining bells, playing each in relation to the first bell, until the correct bell for the second pitch of the tune is found. Starting once more by playing the first two bells, they search among the remaining bells until the proper third pitch is found, and so on. Each time they search for the proper "next pitch," they establish a context by starting the song from the beginning. The task is complete when they have created a row of bells (bell-path) matched one-for-one with the sequence of pitch-events in the tune. In order to play "Twinkle, Twinkle," they need only to play the bells in order. The result is a one-to-one correspondence between bell-path and action-path — that is, the subjects play the tune by simply moving always to the right, or "straight ahead" without ever turning back or

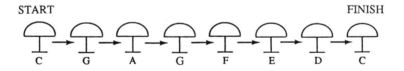

Figure 3

Figural bell-path and action path

playing any bell more than once unless there is an immediate repetition of a pitch. I call this a *figural* bell-path. (Figure 3)

As a result of their consistent and singular construction strategies, trained and untrained subjects differ both in the bell-paths they make and in their action-paths on them. For trained subjects, given a particular tune, it is the action-path that is unique to that tune while the bell-path remains constant across tunes. For untrained subjects, given a particular tune, it is the bell-path that is unique to the tune, the action-path remaining constant across tunes. These strategies appear to be robustly consistent *within* the two groups. As we shall see, gifted children, in striking contrast, switch their strategies significantly as their work evolves.

At the outset of their work, all gifted children seemed to be proceeding like their untrained peers. They began by searching for each bell-pitch as it was needed in the tune, adding them to their cumulating bell-path in order of occurrence from left to right, i.e., C-bell, G-bell, A-bell, etc., representing the opening pitches of the song, C, C, G, G, A, A, etc. But with the next pitch event, all the gifted children made a switch in strategy when compared to the untrained groups. They *reversed the direction* of their action-paths, turning back (to the left) on the word "star" to play the previous G-bell.

What we see here is another dimensional focus. Although the tune-events were first represented and added to the bell-path as simply *next-in-tune*, on this move the children recognize this new event (the reoccurrence of the pitch G) as not only next-in-tune but *lower-than* the previous pitch, A, as well as the *same-in-pitch* as the earlier pitch, G. As a result of their multiple foci, the children are left with a mixed representation of the tune in their

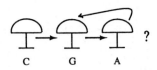

Figure 4

The critical moment

Jeanne Bamberger

work-space and, given what happens next in the tune, a problematic situation. The issue is: what to do with the pitch, F, on the word, "How"?

The problems the children face at this critical moment can be formulated in two ways. First, if the children follow their initial figural strategy (a "straight-ahead" bell-path), the next bell-pitch, F, would be represented as *next-in-tune* and added "after" (to the right of) the A-bell. This move, however, would not take into account the downward pitch motion (*lower-than*) from A, through G, to F. At the same time, it would be inconsistent with a figural straight-ahead action-path because the previous A-bell would be interposed. Second, if they follow their new strategy, the next pitch, F, would be represented as *lower-than* and be placed to the left of the previous G-bell. However, the C-bell already occupies that position in their work space, i.e., the C-bell and G-bell were placed next to each other because of *order-of-occurrence* in the tune.

In confronting the problematic situation, the children made different choices, implicitly assigning differing priorities with respect to these multiple possible dimensions. By way of illustration, let's look at the moves of two children, Keith and Rebecca, at this critical moment (Figures 5 and 6).

Keith, thinking of the F as lower-than the previously struck G-bell, appropriately moves left *on his bell path* — appropriately, that is, if the bells were ordered low-to-high. Striking the C-bell, which is in fact occupying that position as a result of his figural strategy, he confronts the conflict. "Backing up" (moving to the right) at Move 2, he identifies F now as a *place* in the new high-low ordering: "Yeah, it has to go here." Finding the F-bell in his search space at Move 3, he resolves the conflict by giving the problematic F-bell double meaning. That is, he recognizes F as *next-in-tune* as well as *lower-than* G and *higher-than* C. As evidence, we see him push the C-bell to the left (Move 4) and insert the F-bell in the space he has provided for it (Move 5). Continuing with this procedure, he inserts the remaining bells in *order-of-occurrence* (F-E-D). He has, then, created a kind of double classification strategy where each added bell is both *next-in-tune* and *lower- than*.

As a result of his new double classification strategy, the pitch-gap between C and G also visibly emerges. That is, at the outset, when Keith's focus was primarily on next-in-tune, he had appropriately juxtaposed the C and G bells (as one would, in fact, when notating the tune). But as he adds to his focus the dimension, "direction of pitch-motion" (as one does in following a familiar felt-path), he realizes in *table-space* the previously nonrepresented *pitch-space* between C and G. In doing so, Keith also transforms the unique se-

Moves		Description
1	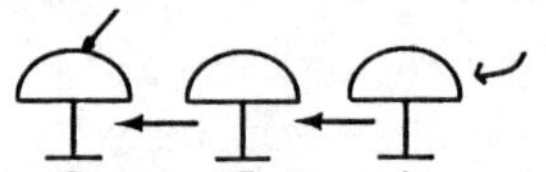	Continues his action-path to left, gently striking the C-bell currently immediately left of the G-bell. K pauses.
2		Swings his mallet between C- and G-bells and says, "Yeah, it has to go here."
3		Moves into search-space. Finds F-bell.
4		Leaving F-bell where it is, goes back to workspace. Moves C-bell to the left leaving a space between C- and G-bells.
5		Picks up bell from search-space and inserts it in space between C- and G-bells.
6		New bell-path.
7-12		Continues with same procedure inserting E- and D-bells.

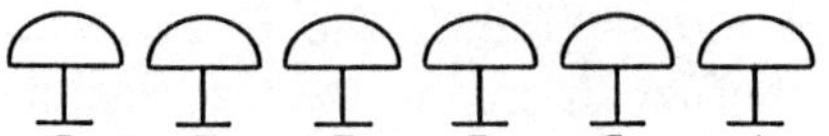

Completed bell path

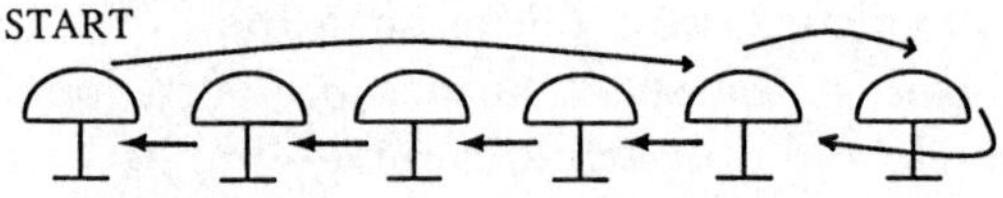

Action-path for Section A

(C C G G A A G 𝄽 F F E E D D C)

Figure 5

Jeanne Bamberger

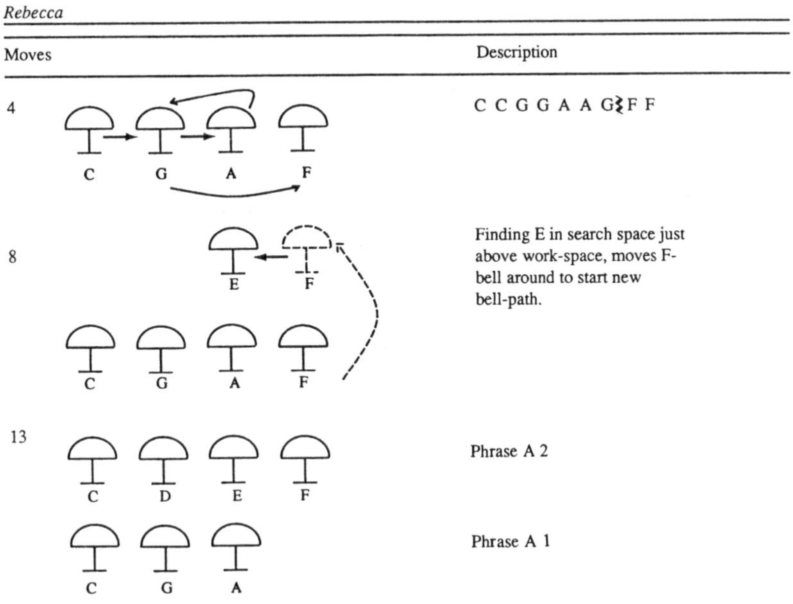

Moves	Description

4   C C G G A A G♯F F

     C   G   A   F

8   Finding E in search space just above work-space, moves F-bell around to start new bell-path.

     E   F

     C   G   A   F

13   Phrase A 2

     C   D   E   F

        Phrase A 1

     C   G   A

Figure 6

quence of pitch-events in *this* tune (C-G-A) into the generalizable, property-ordered sequence, the low-high ordered series: C-D-E-F-G-A.

But notice the difference between Keith's process and that of older, trained subjects. Keith's low-high ordered series evolves *as a result of the particular structure of the tune and in the course of the construction process itself.* This is in marked contrast to older subjects, who feel the need first to orient themselves by building the complete, fixed-reference scale. Only with the scale almost literally "in hand" are they then able to find the tune *on it.*

In contrast, Rebecca thinks of F (Move 4) as simply *next-in-tune* as she places it at the end of her cumulating bell-path. But at Move 8 her attention shifts to thinking of F as the *first event in a second phrase* and also a *higher-than-E.* Unlike Keith, she solves her problem by giving priority to *phrase structure.* This is seen in her two separate bell-paths, one representing the first phrase (A.1) and the other representing the second phrase (A.2)

When the children had finished with the construction of the tune, they were given paper and pencil and asked to "put down some instructions so that a friend who walked into the room right now could play the tune on the bells as they are arranged on the table." The results of their efforts can be grouped into two types of notational strategies which I have called *coordina-*

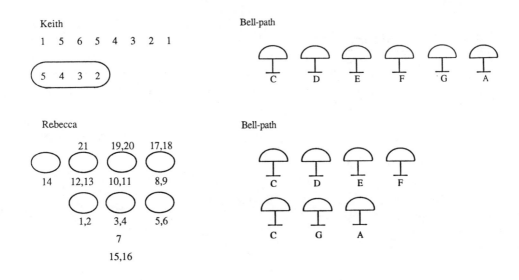

Figure 7

Notational strategies: Keith (coordination), Rebecca (correspondence)
"Twinkle" Sections A and B

tion and *correspondence*. Figure 7, a copy of instructions developed by Keith and Rebecca, illustrates each type.

The notations make a striking contrast. Keith uses his line-up of numbers to *coordinate* two dimensions of the tune, each with its own internal organization: the unique internal structure of this tune and the general structure of ordered pitch properties. His procedure is to use his high-low ordering of the bells on the table as a fixed reference, and from it to assign the numbers 1,2,3,4,5,6 to the ordered series. Each number is a name that stands for the fixed position of a bell in instrument-space as well as the position of its pitch-property in the ordered series. This done, Keith uses the *symbols alone* as objects to be manipulated. The numbers going from left to right in paper-space show the unique *temporal* sequence of events in the tune; the numbers themselves show the fixed *position* of each event along the bell-path in instrument- space.

Notice that Keith's strategy allows him to coordinate three distinct kinds of paths, each with its own meaning and its own trajectory: his bell-path, action-path, and notation-path. Thus, left-right on the bell-path is *low-high*; *left-right* along the notation path shows *temporal sequence* unique tune-events; and each of these is, in turn, different in trajectory from the forward and backward movements of the action-path on the bells in *playing* the tune.

I describe Rebecca's strategy as one of *correspondence* because she makes a direct correspondence between her bell-path in instrument-space and pictures in paper-space. That is, instead of coordinating dimensions by manipulating symbols, as Keith did, Rebecca draws pictures of the bells, taking them, so to speak, one-for-one from instrument-space and putting them into paper-space. Her pictured bells, then, mark fixed places in both *spaces*, leaving numbers to mark unique "places" in time. Focusing her attention on moving numbers about on the pictures, she directly mirrors on paper the distance, direction, and sequence of her actions in actually playing the bells in "real" space. Rebecca's instructions resemble a trail map imposed on a pictured terrain. By following the sequence of numbers through the terrain, you find a path to your destination.

I want to argue now that what we may be seeing in these artificial task situations is a small-scale anticipation of the kinds of cognitive disequilibrium that occur on a much larger scale during the later transition into adulthood. To understand this, it is important to consider a fundamental difference between the activities of the tasks and the children's ordinary musical activities. What we are seeing in the task situations are the children's capacities to *analyze and describe*, neither of which can be said to characterize their everyday work. Analysis and description were obviously involved in the notation tasks. The construction task also involved the children in analysis (albeit in-action) and in description — at times out loud in words, like Keith ("Yeah, it has to go here"), and at times tacitly as they resolved conflict by making new line-ups. Even the results of construction were sometimes partial descriptions of tune structure, such as Rebecca'a phrase rows.

Analysis and description ask the children consciously, even self-consciously, to *reflect on* understandings, actions, and perceptions along with the reciprocal relations among them — things they usually take for granted. Thus it seems likely that this necessity for reflection both contributed to and resulted in the moments of cognitive disequilibrium. And these were the moments, in turn, that triggered the "liberation" of separate dimensions from their usually interwoven web. But it was also reflection that led to insight and to the invention of new ways of coordinating these now separate representations.

My argument, as the preceding suggests, is that the constellation of behaviors that emerged in the artificial and imposed task situations is similar in some important respects to that which occurs naturally and spontaneously during the critical transition into adulthood. The critical connection lies, I believe, in the causal relations between reflection, disequilibrium, and the subsequent invention of new "coordinating schemes."

Although there is yet only anecdotal evidence to go on, I want to propose that a similar dialectic may characterize the transition from childhood into adulthood, but with some important differences. The instability associated with this critical period is a function of *natural* developmental growth occurring over a long period of time and resulting from the *inner* need for reflection. But as in experimental situations, such self-conscious reflection "liberates" problems and conflicts that seemed not to exist before. Choices must be made between *possible* meanings that now emerge and that, in their multiplicity, are often elusive. Conflicts, in turn, must be resolved between *possible* performance decisions that might project these various meanings. This flux of possibilities leads to analysis and description, to looking *at* before looking *through*. In this process, details become detached from the larger design; dimensions are disassembled, and their previously effective interactions break down. It is like a driver looking *at* the streaks on the windshield instead of looking *through* the windshield so as to guide actions in traffic. Just so, reflection here leads, for example, to looking *at* the score (a possible source of answers but also a source of puzzlement) instead, as previously, looking *through* it as a transparent guide to actions on the instrument beyond.

As a result of reflection on actions and on underlying assumptions, dimensions become articulated in all their particularity, and with this, previously confident and well-functioning performance seems to break down. As one sixteen year old performer told me, "It's easy to feel like your playing has gotten worse because we're now listening and hearing so much more." As in the experimental tasks, reflection has spawned disequilibrium, only now it's "for real." These gifted teen-age performers are faced with the problem of building new means for coordinating multiple dimensions, for constructing coherence. They can focus on separate fields of attention, developing each along its independent trajectory. However, as it did for the younger children, this may later mean weighing priorities, for example, between the instrument and structure domains. Sometimes a bowing works technically but not phrasewise, so you have to decide on priorities. Or, at times technique (the instrument field) may be severed from attention to structure. As one fifteen-year-old cellist put it, "I've been practicing the Saint-Saens cello concerto just for technique. I haven't even thought about 'the music' yet."

In other cases, the fear of flux can lead to ritualized, rigidly fixed procedures. For example, well practiced, common configurations on the instrument (what I have called felt-paths) can become undetachably linked to notation, sound, and even meaning. Then, unlike the case for younger children for whom these attachments are still mobile units of action, perception, and notation, can become locked into one another for instant retrieval and security.

Truly artistic performance depends on multiple representations functioning in reciprocal interaction with one another in such a way that events can be related in all their dimensional complexity. This new integration would mark the success of the work of cognitive reorganization. As Artur Schnabel put it:

> "The mature performer works for those rare inspirations when his conception of the score becomes one with its physical realization in performance. At such moments, technique is more than just the disciplined functioning of the body at the command of the ear: It grows into a physical activity which in turn may stimulate the imagination. If all goes well, the conception materializes and the materialization redissolves into conception."

In closing, then, the transitional crisis must be seen as a period of serious cognitive reorganization. There can be neither a return to imitation and the unreflective, spontaneous "intuitions" of childhood, nor a simple "fix-up." As in the microcosm of the experimental situations, reflection that leads to disequilibrium can also be the means toward the invention of new and more powerful understandings. Just as in the other creative acts, the macroprocess is one of evolution and transformation, of quite literally coming to see in a new way.

Presentation of Videotaped Interview with Yo-Yo Ma

Alice G. Brandfonbrener
Medical Program for Performing Artists
Northwestern University Medical School

Introduction

I'm honored to have been asked to participate in this learned meeting. I also feel somewhat overwhelmed by the company I'm keeping. I am primarily a clinician and secondarily a researcher. In fact most of the research in which I am currently engaged has arisen directly from questions and observations that have come from almost two decades of involvement in the medical care of musicians and what has become a fairly large clinical practice in performing arts medicine. We see approximately 65 patients a month.

During the early years and until the recent past, much of my experience was with young musicians; some children, but primarily those of conservatory age. Caring for this special group of patients, and, more recently, professional performers in their active career years, it is difficult not to address some peri-medical issues. For example, is it mandatory to study intensively even as a young child? Do the benefits outweigh the risks? What are the alternatives? Does this early learning create or protect from later physical problems with the instrument?

Many of these very talented youths, propelled by their gifts and by their mentors, find themselves surrounded by an older peer group during their formative years. What does this do not only to their musical gifts but to their maturational processe, their socialization skills, and what are the long range effects? Clearly these are issues that should probably be left to those of you who are psychologists and psychiatrists. As an internist I find these questions haunting and germane to the overall medical care of serious musicians, especially of the young. When there's an indication, therefore, I talk to my patients about some of these issues.

All of us are fascinated by prodigious talent, but my interest comes from the clinical concerns that may accompany the early and fast-tracking of these super-gifted. In medicine we precede the study of illness by a thorough grounding in the normal state. So rather than dwell on failed careers or ones that are otherwise problematical, I am attempting to interview a series of successful performers who have been considered prodigies. This conversation with Yo-Yo Ma is the first one of these that I did. He is not only an international superstar-musician but, as anyone knows who has spent any time with him, a unique young man; well-integrated, thoughtful, intelligent and an altogether delightful person. I hope that you find this tape interesting and stimulating and take away from it the warm feelings that Yo-Yo Ma communicates in his playing and his life. (Filmed interview presented).

Discussion

Although one certainly cannot draw conclusions on the basis of a single interview, it does raise some significant issues to be addressed. Since time is limited, I will simply point out some thoughts that I feel need investigation or at least give some food for further discussion. How is a talent really identified in a young child and, once it is, how should it be appropriately directed in the short as well as the long term? Is it a good or bad idea for the parent also to take on the role of the teacher, and does doing so further complicate the parent-child relationship, both at that time and later on? Does the parent/teacher enhance learning or does the child do better with someone more neutral than a parent as the tutor? If the parent is not the teacher, how should the role be defined? Who makes the career-tracking decision, and how and when? What are alternative pathways, if any, toward the same ultimate goal?

How does one deal with the prodigy's developing self-identity, as well as their peers? Are there ways around the single identity of the child with his talent so that the child has an identity all his own? In the videotape, Yo-Yo Ma has referred with humor but also real poignancy to his "quest for normalcy." How can this be achieved and guarded? How does one deal with the isolation of the talented musician which is, in actuality, a lifetime problem but especially crucial in youth. In using this interview to learn more about the successful resolution and transformation from successful prodigy to successful adult, musically and otherwise, we see that this young man from about fifteen-eighteen was able to go through some very normal adolescent growth to attain not only a degree of emotional and physical independence but to take on his music as his own rather than his father/teacher's. Again, looking at Ma, what about the long term strictly physical risks or benefits of intense training from childhood? Is there a better conditioning for a lifetime of playing an instrument when the pathways and physical skills of handling an instrument are developed as a child? (It has always been a given that a successful career of virtuosic proportions, especially the violin, depends upon a start on the instrument before age ten.) If we do good prospective studies, measuring more data than the success or failure of a concert career, will we find that the tissues, rather than being protected, show significantly increased premature wear and tear? Is it a right or an obligation to protect the prodigy from injuries on the field of play, or are those protecting adults inflicting more serious damage to the physical development and the happiness of the talented child? And competitions — are they anti-educational and destructive, or are they predictive of or essential to a successful career?

The questions raised are unending, and, no doubt, there may be no universally applicable solutions. It will certainly require a multidisciplinary approach to unravel them. I am happy to report that many of the major conservatories are responding to these questions and recognizing their broader responsibilities to their students. Whether it be in achieving increased knowledge of neural pathways and the integration of musical learning, or clinical interests in understanding the challenge of the instruments and the pitfalls that may get our patient into trouble, the level and breadth of interest in these areas assure advances in the near future.

Alice G. Brandfonbrener

Young Narcissus at the Music Stand

Developmental Perspectives from Embarrassment to Exhibitionism

Kyle D. Pruett
Child Study Unit
Yale University

A powerful dilemma faced by the developing young musician that sets him apart from his creative colleagues in the graphic or verbal arts is that he must do his most intimate creating in the least intimate of places: public. The public performance life of the talented musician usually is long and checkered, typically beginning well before most children are accustomed to occupying center stage. This communication is based on an ongoing observational study of musical giftedness which examines performance stress, anxiety, exhilaration, and exhibitionism as it is being actively experienced by talented musicians at different developmental levels. As described previously,[1] the way children experience their own giftedness is quite different from the way the adults around them experience it; this is equally true for performance stress and exhilaration.

An anecdote illustrates many of the problems faced by the gifted young performer. I recently was engaged to sing the role of the Abbot in Benjamin Britten's intriguing liturgical opera, *The Prodigal Son*. Britten scored this opera for a traveling band of monks (adult roles and boy sopranos or trebles) who perform in the manner of a medieval miracle play. The cast is small, so several parts are portrayed and sung by each cast member.

Jonathan, the oldest and head boy chorister, was an exceptionally gifted twelve-year-old musician and performer. We had all enjoyed enormously preparing this elegant, complex piece. Opening night, all warmed up, made up, nerved up, and costumed; the ten-minute call came to the cast for places. The five-minute call came, and it was noted with some alarm that Jonathan was not among those of us assembled in the wings. A frantic search found him locked in the undercroft bathroom, sobbing; he was not coming out. The butterflies were swarming and he had vomited. Benjamin Britten would not hear from him tonight. As a child psychiatrist (by *avocation* in this setting), I was called upon for a quick piece of crisis intervention and brief, *very* brief (as it was not two minutes to curtain) therapy. Through the locked bathroom door, Jonathan and I made a pact that we would share the nervous burden. He was not alone. We were all nervous; we were *supposed* to be. But we weren't all going to be this nervous all night. To reassure him, we arranged a special sign, known only to the two of us, which we would give one another during the first act to indicate when the butterflies had dispersed. A few simple blocking changes were arranged, and the bathroom door opened. Needless to say, things went well; his solo was unusually beautiful. When I gave the private signal, I got back only an elated smile. He had met the butterflies, and they were his, at least on this night. Jonathan had moved with a quickness not uncharacteristic of his age from a moderately severe case of pre-performance anxiety all the way through to a confident exhilaration in his music making.

Jonathan's experience focuses our attention on the problems faced by many gifted children There is a vast difference between playing or singing music, and publicly performing music. What seemed to upset Jonathan was that there were people out there who were going to be watching *him* while in the act of making *his* music. While singing or playing or even dancing alone may be very beautiful, even uniquely creative, the art, itself, dissipates quickly if other hearts do not attune.

This often painful dilemma makes the musician first ignore, then fear, then face and come to appreciate, if not embrace, his audience. If he fails at the beginning of this process, like the tree falling in the woods which no one hears, it becomes a matter for philosophical debate whether or not his music exists, let alone whether it qualifies as music. One way or another, high musical giftedness and talent must display itself for others to hear and see. Whether the young musician finds center stage by himself or is placed there by teacher, parent or agent, few find it a very homey place.

So what are the emotions which mediate the experience of making art in public? How do children of differing ages approach the music stand? How do they experience it? What do they understand about its rules and conventions? Jonathan was the best, the oldest, the most experienced of the choristers, but he was also the most nervous. Does center stage become more comfortable with age? Does the difference between the making of music for oneself and making it for others remain the same over the life cycle? I have chosen to look to the children for answers because somehow I trust grownups a little less. As those of us in child psychiatry and child development seem doomed to learn and relearn, an accurate view of childhood experience simply does not come by talking to grown-ups about their memories. Instead, I've attempted to follow *in situ* how the musically talented child experiences his own giftedness as it is developing. It is a complex question that requires that our data be rooted firmly in developmental psychology. Therein, we discover that what children think of their giftedness often is quite different from what grown-ups may think of it.

Most of what we *feel* we know about growing up gifted comes to us from autobiographical reflections on lives and childhoods by adults who, as grown-ups, turned out to be musical successes. This makes for intriguing, often enjoyable, psychohistorical reading. But the beginning of the unconscious, failed and fulfilled wishes, the notorious vagaries of mid-life memory, and the subsequent omissions of events and facts all combine to portray a *remembered* life. This remembered life is not the actual story of the evolution of a child's giftedness.

There are so few longitudinal studies of musical giftedness because of the difficulty of early identification of such children. By the time such giftedness is obvious, much of the child's early, critical developmental history is long since expired and may be well beyond the memory, even of his parents.

Because of my long-standing involvement in the musical community where I live (primarily, though not exclusively as a performer), I have had the opportunity to be involved with a number of performing musician children and their families over an extended period of time, usually *not* as a clinician but as a fellow performer, family friend, or occasional confidant. Our work together has spanned the operatic, small vocal ensemble, oratorical, and recital repertoire. This has permitted unique access across time to some 18 children who eventually have developed into the complex condition of being musically gifted and achieving.

I usually have encountered the vocal musicians around the age of eight or nine, and the instrumental musicians somewhat earlier. It is to several of these children who have gone on to regional and national prominence that we shall listen for answers to our questions. As adolescence is acknowledged to be the most critical gauntlet which musicianship must run, we shall hear from one pre- and one post-teen representative of the gifted.

But first a word about Narcissus. The image of the young Narcissus at the music stand — the confident, self-absorbed, possibly even grandiose young musician — is known to many who teach, treat, or watch young developing musicians. Yet we also know that public musical stage presence runs the gamut from painfully egotistical and exhibitionistic peacocks in full display, all the way to the exquisitely painful gaze-averting church mice. Are these mere individual variations on a theme, or is there some orderly developmental line which one tows according to ones age and experience?

The natural public comfort and exhibitionism of the primary grade musician is well known. What five- or six-year-old ever has come to the consulting room in search of beta blockers? Center stage is natural habitat for them. But as awareness of peer acceptance and criticism grows in the middle school years, so does anxiety about doing it right, and sometimes, even more important the closer one gets to adolescence, is *looking* as though you're doing it right. This new awareness can be immensely powerful and conflictual for the young musician. Privately, he may be feeling deeply in love with his music in a very vulnerable but driven way. Publicly he must be seen to be feeling cool, in total control, and invulnerable — both socially and musically — whether his medium is rock and roll or Italian baroque. Here is a conflict which makes heavy demands on the young personality's repertoire of defenses and coping strategies. Jean Bamberger[2] refers to this developmental dilemma as the musician's "mid-life crisis" when separate, familiar, expressive musical dimensions seem to float free of their underlying musical representations. The resulting less integrated but powerful intensity of drive to make music, for whatever reasons, forces the personality to come up with a strategy. Two major, vastly divergent paths frequently present themselves here. One is the highly idealized, narcissistic preoccupation with music and the musical life; the other is one of an identification with the important musical adults and peers, most of whom already are involved in the musical and personal life of the musician.

The first path is a dangerous passage, indeed. The Narcissus who spurned Echo's loving advances fell so deeply in love with his own reflected image that he pined away his life, burning with a love of himself, managing to attain his own mirrored loveliness ultimately by drowning in its reflections.

The danger for the young musician in choosing this path is the precarious reliance on the grandiose image of the self. Self-esteem becomes anchored to the possession of certain *qualities,* such as musical talent and musical success, rather than to the more sustaining authenticity of one's own feelings and perceptions. He becomes increasingly dependent on admiration and adulation. Obviously this path rarely is chosen consciously and often occurs as a progression along an already deeply rooted web of troubled early object relationships. The lucky adolescent experiences its tug only transiently, aided by

Kyle D. Pruett

supportive friends, parents and teachers to move onto the other path, that of *joining,* rather than trying to transcend the more ordinary, less deified musical life.

This second path helps the adolescent, through identification with his friends and cronies, work through the struggle over the ownership of his musical talent, i.e., his music ultimately is his to nurture or abandon and is neither a parental nor a public property. He discovers, for example, that he is not the first performing artist in history to struggle with performance anxiety. He even can admit to ambivalence about his music periodically without threatening his value as a human being. He can, like others before him, develop artistic autonomy without attacking the important love relationships in his life — a healthy narcissism, if you will.

With this paradigm of healthy versus unhealthy narcissism in mind, let's listen to the stories of two different, highly gifted, talented and achieving musicians describe their lives at the public music stand.

Ian is a bright, energetic, athletic, eleven-year-old blond who had garnered rave reviews for his vocal renderings of the music of Gian Carlo Menotti, specifically in the role of Amahl in the opera, *Amahl and the Night Visitors.* I first met him at the age of six when he was playing piano for a music school ensemble of eight- and nine-year-old string players. He was notably fearless during these early performances, giving evidence of a lust for public music making that seemed somewhat separate from his actual rendering of the music. He seemed typical of the young five- to eight-year-old talent whose natural exhibitionism and grandiosity gave him a zest for performance more related to the number of people watching than to the music being played.

Unable to confine his musical appetites to the keyboard, he became fascinated with other instruments, notably the trombone. Unfortunately for Ian, the slide was beyond the architecture of his still small frame.

In the meantime, his parents had divorced, ending a long, unhappy marriage, and his father moved to a nearby community. Ian eventually came to rest on choral music and joined a boys' choir at eight, an opportunity easily provided him by his musical family. Three years later, he, like Jonathan, was head chorister and, because of his voice's bell-like timbre and unwavering pitch, was in heavy demand across New England as a boy soprano soloist. Major metropolitan newspapers carried reviews of his performances,

Coping with Life on a Pedestal

and recording contracts were being discussed. What did this twelve-year-old think of the brouhaha?

Ian, in a casual chat after a performance, while inhaling a monstrous ice cream sundae: "It is so neat to get all this attention. But it really spoils you — the TV cameras, the photographers, watching people come into the theater, the microphones. But it doesn't last very long. You're famous for about two days each time. You feel so great when it's over and you didn't screw up the performance too bad. (long pause) Before this concert, I saw this kid riding down the street on a bicycle. And I thought, gee, he's *so* lucky, not a care in the world, and here I am so nervous I can hardly talk, not to mention sing."

"Nerves were a problem?" I asked. Ian: "God, yes! They didn't used to be. When I was little, I never got nervous. Now I do — all the time. I hear this little voice in my head saying, 'You're getting nervous.' "

"So what happens when you get nervous — when you hear that voice?" Ian: "My heart starts beating faster and faster. My throat gets really dry because I'm breathing fast — like my heart. I lose my saliva. But I can't drink too much water because I'd get even more nervous about being scared I'd have to pee and I couldn't."

"So where do the nerves come from?" Ian: "I think it comes from being watched by all those people. Somebody told me once *not* to look at the people, look at the exit signs or over their heads. But that's weird, 'cause you're out there singing *for* the people — you want them to like it — so why not look at them when you're trying to get something across to them? It's weird..."

What does he actually fear when he's out there singing a solo? Ian: "I get afraid of screwing up. That's the worst. Making a big whopper. Cracking on an important note, screwing up the words, missing an entrance. You know, when someone from the audience comes up afterward and says, 'Well, that was interesting.' " What else is he afraid of? Ian: "That I'll disappoint the director or my teacher or even my friends."

"How about yourself?" Ian: "What? Let *myself* down? How could I do that? Letting my friends down is the worst."

"Does anything make performing easier?" Ian: "Yeah, now I psyche myself up. I practice this little pep talk... 'O.K. I know this... I'm good at it... It's going to be great... Nobody can do it better than me.' I also think of my mom. She plays the piano, and she never looks nervous. She says she is; she says everybody is. But she never looks it."

It was clear from Ian's comments that he already had begun to employ a number of complex devices for coping with life on his pedestal commensurate with his developmental capacities. *First,* he could acknowledge the normality of his anxiety. *Second,* he could neutralize it intellectually through rationalizations; and, *third,* he could integrate it into his musicianship by identifying with his teachers, fellow performers, and family members. By and large Ian's mechanisms are quite age appropriate. Peer acceptance, adult approval (both parental and teacher), and avoidance of embarrassment still are the standards for musicianship at his age, not what the critics, Mozart, or the performer himself expect.)

Does Ian worry about the effects of all this attention? Ian: "Kind of. Too much will spoil you. It also bugs your friends. You can get ashamed of being popular. I love being the kid riding the bike while someone else worries. Just because you can sing or play an instrument well does not make you a better person or a smarter person. Besides, life isn't like that. Not really. [Ian paused for a moment, and I had the feeling he may have been thinking about his own life and its imperfections, specifically the divorce.] In life you won't always be on a pedestal. People don't always love you. Some people come up and say you're great. But there aren't many people you can really believe when they say that to you...your teacher, maybe, your really musical friends, and a few others. That's not very many. It's hard to trust what people say."

One can already hear Ian moving toward the more guarded adolescent position and away from the grandiosity of two or three years before with its more generous faith in the adult shepherds of his giftedness. Role models still are important, if simplified, but not for long. His optimism is slightly more realistic than grandiose, and he is getting better at dealing with frustration. Typical of his developmental level, Ian's wish to share his musical gift is genuine, if immature. Issues of even-handed control, adherence to rules, and organized group strivings are quite important to him. Concerns of self and group regard are prominent, and the capacity for self-control is well established. Exhilaration usually comes after, not during, the performance. In summary, Ian demonstrates broad, age-appropriate repertoires of coping strategies for the transient pedestal sitting.

Next in the chronology of human development comes the hormonal flood plain called adolescence. Ready or not, the talented musician now must deal with adolescence as well as music. It is hard to imagine a more incendiary mix.

Ben, a twenty-year-old competition-winning baritone, has, for the most part, successfully run the adolescent gauntlet and, as such, his experience of his own gift is now quite different from Ian's. I first encountered Ben at age eight as a stocky, dusty, red-cheeked, blond-haired drummer in a public school orchestra. The middle son of a working-class, white-collar family, Ben lives in an industrial New England town with his younger brother and twin older sisters. His mother teaches voice privately, and his father is a trades-man. When I first encountered Ben, he was simply "living" drums. He told me he could not wait to get home from school to play. "Nothing's better than my drums," he'd say. He was not studying at the time and played purely on instinct and native talent. When I next met Ben, he was beginning to experi-ment with his voice. His father had noted that Ben had a natural vibrato. Ben, however, did not like to sing for his parents at the time, preferring instead to play the drums "because they were louder."

Ben and I crossed paths again when he was fourteen years old and we were both in a production with a major operatic company. He had abandoned his drums and had "decided to make myself a singing life."

He began by telling me he had "a pretty amazing voice." His mother had become very supportive, having been won over by the strength of his com-mitment and his rapid accomplishments and successes. His father seemed to be receding in significance at this point in life because "We just get in lots of fights all the time."

Ben meanwhile had learned to keep his talent to himself much of the time. Many of his nonmusical friends "treated me like a 'weirdo' whenever I told them I was singing seriously. It was like I was stepping out of line — their line. It got pretty lonely."

My next contact with Ben came when he was eighteen. He recently had won a regional Young Artists competition and was on his way to study voice and music on a full scholarship, having decided not to go to college. I could not say he was an especially happy person, but I could say he was as in love with music as anyone I had encountered. Meanwhile, he also managed to repair a number of his socialization difficulties. He explained, "The way a musician *acts* has a lot to do with whether or not he is accepted by his less talented peers." He had learned to keep his gift to himself and learned how to pick the people with whom to share it. "Acting superior is just a way of

Kyle D. Pruett

dealing with feeling left out — *not smart"* He was busy singing three hours a day. "I think about singing all day long — even when I'm eating...I drink tea and don't have cream in my coffee. I constantly worry about clearing my throat and keeping my vocal chords clean and clear. I watch how loudly I talk in conversation."

At that time Ben was not just a musician — he was also a young adult — and his feelings about his music, his ownership of it, and the external world's value of him and his talent were influenced strongly by all the developmental dilemmas that make up the adolescent passage and subsequent quest for autonomy and self-sufficiency, emotionally and musically. Although it would have been easy to consider Ben a narcissistic, self-involved musician, I still was impressed by how important the audience's response was to his musical performance.

Phyllis Greenacre[3] speaks to this point in what she calls the artist's "love affair with the world":

> "It seems unlikely that the artistic performance or creative product is undertaken purely for the gratification of the self, but rather that there is always some fantasy of a collective audience or recipient, whether this is a real audience as for the stage, or the unseen audience of the writer or painter. The artistic product has rather universally the character of a love gift to be brought as near perfection as possible and to be presented with pride and misgiving." (p. 490)

Ben is now twenty and feels that he's headed for greatness, as do his teacher, parents, and some local patrons. Is he ready? He talked easily after a cast party. Ben: "The attention is getting easier to handle now. It's easy to handle if you can remember that it comes from luck *and* deservedness; luck, because there are plenty of good singers out there, but they haven't had the opportunity yet to sing for Sherrill Milnes — deservedness, because I've worked my ass off for years already!" As though he sounded a little strident on this point, even to himself, he added... "You've got to pump yourself up as a singer. There's nothing to hide behind out there. You're totally naked, no drums, no piano, no violin to hang onto. You've got to *be* larger than life in the way you do it, or what you want to communicate to the audience will never make it off the stage." He laughed. "But that's my New York talk. When I'm home I feel real different. I'm relaxed, no pressure, nice and easy. You really need a place and some time off from the New York stuff. It's so intense — it distorts the way the world looks to you."

How was he feeling about performing? Ben: "Well, I'm not that great with the audience yet. People who watch me think I'm off someplace mentally — some like it and some don't. I really love knowing an audience likes my music. I mean, *God*, why else would a person do it in public? But I make *myself* nervous. It's not the audience." (NB, listen to the difference now from what Ian has told us.) Ben: "I hate it when I don't do well. And there are a lot more things that can go wrong out there than can go right in a performance. I think the better a musician you are, the more nervous you get, because you know how much can go wrong and how great it is when it goes great. Less musical people don't know that, so they have more fun."

How do you manage performance nerves? Ben: "I don't like talking about nerves. I really believe in positive thinking and talking. I talk a lot to myself. I have to *hear* myself say good things before a performance backstage out loud, so I walk around muttering to myself. Everybody has nerves."

What are all those nerves about, do you think? Ben: "Screwing up something major — voice cracking, losing the words, making a big mistake." What's a big mistake? Ben: "Something that ruins the performance for the audience. If you can keep on going — get out of it somehow, and the audience isn't bothered, it's not a big one. The problem for me is controlling my feelings about screwing up so that I don't ruin the performance for me."

What are you doing to cope with the pressure to succeed and perform well? Ben: "My new teacher is helping me a lot. He's slowing me down — cutting back on the competitions and performing. He says I must cut my performing in half in order to keep singing all my life. I also do a lot of things for myself that aren't musical. I do aerobics, ride my bike 60 miles a week, go to a lot of movies, and hang out with nonmusical friends sometimes. Everything I do musically that matters is public, so I go to as many performances as I can afford. Sometimes just watching other people perform makes me nervous, because I know my time is coming. I'll be sitting in the audience and my knees are shaking — isn't that sick?"

Something that Ben did not tell about was his use of what I call the *pre-performance, self-effacement insurance plan*. I had watched him do it several times, and it is a familiar maneuver to all teachers of music. About two weeks before a recital or major public performance, the musician begins denigrating his performance, his musicianship, his program, or even his skill. It insures that there is a psychological escape hatch, a fail-safe mechanism which protects the performer's self-esteem *if* a major blooper occurs in the performance... "Well, I *knew* I wasn't ready. It is just one of those psychological sleights-of-hand that is born of our wish to master *all* the variables — all that is unpredictable, with godlike certainty. Ben preferred to believe, commensurate with his developmental capacities, that practice *does* make perfect — guaranteed.

Was it worth it yet to Ben — the experience, the lessons, the loneliness, the "missed life?" Ben: "Once it was. I was singing some Gershwin stuff for my friends in this little church where the acoustics were perfect. You know, a place that *fits* your voice just perfectly? My teacher played the piano, and I sounded better than I'd ever sounded in my life to me. I felt connected to every single person in the audience — even the ones I didn't know. But I was separate, too, up there with Gershwin, my teacher..I don't know... I just can't say it right."

Susan Langer's lovely quote gives Ben a supporting hand here. "The real power of music lies in the fact that it can be true to the life of feeling in a way that words cannot: Its significant forms have an *ambivalence* of content which words cannot."[4]

Before turning to some thoughts about how gifted children, both with and without our help, figure out how to cope with life on a pedestal, I would like to review briefly some conclusions from a previous study of mine on phenomena commonly found in gifted children's descriptions of their experience of their own talent

First, there is an internal pressure that resembles an aggressive drive to *make* music — to perform, to practice, to learn, to listen; to compose, decompose, and recompose musical forms and symbols. This may be a more predispositional factor and somewhat independent of a musical environment. Second, gifted children report at the time it is occurring the capacity to concentrate intensely on the musical experience to the exclusion of other stimuli, even of human contact. Third, the capacity to make music in a talented and gifted way often is seen by children as a love gift, most characteristically before the onset of adolescence. Fourth, these children seem to hear and feel something in music which they cannot articulate verbally and experience nowhere else. They often appear addicted to repeating it. Fifth, most gifted children articulate the costly negative aspects of owning the musical gift. Sixth, most talented children do not initially see themselves as especially valuable human beings. They are just doing what they need to do, i.e., when the E string breaks, you borrow the nearest fiddle — no big deal. The ensuing media or public attention is often quite surprising to them.

Seventh, a sense of the aesthetic in music begins to coalesce in these children around nine or ten years of age. The difference between what is artistic or beautiful in a thing and what is merely pleasing begins to haunt them and their creativity.

But in the end, owning a substantial musical gift is very different than nurturing it or developing it over a lifetime of public performance. Musical aptitude, combined with achievement itself probably has as little to do with public performance skill as writing poetry has to do with scripting television commercials. Instead, we see a developmental continuum that leads in the gifted child's experience from performing the way his or her teacher did (the Suzuki method is a paramount example here) all the way to performing the way he feels he *must* as an independent adult artist. Seeing that transition is like watching a virtuoso glass blower draw out his molten lump patiently, evenly balancing temperature and physical forces. In using this metaphor, I speak not of the fragile construction of the glass menagerie; the substantial, clear, durable luminescence of great musical talent is anything but fragile. It is sitting on the public pedestal that is precarious.

So what do children teach us about managing life at the music stand? What can or should we be doing as educators, thinkers, patrons, researchers, parents, and fellow music makers to nurture these coping strategies?

Three critically important things: first, encourage these children to think about their musical giftedness in terms of a calendar of the life cycle, not of seasons; second, arm them with the skills, both psychological and behavioral, to render them more durable in the crucible of public performance; third, sponsor their evolution into whole people, not just a few parallel slips of tissue strung atop a larynx, or a particularly skilled eye-ear-hand preparation. Let's look at these important conclusions in some detail.

First, prodigies endlessly fascinate us middle-aged musicians, researchers, and audiences for a multitude of complex reasons. Consequently, they are at some risk even in our empathic hands. We so want to finish or complete the fruition of our own musicianship, whether it be active performing or passive listening, and theirs is so facile — so ready. Yet, one of our most important jobs, since we know more about time than they do, is to help the young talent pace itself. Lifelong careers are the goal here, unlike basketball or football. John Gedo[5] reminds us that "Creative success tends to be extremely stimulating over long spans of time — probably more so than competitive or sexual triumphs, the effects of which tend to wear off relatively quickly. In order to avoid overstimulation, the individual must have at his disposal effective means to reduce tension."

So, resist willy-nilly competitions, performance over-exposure, marathon practicing, even when children want to play, as many of them do, until their fingers bleed. Children almost always have more time than they think.

Second, we can do much to prepare the child for the crucible that is public performance. But our techniques and advice must not simply be founded on building backbone, but rather on preserving the talented child's self-esteem. We can be guided by the self-esteem preserving concept of what Dan Stern[6] has called the "we position" of toddlerhood, as opposed to the "I position" of infancy. Lots of people are out there with the gifted child on stage — parents, teacher — all are part of a holding environment: a holding environment which traces its roots back to the healthy grandiosity of the second year of life in which the infant seems to feel his experiences are shared by *everyone*. That grandiosity provides the child with a sense of shared experience, a fundamental relatedness which preserves self-esteem even in the most adverse circumstances.

By talking with the musically talented about the people out there with them, we can help them begin to see that, first, the audience is not the enemy, and, second, Narcissus was not the best of role models. Nervousness in performance *can* be talked about and anticipated. This helps the child appreciate that he's involved in a commonality of experience. (There is little in life that is more reassuring than that.) And no matter how distinct his gift, it still belongs in the domain of shared human experience. We must help the talented young to take into public what they have mastered in private by acknowledging that what they are feeling about facing the unknown is about as normal a feeling as a human can have; we *can* teach them how to get on and off the stage, how to use relaxation techniques, what to *do* about the audience, or how to manage a media interview. We can talk with them about reviews and what they do and do not mean about their musicianship and their innate worth as human beings. We *can* prepare them for the inordinately powerful, though usually misleading experience, of listening to the tapes or watching the videos of their own performances. We can warn them that what they intend to do musically may not be what an audience either appreciates or understands best from their performance. Although the manifestations of performance and pre-performance stress are easily as varied as prodigious talent itself, I think it wise to presume that is part of the biology of public music making at the music stand. The glib or fluent young, gifted musician who chooses to deny its presence or power, risks some painful surprises sooner or later.

I've left till last what I personally feel is first in importance here — our responsibility to encourage the very gifted to avoid the sense of the asymmetric, misshapen, or unfinished life and self. Over and over again we hear from children that adults need to sponsor opportunities for them to have diverse experiences that permit them to reflect upon their *whole* life, such as the other arts and humanities outside of music, i.e., a fundamental, abiding reverence for one's entire imagination. The most enduring artistic achievements involve the whole person and his careful understanding and intimate expression of his imagination's light *and* dark components, not just his facile fingerings. The single, monocular focus to the exclusion of all else is a menacing promotion of prodigy to prima donna in the most destructive, pejorative sense.

References

1. Pruett. K.P. "A longitudinal study of the musical gift: clinical studies of the blessings and curses of precocious talent," *Medical Problems of Performing Artists,* 2(1):31-38, 1987.

2. Bamberger, J. "Cognitive aspects of development among musically gifted children," In Sternberg R. Davidson C. (eds): *Conceptions of Giftedness,* New York: Cambridge University Press, 1986.

3. Greenacre, P. "The childhood of the artist: Libidinal phase development and giftedness," In Greenacre P. (ed): *Emotional Growth*, Vol. 2. New York: International Universities Press, pp. 479-504, 1971.

4. Langer, L. *Philosophy in a New Key*, New York: Mentor Books, 1951.

5. Gedo, J. *Portraits of the Artist*, New York: Guilford Press, 1983.

6. Stern, D.S. *The Interpersonal World of the Infant,* New York: Basic Books, 1985.

Section VI

Current Concepts and Controversies in Music Education

The Nature and Description of Developmental and Stabilized Music Aptitudes:

Implications for Music Learning

Edwin E. Gordon
College of Music
Temple University

Just before the end of the last century, European psychologists became interested in the source of musicality and in how to describe it objectively and accurately.[1] Depending upon how the word "musicality" is defined, it may be said that either very much or very little has been learned over the past hundred years. If musicality is taken to mean music aptitude, we have learned very much. If musicality is taken to mean music achievement, we have learned very little.

Music aptitude is potential for learning. Music achievement is what has been learned. It is true that if one has a high level of music achievement, he will also have a high level of music aptitude. The reverse, however, is not true. If one has a low level of music achievement, he will not necessarily have a low level of music aptitude. Approximately fifty percent of the students in grades 4 through 12 who do not demonstrate formal achievement in music are in the upper twenty percent of the population at large in terms of music aptitude. Chronological age notwithstanding, they attain composite scores at or above the 80th percentile on the *Musical Aptitude Profile*.[2] The percentage is even higher than fifty percent for children in kindergarten through grade 3, as determined by their composite scores on the *Primary Measures of Music Audiation*.[3]

Though the distinction between music aptitude and music achievement has been made, one may still be unsure of what music aptitude is. Try to recall an experience which you have probably had more than once. You have just attended a recital. You were especially interested in the performance of two students. Both students had studied with the same teacher for the same length of time. They appeared to be performing at a similar level of music achievement in terms of technical skill on the same instrument. They performed compositions of a similar level of difficulty. There were comparable technical errors and lapses of memory in both performances. Yet you were of the opinion that one student might profit musically very much by continuing to take lessons and that the other student might profit only very little by so doing. How did you come to that conclusion? Though you probably still cannot describe precisely what music aptitude is, your thoughts were based either consciously or unconsciously upon what you considered to be the comparative music aptitudes of the two students.

There is little to suggest that the early European music psychologists thought in such terms. I'm not sure that the concept of music aptitude existed or that there was a word to represent it. Musicality was unabashedly described as music achievement. For example, Revesz said that the abilities to recognize chords and intervals and to transpose, improvise, and compose music are the bases of musicality.[4] Stumpf asserted that "perfect pitch" is the basis of musicality.[5]

It was Carl E. Seashore, an American, who defined music aptitude and music achievement as being different from each other, and who emphasized the importance of music aptitude. For him, the words "musicality," "ability," and "talent" were ambiguous. Yet Seashore wrote and published the first standardized group test battery of music aptitude in 1919, and called it the *Seashore Measures of Musical Talent*.[6] Five subtests were included in the battery: *Sense of Pitch, Sense of Time, Sense of Consonance, Intensity Discrimination*, and *Tonal Memory*. A sixth subtest, *Sense of Rhythm*, was added in 1925, and the *Sense of Consonance* subtest was replaced by the *Sense of Timbre* subtest in 1939. The content of the subtests is not of great importance to the purpose of this paper. What may be of interest, however, is that although the *Sense of Consonance* subtest was a preference measure, the *Sense of Timbre* was not.

What is significant to the issue at hand is the conclusion that Seashore drew as a result of being influenced by the European psychologists. His conclusion seemed to be supported by the results derived in the controlled research in which his subtests were used. It had to do with what became known in the literature as the "nature-nurture" issue. Persons who took the nature position believed that music aptitude is innate. Persons who took the nurture position believed that music aptitude is based on environment. There seemed to be no middle ground.

Seashore placed himself on the nature side of the disagreement primarily because of the research findings of Haecker and Ziehen,[7] Koch and Kjoen,[8] and Feis[9] in Europe, and of Stanton[10] in the United States. Through the use of interview and questionnaire techniques, the Europeans concluded that 1) if both parents are "musical" their children will very likely be "musical," 2) if only one parent of the two is "musical" the children will probably be "musical," and 3) if neither parent is "musical" the children will have less "musicality" than the parents. In the United States, Stanton[11] came to a similar conclusion as a result of working with eighty-five members of six families in each of which at least one member was a professional musician. Their higher scores on the *Seashore Measures of Musical Talent* when compared with those of individuals from families who achieved less in music give rise to the supposition that innate potential, rather than environmental influences, is the basis of music aptitude.

Had Seashore lived long enough to be able to read Amram Scheinfeld's book[12] in 1956, he probably would have been thoroughly convinced of the validity of his own position. Scheinfeld investigated the backgrounds of thirty-six well-known instrumental musicians and thirty-six renowned vocalists. For the former group it was estimated that seventeen mothers, twenty-nine fathers and about one-third of the children had attained high levels of music achievement. For the latter group, thirty-four mothers, thirteen fathers, and more than half of the children had attained high levels of music achievement. Although the implication of Scheinfeld's work is that music aptitude is innate, the results are questionable. Was it possible that simply sharing an environment and working with one or more fine musicians would allow one to achieve high levels of music achievement? Moreover, there are many exceptions to the rule in Scheinfeld's study. For example, the parents of Toscanini, Rubinstein, and Schnabel were found to be, by definition, untalented. Also, the offspring of some of the renowned musicians were found to be untalented.

Embroiled as they were in the nature-nurture issue, researchers were trapped into combining the nature theory with inheritance. That is, some researchers went beyond the nature-nurture issue to state that music aptitude is not only innate, but that it is inherited. For example, Seashore claimed that "the inheritance of music capacities seems to follow Mendelian principles."[13] That claim was not justified in research. To say that music aptitude is innate suggests no more than that a child is born with a certain level of music aptitude. That statement should carry no implication as to why a child was born with that level of potential. Though one may wish to believe that a child inherited his music potential from his parents or grandparents, such a conclusion is not warranted. It is possible, of course, that future research may indicate that music aptitude is recessive. Nonetheless, all that can be reasonably assumed at this time is that if a child is born with a high level of music aptitude, it is a matter of chance, and if a child is born with a low level of music aptitude, that also is a matter of chance. Whether a child will be born with a high level or low level of music aptitude cannot be predicted.

Some persons were persuaded to accept the idea that music aptitude is innate by Seashore's belief about the effect of practice and training on music aptitude. Seashore maintained that regardless of the amount of music training students received or the amount of time they practiced, their scores on the *Seashore Measures of Musical Talent* would not increase. Though the experimental designs of the studies were not always adequate, the consensus was that scores on the Seashore battery do improve with practice and training. Wyatt[14] was the most outspoken on the issue. Nonetheless, it was not clear whether the *Seashore Measures of Musical Talent* was a music achievement test, or whether music aptitude was a matter of nurture, or both.

Many of Seashore's adversaries in this country, Canada, and abroad believed that cultural influences are the bases of music aptitude. Heinlein, on the basis of his own research, criticized Seashore's experimental methodology and conclusions.[15] Mursell, primarily on philosophical bases, disagreed with Seashore's test validation procedures and the interpretation of data.[16] In general, it was difficult for the critics to understand how the discrimination of pitches less than a semitone apart, and particularly those which differ only nine cents (there are 100 cents in a semitone), has a significant relationship to music aptitude; how time discrimination contributes to an understanding of musical expression; or how timbre discrimination contributes to an understanding of tone quality. Also, they took the position that the ability to discriminate between pairs of tones in terms of pitch, time, loudness, and timbre are measures more of acoustical acuity than of music aptitudes, and that one's ability to draw conclusions about a series of unrelated pitches in tonal memory has little if any value for predicting how well one can be taught to recognize and identify a key center, let alone a resting tone.

In the main, those concerns led to what has been referred to as the Gestalt-atomistic controversy. The critics argued that music aptitude cannot be divided into component parts, because music aptitude does not have component parts; even if it does, the whole is different from the sum of its parts. Seashore, a steadfast atomist, maintained that indeed music aptitude comprises several different capacities, and in order to describe music aptitude, each of its component parts must be considered as being independent of every other. To emphasize his point, he changed the word "talent" to "talents" in the title of the 1939 revision of his test battery. The Gestaltists went on to say that music aptitude should be described in terms of one general score and not in terms of two or more scores which supposedly represent different aspects of music aptitude. Moreover, the critics believed that in order to measure music aptitude validly, the content of test items must consist of musical material, and the means of presenting the musical material must be a music instrument.

Though several music aptitude tests were published in the quarter-century following Seashore's initial publication, none made as great an impact as that of Herbert Wing's in England. Wing, a Gestaltist, whose test was described as "judicious musical" in contrast to Seashore's which was labeled as "mechanical acoustical," believed that music aptitude is a general factor, including general intelligence, which cannot be separated into parts. In his *Tests of Musical Ability and Appreciation,* Wing included three non-preference subtests[17] (constructed differently but measuring attributes similar to some found in the Seashore battery) and four preference subtests.[18] With regard to the preference components, Wing maintained that music aptitude is manifested by the ability to indicate a preference for a section of a piece of music performed as it was written by a master composer rather than for a section of a piece of music performed with unmusical alterations in rhythmic accents, harmonization, dynamics, and phrasing. Their disagreements notwithstanding, Wing, on the basis of his own research, agreed with Seashore that music aptitude is innate.

The *Musical Aptitude Profile* was published in 1965.[18] The manual and recordings are being revised this year. It is an eclectic test battery that combines so-called Gestalt and atomistic principles of music aptitude test construction. Four of the seven subtests included in the test are non-preference measures: *Melody, Harmony, Tempo,* and *Rhythm.* The three preference measures are *Phrasing, Balance,* and *Style.* All of the subtests consist of original short selections that are performed on stringed instruments. In addition to its extensive standardization, the test battery is unique also as a result of the number of pre-publication and post-publication longitudinal predictive validity studies associated with it.

The results of the research undertaken with the *Musical Aptitude Profile* from 1960 to 1975, particularly those derived from the three-year longitudinal predictive validity study, indicated that music aptitude is innate.[19]

That is, after three years of intensive music instruction, students maintained their relative positions on the pre-instructional and post-instructional administrations of the *Musical Aptitude Profile*. As expected, raw scores increased, but percentile ranks remained stable. The predictive validity coefficient and the corrected for attenuation stability coefficient for the composite scores were .75 and .93, respectively. Thus I found myself in agreement with Seashore and Wing in unequivocally supporting the role of nature over nurture. Moreover, given the diagnostic validities of the individual subtests and the low intercorrelations among them, it was clear that music aptitude is not only normally distributed, but multi-dimensional. Though not relevant to the topic at hand, it should be of interest to those of you who work with talented and gifted children that music aptitude and IQ share less than a 10 percent relationship.

The more reputable music aptitude tests were standardized for students nine years old and older, beginning in fourth grade. Though attempted many times, it did not seem possible to obtain a desirable level of reliability when the tests that were used with older students were administered to younger students. It was discovered in 1979, however, that with the use of different types of test content, stimuli, directions, and answer sheets, valid music aptitude tests could be developed for use with children five through eight years of age. It was found that only the tonal and rhythm dimensions should be measured, that the tonal dimension must be void of rhythm elements and the rhythm dimension must be void of tonal elements, and that a synthesizer should be used as the stimulus. Moreover, preference tests were found to be invalid with younger children. Those discoveries led to the publication of the *Primary Measures of Music Audiation* and the *Intermediate Measures of Music Audiation*.[20] Of the longitudinal predictive validity studies of the two tests, the three-year study is especially comprehensive.[21] The most important aspect of that study was the confirmation of an earlier discovery that the music aptitude of younger students fluctuates from five years of age, if not earlier or even prenatally, until nine years of age, depending upon quality of the music environment to which the student is exposed. The results of concurrent and construct validity studies offer corroborative and additional evidence on the matter.[22]

It is safe to say that both those who supported the nature theory and those who supported the nurture theory of music aptitude were correct. Research findings over the past few years indicate that music aptitude is a product of both nature and nurture. The potential with which a child is born and his early environmental experiences interact and contribute in unknown proportions to his music aptitude. Whether innate potential or environment is more important, or if they are of equal importance, is not known. Also, the role of inheritance in innate potential is still far from clear. Although part of music aptitude is innate, the level of music aptitude a child is born with still cannot be predicted on the basis of ancestry.

From direct and indirect results of research, both applied and observational, it appears that regardless of the level of music aptitude with which a child is born, he must have favorable early informal and formal experiences in music in order to maintain that level of potential. Further, unless he has favorable early informal and formal environmental experiences with music, that level of music aptitude will never be realized in music achievement. Regardless of how favorable a child's early informal and formal experiences in music are, his music aptitude will never reach a level higher than that with which he was born. Although environmental influences cannot raise the level of music aptitude with which a child was born, favorable environmental influences are necessary for a child to maintain the level of music aptitude with which he was born. Unless a child has favorable early informal and formal environmental experiences, the level of music aptitude with which he is born, be it high or low, will atrophy. The higher the level of music aptitude with which a child was born, the more and the more varied the informal experiences are required for him to maintain that level. The lower the level of music aptitude with which a child was born, the fewer early informal and formal experiences are required for him to maintain that level.

Because the level of music aptitude a child has at birth will change according to the quality of the early informal and formal music experiences he has, the music aptitude of children up to nine years of age is called developmental music aptitude. Music aptitude does not continue to develop, either positively or negatively, after a child is approximately nine years of age. The music aptitude of students nine years of age and older is called stabilized music aptitude.

The level of developmental music aptitude a student has acquired at age nine becomes stabilized and remains relatively the same throughout his life. That should not be interpreted to mean that after age nine a person cannot successfully be taught music. What it does mean is that he can be expected to reach in music achievement throughout his life a level no higher than that at which his potential to achieve has stabilized. He can reach at any time during his life a level of music achievement as high as that at which his potential to achieve has stabilized. Unfortunately, it seems that many of us have not developed our music aptitude to its highest possible level by age nine. Moreover, none of us achieve in music as much as our level of stabilized music aptitude would allow.

It must be emphasized that early informal and formal instruction in music, particularly from birth to age nine, is of greater consequence than formal instruction in music after age nine. The more appropriate early informal experiences and formal instruction in music are, the higher the level at which a student's music aptitude will stabilize. Possibly of even greater importance is that the younger a child is when he begins to receive appropriate early informal and formal instruction, the more he can profit from such instruction and the higher the level at which his music aptitude will eventually stabilize. A child can profit from appropriate informal and formal music instruction very much more at age five than at age six, more at age six than at age seven, and very little more at age seven than at age eight. The implications are, at the very least, compelling.

Footnotes

1. Carl Stumpf, *Die Anfänger der Musik* (Leipzig: Barth, 1911; Trans. H. Pear, "The Classification of Observers as 'Musical' and 'Unmusical', *British Journal of Psychology*, 4 (1911), pp. 89-94; Géza Révész, trans. by G.I.C. de Courcy, *Introduction to the Psychology of Music* (Norman: University of Oklahoma Press, 1953); Hans Rupp, "Über die Prufung musikalischer Fähigkeiten," *Zeitschrift für experimentelle und angewandt Psychologie*, 9 (1919), pp. 1-76; JA Mjøen and F. Mjøen, "Die Bedeutung der Tonhohenunterschiedsempfindlichkeit für die Musikalität und ihr Verhalten bei der Vererbung," *Hereditas*, 7 (1926), pp. 161-188; V. Haecker and T. Ziehen, "Betrag zur Lehre von der Vererbung und Analyse der zeichnerischen und mathematischen Begabung insbesondere mit Bezug auf die Korrelation zur musikalischen Begabung," *Zeitschrift für Psychologie und Physiologie der Sinnesorgane*, 79 (1930), pp. 1-45; Hans Koch and Fridjof Mjøen, "Die Erblichkeit der Musikalität," *Zeitschrift für Psychologie und Psysiologie der Sinnesorgane*, 80 (1931), pp. 136-140; Oswald Feis, *Studien über die Genealogie und Psychologie der Musiker* (Wiesbaden: J.F. Bergman, 1910) and Heinrich Schüssler, "Das unmusikalische Kind," *Zeitschrift für angewandte Psychologie*, 11 (1916), pp. 136-166.

2. Edwin Gordon, "A Comparison of the Performance of Culturally Disadvantaged Students with that of Culturally Heterogeneous Students on the Musical Aptitude Profile," *Psychology in the Schools*, 15 (1967), p. 260-268.

3. Edwin E. Gordon, "Developmental Music Aptitude as Measured by the Primary Measures of Music Audiation," *Psychology of Music,* 7 (1979), pp. 42-49; Edwin E. Gordon, "Developmental Music Aptitudes Among Inner-City Primary Grade Children," *Council for Research in Music Education,* 63 (1980), pp. 25-30; and Edwin E. Gordon, "The Assessment of Music Aptitudes of Very Young Children," *Gifted Child Quarterly,* 24 (1980), pp, 107-111.

4. Géza Révész, *The Psychology of a Music Prodigy* (New York: Harcourt Brace, 1925).

5. Carl Stumpf, "Akustische Versuche mit Pepito Areola," *Zeitschrift für Experimentelle und angewandte Psychologie,* 2 (1909), pp. 1-11.

6. Carl E. Seashore, *Seashore Measures of Musical Talent* (New York: Columbia Phonograph Company, 1919).

7. V. Haecker and T. Ziehen, "Beitrag zur Lehre von der Vererbung und Analyse der zeichnerischen und mathematischen Begabung insbesondere mit Bezug auf die Korrelation zur musikalischen Begabun," *Zeitschrift für Psychologie und Physiologie der Sinnesorgnane,* 79 (1930), pp. 1-45.

8. Hans Koch and Fridjof Mjøen, "Die Erblichkeit der Musikalität," *Zeitschrift für Psychologie und Physiologie der Sinnesorgane,* 80 (1931), pp. 136-140.

9. Oswald Feis, *Studien über die Genealogie und Psychologie der Musiker* (Wiesbaden: J.F. Bergman, 1910).

10. Hazel Stanton and Wihelmine Koerth, *Musical Capacities Measures in Adults Repeated After Musical Education* (Iowa City: University of Iowa Studies, Series on Aims and Progress of Research, No. 42, 1932).

11. Hazel Stanton, "The Inheritance of Specific Musical Capacities," *Psychological Monographs,* 31 (1922), pp. 157-204.

12. Amram Schienfeld, *The New Heredity and You* (London: Chatto and Windus, 1956).

13. Carl E. Seashore, *Psychology of Music* (New York, McGraw Hill, 1938).

14. Ruth Wyatt, "The Improvability of Pitch Discrimination," *Psychological Monographs,* 58 (1945), pp. 1-58.

15. Christian Paul Heinlein, "An Experimental Study of the Seashore Consonance Test," *Journal of Experimental Psychology*, 8 (1928), pp. 408-433 and Christian Paul Heinlein, "A Brief Discussion of the Nature and Function of Melodic Configuration in Tonal Memory with Critical Reference to the Seashore Tonal Memory Test," *Pedagogical Seminary and Journal of Genetic Psychology*, 35, (1928), pp. 45-61.

16. James L. Mursell, "Measuring Musical Ability and Achievement: A Study of Correlations of Seashore Test Scores and Other Variables," *Journal of Educational Research*, 25 (1932), pp. 116-126 and James L. Mursell, *The Psychology of Music* (New York: W. W. Norton, 1937).

17. Herbert D. Wing, *Tests of Musical Ability and Appreciation* (Cambridge, England: University Press, 1971.

18. Edwin Gordon, *Musical Aptitude Profile* (Boston: Houghton Mifflin, 1965).

19. Edwin Gordon, *A Three-Year Longitudinal Predictive Validity Study of the Musical Aptitude Profile* (Iowa City: The University of Iowa Press, 1967).

20. Edwin E. Gordon, *Primary Measures of Music Audiation* (Chicago: G.I.A., 1979) and Edwin E. Gordon, *Intermediate Measures of Music Audiation* (Chicago: G.I. A., 1982).

21. Edwin E. Gordon, *The Manifestation of Developmental Music Aptitude in the Audiation of 'Same' and 'Different' as Sound in Music* (Chicago: G.I.A., 1981).

22. Edwin E. Gordon, "Developmental Music Aptitude as Measured by the Primary Measures of Music Audiation," *Psychology of Music*, 7 (1797), pp. 42-49; Edwin E. Gordon, "Developmental Music Aptitudes Among Inner-City Primary Children," *Council for Research in Music Education*, 63 (1980), pp. 25-30; and Edwin E. Gordon, "The Assessment of Music Aptitudes of Very Young Children," *Gifted Child Quarterly*. 24, (1980), pp. 107-11.

Selected Bibliography

Gordon, Edwin. *Musical Aptitude Profile,* Boston: Houghton Mifflin, 1965.

Gordon, Edwin E. *A Three-Year Longitudinal Predictive Validity Study of the Musical Aptitude Profile*. Iowa City: The University of Iowa Press, 1967.

Gordon, Edwin. *The Psychology of Music Teaching*. Englewood Cliffs: Prentice Hall, 1971.

Gordon, Edwin. *Tonal and Rhythm Patterns: An Objective Analysis*. Albany: State University of New York Press, 1976.

Gordon, Edwin E. *Primary Measures of Music Audiation*. Chicago: G.I.A., 1979.

Gordon, Edwin E. *Intermediate Measures of Music Audiation*. Chicago: G.I.A., 1982.

Gordon, Edwin E. *The Manifestation of Developmental Music Aptitude in the Audiation of 'Same' and 'Different' as Sound in Music*. Chicago: G.I.A., 1981.

Gordon, Edwin E. *Learning Sequences in Music: Skill, Content, and Patterns*. Chicago: G.I.A., 1984.

Gordon, Edwin E. "A Factor Analysis of the Musical Aptitude Profile, the Primary Measures of Music Audiation, and the Intermediate Measures of Music Audiation." *Council for Research in Music Education*, 87 (1986), 17-25.

Gordon, Edwin. *Musikalische Begabung, Beschreibung, Messung und Beretung*. Ubersetzung aus dem Amerikanischen von Michael Roske. Mainz: Schott, 1986.

Gordon, Edwin E. *The Nature, Description, Measurement, and Evaluation of Music Aptitudes*. Chicago: G.I.A., 1987.

Hodges, Donald A., ed. *Handbook of Music Psychology*. Lawrence, Kansas: National Association of Music Therapy, 1980.

Radocy, Rodolf E. and J. David Boyle. *Psychological Foundations of Musical Behavior*. Springfield, Illinois: Charles C. Thomas, 1979.

Shuter-Dyson, Rosamund and Clive Gabriel. *The Psychology of Musical Ability*. London: Methuen, 1981.

Thorndike, Robert and Elizabeth Hagen. *Measurement and Evaluation in Psychology and Education*. New York: Wiley, 1977.

An American School of Music Education

Richard Colwell[1]
Department of Music and Secondary Education
University of Illinois

L ewis Carroll, the author of *Alice in Wonderland*, loved words and language; his spoofs on English entertain us today. Marilyn London[1] completed a doctoral dissertation in music in 1982 reminding us of the importance of interpreting both music and language in our efforts to understand meaning in music. Language and experience are the two important elements in this brief survey of whether there is an American school of music education.

Lewis Carroll created the mock turtle, who said to Alice: "Don't speak a word until I have finished." Following a long period of silence, Alice remarks "I don't see how he can ever finish if he doesn't begin." Once the mock turtle did begin, he and Alice compared their education. They quickly agreed that one could not have a quality education that did not contain extras. For Alice, her "extras" were music and French. (Lewis Carroll explains in the margin that it was customary to pay for these extras; sound familiar?) The mock turtle bettered Alice, having taken music, French, *and* washing.

Carroll offers other similarities with American education as one follows the conversation between Alice and the mock turtle. Classes in school are called lessons because they "lessen" from day to day. The subdisciplines of arithmetic were ambition, distribution, derision, and uglification. When queried, the turtle explains to Alice that beautification is often desired and when such an objective is attempted, the converse must be considered as well. In our survey of music education's research literature we found no reports of uglification although there was considerable emphasis on attaining beauty in art, music, and life.

Americans use folklore like *Adventure in Wonderland* and *Through the Looking Glass* to enrich education and our lives. We employ folklore in music education although it is often not so labeled. Because a practice or belief

---

1 Professor Colwell is currently at the University of Northern Colorado, Greeley.

arises out of folklore does not mean that it is invalid. There are many hidden truths conveyed through Carroll's frolic with the English language. So it is with music. Practices in music education have often not been developed and tested systematically, resulting in considerable professional folklore which today influences practice and colors our beliefs. The idea that learning proceeds best when the learning sequence of rote to note is followed is folklore. This bit of folklore is easy to believe because there is some logic to it — we all know at least one example of where it has been true, and folklore thrives in a profession where ideas are seldom challenged. We also have folklore on when to practice, how to memorize, and the merits of various counting systems. Language is important if the folklore of rote to note or other practices are to be challenged; definitions become crucial. What does one mean by "learning music"? Will one sight read more accurately, enjoy the music more, learn faster, or reach a higher level of understanding or discrimination? Many additional examples of "tradition" which Zero Mostel described for us in *Fiddler on the Roof* could be given. These include: if you can't sing it, you can't play it; moving to the beat is essential for understanding the structure of music; and thick lips are a disadvantage to trumpet players.

Expert opinion is often based on folklore. One might guess that teaching methods are more apt to be accepted when revealed by a distinguished member of the profession. In searching for answers to the question of whether there is an American school of music education, I found that much of my data were based on accepted folklore. For example, authorities often suggest that creativity and improvisation lie at the heart of arts education. In an informal poll, I found agreement that ability to improvise was a neat trick but little agreement that improvisation was essential. Recent research studies by LaRue,[2] Bryant,[3] and Bell[4] provide evidence that improvisation is not highly valued by high school students, band directors, instrumental music education instructors, parents, or school administrators.

Related to folklore, the use of logic as a way of knowing may not discriminate among those beliefs that should be retained and those that should be abandoned. Logic would inform us that the tremendous acceptance of the Suzuki string program in the United States has alleviated the problem of too few violinists.

Frank Wilson's question, "Is there an American School of Music Education?" intrigued me and I appreciated the opportunity to reread the research literature, to do computer searches that turned up nothing, and to reflect on practices in American schools that might indicate the presence or absence of an identifiable set of beliefs comparable to Orff, Kodaly, Dalcroze, and Suzuki. The absence of a name, a promoter, or media hype made the search perilous, yet, like the old story, I knew there had to be a horse around someplace because the quality of American music education was so pervasive.

American general music is the envy of the world. For more than 100 years a higher percentage of American students have received instruction in school music than have students in any other country in the world. Elective music is prized in the U.S. Large percentages of students perform for one or more years in high school ensembles. The study of group and private piano is considered to be good for children and maybe even helpful in their school music endeavors. A quick analysis indicates that although the product of these experiences is valued — in that students, parents, and administrators attend and appreciate electrifying concerts — it would appear that the process, not the product, is perceived as being the goal in most American schools. There is little concern for grades, minimum standards, or these other characteristics appendant to subjects that are prized for what is learned. It's a bit comparable to the religious dictum that it is the journey that counts.

Despite the success of music education in the United States, many American music educators have been willing to abandon their traditional general music programs for music programs that were developed in elitist cultures or in cultures that have not made major contributions to civilization. Also ideas stemming from educational systems that are undistinguished for their creativity or the excellence of their graduates have been unquestioningly adopted. Can one subject, in this case music, be plucked from an educational system or a culture with any success? Can one select a program out of context? Do we want our graduates to be connoisseurs of folk tunes?

American music and American musicians are the dominant force in today's world culture, rivaled only by British musicians, but is anyone exporting or touting British music education programs?

Initially I admonished you on the importance of language; thus, I find that defining American music education is the only acceptable way to begin. I can't do that, so I'm forced to proceed in unacceptable ways. The research on teaching practices should have been helpful; the research on objectives was. Research in music is not unlike that in medicine. Progress is not made solely through the study of sick people. Chemistry, microbiology, genetics, and other subjects have really helped in advancing the cause of medicine. So it is in music education. I discovered the core of American music education through research in philosophical foundations.

American music education is a way of thinking — classroom practices, activities, experiences, and standards have been accepted that fit a philosophy of music. I have to depend on language and describe the goals in philosophical terms and ask that you reflect on your own experience in school music including early childhood to understand the unity of this American approach.

What teaching practices are uniquely American? Not many. One prized objective is the ability to read music. Possessing that skill allows one to perform music independently. An important American contribution to reading was the use of shape notes. Never mind that the method is not in common usage, some insights into what is American music education might still be gained. Shape notes appear to have been the concern of only a few music education researchers and their concern was a fascination for a technique that worked rather than any serious study of pedagogy. In 1969 Jim O'-Brien[5], using materials from Aikens' *Christian Minstrel* of about 1846, compared two classes of intermediate level students. As measured by the Hammer Sight Singing Test, both groups were successful readers at the end of seven months of instruction. As the control group was taught with traditional notation, the research finding provides evidence that music reading can be taught as well with shape notes as with traditional notation. More extensive ethnographic studies of shape notes have been conducted in musicology. Doris Dyen's, *The Role of Shape Note Singing in the Musical Culture of Black Communities in Southeast Alabama,*[6] is typical of this genre. Ms. Dyen investigated the four shape note system that was used by blacks in this corner of Alabama, although she also provides interesting data on the more common seven note systems that are found in most Sacred Harp publications. Investigating shape notes, however, does not seem to be profitable for identifying a formal educational system. Lining out and shape notes are a more systematic method than oral transmission of music; in the U.S. both techniques were used informally and usually outside the school system. School music utilized sacred or art music with traditional notation while American folk songs, with their descriptive verses, flourished in pubs, in the field, and community gathering places that profited from shape notes. What I want you to remember is the kind of music that was transmitted and the impact this type of music had upon performer and participant-listener.

A second practice that is uniquely American is the use of jazz. The argument for its influence is weak in that jazz is not a major component of music education. Also, finding jazz in a community does not mean that jazz has been successfully taught in that locale. Where there is systematic study of jazz, it is of recent origin and usually limited to high school and colleges.

Jazz has been more extensively researched than shape notes, although the preponderance of research studies are analyses of individuals or groups that have been successful in that genre. Only on occasion have there been successful investigative attempts to teach those characteristics that have been identified as common to successful jazz musicians. Quality research studies would include Wilmot Fraser's thesis on "Jazzology: A Study of the Tradition in Which Jazz Musicians Learn to Improvise,"[7] and William Carlson's "A Procedure for Teaching Jazz Improvisation Based on an Analysis of the Performance Practice of Three Major Jazz Trumpet Players: Louis Armstrong, Dizzy Gillespie, and Miles Davis."[8] Many of these quality studies, including that of Fraser, were completed in the department of folklore and folk life, not music. Much of what we know about jazz is certainly folklore. The molting stages that have been identified for jazzers include: attraction to music; emulation of models; and refinement and self actualization (sometimes called individual stylistic development). Note a commonality, however: the language used to describe music by those who read shape notes is imprecise; the focus is on the emotional component. The language of jazz musicians is also nonverbal. There is some match with the objectives for education espoused by those of liberal persuasion: self actualization, stylistic development, and the search for self expression. These objectives have been vague and often assumed a mystical character.

The performance and appreciation of jazz approximates a religious attitude. The true believer can perceive a commonality among an inspired human life, a valuing and appreciation for one's emotions, and the experiencing of jazz. Analyzing the jazz experience reveals the role of gestalt psychology in understanding that experience. Rhythm is the organizational principle in the Gestalt, and for the jazz aficionado there is a perceived relationship between physical movement and human creativity. Can you imagine an inspired solo being rendered by a jazz trumpet player without envisioning accompanying movement? Jazz is not an individual sport; great jazzers are aided by performing with equally talented cohorts. To the jazz buff, there is a compelling belief that the human group is the fundamental human social institution, an institution that reaches one of its peaks with the performance of great jazz music. To know jazz is to appreciate the physical, social, technical, and artistic aspects that are a part of successful jazz music.

The jazz musician appreciates the importance of high degrees of skill and it is this skill coupled with technical expertise in the genre that enables one to be fully effective in communicating human self expression. Through learning, the student recognizes the importance of self expression and this respect for human expression is handed down through the study of and with exemplary individuals who are worthy of emulation. Language remains imprecise because philosophy is expressed in action and symbolic music rather than through words.

Jazz may be trial and error but even the errors are expressive of human feeling. The value of jazz music comes from a belief that in the interaction of musical and human ideas, those ideals and symbols which are best organized, most unique, and authentically expressive of human feeling will eventually prevail, and that universal human understanding may be achieved through organized free self expression of ideas around universally common themes. Compare these ideas with the ideas about general education by certain elements of American society and one gains understanding.

A quick look at the research interests of music educators in jazz is informative. Joseph Briscuso[9] found some relationship with scores on the sensitivity section of Gordon's *Musical Aptitude Profile* and one's ability to improvise, but not with the total test score. Robert Hores[10] found no relationship even with the sensitivity test subscores. He also discerned that aural instruction was no better than visual instruction in teaching jazz improvisation. Another pedagogical study[11] found that instruction aided one to improvise but that participation in a jazz ensemble did not! Research in creativity is closely related with these results, also indicating a gap between the use of and learning of creative experience with achievement in music education classes. Wayne Gorder found the constructs of creativity to be unrelated to musical training and musical experience.[12] Studying fifth grade students, Douglas Freundlich[13] found that ability to use notation was not a critical skill for these students. Students were able to develop musical ideas, at least those useful in a short phrase, even though his two subjects had not become proficient with music notation. Teacher evaluation of musical growth is not affected by creative experiences and the accomplishment of creative exercises does not seem to impact upon one's attitude toward music.

If the way technique is taught is sufficient to define a school of music education, American music education is unique in its use of instructional devices advocated by behaviorists. Programed instruction, computer assisted instruction, Tap and Pitch Masters® and interactive video discs are promoted for their instructional efficiency. Some educators have used sound mixers and synthesizers of many shapes and sizes in their search for improved education.

Despite a growing body of research, this reviewer could not identify a coherent thread that unifies the activities behind the use of technology in music education. There seems to be no theory of instruction and no effort is being made to investigate developmental characteristics of students concurrent with the improvement of software and hardware. Most of the research is based upon a linear organization of ideas. Extant materials and ideas are cast in a new format. Branching programs allow the student to skip ahead or back but the material is primarily a linear organization of extant materials. Computers have made instructional material more accessible but some of the material is dead on arrival. The fascination of the developers has been and continues to be with the hardware, and that hardware is truly amazing. When technology has been used in music education research, the results indicate achievement nearly equal to that attained with traditional approaches but with an enormous savings of teacher time plus the advantages of individualized pacing of instruction. At this point, however, there seem to be too few unique characteristics for technologically inspired instruction to constitute an American school.

Learning theory is a bit American and a fifth possible unifier. The body of systematic research in music education provides few clues about the fundamentals of American music education. Investigators have focused on describing the process of musical development. We have many one-shot conclusions that reveal that instrumentalists do not use patterns in learning notation,[15] that children of eight and nine do not connect aural and visual patterns,[16] that there is no difference in reading achievement whether patterns are learned in isolation or in context,[17] that individual grade levels make little difference,[18] and that use of the Orff method does not facilitate reading.[19]

Following the lead of Marilyn Zimmerman, music education researchers were intrigued with the existence of conservation and the impact of training upon a child's ability to conserve. Ronald Larsen,[20] Thomas Ashbaugh,[21] Stephen Schultz,[22] Herbert Kress,[23] and Noel Gantly[24] are among those, but little clarity is provided by the findings as each study reports a different revelation. One of the more clever studies is that of Robert Cutietta[25] who identified listening strategies employed by eleven to sixteen-year-old students. He found that students tend to focus on the properties or elements of the music rather than the type or style. Timbre, beat, and tempo were commonly recognized but broad stylistic classifications were often used incorrectly. Usable categories were predominantly opera, church, or rock.

A small corpus of materials was found; scholars such as Gretchen Beall[26] and Rosemary Watkins[27] investigated the applicability of Ausubel's advance organizer model for the acquisition of basic music concepts. Jackie Boswell[28] applied Bruner's theory of mental growth to the teaching of concepts in beginning instrumental music. Frank Abdoo[29] compared the effects of gestalt and associationist learning theories on beginning wind and percussion instrument students. Even Maslow's psychological concepts have been inspected for clues to determine whether self actualization might not occur through the singing of folk songs.[30] Max Camp[31] compared Mursell, Piaget, and Bruner in developing an instructional approach to piano study. Most of these studies are theoretical and although chock full of hypotheses, they point more to what might be done rather than what is being done.

More clues about American education are available in those few studies that have investigated phenomena that are closely related to learning theory. For example, James Major[32] was interested in the effect of rhythmic subdivision activity upon rhythmic performance skills of high school choral students. In establishing groups for his own study, it was necessary to investigate four theories of learning: instinctive theory, cognitive theory, physiological or muscle change theory, and motor theory. Folklore would have it that movement aids rhythmic performance following the British psychologist, Mainwaring, who advocated movement. Ruckmith[33, 34] found movement initially helpful but its usefulness quickly diminished. After the subject perceived the pattern, movement was unnecessary. Major's results confirmed the more cognitive or subdivision approach in improving rhythmic performance skills. Likewise, Archie Sharretts[35] provides a peek under the tent from the results of his investigation of rhythmic reading event using Gagne's psychology. Like Major, he sees that the music profession has been overly concerned with the motor-theory rhythm especially to the neglect of the intellectual aspects of the task. In line with his hypothesis that the processing of meter is a complex mental function and not a perceptual problem, Sharrett advocates the need to internalize metrical concepts. Using Gagne's learning psychology and selected works on notation reform, Sharrett develops a notational system based on meter hierarchy.

The three basic approaches to music reading pedagogy which might be identified are to present sound and symbol contiguously, move from sound to symbol, or move from symbol to sound.

Research and learning have received scant treatment from music education researchers but those who have been intrigued with the effectiveness of instruction have provided the key to looking at practices which might shed light on an American school of music education. Beginning band programs follow Gestalt psychology with the symbol and the behavior learned simultaneously. Many programs for music reading in the general music programs are based on the concept of prereading; the music must be learned first and then the music is matched to the symbol. Suzuki, Gordon, and Richards as well as others follow this line of logic. Most of the public school methodologies are sensorimotor — Dalcroze, Kodaly, Orff, Suzuki, Carabo, Cone, all seemingly following the ideas of Mursell who emphasized motor development. Gordon combines skill and perception but seems to ignore the cognitive or conceptual aspects of the task. The difficulty of internalizing intellectual skills may signal a caution light to many scholars in the profession. The ability to inspect practice and infer a set of beliefs may allow one to identify the elusive American school of music education.

My attempt to associate beliefs and practices requires the interpretation of language which, as Lewis Carroll knew, in itself creates a serious problem. Often words mean different things to different individuals. For example we might ask teachers whether they believed in accountability. An affirmative answer might indicate agreement with either the internal or external criteria. Internally one might believe in accountability, but to mean external criteria, one has to be willing to act. Music educators might agree that musical literacy or musical independence is critical (internal criteria) but not be willing to insure that each student be able to read pitch and rhythm patterns. Secondary school music teachers may have music discrimination as a stated goal of instruction but in practice the objective is to learn the notes and rhythms and be able to put the parts together into an acceptable sounding performance.

In an historical context, there was no discernible American school of music education from the time of Lowell Mason until the turn of the century. The influence of Pestalozzi and other European psychologists dominated instructional practices. As Americans became more self confident in industry, commerce, and politics, so it was in education. Here, the ideas of one individual have formed the basis of an American school of music education and that individual is John Dewey. Dewey competes only with Plato in his influence in shaping educational practice. But for all of his systematic exposition of ideas, he is still not the author of an educational system. The variety of his thought was such that music educators have sought his support in justifying opposing courses of action.

Although Dewey modified the purely liberal views on education, it is to liberal thought that one must first turn to understand the present status of American music education, our objectives, and our procedures. For the liberal there is to be a social regeneration, a moral vision of what life can be through education. Liberal philosophy requires that the schools be a part of this regeneration and if an objective of schooling is *not* to be able to correctly spell 1000 common words, new objectives have to be formulated. Objectives such as truth, justice, and progress were substituted. These words appeared to have universal meaning, but even they do not. The language of the liberal can be used to address substantive issues or it can be used in the most vapid and innocuous way. Caring, self-fulfillment, expanding consciousness, feelingful state are a few examples of putative school objectives.

A problem arises because the individual is the important social element for the liberal but the language that describes the general goals of education is devoid of any concrete referent; thus educational language becomes a description of process more than that of the finished product, e.g., the musically educated person.

For Dewey and others, educational jargon became one of metaphors: equality, freedom, self realization, critical consciousness, efficiency, and predictive control. What is of interest and intriguing to us is that the language of the educational liberal has some of the same qualities and meaning as that used by the jazz musician in describing meaning in his music and that used to describe the objective of music at the time of the shape notes.

Dewey's thinking and writing have been so pervasive that almost all educators who have written about the language of possibility have been liberals. School music was not omitted from this philosophical revolution. Music objectives also became focused on process, not product, and the process of music education contributed materially to the general goals of education. Metaphors created problems for organizing music instruction. Different interpretations changed the definition of the end result. These problems can be better understood when change is equated with progress, rationality with human betterment, and individualism with emancipation. In our society, there were educators who had separate agendas. For some, the rebellion or change was against the overly materialistic world. For others, the adoption of liberal ideas in education was a means of consciousness training. In the process, metaphors became the language of instruction, both process and product. Students were being asked to sing as if their hearts were full of love. Their tone quality was to be nasty. Even more colorful expressions have been reported. Evaluation became moot; who could tell whether the phrase was sung as if one's heart were breaking?

Liberal education philosophy was not limited to Dewey; most Americans became involved with teaching the individual. Skinner's emphasis on individualism is apparent through his research with rats and pigeons and his individual behaviorism. Carl Rogers is one almost of the opposite persuasion, and his search for the individual's inner quest for meaning identifies him as a liberal in his advocacy of personal discovery and wholeness. Rogers, of course, also believed that the schools were the most traditional, conservative, rigidly bureaucratic institutions of our time.

Despite problems, liberal ideas captured the learning theories and philosophers. These ideas in education grew out of John Stuart Mill's and John Locke's idea that change is inherently progressive. When change is equated with good, a major purpose of the school, and for all social institutions, is to work for change. Changes that lead to betterment of one's life are to come about through the process of the scientific method. With the individual as the basic social unit, the actions of the individual are evaluated. Success is determined by the degree of freedom afforded the individual and by his or her rational acts.

Understandably, the optimism of liberal thought is exciting and challenging even when it borders on the point of naivete. The role or lack of objectives is apparent when one observes how uncomfortable music educators are with words such as authority, discipline, and tradition. Rational thought replaces cultural authority. Values in life and in art are not the products of reason. Values are individualistic, arrived at through use of the scientific method by each individual. Educated judgment enables the individual to stand for truth, truth which also changes as progress is made. The creative man is a substitute for the good man, and there is not just one good life but many, none of which can be compared to the other. It would appear that in the purist liberal philosophy that frenzied work and frenzied play are acceptable in lieu of referent objectives and goals. Influenced by change, process becomes seminal, not product. A true liberal needs to ignore, to a certain extent, present good and that which is presently valued because even the exemplars must be changed. Is that why we're continually looking to import new methods? Right and wrong, good and bad are individual choices based on educated judgment rather than on enduring principles. Teachers do not interfere or attempt to change student judgments about good and bad or right and wrong as long as the student has done the best job he can in following the process of scientific thought and in weighing the alternatives. This paper is not the place to describe any faults in liberal thought although no process in that system exists for determining what music will be heard and what ignored. Obviously with such a question unanswered, different interpretations of what liberalism means for music have resulted.

Dewey believed more in society than in the individual but he found it impossible to argue against the basic liberal ideas, as only through liberalism is one able to examine the connection between education and the problems of society. Liberal thought integrates all social institutions in bringing about change for greater good. Dewey, however, could see that when the individual is encouraged and becomes the final authority, there is a crisis in command and in social purpose. This philosophy values individual good above the collective good. Thus with liberal thought, society can have an ecological crisis because the individual good and the collective or social good may operate at cross purposes. If carried too far, one could lose all sense of community life and a type of nihilism creeps into the thinking of the educated element of society. We are fortunate in having had Mr. Reagan as president because he provides such excellent examples of inconsistent thinking. Reagan's initial reaction to AIDS was that the problem was one of individuals not taking responsibility and the solution would be the responsibility of education, a nice liberal bit of reasoning. He veers away from liberalism, however, with abortions. The mother to be is not free to decide what is best for her in her situation through any rational scientific process.

Dewey successfully challenged the liberal idea that power and authority of an individual must be progressively strengthened either through skill development or consciousness raising. Dewey prompted the importance of collective action for social good even when the individual might be inconvenienced. He realized that ideas have consequences and he advocated that the test of any idea is the consequence that would likely result.

Dewey made other modifications in liberal thought that insured its survival. There were to be two purposes for continual change. The individual works to change society to make things better, and he also had to have change in order to discard old ways of thinking and acting that were preventing individuals from experiencing the growth that represented the promise of the modern world. Intelligence was an organizing factor within experience and therefore an important component in making decisions, but it could play no greater role. Major decisions that affected everyone were impossible for Dewey because for him there is no fixed body of knowledge that everyone has to master. Dewey would be happiest when, through self analysis, an individual finds himself and learns to like himself, but he would disapprove if one found God instead and learned to despise himself as a sinner. For Dewey, true happiness is to occur through accomplishment.

Art for Dewey is, however, individualistic. It grows out of one's own experiences. Art is not set apart from the world. With continuity in nature and in experience, art is part of nature and part of the human experience. The lived experience should be full of meaning and value and without art the lived experience will be less than desired. Aesthetics is the realization of the human spirit toward lived meaning and value with the aesthetic experience being both expressive and communicative. Dewey addressed the question of meaning in art and suggests that meaning results from the creative interaction of or participation in a social situation. Meaning is primarily creative and developmental; it operates in an intelligible context which makes sense to the individual. Thus meaning may depend upon certain biological and habitual structures, not to mention social and cultural conventions.

As Dewey influenced American education, James Mursell, speaking as a disciple of Dewey, influenced music education. I conclude that it was Mursell who established and continues to speak for the American School of Music Education. For Dewey the purpose of education was more education and the primary purpose of life was growth; so it was for Mursell. The process of musical growth was the purpose of music education and the purpose of that process was to enhance musical responsiveness. To Mursell all power and fulfillment in life come through growth. Musical skill was not of prime importance. The heart of music education was to perceive directly and become responsive and sensitive to the tonal and rhythm patterns of music. The language for the objectives of music education parallel the language that I have described for liberal education. Like Dewey, there was to be no accumulation of musical knowledge; education was continual growth that would enable the individual to realize his musical potential and develop into a musical person. Mursell was actually more of a pure liberal than Dewey. The avenues to musical growth were through musical awareness, musical initiative, musical discrimination, musical insight, and musical skill.

General music is the trunk of a liberal developmental program of music education. Here, one was to do music and not to learn about music as an end in itself. Standards and exemplars as well as one's past culture were relatively unimportant. Mursell would use music that the learner wished to sing or play and through that music show the student the expressive components. Mursell was opposed to learning notes in order to make an expressive performance; the learning of notes and the responsive performance were to go together somehow.

Stressing individualism, Mursell argued against mechanistic approaches because he did not believe that the order of difficulty is the same for all learners. Sequential learning was unfeasible as earlier lessons often did not remain firmly in the learner's mind. When one cannot work through externals to the essentials, there was no reason to explore known to unknown, simple to complex, or any other organizational system of learning music.

Music reading was to be treated as one special phase of a continuous sequence of musical growth. Children were little adults. Mursell believed, and I quote, "the youngest child should sing or play as the masters sing or play, compose as the masters compose, listen as the masters listen. The student should be doing on his level of capacity the selfsame things that they do in theirs."[36]

For Mursell there was no separation of cognitive, affective, and psychomotor development, as the human mind and personality always develop as a whole. Bearing in mind the expressive content of music, one should define a musical experience as arresting, impelling, revealing, fulfilling, and conscious. Accomplishment in music could be observed in the eyes of the children. His philosophy centered on more understanding, achieving deeper feeling or greater awareness with nothing determinant, and teaching nothing that had a referent. Accomplishment in skill development was designed primarily to heighten the musical experience.

The ideas of James Mursell were employed by Charles Leonhard and Robert House. These two individuals attempted to add identifiable behavioral and expressive objectives to the instructional process without losing the essence of the musical experience advocated by Mursell. Without objectives, Leonhard and House could find no basis for organizing a program of instruction, selecting experiences, selecting methods of teaching, establishing any administrative procedures, or evaluating the program. Systematic teacher education was also unfeasible without objectives. Apparently Mursell did not concern himself with methods courses; methods would constitute a body of content not compatible with sound liberal philosophy. In analyzing the purposes of education, Leonhard and House discerned that objectives needed to be further divided into levels because with vague language individuals talked past one another, applying broad ideas to diverse and specific situations in the arts. The suggested levels of Leonhard and House were broad social objectives, concrete social objectives, program objectives, and instructional objectives.

Leonhard and House believed that they could add clarity to music education by suggesting principles for music education. These principles were to come from scientific experimentation which Dewey and Mursell would have found acceptable, but they were also to come from expert opinion or were to be based on logical reasoning and personal and collective experience. Leonhard and House clearly moved too fast; their ideas could be accepted at the belief level but music educators were unwilling to put them into practice. Remember the two levels of acceptance? Music educators were unwilling to internalize. Leonhard and House were too conservative with their principles and with their levels of objectives for their philosophy to be compatible with the American school of music education. Other music educators have attempted to go even farther and suggest grade level objectives and grade level standards. These ideas also have been rejected by the profession.

There *is* an American school of music education, one built on folklore and the processes in liberal political-educational philosophy. Curriculum guides suggest little more than continued experiences, continued development of skills, further opportunities to develop discriminative powers and the addition of knowledge that might contribute to increased responsiveness to music. Awareness of contemporary and ethnic music is advocated along with alerting students to the occasional uglification of music. What enables us to have an American school of music education is that there is consensus at the operational level on accepted practices in music education. The purpose of music education is more music education. A vague disquiet has settled on American music education punctuated only by school performances. These performances, however, are viewed as relating more closely to private music instruction than to the trunk of school music, Mursell's general music education. American music education may only be a mood but it is an identifiable mood reflecting the ambiance established for it by James Mursell.

Footnotes

1. London, Marilyn. *Music and Language: An Ethnographic Study of Music Learning and Interpreting Situations*, EdD, Rutgers Univesity, the State University of New Jersey (New Brunswick), 1982.

2. LaRue, Peter. *A Study to Determine the Degree of Consensus Regarding Outcomes of Band Participation and the Competitive Elements in Band Programs Among Band Directors, Band Members and Members of Parent Booster Groups*, EdD, University of Illinois, 1986.

3. Bryant, William. *The Importance of Objectives for Secondary School Music Programs and the Opinions of Five School Related Groups*, EdD, University of Illinois, 1986.

4. Bell, John. *The High School Band: Instructional Tasks, Administrative Tasks, and Terminal Outcomes*, EdD, University of Illinois, 1986.

5. O'Brien, James. *An Experimental Study of the Use of Shape Notes in Developing Sight Singing*, PhD, University of Colorado, 1969.

6. Dyen, Doris. *The Role of Shape Note Singing in the Musical Culture of Black Communities in Southeast Alabama*, PhD, University of Illinois, 1977.

7. Fraser, Wilmot. *Jazzology: A Study of the Tradition in Which Jazz Musicians Learn to Improvise*, PhD, University of Pennsylvania, 1983.

8. Carlson, William. *A Procedure for Teaching Jazz Improvisation Based on an Analysis of the Performance Practice of Three Major Jazz Trumpet Players: Louis Armstrong, Dizzy Gillespie, and Miles Davis*, DMA, Indiana University, 1980.

9. Briscuso, Joseph. *A Study of Ability in Spontaneous and Prepared Jazz Improvisation Among Students Who Possess Different Levels of Musical Aptitude.* PhD, University of Iowa, 1972.

10. Hores, Robert. *A Comparative Study of Visual and Aural-Orientated Approaches to Jazz Improvisation with Implications*, EdD, Indiana Univ. 1977.

11. Damron, Bert L., Jr. *The Development and Evaluation of a Self Instructional Sequence in Jazz Improvisation*, PhD, Florida State University, 1973.

12. Gorder, Wayne. *An Investigation of Divergent Production Abilities as Constructs of Musical Creativity*, EdD, University of Illinois, 1976.

13. Freundlich, Douglas. *The Development of Musical Thinking: Case Studies in Improvisation*, EdD, Harvard University, 1978.

14. McClellan, Lawrence Jr. *The Effect of Creative Experiences on Musical Growth*, PhD, Michigan State University, 1977.

15. Roach, Donald. *The Development and Evaluation of Programmed Instruction to Facilitate Upper Elementary School Children's Perception of Music Notation*, EdD, Pennsylvania State University, 1970.

16. Boekelheide, Viola Ethel. *Some Techniques of Assessing Certain Basic Music Listening Skills of Eight- and Nine-Year-Olds*, EdD, Stanford, 1960.

17. Marquis, James Henry. *A Study of Interval Problems in Sight-Singing Performance with Consideration of the Effect of Context*, PhD, State University of Iowa, 1963.

18. Petzold, Robert G. *Development of Auditory Perception of Musical Sounds by Children in the First Six Grades*, University of Wisconsin, 1960 USOE.

19. Olson, Rees Garn. *A Comparison of Two Pedagogical Approaches Adapted to the Acquisition of Melodic Sensitivity in Sixth Grade Children: The Orff Method and the Traditional Method*, PhD, Indiana University, 1964.

20. Larsen, Ronald. *Levels of Conceptual Development in Melodic Permutation Concepts Based on Piaget's Theory*, PhD, University of Minnesota, 1972.

21. Ashbaugh, Thomas. *The Effects of Training in Conservation of Duple and Triple Meter in Music with Second-Grade Children*, PhD, University of Iowa, 1980.

22. Schultz, Stephen William. *A Study of Children's Ability to Respond to Elements of Music*, PhD, Northwestern University, 1969.

23. Kress, Herbert. *An Investigation of the Effect Upon Musical Achievement and Musical Performance of Beginning Band Students Exposed to Method Books Reflecting Piaget's Theory of Conservation*, PhD, University of Colorado at Boulder, 1981.

24. Gantly, Noel. *Cognitive Behavior of Preschoolers on Auditory Pitch Discrimination Tasks: A Neo-Piagetian Investigation*, EdD, Brigham Young University, 1985.

25. Cutietta, Robert. *The Analysis of Listening Strategies and Musical Focus of the 11 to 16 Year Old Listener*, DEd, Pennsylvania State University, 1982.

26. Beall, Gretchen. *Meaningful Reception Learning and Secondary School General Music*, EdD, University of Illinois, 1967.

27. Watkins, Rosemary. *The Effects of Ausubel's Advance Organizer Model on the Acquisition of Fundamental Music Concepts and Skills by Nonmusic Majors*, PhD, University of Texas at Austin, 1982.

28. Boswell, Jacqueline. *An Application of Bruner's Theory of Mental Growth to the Teaching of Musical Concepts in Beginning Instrumental Music*, EdD, University of Illinois, 1969.

29. Abdoo, Frank. *A Comparison of the Effects of Gestalt and Associationist Learning Theories on the Musical Development of Elementary School Beginning Wind and Percussion Instrument Students*, DMA, University of Southern California, 1980.

30. Kaufman, Sula, *The Aesthetic Development of Young Children Through the Folksong*, PhD, New York University, 1979.

31. Camp, Max. *An Instructional Approach to Piano Study With Reference to Selected Learning Theories*, DME, University of Oklahoma, 1977.

32. Major, James. *The Effect of Rhythmic Subdivision Activity Upon Rhythmic Performance Skills of Subjects in High School Mixed Choirs*, PhD, University of Wisconsin-Madison, 1976.

33. Ruckmith, C.A. "The Rhythmical Experience from a Systematic Point of View," *American Journal of Psychology*, Vol 39, 1927, 357-366.

34. Rucksmith, C.A. "The Role Kinesthesis in the Perception of Rhythm," *American Psychology*, vol 24, 1913, 303-359.

35. Sharretts, Archie, *A Task Analysis of the Music Rhythmic Reading Event Using Gagne's Psychology: A Revision of Conventional Musical Notation*, PhD, Florida State University, 1979.

36. Mursell, James, *Education for Musical Growth*, Boston: Ginn and Co., 1948, p. 57.

Movement in the
Music Education of Children

Patricia K. Shehan
Department of Music
Butler University, Indianapolis

I hope that you will not be bothered by this attempt to convey the meaning of movement and music for children in a manner that is the antithesis of the topic. This space is not conducive to movement for us all, and so we will turn to paper-reading as the mode of presentation. I am midway through a Dalcroze program at the Longy School in Cambridge, Massachusetts, and am prepared to use words to describe a subject which is better understood through experience, but which nonetheless clamors for an analysis that can be verbally communicated. The use of movement as a pedagogical tool figures prominently in the music education of children, and so we will examine it this morning in the context of research, and historical and contemporary perspectives.

It is an intriguing notion that the foundation of music as performance parallels the manner in which children learn best; both are closely associated with the physical self. Music, the aural art, is also music, the kinesthetic art. The ear, the muscles and the brain are inherently related in their functions as receivers and conveyers of musical sound, and thus, they play important roles in the training of musicians, and in the music learning of children.

We know that musicians are mobile creatures. The activation of their voices and instruments in producing musical sounds require movement, and the precision of sound they offer to the listening audience is often in direct proportion to their exacting movements. The intricate motor tasks of the musician's fingers, bow arms, pedal feet, and embouchure become finely tuned through repetition, and the aural channel serves to prompt great musical accuracy over time.

Neurologists have provided explicit descriptions of the physical impulse of our movement as musicians: the brain triggers messages in the form of electrical impulses to certain designated nerves, which deliver them to the attached muscles in the form of chemical codes. The complex motor system of the brain provides the mind-body connection vital to the musicians' performance.

What is movement in the context of school music programs? There is a broad array of images. Elementary school children are led to an understanding of rhythm, phrasing and form through marching, clapping, snapping, stepping, patting and dancing. Junior high school students experience a tremendous challenge to the motor coordination of their feet, hands and fingers in their first marching band season. Choral groups use movement as an expressive device, from subtle gestures and swaying movements to complete song-and-dance presentations in the popular show choirs. Conductors of school ensembles also employ movement in their gestures, cues, body position, baton technique, and coordination of physical and rhythmic skills so vital to effective conducting. Music in performance and in music education — which is also performance — appears to be inseparable from movement.

The target of this talk is elementary and preschool children. How are they engaged in the perception and conceptual understanding of music? We know that movement activities form an integral part of most music education programs. The basal music textbooks advocate movement as the important activity for music learning for preschool and kindergarten through at least the sixth grade. Teachers employ music and movement as avenues of self-expression, for physical release after academic tasks, and as a means of social interaction.

There is a certain perspective, even a universal truth, that pervades elementary curricula, advocating "holistic learning" with the belief that children learn best when the whole self is involved. Children are thought to become better acquainted with music, and to truly develop a musicianship, when they think, feel, and do music. When their bodies are used as musical instruments, receiving and responding to music, there is the view that music learning fully occurs. [This week in a Dalcroze technique called "plastique," we set a portion of Messiaen's *Vingt Regards sur l'Enfant Jesus* to movement — not dance — but movement which conveyed the rhythm, melody, texture, and dynamics of that monumental work. I finally understand that piece, because my body became an instrument of musical expression. So it can be with children as well.]

It is unfortunate that however many music and movement experiences are found in school programs, there are seldom well-defined objectives to accompany them. We often hear of the extramusical goals of a movement activity: the development of motor coordination, laterality, eye-hand perspective, a sense of community and cooperation. Although these goals are important in the greater context of school and society, they do little toward developing musical beings. In fact, sometimes these broader goals distract from the mission of making children more musical.

In order to best utilize movement in the music education of children, it may be important to understand their movement potential, and in this way, to know their physical and intellectual levels of development. We will briefly outline the historical significance of movement in school programs, refer to learning theories of music and rhythmic movement, highlight empirical evidence of the effects of movement-based instruction, and review the treatment of movement by such classic music educators as Emile Jaques-Dalcroze, Carl Orff, and Zoltan Kodaly. The underlying thought should surface throughout: that movement in the music education of children is vital, fundamental, natural, and most effective in facilitating learning when designed by the informed specialist.

Movement and Music in History

The most predominant use of movement historically has been the development of rhythmic concepts and skills. Rhythmic activities were a part of the elementary school curriculum in isolated instances even before the turn of the century. There were conflicting views, however. Some felt that physical exercises were innocuous and might serve as diversions or periods of rest between academic lessons, while others felt that physical activity was harmful to the mental processes, and that the mind could not function at maximum capacity if the muscles were exercised. Most movement and rhythmic exercises at the time fell within the domain of physical education. Among the more common goals for the use of movement was "the elimination of poor posture" (Chicago Schools, 1896); marching at various tempos was held by some as the most likely remedy.

Physical education instructors brought gymnastics and dance into their programs because these were believed to develop a sense of rhythm and give the body grace, control, and distinction. Fundamental movements such as walking, running, skipping, hopping, jumping, and sliding were included. In the hands of physical education instructors, rhythmic perception and musical understanding was only a by-product, and then a rare one.

In Switzerland at the turn of the century, Emile Jaques-Dalcroze formulated a system of rhythmic training that established physical experience as a prelude to intellectual understanding. He established the technique of eur-hythmics as an alternative to dance, and delivered to his students a fuller rhythmic consciousness through their physical responses to music in directed and improvisatory ways. Jaques-Dalcroze asked his students to follow the tempo, rhythm and meter of his improvised music with their bodies, and to react quickly to changes in any aspects of the music (meter or, for example, a shift of rhythmic patterns, dynamics, extended or reduced phrases, for example). He recognized movement as the foundation of a thorough musician-ship for naive children as well as for experienced performers in the conser-vatory.

In the United States, the impact of Dalcroze instruction was considerable. The New York School of Dalcroze Eurhythmics was founded in 1915, and eurhythmics was incorporated within music classes in a number of conser-vatories and colleges, in preparatory programs for children, in private piano studios, and in some elementary school programs. By 1930, eurhythmics was widely known although its practice was still somewhat limited, due to the extensive training necessary for the Dalcroze specialist.

Music educator James L. Mursell (1931) wrote extensively on the nature of rhythm and rhythmic behaviors, proposing that rhythmic understanding is closely related to the capacity for muscular response. From the late 1920's until well into the 1940's, he supported eurhythmics as a style of music learning that involved the muscles in kinesthetic response. Mursell's motor theory of rhythm suggested that we are capable of producing rhythms be-cause we have a bodly machinery which can be trained to pulse and react in ordered sequence. He wrote of the human potential to perceive and respond to great rhythmic complexities because of a nervous and muscular machi-nery which can be finely and delicately educated. He postulated that these responses, beginning with large and overt muscle movement, are modified until only the smallest muscles respond to a rhythmic pattern. Hence the rhythmic impulse proceeds from overt to covert movement.

As Mursell set thoughts in theory, children were provided with rhythmic movement experiences in school music programs. Under the leadership of Maybelle Glenn and Marguerite Hood in the 1930's and 1940's, teachers were trained to incorporate movement into music classes along with the more traditional singing and note-reading activities. The natural rhythmic movements for walking, running and skipping were integrated into listening lessons and song activities, and were eventually correlated with notation. A repertory of rhythms was thus developed and understood by the ear, the eye, and the body.

In Europe, other philosophies and practices for the music education of children were in developmental stages. Because of the "radical" nature of Jaques-Dalcroze's eurhythmics, he was first dismissed and then recalled to the Geneva Conservatory. During the interim period, he founded an institute for dancers and musicians at Hellerau, Germany, which had a tremendous impact on all the performing arts. A young Carl Orff went to Hellerau, and was much influenced by the merging of music, dance and theatre. The emerging "Orff Approach" quite likely was formulated as a result of Orff's experience with Jaques-Dalcroze at Hellerau.

Soon after Jaques-Dalcroze developed his solfege techniques, they were employed in English school programs. It was there that Zoltan Kodaly observed the blending of Dalcroze solfege with the principles of John Curwen, including the hand signs of the tonic sol-fa. The Dalcroze influence of the solfege-rhythmique practice was evident, using kinesthetic techniques to complement ear training and sight singing exercises. Kodaly added numerous innovations of his own in his sequence for learning, as did Carl Orff, but the Dalcroze principles of movement laid some of the foundations for their evolving practices. By the 1950's, American teachers of elementary school music began to hear of these approaches to music education, and they creatively adapted them to the special needs of American children.

Research in Music and Movement Instruction

There are empirical and theoretical bases for movement in developing musical ability. The views of two educational psychologists provided strong support for rhythmic movement several decades ago, and their foresight was extremely keen and relevant to contemporary music education practices. Jean Piaget placed much importance upon early sensorimotor learning as the basis of intellectual development. "Movement precedes perception," he said, and results in perception. From their earliest growth stages, Piaget noted that children explore their environment in active and physical ways in order to know it thoroughly. Jerome Bruner's theory of learning stressed the development of the child in three stages: enactive, iconic, and symbolic. Clearly, the younger the child, the greater the importance of participatory activities. Rather than passive and abstract modes of presentation, Bruner recommended that active experiences lead the way to symbols. Piaget and

Bruner agreed that, like a picture, an experience is worth far more than words can express, at least initially.

Movement as an instructional tool is an issue addressed by researchers in recent years. At his presentation at the Ann Arbor Symposium (1981), Robert Sidnell advocated the building of a theory of motor learning which would address items such as the optimum periods of motor growth, the transfer of motor skills to music learning, and efficient methods of motor skill development. Several studies have investigated these issues.

It appears that movement ability and the psychomotor skills necessary for performance improve with advancing age. Chanting, tapping, clapping, patting and stepping the beat may depend upon gender as well. Robert Petzold's classic study (1966) reported that by third grade, most children can accurately maintain a steady beat by tapping. Lois and Stanley Schleuter (1985) confirmed the thesis that for primary grade children, the large muscles required of stepping were more difficult to maneuver than the smaller muscle movement of clapping and chanting. The results also indicated that girls seem to demonstrate a greater capacity for rhythmic movement than boys, through the age of ten.

Edward Rainbow issued a final report (1981) from a series of studies on the rhythmic responses of preschool children, and as such provided a hierarchy of normal expectations in regard to the movement of four-year-olds. While up to 90% were able to vocally echo a rhythmic pattern presented to them through word-chants, only about half of them could keep a steady beat to recorded music by clapping and tapping rhythm sticks, and only 20% could march in time to the pulse of the music. With maturation or with specialized study such as eurhythmics, these rhythmic movement tasks become increasingly easy.

Some authors of music education materials recommend that first free and then directed movement be used to develop rhythmic accuracy. Each style demands a certain discipline, with free movement requiring imagination and sensitivity to the flow of music, as well as a repertory of movement behaviors. John Flohr and Jacqueline Brown (1979) studied the influence of peer imitation on the expressive movement to music of preschool and kindergarten children. The children were videotaped as they responded to music with and without blindfolds. They concluded that expressive movement was significantly influenced by the tendency of children to imitate their peers. Teachers might consider their roles as models in providing a richer vocabulary of movement for children.

Among the results of an exploratory study of children's creative movement qualities, Wendy Sims (1985) noted that there were considerable discrepancies among three-, four-, and five-year-olds. While children listened to music, nearly half of the three-year-olds remained still, and the remainder were mostly engaged in non-locomotor movement. The amount of rhythmic movement by five-year-old children was over three times as much as that used by three-year olds; movement of the older children also corresponded to the beat almost three times as often as those of the youngest group.

The integration of movement into elementary general music classes appears likely to enhance perception, performance, and attitude toward music. Following twelve weeks of instruction in a kinesthetic mode, Barbara Lewis (1936) reported that first and third grade children showed greater achievement in the aural perception of dynamics, while third graders also increased their aural perception of melodic direction. The lessons were based upon textbook modules for tempo, dynamics, melodic direction, meter and rhythm; the experimental group lessons were enriched by the addition of movement-based instruction. Deborah Carlson noted the effect of movement on attitudes of fifth grade students toward their music class (1983). Males tended to respond more favorably than females to the addition of movement in their classes. There was no inquiry as to the relationship between movement activities and cognitive gain, but nevertheless, we know that attitude is a significant factor in music learning.

Two investigations point to the positive effects of Dalcroze eurhythmics as a technique in developing musical understanding. Sue Crumpler (1982) demonstrated the impact of eurhythmics on melodic discrimination ability of first grade students. Given only eight weeks of instruction, children were capable of discriminating between tonal patterns from familiar songs which they had previously responded to through movement, as well as to make the transfer in the discrimination of unfamiliar patterns. In another study, Annabelle Joseph (1982) found that as a result of the application of Dalcroze eurhythmics and improvisation techniques, children were able to recognize and respond to familiar rhythm patterns in unfamiliar music. The treatment period lasted 44 lessons, in a format that incorporated ear-training, movement exploration, rhythmic movement, rhythmic games, relaxation, and improvisation.

Contemporary Approaches to Music and Movement

The contemporary application of movement experiences in music classes for children center around three prominent teaching techniques: Dalcroze, Orff, and Kodaly. Their philosophies support the walking, running, skipping, hopping, jumping, hand-clapping, and gestures of children's play experiences, and their practices incorporate these natural movements as avenues to musical understanding.

Of the three widely-known approaches to music for children, Dalcroze is the least practiced in American schools. Few licensed Dalcroze teachers exist. The training is intensive, and is found only at five locations in the eastern U.S.: The Dalcroze School, New York; Manhattan School, New York; Ithaca College, Ithaca, New York; Longy School, Cambridge, Massachusetts and Carnegie-Melon in Pittsburgh. The teacher examinations are difficult: extensive piano improvisation, solfege using the European Fixed-Do system (when most American-trained teachers are accustomed to Movable-Do), and teaching practicums in eurhythmics and solfege. The highest standards of musicianship are maintained in the certification process, and the one to two years of instruction necessary to internalize the Dalcroze techniques cannot usually be reduced.

The eurhythmics technique requires the development of a rather complex set of kinesthetic reactions. Children dress in comfortable clothing, and are usually barefooted. Their movement may include any number of possibilities: in place and in locomotion across the floor, in isolated gestures using the hands, arms, head, shoulders. They may move independently, with partners or in groups. Their movement is a personal and immediate response to the music which sounds on the piano, on percussion instruments, vocally, or (rarely) on recordings.

Eurhythmics is commonly misinterpreted as dance. Like dance, eurhythmics requires physical conditioning. Like dance, eurhythmics has a visual component. Dance is an art, however, while eurhythmics is a means to an end: refined musicianship. The student of eurhythmics is first evaluated for accuracy and immediacy in responding to the characteristics of the music; the quality of the movement is an important, but not primary concern. The body is trained as an instrument, realizing the music through the limbs by stepping, clapping, and gesturing.

Dalcroze eurhythmics calls for attention, concentration, and memory. In practice, the movement reflects rhythm. It spins from the music itself. The concept of music as existing in time is expanded through eurhythmics, which allows that music can be expressed through movement, which exists in space. Dalcroze instruction suggests that musical understanding is more complete because students experience music in more than one dimension: through the ear and through the body.

For children in the elementary school, there is a progression of experiences: stepping, running, skipping, galloping, moving in different meters, moving to different rhythmic patterns, strengthening the memory through canons of rhythmic movement. Used well, Dalcroze provides the underpinnings for the complex musicality which is the goal of music education.

Carl Orff found movement to be at the foundation of music learning. He saw movement as part of the natural developmental process of the child, and incorporated the movement of free play into his *Schulwerk*. He observed children as capable of a variety of movements which were fluid and free, and unhampered by the inhibitions which define most adolescents and adults. Orff's philosophy on movement was evident when he stated in his *Music for Children*: "Out of movement, music; out of music, movement."

The Orff approach to music education encourages children to explore a variety of movements, and to experience music with their bodies. The ultimate goal of Orff is the development of creativity, as demonstrated through the composition and improvisation of music. Free movement derived from natural and play activities, rather than from structured dance, is the ideal goal. Movement is more than ancillary in directing that course, and is viewed as an aid in nurturing expressive ideas that may be channeled toward the creation of music.

In a very real sense, teachers of the Orff approach view movement and sound as interlocking events. Four body movements are central to Orff experiences, all of which create sounds as they are performed: clapping, stamping, finger-snapping, and patschen or patting the hands on the lap. These movements are isolated or combined in multiple ways, and the rhythms of songs and chants are reinforced through these movements. By associating movement patterns with words, rhythms and melodies, songs are often better learned and retained.

Patricia K. Shehan

Movement, chant and song are preliminary steps toward the playing of instruments of the Orff ensemble. The four principal movements, in particular the patting, are practiced while rhythmically chanting a song or verse. Only after sufficient repetition are the hand movements transferred to the instruments. Ostinatos, bourdons comprised of parallel fourths and fifths, and complete melodies are played more easily by children when they have been prepared for the hand and arm movements in advance.

Zoltan Kodaly recognized that music and dance are often integrated in the national culture of a people, including that of his beloved Hungary. He sought to preserve the heritage of Hungary through school music programs that are unique in their intensity, and whose teachers are committed to developing musically literate children. Folk dances are taught early on in the sequence of Kodaly-inspired music education. The ancient circle and line dances are a part of childlore in nearly every culture, and are thus important to the practice of Kodaly teachings worldwide. In American schools, the older stratum of play-party games, reels, and square dances are introduced.

Children's hand-clapping games as found on the playgrounds and in neighborhood streets are viewed as further events of a musical nature — and part of a musical heritage — that should be kept alive in the music classroom and from which the learning of musical concepts can occur. Songs of children are rich with natural movement, from *Ring around the Rosie* to their parodies of McDonald's commercials. Clapping, patting, finger-snapping, criss-crossing the hands and arms, turning, bending, jumping are movements performed by children alone or together in the songs they possess. Kodaly teachers recognize the importance of childsongs and their associated movements, and design their curriculum to include these experiences.

The Kodaly adaptation of the Curwen signs for singing solfege provide effective kinesthetic accompaniment for learning tonal patterns and relationships. Through the association of sound with a spatial level, the hand positions represent the melodic pitches in a concrete way. The aural, visual and kinesthetic senses provide a three-way channel that cover the possible modes of instruction. This technique espoused by Kodaly is one of the most carefully structured fusion of music and movement practices to be found in the course of music instruction for children.

There is every indication that movement is integral to a child's musical experiences. The physical self is vital to music learning; the body is an important pedagogical tool. As music flows in time, children are triggered into movement. The total participation of children in music-making includes the activation of the kinesthetic sense, and permission for the child to use his body in the music experiences. Current learning theories are solid, and the results of current research are in, attesting to the significance of movement as a means to musicianship. The key to the successful music education of children appears to rest heavily in the arena of movement.

References

Carlson, Deborah Lynn. "The effect of movement on attitudes of fifth grade students toward their music class," Doctoral dissertation, 1983. (University Microfilms DA 8319315)

Crumpler, Sue E. "The effect of Dalcroze eurhythmics on the melodic musical growth of first grade students," Doctoral dissertation, 1982. (University Microfilms DA 8829498)

Flohr, John and Brown, Jacqueline. "The influence of peer imitation on expressive movement to music," *Journal of Research in Music Education* 27:3, Fall, 1979.

Joseph, Annabelle. "A Dalcroze eurhythmics approach to music learning in kindergarten through rhythmic movement, ear-training and improvisation," Doctoral dissertation, 1982. (University Microfilms DA 831454).

Lewis, Barbara E. "The effect of movement-based instruction on the aural perception skills of first-and third-graders," Doctoral dissertation, 1986. (University Microfilms DA 8607396).

Mursell, James L. *Principles of Music Education,* New York: The Macmillan Company, 1931.

Petzold, Robert G. "The development of auditory perception of musical sounds by children in the first six grades," *Journal of Research in Music Education* 11, Spring, 1963.

Rainbow, Edward. "A final report on a three-year investigation of the rhythmic abilities of preschool aged children," *Bulletin of the Council for Research in Music Education* 66-6, Spring-Summer, 1981.

Schleuter, Stanley L. and Schleuter, Lois J. "The relationship of grade level and sex differences to certain rhythmic responses of primary grade children," *Journal of Research in Music Education* 33, Spring, 1985.

Sidnell, Robert G. "Motor learning in music education," In *Documentary Report of the Ann Arbor Symposium*, ed. R.G. Taylor, Reston VA: Music Educators National Conference, 1981.

Sims, Wendy L. "Young children's creative movement to music: categories of movement, rhythmic characteristics, and reactions to changes," *Contributions to Music Education* 12, Fall, 1985.

What Children Teach Us About Learning Music

The Philosophy of the Yamaha Music Education System

Elizabeth Jones
Director of Instruction
Yamaha Music Education System

Babies and children are in the biologic business of creating themselves. It is our mandate to merge with this eternally mysterious matrix, to once again catch ourselves in the web of wonder of our own early self-creating powers. In that reawakened, wide-eyed place we are open to learn from them, how to teach them; watching them as they watch us; listening to them as they listen to us; noticing them as they notice us; paying non-judgmental attention to them and making the world safe for their discoveries and growth; or dancing with them an ancient dance with ever renewable steps.

Human infants are "bio-logic" learners, designed to take entire lifetimes in the process of becoming. By nature's design, this is a process slower in humans than in any other species. There's a precise word for this gradual unfolding of lifelong learning; the word is neoteny.

Ashley Montagu wrote a significant book about neoteny and its part in both evolution and education. In this book, *Growing Young,* he wrote: "We know that children are developing human beings who will continue developing all their lives if not prevented. And now, we begin to see that the goal of life is to die young as late as possible." To which I would add: and certainly not slip heedlessly into what he terms psychosclerosis (hardening of the mind).

Plainly then, to learn what children teach us about how they learn music or indeed anything, we must stay open-minded, curious, playful, inquisitive, trusting, and willing to learn by trial and error — in short, able to tap the genius of our own childhood learning on behalf of those who arrived later on the planet than we did. That is the philosophical pivot around which the practical points in this presentation revolve.

Now about learning how children learn music. First, let's look at and listen to children making music. The first example shows a student who plays a standard repertoire piece rather well, and is also capable in other musical skills, specifically ensemble performance and composition. [Video example]

Improvisation is important to the Yamaha system, too, so we'll also hear a duet improvisation by two very young Japanese girls at a United Nations Concert. [Video example]

The aim of this particular teaching system, then, is not only solo performance of repertoire. It is comprehensive musicianship based on the notion that inside each individual resides not only a listener, but a performer and creator of music.

In Japan, literally thousands of children can function musically at this level of achievement and beyond, astonishingly proficient in musical performance and comprehension. For in the wake of the migration of Western classical, pop, jazz and folk music to Japan, teaching systems were spawned with the capacity to make this music accessible to wide segments of its populace, even in preference to the music of their own country. Paradoxically, these Japanese teaching systems have within the past 30 years migrated back full circle to the western hemisphere.

Suzuki, the more widely known of the two, involves repertoire as an end in itself. Yamaha utilizes standard repertoire (in all kinds of music) as a musical model of possibilities for improvisation, arranging and composition. In other words, Yamaha specializes in teaching comprehensive musicianship, which becomes the springboard for creative music making. The pedagogy thread which weaves the fundamental skills of musicianship together in this system is "keyboard harmony"— keyboard harmony taught in a group, using electronic keyboards in a setting that uses parent/child bonding to facilitate learning a sequence of sensorimotor patternings.

Before telling you in greater detail about what we've found to accelerate teaching keyboard harmony to American children, I want to return briefly to the transplant of the Yamaha system to cultures other than Japan, specifically, of course, America. Two quotations serve to focus on this issue. First this quote from Genichi Kawakami, the founder of the Yamaha Music Education System:

> "If the education method is correct, the same results will be obtained anywhere in the world."

Let us take "correct" to mean merging with natural blueprints for learning which characterize children, *plus* the cultural influence which acts upon them. We have from Howard Gardner's book, *Frames of Mind*, this quote:

"The key to the success of the Suzuki (we may add or substitute Yamaha) program in Japan lies in the comfortable fit between the abilities and inclinations of the target population (young children) and the particular values, opportunities and institutions of the society in which they happen to be growing up.

Such programs can be successfully exported only if similar support systems exist in the new host country or alternatively if suitable alterations are made so that the educational program meshes with the dominant values, procedures and intellectual orientation of the host land."

Facilitating such a meshing of the Yamaha System in the U.S.A. has created challenge (always) and difficulty (at times). However, devising suitable alterations has led to some solutions.

Let me identify for you the components of the system which not only didn't mesh with the dominant values here, but appeared to be antithetical. In a quick run-through, I'll name the component, and the dominant conflicting value, procedure and/or intellectual orientation.

1. The use of group lessons for beginners and intermediate, in an atmosphere of cooperation, *not competition*. Parents are part of the group. In this setting, the course encourages:

- cooperation of one's own body parts to hear or see sound patterns, then master the motion to re-create the sound patterns;

- cooperation with and between the instruments, learning their capabilities; cooperation with others.

Though the individual is patterning only one musical part, the division of labor among the group creates a total sound. One can perform one line of music while still listening to the others. This cooperative mode is referred to in the system as *harmony among friends*. Ultimately, individual accomplishment emerges. The dominant values in the U.S.: Parents compare and compete. Prevalent idea is that private instruction is better at any age. Talent is a big issue. Faster is considered better.

2. We use electronic keyboards. Keyboards are considered learning tools in two main ways:

- first, as a means to teach all the fundamental skills — hearing, singing, playing and reading, rather than keyboard solo playing as an end in itself. On these keyboards, repertoire playing and keyboard harmony skills can expand into comprehension of instrumental possibilities, a dimension which enhances arranging and composition;

- second, as a means to integrate the highly developed sensory capabilities of every child with the less developed motor abilities. Fixed-do solfege singing is combined with many left and right hand finger preparation activities which are applied to the keyboard.

The dominant, yet changing, view here (in the large and diverse community of music educators) is that such technology threatens the supremacy of the piano as an instrument for learning music. Also, piano teachers are concerned with faulty hand position and sense of touch.

3. The program is most successful when reinforced by the parent and child bond. In Japan, such training is the cultural expectation. The Kyoiku mama (education mother) is heavily invested in time and effort in the child's music training.

The dominant realities *here* are: many working mothers, split families, tendency to pay specialists to teach children, and diverse modes of parenting due to multi-ethnic population. As consumers, Americans like instant gratification. Stick-to-itiveness and participatory support are not so prevalent and deeply rooted as in Japan.

4. The system requires teachers to be equipped with a battery of musical skills which balance performance, theory and applied skills.

In the colleges and conservatories of this country, performance of standard repertoire is emphasized, since most concert going is based on comparative listening of standard works. Competition is based on that. In testing hundreds of American teacher candidates, we have found that they score high on performance and theory and low on applied skills.

Another factor is the difference in cultural attitudes about teachers. The "those who can, do; those who can't, teach" attitude still holds sway here, whereas teachers in Japan are held in high esteem.

Also, most American college graduates in music receive little or no training in child development and human learning. In a polyglot society, this type of training is necessary. In Japan, a homogeneous society, child rearing is a manifestation of the total acculturation. Piano teaching here is often based on techniques which approach *all* children as if they were training to be professionals. Average learners can be predestined to fail. This creates feelings of musical inadequacy and threatens enjoyment of music.

5. A final and important consideration in Gardner's hypothesis concerns the "abilities and inclinations of the target population of young children." Japanese children excel in fine motor coordination. Thus the musical materials and developmental sequences designed in Japan for the course require a fairly high degree of two-hand coordination. These materials and sequences have proven to be difficult for average learners here. Bringing this coordination about in large numbers of children, not only the "talented" few is a major challenge in this country, due to the diversity of cultural and developmental factors.

Those have been the challenges. At this point, I want to present two of the major solutions worked out through Yamaha's two experimental schools in Southern California. These solutions, I believe, have significance to educators and researchers outside the system. But before I do, let me clarify for you the type of research which goes on at these schools: it is a practical blend of consumer and educational research which I call "double bind" studies. That is, dollars get pulled away by the consumer if we do not provide the musical and educational results we promise!

Because the system is global and students can transfer internationally as well as locally and from state to state, all musical materials (published in Japan) are the same worldwide. Children and parents can feel at home musically anywhere in the Yamaha world.

Nonetheless, each country, Germany, Mexico, England, America, must, through research and development, adjust the *psychological* and *developmental* approaches to teaching the international *musical* material with the cultural realities (i.e. the "dominant values, procedures and intellectual orientation" in Gardner's notion) of each particular country in mind.

Now, to our R & D solutions for adaptation of the Yamaha program to the American music education scene.

To shift the paradigms I listed for you, i.e. group instruction, cooperation not competition, family support, etc., we created a sophisticated mutual reference guide for teachers and parents. It is called the *Parent Guide*. In a pleasant but authoritative format, it covers *musical, developmental* and *psychological* aspects of becoming co-learners with the children. Each semester, a unit of the guide is issued for that semester. Tab index dividers indicate the basic components of the guide: e.g. *Together in Music*: the parent-child-teacher bonding and group process; *Singing*: the solfege connection; *The Beat Goes On*: rhythmic training; *Switches, Buttons and Keys;* and *Super Eyes*. All inform parents and teachers the whys and how to's of acquiring all the fundamental skills).

Each semester issue portrays the goals of that semester in the first six sections. The last section, *Finale*, surveys the fundamental skills for that semester, providing the means to measure group accomplishments as well as individual progress. Practical suggestions for what to look for in class and ideas for at-home learning are given. Parents and children are involved in co-learning and co-practicing.

Strong guidelines to adult classroom etiquette are included. Called the three R's, (Figure 1) they are: respond for yourself; respect the bio-logical way your child learns; restrict adult chatter. The musical, developmental and psychological rationale for each is described and reviewed for both teachers and parents.

Pages are devoted to dissuade parents from placing eight-year-old expectations on four-year-olds through illustrations and descriptions of sequential learning tasks. Parents are shown how to support children's hands in the very early times at the keyboards — encouraging a loving, touching relationship at the keyboard. Parents learn all fundamental skills, too.

The guide is and has been since we began using it in 1985, a tremendous help in dropout prevention and in improving the quality of instruction, by raising adult (parents and teachers) levels of understanding, shifting consciousness toward the child as he or she really is.

The second major adaptation of the Japanese Yamaha course for American children has been in the developmental sequencing of tasks for teaching children how to coordinate right and left hands in repertoire pieces, which leads to teaching keyboard harmony, our pathway to creativity. Specifically, we set for the left hand the task of being able to play chords, and for the

THE THREE R'S

RESPOND

Respond to the music for yourself, not for your child.

Musical Reasons. The solidness of sound and quality of expression depend on every person's unaffected, unguarded, spontaneous response.

In singing, solfege, rhythm activities, reading exercises, and all other lessons, **respond** to the music as "musically" as you can—*for yourself!* Your child will "feel" and "see" your freedom and respond for himself or herself.

A truly successful class is one in which everyone—parents, teachers, and children—responds naturally…and improves musically…week after week.

Psychological Reasons. When you respond for your child, you teach your child to respond the way you think he or she should respond.

Your son or daughter needs to be encouraged to respond freely—without any apprehension about being right or wrong in your eyes.

When you respond for your child or expect a specific response from him or her, **your child's attention focuses on your approval and not on the lesson.**

Developmental Reasons. You are the first and foremost role model for your child.

Your son or daughter's ability to accomplish musical tasks depends on his or her willingness to repeat patterns many times over. If you're also willing to repeat the patterns (and your child can "see" your willingness!), skill development will become accelerated…and more effective.

RESPECT

Respect the physical way your child learns and grows.

Musical Reasons. How well you understand and appreciate your child's normal, natural growth rate will determine how well you and your child progress in the YMES Primary Course.

Don't *over-estimate* what your child can do on keyboards, and don't *under-estimate* the sophisticated ear development taking place in your child at this age. Trust your son or daughter's ability to learn *many* musical skills in the group setting.

Psychological Reasons. If you want your child to take learning cues from you, you must take learning cues from him or her.

Watch and listen for how your child learns. Then provide the kind of emotional support to make that learning the most effective possible—for both of you. You may still use "adult" ways for yourself, but try to get the "child's feeling" for learning, too.

Developmental Reasons. Your child tries and your child imitates—that's the true developmental learning process.

To fully develop sensory-motor coordination, your child needs to have many successful repetitions of physical patterning before he or she can be expected to label the patterns or explain what he or she is doing.

If you interrupt your child's physical concentration with intellectual questioning, you'll be depriving your child of his or her best learning tool.

RESTRICT

Restrict adult chatter so your child can concentrate.

Musical Reasons. Your child's ear needs to be free to "hear" the new language: Music—with its rhythmic, melodic, and harmonic patterns given by the teacher.

The highest priority in YMES Primary Course musical training is listening. If you talk during ear training sessions, you will interfere with your child's ability to hear this language and to acquire the necessary motor skills to sing and play it.

Psychological Reasons: Give your child the freedom to learn.

At times, it will seem easier for you to explain the teacher's instructions than it will be for you to let your child learn on his or her own.

Remain quiet, especially when the teacher is giving ear training lessons at the keyboard. In the YMES learning process, we want your child to learn to *trust his or her own ears*—so they become musically independent.

Developmental Reasons. Your words can be like static, interfering with your child's "reception" of the teacher's "signals."

Think of the teacher as the transmitter of musical patterns and cues. Your child is the receiver.

Your oral interpretations of the teacher's directions, cues, and patterning are like microwave signals that block or distort your child's reception. This interference "short circuits" the transmission of musical information your child needs to become musically sure of himself or herself.

Figure 1

Elizabeth Jones

right hand being able to play melody. This, by the way is but one of the ways children in Yamaha combine the two hands in playing repertoire pieces.

Only recently, through empirical means, we have made some significant advances in comprehending how children of average ability can accomplish this task of integration. Simple approaches to teaching the left hand chord, right hand melody task have been devised. This is what we have found in the training of hands *separately:*

- The *right hand,* to perform the motions of a melody line in rhythm, receives significant assistance from the child's voice singing fixed-do solfege as the melody is played. In other words, the musical language helps the right hand. The ability to do this while playing at the same time must be preceded by: 1) complete memorization of the melody line of a given piece through singing *separately from playing;* 2) preparation of the motions and sequences of the hand and fingers of the piece *away from the keyboard,* with the *eyes watching* these motions and sequences; 3) gradual playing and singing of one and/or two measure patterns of a repertoire piece *at the keyboard* while watching the hand and fingers in motion. 4) playing the memorized piece with the eyes closed.

- The *left hand* receives some help from solfege primarily as a handy label. More powerful sensorimotor assistance comes from visual patternings. Right brain gestalt is invoked to help left hand patterning as follows: 1) while singing a memorized melody students watch the teacher perform the motions of a chord sequence in a piece at his/her keyboard; (Teacher doesn't play along with the melody as the children sing.) 2) students shape their own hand and fingers to model that of the teacher — we call this playing *air piano.* Children learn to create the shape and downward motion as they watch the teacher play the chord and simultaneously sing the memorized melody line. This is called two-line listening; 3) reinforcement of the motion and shape results from playing *air piano* and seeing the notation of a bass line simultaneously. The teacher first checks hand shapes using solfege labels: "Let me see the *mi-sol* shape in your fingers. Now the *fa-sol* shape. Use your eyes to see your fingers make the *mi-sol* shape, now your *fa-sol* shape;" 4) pointing to the pattern on the board, she encourages the children to "play the shapes." At this time, the students disengage from watching their hands, and watch the notes as they "play their hand shapes" either on *air pianos* or *arm pianos* (playing one hand on the opposite arm). This preparation allows the left hand to be "in automatic" and frees the eye to receive visual information, an important element of reading musical scores.

Because the right hand imprints quickly from the left brain musical language cues of solfege, and the left hand imprints quickly from the right brain gestalt and because both benefit from rehearsing and memorizing shapes, motions and sequences away from the keyboard along with a sound and pitch source (i.e., voices singing melody in solfege and/or teacher or parent playing the chords), we have devised simple exercises which can be divided among members of the group to accelerate individual accomplishment of two hand playing *much* earlier in the course than before, and by many more students.

Prior to the approaches described above, other left and right hand preparation activities which take about 15 weeks are undertaken in class as a group, and co-practiced in the partnership at home. For example, in the early weeks of the course, all finger awareness and preparation exercises (finger play) are done hands separately, not bilaterally. The contrary motion action of bilateral finger plays makes it harder for children to get each hand to do differing motions later when they need to learn repertoire pieces. Parallel playing of octaves too early also specifically slows the aural and tactile assimilation of keyboard harmony, i.e., chords in left hand, melody in right. Also, children need their eyes to watch their own fingers in these activities, until such time as they can close their eyes and bring out the correct finger, then check.

At approximately week 9 of the first semester (with four and five year olds), a series of two-hand separation activities begins, using clapping and tapping gestures, less complicated than those required to play on keyboards in rhythm. These exercises emerge from two-measure clapping patterns in which the first measure is a static pattern, the second a changing pattern, both taken from the one measure pattern clapping accomplished in the first 8 weeks of the course.

Using various combinations of sensorimotor differentiations, first separating the task each hand does, repeating until one hand is "in automatic" while the other attends to changing patterns, children can gradually integrate the two hands to accomplish what we call *two-hand by copy* and/or *by ear* playing of 1 and 2 measure patterns at the keyboards.

The sequence, which takes from 5 to 7 weeks goes like this:

In Semester one, between Lessons 9 and 17, two-hand separation activities emerge from dividing two-measure patterns, and using by ear timbre cues. Room is quiet; teacher gives patterns from behind the group, or children close eyes.

- first, through body and gesture differentiation;

- second, through body and instrument differentiation;

- Third, through left and right differentiation of two-measure patterns; of gesture and sound (by ear timbre); of pitch and differing registers at the keyboard, using ostinato and by-ear playing;

- fourth, through left and right hand integration of combined rhythmic patterns (left hand, whole note ostinato and right hand changing patterns); of gesture and sound; of pitch and differing registers at the keyboard.

Two hand by-copy/by-ear playing, i.e., teacher plays a pattern, children imitate; teacher gives another pattern in which left or bass remains the same and the right or treble pattern changes, is possible when students have accomplished a simple two-hand ostinato in which both hands come down, but left hand plays and holds, right hand plays and moves melodically. A developmentally significant ear-hand accomplishment is made here. That is, the left hand is getting in "automatic" which frees the ear to listen to and transmit a changing pattern to the right hand, an accomplishment of language (musical language) to trigger rhythmic motion.

These rudimentary underpinnings are currently being refined at the R & D centers and key account schools. Implementation is beginning nationwide this year.

Our subject has been what children teach us about learning music. In this talk, I've tried to show how those of us providing music to children, even in the corporate setting, receive the most relevant lessons from watching and listening to the children themselves.

To me the most appropriate way to bring the presentation to a close is to let a child teach us once again. From a San Jose, California newspaper article comes a genuine Biology of Music-Making story reported by a mother of two young children.

> When my son, Charlie, was a few days old I had to take a 30-mile trip with just him and his four-year-old sister, Audrey, in the car, and he began to cry. I asked Audrey if she'd sing to her brother, mostly just to distract her from the noise of a screaming baby beside her.

> She made up a song called "milk," sung to a tune that resembled a Gregorian chant. "Milk is coming," she sang. "Milk is on the way." She sang all the way to the doctor's and home again, and her brother didn't make a sound the whole time — or ever anytime Audrey sang him "milk." The song and its many variations remained in our lives over the year and a half. It worked only when Audrey sang it, and it had to be about milk, had to be that same non-tune. The moment she started singing, he stopped his crying. and the lesson my daughter learned from the milk song stayed with her. Music can be magic.

The Suzuki Method

William Starr
Department of Music
University of Colorado, Boulder
Chairman of the Board, The International Suzuki Association

"All Japanese children speak Japanese!" exclaimed Suzuki to his friends one day. He had suddenly realized the astonishing fact that every normal child old enough to talk had been successfully educated by the mother-tongue method.

> "Children everywhere learn to speak their own tongues fluently which shows that they have a very high level of ability. The most successful example of the learning process is the mother-tongue method. Not only do normal children all over the world learn the basics of their mother-tongue without text, test, or classroom, but they also learn to speak the dialect with its often subtle nuance, and they are able to build an amazing vocabulary before they ever set foot in a school."

> "If these same children do not do well in school, is it because they have used up their allotment of ability acquiring their mother-tongue, or because the educational method is so drastically different?"

> "I was determined to study the mother-tongue method and to try to apply it in the teaching of violin to small children. The results of my endeavors came to be known as the 'Suzuki Method,' but it is nothing other than my adaptation of the principles of the mother-tongue method of music instruction."

Suzuki saw that the baby learns with joy and confidence, is fascinated with learning, expects to learn, learns at his own rate often with a staggering number of repetitions, knows what his own rate is, learns in order to retain and use his knowledge and skill, moves very slowly at the beginning, chooses to learn in small steps, doesn't move on to the next step until he is ready, and hasn't the faintest idea what a negative self-image is! He is inspired by loving teachers who demonstrate again and again the skills he wants to imitate. He is excited by the fascination, delight and praise with which these loving teachers greet each new step of learning. He is encouraged because everyone expects him to learn and allows him the time he needs to do it. His desire to learn grows and grows.

In truth, how many educational experiences does one have in life that have the same ingredients that make the mother-tongue method so successful?

Putting the development of a desire to play at the top of the list, Suzuki drew up these aids to instruction for his teachers and parents:

1. Constantly think of new ideas to help awaken and develop desire in the child.

2. Be aware of the effect of teacher and parent attitudes, particularly expectations.

3. Always expect the best from the student.

4. Remember that beginners learn very slowly.

5. Do not allow any child to feel that he has failed.

6. Remember that each child has his own rate of advancement.

7. Remind yourself daily that every child has high ability.

8. Review constantly to develop fluency, refine skills and to keep a certain amount of repertoire "in the fingers."

9. Provide early participation in concerts.

10. Make the private lesson a social affair.

11. Provide many opportunities for performance

12. Encourage weekly home concerts.

13. Encourage regular attendance at group lessons.

14. Encourage frequent listening to recordings to motivate the child and educate him.

15. Motivate the child with graduation from one level to another.

16. Praise and encourage the child often.

17. Teach in small steps that the child can learn easily.

18. Work to develop the child's attention span, and his visual, aural, and kinesthetic sensibilities.

19. Remember that the goal is to enable the child to play fluently at each level of advancement so that he will enjoy performing for himself and others.

20. Remember that you are educating the whole child — heart and mind and body. His study of music should enrich his whole life and make him a more beautiful human being.

Now I would like to expand on several aspects of the Suzuki method to illustrate how Suzuki carries them out in practice.

In his book, *Nurtured by Love*, Suzuki describes what he feels is the ideal way to begin instruction:

> Although we accept infants, at first we do not have them play the violin. First, we teach the mother to play one piece so that she will be a good teacher at home. As for the child, we first have him simply listen at home to a record of the piece he will be learning. Children are really educated in the home, so in order that the child will have good posture and practice properly at home, it is necessary for the parent to have first-hand experience. The correct education of the child depends on this. Until the parent can play one piece, the child does not play at all. This principle is very important indeed, because although the parent may want him to do so, the three or four-year-old child has no desire to learn the violin. The idea is to get the child to say, "I want to play, too," so the first piece is played every day on the phonograph, and in the studio he just watches the other children (and his mother) having their lessons. The proper environment is created for the child. The mother, moreover, both at home and in the studio, plays on a small violin more suited to the child. The child will naturally before long take the violin away from his mother, thinking, "I want to play, too." He knows the tune already. The other children are having fun;

he wants to join in the fun. We have caused him to acquire this desire.

This situation having been created, lessons are led up to in the following order: first the parent asks, "Would you like to play the violin, too?" The answer is "Yes!" "You will practice hard?" "Yes." "All right, let's ask the teacher if you can join in next time." This always succeeds. What a thrill the first private lesson always is! "I did it, too," the child boasts. "Now I can play with the other children." Parents who understand children make fine teachers. In the studio there are private lessons and group lessons. Parents who do not understand children think they are paying for the private lessons and that the group lessons are just recreation periods. So although they make sure that their children attend the private lessons, they often fail to bring them to the group lessons. But the fact is that what the children enjoy most is the group playing. They play with children who are more advanced than they are; the influence is enormous, and is marvelous for their training. This is real talent education."

Although teaching the mother first is generally accepted as being the ideal way for a beginner to start in Talent Education, for one reason or another not all Talent Education teachers do this. Some are content that the mother knows how to teach the child at home. If the child is older than three, the desire to imitate the mother may be overshadowed by the desire to be independent. At any age, Suzuki has found it normal that the child wants to please the parents and the teacher. The child expects his parents to be vitally interested in what he is doing, and wants praise for his successful development. In Japan often the whole family shows great interest in the child's violin playing.

Praise

In a lesson for a beginning three-year-old, Suzuki was heard to say "umai" (good) after every effort the child made. He never said, "No, that is not good," but only "Good. Can you do this better? Let's try again." He urges the mother also to praise the child at every step. Many mothers withhold praise if the child does badly, thinking that if they then praise the child he will not know when he is doing well and when he isn't. Suzuki explains that there can be degrees of praise and that it is better to be silent than to be critical.

In most cases, the ingenious mother can find something worthwhile to call to the child's attention. "That tone was better." "You remembered all the notes." "You held your violin higher." "Your bow hold was good." If the teacher and mother are guiding the child properly they need not worry about a little undeserved praise. "Very good. Can you do better?" is the basic Suzuki formula.

Home Concerts

Suzuki urges each mother to stage weekly home concerts for the father to see the child's progress. These concerts can be scheduled at the beginning of instruction even before the child can perform anything. Many mothers have made this a real event, making small stages or platforms out of boxes for these concerts. At first, the child walks up onto the "stage" with his violin tucked under his arm and his bow in his hand. After facing the father, he bows solemnly and then leaves the stage. He has shown the father how well he can hold the violin "at rest" In the early months when the progress is very slow as the teacher and mother are trying to prepare the child's postures and bow hold properly, the weekly home concert can be quite an incentive for the child. Every small step forward is noticed and applauded.

Private Lessons

Suzuki finds that private lessons provide a great deal of motivation if the teacher really loves children and enjoys teaching them. The private lesson is always a public affair in Talent Education. Suzuki says that the child should always watch lessons of other children. He considers this environment essential, observing that the child learns from the advanced students perhaps more than he does directly from his teacher. In a typical Talent Education private lesson the studio is filled with mothers and children who wait patiently watching private lessons of other students.

Early Participation in Concerts

Suzuki believes early participation in concerts is a fine motivating force for beginners, not only in the home concert, but also in public recitals and concerts. I witnessed a charming demonstration of this idea of early participation at a prefectural concert performed by over four hundred students. Immediately after intermission, members of the audience hurried to their seats to see the beginners bow. The children came on stage solemnly, violins under their right arms and bows clutched in their fingers. After they had been lined up, a chord was played on the piano, and they bowed, staring out at the audience which responded with resounding applause. They then ran happily off the stage. Some had come sixty miles by train for this event!

Graduation

To increase motivation in the young children, Suzuki has created a system of "graduations" throughout Talent Education in Japan. Talent Education youngsters from all over Japan send tapes to Suzuki to qualify for "graduation" from one level of difficulty to the next. This means that Suzuki listens to approximately one thousand tapes every year. All of the children graduate, and all are rated "excellent" or better by Suzuki!

At the end of the student's selection, Suzuki records comments and advice for improvement. Not all of these remarks deal with technique, tone, or musical sensitivity. For instance graduates progressing on to the Bach *Concerto in A Minor* have been given words of advice that must have received warm welcomes in Japanese households:

> Now you are going to play great concertos of Mozart and Bach, and you must try to catch the heart of Bach and Mozart in their music. You must practice every day to catch the feelings of others without words. Look at your mother and father. Can you see how they feel? Try to see when your mother needs your help — before she asks. Then it is too late. If you practice every day, watching not to harm anyone by what you say, and also trying to catch how they feel, then you will develop sensitivity toward the feelings of others. Perhaps later you will also catch the heart of Bach and Mozart in their music."

Suzuki receives many letters from mothers expressing their gratitude to him for these words of advice to their children.

Some Suzuki teachers in the West give pins or certificates to students in recognition of their graduation to another level. These are usually presented at the recital at which the children have performed their graduation pieces.

William Starr

Constant Review

Both parent and child should know that the rate of improvement during practice on a specific complex task is by no means stationary. The rate of improvement is often very fast at the start. The first repetitions contribute a great deal to the mastery of the problem. Children are sometimes quite disturbed by the fact that the following repetitions seem to contribute increasingly less to the total performance.

This is one advantage of the Suzuki review work. In fact, Suzuki doesn't expect the student to have complete mastery of a piece before he goes on to the next one. Hundreds of follow-up repetitions are scattered through the student's practice days as he reviews earlier material.

These repetitions, contributing more slowly to the learning process, are not as stressful as they would be if the student were to do all of them immediately after the notes and fingerings were learned. Refinement and growth are very gradual, perhaps not perceived by the child, yet very real, contributing significantly to the child's developing skill.

Slow Rate of Progress, Many Repetitions

"Beginners learn so slowly. Same as mother-tongue. The baby does not say 'Mama' and then immediately speak many different words. No! The mother does not say to the child, 'You have said "Mama" enough times. Next word.' No. The child must repeat and repeat if he is to learn. Knowledge is not skill. Knowledge plus 10,000 times is skill."

In the group lesson following this talk, I will illustrate several of the principles upon which the success of Suzuki's method rests. And successful it is, capturing the imagination of parents and teachers all over the world. In the last twenty years it has spread to include thousands upon thousands of children in thirty countries, children studying not only violin, but also piano, cello, bass, harp and guitar.

Although only a small percentage of these Suzuki students have made, or will make careers in music, Suzuki, ever the idealist, insists that the child's study of music should enrich his whole life and make him a more beautiful human being.

Teaching Tots and Toddlers

Donna Brink Fox
Department of Music Education and
Cluster on Musical Development and Cognition
Eastman School of Music

In the fall of 1985, the youngest student at the Eastman School of Music was five months old. Today, Gregory Stern, already a two-time alumnus of the MusicTIME program, is enrolling with his father, Michael, for "Music Times Two," marking his graduation to the two-year-old classes. Gregory's mother, Donna, is an operating room supervisor and visits occasionally on her day off. Why did this father, a non singing factory worker who played the trombone as an elementary student, elect to participate in a music class with his young son? Because Michael had noted how naturally and spontaneously the baby reacted to all types of music, and as a parent, he wanted more information and ideas on how to keep Gregory interested and responsive.

Michael's observations of Gregory were not unique. Researchers and teachers repeatedly have observed the enthusiasm and interest of young children in relationship to music. Those who have formally studied the relationship between home environment and musical development consistently have identified the important role of parents in influencing the musical behavior at an early age (Bloom, 1985; Jenkins, 1976; Kirkpatrick, 1962). Katz (1986) suggests that parents can provide for children the opportunity to develop skills and knowledge about music, but even more important, can help them acquire positive "disposition" toward music by spending time with them in musical activities.

The research literature documenting the musical behaviors of infants and toddlers is scant; some dozen studies in nearly twenty years have been conducted by musicians. Researchers in various fields of psychology have made us aware, however, of the tremendous capacity of the very young child to respond to sound and to initiate sound-related behaviors. The MusicTIME program at the Eastman School of Music was designed to explore further the nature of music behavior in children under the age of three years, and how that behavior might be nurtured by adults. The purpose of the program is to provide an interactive educational experience for adults and children, with the emphasis throughout the sessions on active involvement in both making and responding to music. The training of new teachers is an integral component of the program, along with observation and research.

Program Organization

MusicTIME classes are offered through the Community Education Division of the Eastman School of Music, which is one of the colleges within the University of Rochester. Parents pay a fee to the Community Education Division, which handles all registration and billing for the classes. Space for the program has been provided by the Metrocenter YMCA, built in 1983 and located directly across the street from the school. The staff for the program includes one faculty member from the Music Education Department, graduate and undergraduate students in a variety of majors, as well as community .personnel. The program is organized into 10-week sessions, with each class approximately 40-50 minutes in length.

In the fall of 1986, a second level of the program was initiated, called Music Times Two, and intended for children two to three years. The emphasis in these classes is on more independent responses and taking turns, as children develop the social skills to be part of a musical group. (See workshop handout for specific activities appropriate for this level.)

Observation

At the close of the 10-week session, parents are asked to observe and assess their own child's at-home musical behavior using a tool developed for that purpose by Donna Brink Fox. The MusicTIME Behavior Profile is a listing of 55 categories of musical behavior, divided into areas of vocal development, movement response, exploring sounds, and participation. Each individual behavior is coded according to its frequency or consistency of occurrence using this scale:

> 0=Not observed
> 1=Seldom or occasionally observed
> 2=Frequently observed
> 3=Always or consistently observed

In addition, parents are encouraged to comment on, explain, or amplify their numerical assessment by providing examples of their child's specific musical behavior at home.

Finale

In the introduction to her guidebook for *Music Play Unlimited*, Barbara Andress suggests that what young children need to help them make music are adults who reflect interest in making/becoming involved in music, and who are willing to enter the child's world of play, model and/or otherwise motivate music making. MusicTIME provides that place for parents, as Michael and Gregory learn from each other and from the other children and adults, developing a life-long disposition to be a music-maker.

References

Alford, D.L. "Emergence and development of music responses in preschool twins and singletons: A comparative study," *Journal of Research and Music Education*, 19, 222-227, 1968.

Alvarez, B.J., (1981). "Preschool music education and research on the musical development of preschool children: 1900-1980," Doctoral dissertation, The University of Michigan, 1981.

Andress, B. "Toward an integrated developmental theory for early childhood music education," *Council for Research in Music Education*, 86, 10-17, 1986.

Bloom, B.S. (Ed.), *Developing talent in young people*, New York: Ballantine Books, 1985.

Brand, M. "Relationship between home musical environment and selected musical attributes of second-grade children," *Journal of Research in Music Education, 34*(2), 111-120, 1986.

Chang, H., & Trehub, S. "Auditory processing of relational information by young infants," *Journal of Experimental Child Psychology*, 24, 324-331, 1977a.

Chang, H., & Trehub, S. "Infants' perception of temporal grouping in auditory patterns," *Child Development*, 48, 1660-1670, 1977b.

Fox, D.B. "Development of the MusicTIME program at the Eastman School of Music," Unpublished paper presented at the ISME Early Childhood Commission seminar, Reaching the Young Child Through Music, Keskcemet, Hungary, 1986.

Fox, D.B. "The pitch range and contour of infant vocalizations,"Doctoral dissertation, The Ohio State University, 1976.

Greenberg, M. "Research in music in early childhood: A survey with recommendations," *Council for Research in Music Education,* 45, 1-20, 1976.

Honig, A.S. *Parent involvement in early childhood education* (2nd Ed.). Washington, DC: National Association for the Education of Young Children, 1979.

Honig. A.S. "Parent involvement in early childhood education," In B. Spodek (Ed), *Handbook of research in early childhood education* (pp. 426-455). New York: The Free Press, 1982.

Jenkins, J.M.D. "The relationship between maternal parents' musical experience and the musical development of two-and three- year-old girls," Doctoral dissertation, North Texas State University, 1976.

Katz, L.G. "Current perspectives on child development," *Council for Research in Music Education,* 86, 1-9, 1986.

Kenney, S. J. "A parent/toddler music program," In J. Boswell (Ed.), *The young child and music: Contemporary principles in child development and music education* (p.103). Reston, VA: Music Educators National Conference, 1985.

Kessen, W., Levine, J. & Wendrich, K. "The imitation of pitch in infants," *Infant Behavior and Development,* 2, 93-99, 1979.

Kirkpatrick, W. "Relationships between the singing ability of pre-kindergarten children and their home musical environment," Doctoral dissertation, University of Southern California, 1962.

Kucenski, S.D. "Implementation and empirical testing of a sequential music sensory learning program on the infant learner," Doctoral dissertation, Northwestern University, 1977.

Larsen, J. M. "Influences of home and family on musical opportunities of educationally advantaged preschool, kindergarten, and second grade children," In J. Boswell (Ed.), *The young child and music: Contemporary principles in child development and music education* (p.117). Reston, VA: Music Educators National Conference.

Missouri Department of Elementary and Secondary Education, 1986. *New parents as teachers.* Jefferson City, MO: Author.

Reis, N.L.L. "An analysis of the characteristics of infant-child singing expressions," Doctoral dissertation, Arizona State University, 1982.

Simons, G.M. "Early childhood musical development: A survey of selected research," *Council for Research in Music Education, 86* 36-52, 1986.

Simons, G.M. "Comparisons of incipient music responses among very young twins and singletons," *Journal of Research in Music Education,* 12, 212-226, 1964.

Summers, E.K. "Categorization and conservation of melodies in infants," Doctoral dissertation, University of Washington, 1984.

Tims, F.C. "Contrasting music conditions, visual attending behavior, and musical preferences in eight-week old infants," Doctoral dissertation, The University of Kansas, 1978.

Trehub, S.E., Bull, D., & Thorpe, L.A. "Infants' perception of melodies: The role of melodic contour," *Child Development,* 55, 821-830, 1984.

Wendrich, K.A. "Pitch imitation in infancy and early childhood: Observations and implications," Doctoral dissertation, The University of Connecticut, 1981.

Zimmerman, M.P. "State of the art in early childhood music and research," In J. Boswell (Ed.), *The young child and music: Contemporary principles in child development and music education* (pp. 65-78). Reston, VA: Music Educators National Conference, 1986.

Teaching Music for Life

Sharon Jones
Sebastopol, California

I would like to begin my paper with a short story. The author is unknown.

> A young boy traveled across Japan to the school of a famous martial artist. When he arrived at the *dojo* he was given an audience by the *sensei*. "What do you wish from me?," the master asked. "I wish to be your student and become the finest *karateka* in the land," the boy replied. "How long must I study?" "Ten years at least," the master answered. 'Ten years is a long time," said the boy. "What if I started now and studied twice as hard as all your other students?" "Twenty years," replied the master. "Twenty years! What if I practiced day and night with all my effort?" "Thirty years, was the master's reply." "How is it that each time I say I will work harder you tell me that it will take longer?" the boy asked. "The answer is clear. When one eye is fixed upon your destination, there is only one eye left to find the way."

It is becoming painfully clear in our current American society that stress is destroying us as a nation in the world and internally as a people. Not only does the threat of nuclear destruction hang over us but the effects of overwhelming stress are wreaking havoc in our mind-body-emotional organism. Increasingly, the symptoms of debilitating stress are showing up in our children and students. It is my belief that our old world music paradigm must change as we move towards the twenty-first century. The study of music as it is now taught is one more added stress to a child's life and can place considerable pressure on a family that is already overburdened and quite literally overwhelmed by regular day-to-day living.

As a culture we have accepted the premise that the study of music is an end in itself. However with new research emerging from the fields of music/medicine, music/psychology and music/science, past assumptions are being challenged, discarded and amended. It is my thesis that the focus of music study should be to foster self-knowledge, self-expression and creativity, self-fulfillment, healing, and to encourage family and community music making amongst people of all ages through improvisation. The mastery of an individual instrument will evolve naturally, not as a goal in itself, but as the outcome of a healthy music relationship with the child's teacher, parents, siblings and community.

My interest and first steps as a fledgling piano teacher began thirty-five years ago at the age of eighteen while I was a music student at Stanford University. My teaching has taken me all over the United States. My last position was at the Harlem School of the Arts in New York City where I was Chairman of the Piano Department for six years. In addition I have four children; one a concert pianist, another a professional dancer and teacher, another a violinist and stage manager for the Performing Arts Series at St. John the Divine in New York City, and the fourth, a college student who passionately loves music and dance as an avocation. My experience as a music student, parent, teacher and administrator has led me to ask many questions. These questions precipitated a major crisis during my stay at Harlem.

At my initial interview for the position of Chairman, I was asked if I could develop a pre-professional piano conservatory program which would co-exist with an open school type of environment. The teachers were to track the students according to ability, motivation, coordination, cognitive skills, talent/promise and family support. We were encouraged to teach the students to enter the outside world, compete with the finest students anywhere, and win.

We began to develop a 12-year curriculum, with juries planned at the end of each year. We set up honor recitals — winners determined by audition and competitions within the school. As is our way in America, we taught the children how to pit themselves against each other, with winning or losing becoming the only relevant outcomes of musical study despite our assurances that: "This will be a learning experience for you. It doesn't matter whether you win or lose." We also presented many achievement recitals to recognize children for any significant improvement in interest, mastery, ability, performance, creativity, etc. And there were regular recitals once or twice a month.

We taught the students well. They began to compete outside the school and they often won. Our program rapidly became known on the East Coast. The number of students grew from approximately 50 to 200 with an additional 150 on the waiting list. Students came from all five boroughs of New York

City, New Jersey and Connecticut. Some commuted two hours each way for a one-hour lesson.

The piano faculty grew from 8 to 16 members. Most of the teachers either had received or were working on their Master's or Doctorate from Juilliard, Manhattan, Leningrad, etc. The teachers were from Russia, Germany, South America, Japan and the United States. Many of the teachers were performers and were entering competitions such as the Leeds.

As the program entered its fourth year I began noticing problems with the students. There were psychological and physical problems: free-floating anxiety; nightmares, headaches and stomach aches; performance phobias; sleeping disorders; music-related physical pain; increased sibling rivalry; decreased spontaneity, with observable inhibitions beginning to develop. With demanding, over-concerned and over-involved parents being commonplace, increased family tension and illness due to the stress of music study also became commonplace. Most of the open school children eventually quit music study completely because they felt they were not "good enough." The ones who stayed were there primarily because their parents insisted.

The teachers also went through their own transformation. When I arrived at Harlem, the school had not had a Piano Chairman for a year. The department was disorganized and lacked focus, structure, or goals for the students. A black cellist in the String Department remarked that, "Third world children are taught that they are disadvantaged." As I observed the teaching that was going on, I agreed completely. The program was in difficulty.

Over the next three years, after I had taken over the department, we became cohesive, supportive, committed and enthusiastic. However, as we moved into the fourth year, I noticed a change. The teachers secretly began comparing themselves with each other. Everyone pushed harder. The "losing" teachers were motivated by a fear of inadequacy, while the "winning" teachers were motivated by their need to remain on top. Competition had become a runaway horse with the teachers having lost the reins. Teacher's jobs were at stake and the children unwittingly became the sacrifice.

Some of the teachers were also concerned. When we realized how destructive the atmosphere had become, we agreed to address the problems seriously. Each child played for me at least once a month to work on the physical or psychological problems associated with practice and performance. The teachers and I held monthly pedagogy classes to discuss problems of particular students and personal concerns of the teachers. I had many meetings with the families of students I was particularly concerned about. In short, we did everything we knew how to do to alleviate these problems. We were not successful.

To the world outside of Harlem (and even to most within the school), we appeared enormously successful. I was approached by a faculty member at Columbia University with a proposal to start an internship program for their graduate students in music pedagogy. The intention was to start a collaboration sometime in 1987.

It was becoming clear to me I had helped create a monster. I worried incessantly about the "losers" and the open school children who supposedly had no aptitude for music. I kept remembering the words of Thoreau: "The woods would be very silent if no birds sang except those that sang best." The problems of the "winners" haunted me. What did I really want for these children? Did I want them to go out into the world prepared as pianists, albeit with problems exactly like the rest of the world's pianists, but not prepared for life? Did they and their parents in their innocence understand and ultimately want for themselves the psychological and physical distress that plague so many of our musicians today? How in all honesty were these kids going to *support* themselves? Did I want to take personal responsibility for encouraging these students to make competition their God? What did I really want the children to learn? What would benefit them the most as they faced this rather terrifying world of ours?

At this point, during the summer of 1985, I approached the administration of Harlem and New York University (N.Y.U. had just put on an international conference on "Stress and the Performing Arts") and proposed a collaboration between the two schools to examine our music program from the point of view of the students, teachers, "teaching music in general," and families; to consider career possibilities, minorities in music, the prevention of physical injuries and psychological distress; to consider music in relation to human biology and the treatment of illness. Several departments at N.Y.U. were eager to be involved; approval was given to this project and in the fall of 1986 we thought we were prepared to begin. Then, rather abruptly, and for reasons I can only surmise, enthusiasm for the project at Harlem simply evaporated. Seeing this collaboration as indispensible to my personal commitment to the healthy education of these children, I resigned. The words of Pablo Casals rang in my head:

> "Each second we live in a new and unique moment of the universe, a moment that never was before and never will be

again. And what do we teach our children in school? We teach them that two and two are four and that Paris is the capital of France. When will we also teach them what they are? We should say to each of them: Do you know what you are? You are a marvel. You are unique. In all of the world there is no other child exactly like you. In the millions of years that have passed, there has never been a child like you. And look at your body — what a wonder it is! Your legs, your arms, your cunning fingers, the way you move! You may become a Shakespeare, a Michelangelo, a Beethoven. You have a capacity for anything. Yes, you are a marvel. And when you grow up, can you then harm another who is, like you, a marvel? You must cherish one another. You must work — we must all work — to make this world worthy of its children."

How do we teach our children music for life? In a quote from the current best seller, *Codependent No More,* Melody Beattie quotes from the 1983 publication, *Honoring the Self,* by Nathaniel Branden:

"Of all the judgments that we pass in life, none is as important as the one we pass on ourselves, for that judgment touches the very center of our existence...

No significant aspect of our thinking, motivation, feelings, or behavior is unaffected by our self-evaluation...

To honor the self is to be willing to know not only what we think but also what we feel, what we want, need, desire, suffer over, are frightened or angered by — and to accept our right to experience such feelings. The opposite of this attitude is denial, disowning, repression — self-repudiation.

To honor the self is to preserve an attitude of self-acceptance — which means to accept what we are, without self-oppression or self-castigation, without any pretense about the truth of our own being, pretense aimed at deceiving either ourselves or anyone else...

To honor the self is to be in love with our own life, in love with our possibilities for growth and for experiencing joy, in love with the process of discovery and exploring our distinctively human potentialities."

We know now that music is a biological, therefore essential, part of human life. The fetus in the womb not only hears but actively listens to the sounds around it: its mother's breathing and heart beat; the soothing voices of the parents; the sounds and rhythm of music.

Studies with Alzheimer's patients suggest our sense of hearing may be the last sense retained as we age and move into the dying process. Music/sound is as integral to life as breathing, moving, seeing, talking, and sleeping. Have we been blinded by an obsession with the *performance* of music? Isn't it time to enlarge our limited concept and acknowledge music as a way of life, perhaps a vehicle *for* life; to view the student-teacher relationship as a healing relationship, a spiritual relationship or at the very least a relationship built on mutual respect and love of discovery? When will we see that music study can be a preparation for life only if it makes the student's positive self-image its highest priority?

When, where, and how can the child learn to "honor the self...be in love with its own life, in love with its possibilities for growth and experiencing joy, in love with the process of discovery and exploring its distinctively human potentialities?" Who gives children the tools for living, coping, caring and sharing? If our children have no childhood, they have no future. Stress permeates our homes, our schools, our streets, country and the world. We want them to learn to act; we teach them to *act out*.

Teaching music for life. Is this possible, realistic? It is being done in other cultures, why not ours? Private music teachers are probably the most significant adult in a child's life other than the parents or care-taker. A teacher spends one-half to one hour each week at a specified time with a student. This learning relationship may go on for years. It is one of the most critical learning relationships the child will ever have. How can you overstate the enormous and awesome responsibility that is placed on the shoulders of our teachers? What goes on during the lesson will impact your student's life forever.

Some of us have thought of the study of music as a discipline; others a kind of fluff — the frosting, if you will, on life. I don't think it matters *what* the real reason for music study turns out to be in any student's case. What *does* matter a great deal is the teacher's commitment to the emotional and physical health of the child.

We need finally to admit that the seeds may be sown in the teacher's studio for physical and psychological pain associated with music learning. It is now time for us to educate ourselves so that our influence will only be positive. What is the *very least* we can hope for in a good student-teacher learning relationship? I will speak for teachers, but the same holds true for anyone in a musical relationship with a child.

1. Create an environment in your studio of calm, peace, support and unconditional acceptance, a haven and refuge where your students can let go and totally be themselves. Encourage them in their total acceptance of themselves as they see themselves mirrored in you.

2. Determine how each child learns best — whether through intuition, reason, sensation or feeling. If the child learns best through sensation, which sense — aural, visual, kinesthetic or touch? How important is imitation, or, at the other extreme, individuality and independence? Gradually, as the child is ready, enlarge his/her modes of learning. Howard Gardner, in *Frames of Mind,* discusses his theory of multiple intelligences and the crossover in most disciplines. It is helpful for the teacher to be aware of the style of learning a student uses. In my opinion, the study, transmission, performance, and creativity (improvisation and composition) involved in music-making include all of Gardner's categories: musical intelligence, bodily-kinesthetic intelligence, spatial intelligence, logical-mathematical intelligence, linguistic intelligence, and the personal intelligences. The teacher can identify learning problems and blocks more easily with an awareness of these learning intelligences.

Question and tear to shreds everything you have learned and accepted as necessary to the building of technique — the way you teach scales and arpeggios, exercises and etudes. Examine "givens" such as: "Practice this passage until you can play it 3 times without a mistake." Keep constantly in your mind that physical injuries develop through overuse and misuse of our muscles, tendons, joints, etc. Each student is unique with completely different bodies, body tension, weaknesses, strengths, needs and goals. Pay attention! Keep abreast of new information regarding the body: massage techniques for the hand, warm-up body movements, relaxation techniques, new practice techniques for mastery and memorization; in short, *every aspect* that pertains to the musician and his instrument. Your primary musical goal is to equip the student ultimately to teach himself.

Examine your students' repertoire closely. Give up your past assumptions regarding what *all* students need to play and the old logical progression. Consider the possibility that some repertoire might even be dangerous for certain students — pushing their bodies beyond what is possible and healthy for them. Rethink our past emphasis on speed (we must achieve the metronome marking or...?) and perfection as the unstated goals of practice and performance. Re-examine all fingerings and approach them with fresh eyes from the standpoint of prevention rather than speed and volume, and how it applies to the individual student.

3. A part of each lesson should be devoted to improvisation and composition. In this way a child begins to hear and trust her own unique voice, her precious gift to the world. She can then actively participate in creating music with others, thereby experiencing a sense of unity and belonging. Many children may want to include, or prefer, chamber music and orchestral experiences. It is the teacher's responsibility to encourage and suggest opportunities for community music-making.

4. A lesson is not wasted if it is spent listening to a child talk. If he is upset by something that has happened, he won't be able to learn anyway. He will just draw further into himself. Be with him, where he is, every moment. Give up your agenda. It may not be his agenda. He is or should be teaching you and guiding you. The student may bring you a poem, a story he has written, a picture he has painted, a scene he has photographed, a little piece he has composed. In short, he offers you a gift of himself. He may want you to listen to a piece of music on a tape by which he has been moved. He might speak of something beautiful he has seen and experienced in nature. You in turn might share those things that have touched you. You can help him to see and appreciate the majesty, beauty and wonder of the world around him as it unfolds anew every moment; what a miracle life is and how we must protect it!

Again, the student must guide you. Reflecting on the period of her adolescence, Wanda Landowska asked the question:

> "What did I learn? Nothing, really nothing. I was refractory to rules and laws. As soon as they were imposed on me, I stiffened, terrified. My music was covered with exercises in which I had no interest at all. Counterpoint? Yes, but through the direct channel of Bach. I sang the voices separately with a limitless joy. I

punctuated them and they became lively; they sprang forth. Was my teacher inadequate? Or was I a bad pupil?"

When a teacher is controlling and authoritarian, his behavior may be springing from a deep well of inadequacy and fear within himself. In the words of Stephen Levine:

> "Coping makes one long for control. It may make one attempt to appear very together as a mask for feelings of powerlessness. Indeed, it is the remarkable power of letting go that creates balance instead of a need to maintain control: it is trust in our vast 'don't know' that allows room for the truth, that allows the next intuition to float to the surface. In a funny way it is your models, your knowing, your training, that keeps you from becoming the 'teacher' (substituted for the word "healer") you have always wished to be. All training is a preparation to go beyond training. It is the effort we make to reach 'the effortless.' There are no rules. There is only a sense of the appropriateness that floats in the heart, changing from moment to moment."

5. Be with your students, wherever they are; participate in and encourage their joy — their actual love affair with music. Be with them in their child-likeness, their pain, their rapture and spontaneity. Encourage them in their fearlessness, their freedom. Stephen Levine asks:

> "How do we prepare students to jump off the edge? The edge is where all growth occurs and growth is really a letting go of those places of holding beyond which we seldom venture. That is the edge of our cave, our imagined limitations, our attachment to old models of who we think we are or *should* be. It is our edges that define what we consider 'safe territory.'"

6. Expose *yourself* to your students. Share your joy, your laughter, your child-like nature, your spontaneity and play. Let them see, experience and participate in the deeper spiritual side of your nature. Show them your weaknesses, your mistakes, your fears, your pain — so they know they are not alone. It is this the student will take away from the lesson — participation with you and your joy and love of music, life and growth.

Openly love your students and show them how much you care about all aspects of their lives; their uniqueness and individuality, the way they relate not only to music but more importantly, to their journeys through life. Help give them tools for self-discovery. Edward Crankshaw said of Artur Schnabel:

> "In every situation what he gave was invariably himself and his life was basically an endless exploration into the truth of everything that came his way...His whole life, his whole conversation, was unending discovery, and it applied to everything he touched or that interested him; there was only one tabu, and that was (anything) second hand. The whole of his teaching was bent to one end: to make his pupils think for themselves...There was only one thing forbidden: received authority including his own. 'Tradition,' he would say — and this applied to tradition in piano playing as in everything else — 'too often means a collection of bad habits.' "

7. During a lesson with any student, no matter the age, there is *never* a place for anger, intimidation, sarcasm, irritation, belittling or embarrassing imitation. There is a place for firmness, directness, respect, clarity, gentleness, kindness, interest, humor, laughter, patience, support, humility, encouragement, *unconditional love and absolute faith*. The interaction with a teacher is where a child can learn about honesty, integrity, consistency, independence, courage, concern for others, optimism, considerateness, and consistent availability, stability and predictability from another human being. The child learns about the tiny necessary steps that lead to growth, success and achievement. In the words of Abraham Maslow:

> "Education for the child is growth through delight. How do we know when the child feels safe enough to dare to choose the new step ahead? Ultimately, the only way in which we can know is by *his* choices, which is to say only *he* can ever really know.

> Growth forward customarily takes place in little steps and each step forward is made possible by the feeling of being safe, of operating out into the unknown from a safe home port of daring because retreat is possible.

> Ultimately the person, even the child, must choose for himself. Nobody can choose for him too often, for this itself enfeebles him, cutting his self-trust and confusing his *ability* to perceive his own *internal* delight in the experience, his own impulses, judgments, and feelings and to differentiate them from the interiorized standards of others."

During the lesson the child learns about himself in relation to others. He learns to care for others as his teacher cares for him and he learns about the reciprocity of love.

We still know so little about man and his true relationship to music — what it means to his soul. In conclusion I will end with an Armenian folk legend entitled, *Listening to One's Own Note:*

> "A man had a cello with one string which he would bow for hours and hours on end, always holding his finger at the same place on the string. For seven months his wife put up with the noise in the patient expectation that her husband would either die of boredom, or smash the instrument. However, since neither happened, she gently said one evening: 'I have noticed that when others play this wonderful instrument, it has four strings for bowing, and the players keep moving their fingers up and down.'
>
> The husband stopped playing for a moment, shook his head, and replied, 'Of course the others move their fingers up and down. They are looking for the right place. I have found it.' "

References

Beattie, M. *Codependent No More,* New York: Harper & Row, pp. 115-116, 1987.

Gardner, H. *Frames of Mind, The Theory of Multiple Intelligences,* Basic Books, Inc., 1985.

Landowski, W. *Landowska on Music,* Edited by Denise Restout Stein and Day, New York, p. 7, 1965,

Levine, S. *Meetings at the Edge,* Anchor Press, New York: Doubleday & Company, pp 47, 44, 1984.

Maslow, A. *Toward a Psychology of Being,* New York: Van Nostrand Reinhold Company, p. 49, 1968 .

Schnabel, A. *My Life and Music,* Longmans, Green and Company, Ltd., Great Britain, p. xv, 1961.

Breaking 100 in Music

Panel Discussion

Moderator: Roy Ernst, Chairman, Department of Music Education, Eastman School of Music, University of Rochester

Panelists

Paula Bernstein, Assistant Clinical Professor of Psychiatry, University of Colorado School of Medicine

Richard Colwell, Professor of Music and Music Education, University of Illinois at Urbana-Champaign

Edwin Gordon, Professor of Music, Temple University

Sharon Jones, Former Chairperson, Piano Faculty, Harlem School of the Arts

Helen Myers, Consulting Ethnomusicologist, *The New Grove Dictionary of Music and Musicians*, London

Rosalie Rebollo Pratt, Professor of Music; member, Graduate Council, Brigham Young University

Kyle Pruett, Associate Clinical Professor of Psychiatry, Yale Child Study Center

Lauren Sosniak, Assistant Professor of Education, University of Illinois at Chicago

At one of the planning meetings for this conference, a committee member told the following story:

> Some years ago, a bowling ball manufacturer became concerned over declining sales of his product and ordered a market survey to learn something of the feelings of the typical bowler for his sport. It was reported to him that as soon as someone begins regularly to bowl scores over 100, this person begins to regard himself or herself as a "bowler." Similarly, it seems that golfers respond

positively when their scores begin to fall under 100. The number 100, then, is in some cases a benchmark for achievement in an important recreational endeavor, warranting feelings of success and worthiness. The teller of this story then noted that there does not seem to be a similar benchmark in music — an identifiable marker that signals to the individual entitlement to membership in the world of music-makers. This panel will explore, in view of the discussions earlier in the week and in view of their own personal feelings on the subject, just what it means to "break 100" in music.

ROY ERNST: The topic Breaking 100 in Music is large and unfocused, but our panel approaches its challenge with a wonderful diversity of background. We will define the topic in several different ways, including a world music perspective, the perspective of persons who deal mostly with children who have developed a feeling of incompetence and a lack of success, and from the standpoint of nurturing a feeling of success and competence in making music, and also a feeling of success and confidence in listening to music.

The panel thought that I would be getting off too easily if I only had to direct traffic here, so they insisted that I make a comment on the topic also. I will place myself at the end of the line in doing that, however, so we will begin with Paula.

PAULA BERNSTEIN: Last night at the conference banquet, someone called this question a verbal Rorschach; it seems to mean something different to each of us. I think of the idea "Breaking 100 in Music" not so much in terms of the attainment of a certain level of musical competence (the threshold of which we would have to determine) but as a change in self-concept. "Are you a musician?" "Yes, I think I am." Or, conversely, "No, I'm not."

As a therapist concerned about the ways in which we thwart our own self-development, I'm not only curious about what makes that shift in one's sense of identity and sense of special competence happen, but also interested in what prevents it from happening. So I puzzle about it, from the point of view of a psychoanalyst and a student of infant development, trying to integrate what I brought with me with what was given here. I think of parallels between musical development and development in general. I think about a *musical self*.

The sense of self always develops in a context, along with a developing sense of the other, in close communion with the other — the beloved needed partner. The parent helps to inform the infant's behavior with meaning, by understanding what the infant wants or is trying to do. The parent affirms (or disaffirms) the infant's sense of self by reflecting back the emotional meaning of what the infant is experiencing. Infants and parents communicate by means of a nonverbal attunement that has been beautifully described by Daniel Stern in his book, *The Interpersonal World of the Infant* (New York, Basic Books, 1985). The attuned parent validates the infant's sense of having a self that is coherent, instrumental, and intersubjectively related to another. The parent also "tunes" or shapes the infant's experience. The parent helps the infant organize himself: from tension to *intention* — *from activity to act.* (See David Shapiro, *Neurotic Styles*, New York, Basic Books, 1965, p. 189.)

I was fascinated to see that in order to objectify the study of mother-infant attunement, Stern used dimensions that belong in a text of music: timing, rhythm, beat, crescendo and decrescendo. I came away from his book with the feeling that the early, preverbal relationship is made out of music. And, of course, nonverbal affective communication is not totally superseded by verbal communication. "The beat goes on" our whole life long.

I think of the African infant Dr. Blacking showed us, banging the pot. The adult hears not noise, but music — and joins in with the infant to add a more complex overlay of rhythmic pattern. The baby is transformed instantly into a functioning member of a musical community. If I understand Dr. Blacking correctly, every infant in the Venda culture will break 100 in music.

In contrast, as Dr. Bailey showed us, music in Afghanistan is regarded with great ambivalence. It is suspect because of its perceived alliance with the instincts, with dangerous untamed emotional forces. Music is split off from the religious and moral structure of that society. Like the women of that society, it continues to exert its mysterious power — but must be sequestered and veiled. A musical self means something very different to an African child and an Afghanistan child.

Why is it so hard to break 100 in our own culture? What are we really transmitting and receiving, consciously and unconsciously? Somehow our musical self — our *major* self in infancy — has become split off and lost. For some reason we acquire a terribly self-critical attitude. We are terrified down deep of performing music in front of other people. Many people don't break 100 in music because they don't think of themselves as *worthy* to.

It seems very clear to me after attending this conference that musical ability is developed in a relationship — in a succession of relationships — musical self in relation to musical selves. Those relationships are embedded in a culture which is, simply put, a distillation of the history of each teacher's relationships — musical and anti-musical. In one of the open discussions here, someone asked the question: "Why do fairly accomplished pianists still feel like imposters when they leave the stage?" The sense of falling short, the lack of a sense of ownership, authenticity, and joy in one's music making, keeps too many people from breaking 100 in music — from reclaiming and integrating into their lives a musical self.

RICHARD COLWELL: I will make a few brief comments about what I think breaking 100 would mean to most students who are studying music. First, what it is not. No matter how capable a student becomes in imitating songs, mere imitation will never lead to a feeling of musical competency. It seems to me that students would have to be able to read some of the music they are interested in singing or playing. Going from not being able to make sense out of musical symbols to making some sense of them independently is a very big step.

Second, it is important that students be able to recognize some of the more basic elements of music, such as melody, harmony, rhythm, and texture. These are things which one should be able to discern in music, things that one can feel good about, that lead to the self-confidence that Paula mentioned. When, for example, one can hear in music those things that people talk about during the intermission and after a concert, then I think one feels independently self-confident about music.

Third, in the area of performance, I think one should be able to harmonize without music, as one might do when singing around a campfire, or in church or school. I'm not suggesting that one needs to go as far as Dr. Zeitlin did during last night's performance; but I do think the ability to harmonize in the context I've described is basic to the idea of musical independence.

EDWIN GORDON: It is my sense that being able to audiate in addition to imitate would bring a person to feel they are breaking 100. Many people don't break 100 because they lack self-confidence; because they realize that all they can do is imitate what is taught to them, either in the context of a private music lesson or in a class learning a song by rote. Without knowing it, they lack the capacity to audiate. They know something is wrong, but don't know what.

We have a tendency to teach music by imitation, whether it be at the pre-school level or in the glorified trade schools we call music conservatories. As a graduate of a conservatory, I was trained to imitate, knowing full well that I was not being challenged to think. I had no self-confidence. All that belonged to me was given to me by my teachers. "Do it this way," I was told.

To me, breaking 100 is not necessarily a matter of being able to read music. Rather, it is being able to audiate. It is this ability that leads to the development of self-confidence and the capacity to read, improvise, and create music. Audiation is, therefore, at the core of all musical understanding.

SHARON JONES: Speaking from the perspective of a teacher, I am convinced that the student's overall well being and positive sense of self is central to both the joy and mastery he or she associates with music making. My Harlem experiences have led me to believe that the role of a teacher is to love the child. The child instinctively feels tension in the absence of love. If you can't love the child sitting next to you at a lesson, send the child to another teacher — the lessons with you will not be successful. The child's uniqueness and individuality must be recognized; not only his or her music but also his or her particular journey through life.

I would like to follow up on a point made earlier at this conference, explaining a child's breaking loose from or losing interest in music at age twelve or thirteen. I tend not to agree with Jeanne Bamberger's thesis that the child's crisis is basically a cognitive crisis. I think the musical crisis has to do with breaking away from the parent, and with the child's search for personal identity and ownership of his or her own interests. This, I think, is a part of the normal process of breaking away from the parent. If the parent is really involved with the child and its music, part of the breaking away from the parent may require breaking away from the music. I think that's how we lose many of our students.

Additionally, I believe the first interaction a teacher has with the child, and hopefully the entire family, is absolutely crucial. It's amazing how much can be found out in thirty minutes that enables one to find how best to reach the child. You can, for example, observe the dynamics between siblings, or take note of an illness in the family. These and similar matters, which can often be assessed very quickly, are very important to the development of a positive student-teacher relationship.

HELEN MYERS: My thoughts about this topic are grouped around the idea of "Breaking 100 in Music — The World Within and the World Beyond." We have reports of musicians from the world beyond our own culture, about their inner world of musical inspiration and about the circumstances of their first musical inspiration. As one might expect, although they share a number of common features, these reports are quite diverse. Often these experiences are propelled by a specific event. Generally, the musician describes an interaction with some external stimulus which may, for example, catapult him into the world of music. Or there may be a more gradual easing into the musical world. The event may occur in the context of a group of musicians, or it may occur in the presence of a witness who is listening, or it may occur in the presence of what are believed to be supernatural beings. I would like to offer you a small sample, seven short statements from or about musicians of different cultures, about the notion of the onset of musicianship.

One common concept is that the start of musicianship coincides with the acquisition, with the actual ownership, of a song or other piece of music. Accordingly, Frank Mitchell, who was a Navajo singer of the Blessingway ceremony, stated, "So during that time after I stopped hauling freight and began working more around home, I used to go out with my father-in-law, Man Who Shouts, whenever he was asked to perform the Blessingway. At first I just watched and then, finally, I felt I had learned practically everything he was doing, and before I knew it I was helping him with the ceremony. Finally I reached the point where I had learned it well enough so that I had a ceremony of my own." (Charlotte J. Frisbie and David P. McAllester, eds., *Navajo Blessingway Singer: The Autobiography of Frank Mitchell, 1881-1967*, Tucson, Arizona: Arizona University Press, 1978, p. 193). This was not sudden. This was a gradual easing into the world of music until the ceremony belonged to him.

Another example of musical ownership from American Indian culture is the Plains Vision Quest. Musicality and song ownership is achieved through a rite of passage. The individual goes into the wilderness, he isolates himself from the social group, he may fast. Finally, a supernatural being will present itself, often in the form of an animal, and will give the individual a song. We have a report from Alan Marriam recalling a statement by a Flathead Indian: "There was a man who was out hunting. He was sneaking up on the game by sitting at a spot on the game trail when he heard somebody singing. He thought, 'There must be people around.' So he stood there and waited to see who was coming. Pretty soon a spike bull elk came out from the brush and told him, 'This is your song. If you really need this song, sing it.' It was a love song. So he didn't kill the spike, and never killed an elk again." (Alan P. Merriam, *Ethnomusicology of the flathead Indians*, Chicago: Aldine Publishing Co., 1967, p.7).

Inspiration from dreams is quite common around the world. Among the Shona people of Zimbabwe we have this report about an mbira player (from the ethnomusicologist Paul Berliner). "When he was very young, two old men use to come to him in dreams and teach him the mbira. He recognized them as Zhanje and Makunde, both great mbira players in the Mujuru family; they had played for Chaminuka in his court at Chitungwiza. Mujuru remembers the dreams as being 'as clear as daylight.' The old men told him what to play on the mbira, and he would awake the next morning and perform the new parts he had learned during the night." (*The Soul of Mbira: Music and Traditions of the Shona People of Zimbabwe*, Berkeley: University of California Press, 1978, p.138).

The onset of musical inspiration may extend directly from the expression of an inner emotional state. From the Tiv people of Nigeria we have this report from Charles Keil concerning a man whose mother had just died. "When his mother died, he was very miserable because there was absolutely no one to provide for him. His father was dead long before that, so not knowing what to do to comfort himself, Chen starting crying [vaan]. In his cry Chen recalled all the nice treatment and provisions his mother had given him when she was alive. He sang them out in his cry. He did this repeatedly and it finally ended up in a beautiful song of condolence. Therefore, Chen, on being successful for the first time, went ahead composing." (Charles Keil, *Tiv Song: The Sociology of Art in a Classless Society*, Chicago: University of Chicago Press, 1979, p.128). Also from the Tiv we have an example of a first musical inspiration being stimulated by a combination of drugs or medicine and illness. "After being in his company for a little over a month, he decided to teach me to compose by giving me medicine. I never requested it. I took some for five days, and two different ones for eight days. Uduwua told me not to leave my house on the eighth, day, and soon after I woke up that day I fell suddenly ill. No one thought I would recover, and I too thought it was my end, but the next morning I was well again. From that day I was able to compose my own songs." (Keil, p. 147)

These reports of musical inspiration from dreams, fasting, inner emotional states, and so on, are quite sudden, quite abrupt. Moreover, they have a certain solitary quality about them, although they by no means occur in social isolation. In contrast, however, is the individual who discovers music in the context of a group. This next example, from the book *Akenfield* by Ronald Blythe, is about bell ringing in English churches. "During the war, in 1916, the parson here had two daughters who did a bit of ringing. I once saw them what they call 'raise the bell,' that is bring it full circle. So one day I went into the church and climbed the belfry, wound a sack round the clapper, went downstairs, — and pulled! To my amazement I got the bell up, so then I started practising. That is how I first came to ring. I then brought other boys to the tower and taught them how to do it, and then one day we all walked to Burgh and rang the six bells there — we couldn't stop. A ringer is first attracted by the sound of the bells, then he comes to see how it is done and something quite different gets a hold of him. Some people say it is the science of the thing." (Ronald Blythe, *Akenfield: Portrait of an English Village*, London: Allen Lane the Penguin Press, 1969, pp. 73-4).

Similar group experiences among the Bali, for the Balinese gamelan, are described by Colin McPhee; others are described by Hugh Tracey reporting on the xylophone orchestras of Mozambique. In these two settings the experience seems to be more gradual, more of an easing into the world of music, in contrast to our English bell ringer, whose musical initiation was quite abrupt.

My final example is from the world of Indian classical music. The model here has clearly defined stages of musical development. Although it may be possible to identify the single event which marked the onset of musical inspiration, that is not the full story. There is an advance and retreat, of progress and regress, an ebb-and-flow model of musical creativity. This can be seen fairly clearly in Ravi Shankar's autobiography, *My Music, My Life* (New York: Simon and Schuster, 1968). In his account we find four clearly defined stages where musical inspiration comes to him afresh. "As far back as I can remember, I used to love to sneak up and tickle the instrument while my mother was busy in the kitchen. I had the feeling I might be scolded for it if anyone found out, but I later surprised the whole family by playing some of the songs I had heard Rejendra practice" (p. 60). Later, as a teenager, he went on tour with his older brother to Europe where he choreographed a dance solo for himself. He performed it and was extremely successful, receiving very good reviews. There was a certain musical transformation which occured at this point of his career. In the third level of transformation, he discovered that the sitar belonged to him. "In the summer of 1936, we spent a few months at Dartington Hall in Devonshire, England. I had a great deal of time to practice on the sitar and to have lessons with Baba. This was the first time I had played scales and exercises and not just whatever pleasing melodies came into my head... I sensed something new and very exciting; I felt that I was coming close to music and that this music is what I was meant to devote my life to." (p. 70) After years of arduous training with his guru, which in India is a stripping away of individual expression while building musical skills, Shankar described a spiritual encounter with a holy man which marked the onset of his musicianship in the fullest sense. This complex model from classical Indian music is, one we need to consider seriously because of its parallels with the training of musicians in the West.

ROSALIE PRATT: I must be the only one who is uncomfortable with this metaphor, and I've finally figured out why. For quite a few years, I have been working with children who, because of various impairments, are penalized by notions of breaking 100 in test scores. When I reflect on it, the most successful musical experiences I have had and have been witness to have been those where the person (or myself) was very involved in the experience and very happy doing it. That's breaking 100, whether it's my friend, a Metropolitan Opera singer who happens to be a magnificent performer, or the child who is finding a wonderful avenue out of autism with a melody of his or her own.

I had that feeling earlier today when Chava Sekeles gave us those beautiful examples of her work with Alon. That was breaking 100 for me. I had the feeling we were all breaking 100 when we participated in a song game, as simple as that may be. There is a joy connected with it. Musical understanding is important; but it is the joy, the touching of the inner nature that Abraham Maslow speaks of so movingly, that is breaking 100 for me.

KYLE PRUETT: I don't know about the rest of you, but when I play golf or bowl I may or may not break 100. There are times when I feel very complete in the experience and times when I don't.

Tabulated performance results are not causally related to successful music making for the performer; teachers, critics and mothers rarely speak with one voice. I'd like to take a few moments to talk about the issue of mastery. It is an issue that has great power in human development, not just in terms of musical evolution and competence, but more broadly in the wish to master the human experience. The drive to mastery is an innate human given.

Watch a newborn, hours after birth, working to get its hand into its mouth. It may not seem like much, yet why does the child bother? It bothers for the simple reason that it wants to soothe and comfort itself, and will do what it takes to become a little more comfortable. The child would not ask, "Why am I doing this?"

The issue of emotional ownership of one's musicianship intrigues me, because the capacity to perceive musically cannot be taught. It is something close to what Ed Gordon describes as audiation. But the capacity to own the experience of musical expression is another issue altogether. It would be nice if, as Sharon says, we could love all our students, but I don't think we can. I do, however, hope that we can all sponsor and *appreciate* the child's ownership of his own musical expression. That is, after all, a kind of love.

Finally, there is for me the issue of fullness and completeness of musical experience in young children. Bill Westney, who is here at this conference, is a pianist with whom I performed a recital some years ago. We reminisced about this experience and were aware that something we had shared many years ago for about an hour and a half had completed us as human beings — at least for a while. Children are very complete people; they have other humans close by, they have the world in which they live, they have their imagination, and their bodies. They are proud of what they have, and they know it's all there to be used. By the time we are adults we have lost many things: our naivete, our youth, as well as some friends and loved ones. One of the ways we recover certain lost parts is through the musical experience. The problem is that the musical experience is nonverbal, which is why I find it difficult to talk about this metaphor.

LAUREN SOSNIAK: I, too, am troubled by the metaphor, but for a different reason. I think the music maker's feelings of success and worthiness have many things in common with the feelings associated with breaking 100 in golf or bowling. On the other hand, the problem we are considering is far more complicated than mere analogy.

Pianists suggest that for them breaking 100 might be comparable to being invited to perform at some legitimate musical occasion such as a concert sponsored by a local music group, perhaps as part of a chamber music group. Here the sense of identity as a musician is clear; one has been invited to make music and people will probably pay an admission to attend the performance. It is not essential to perform expertly at these occasions, in the same sense that not every golfer or bowler who breaks 100 is an expert at the sport. Even so, the golfer and bowler are working in a manner consistent with good golfing or good bowling. They are aspiring to competence in the same way that a pianist of any age would strive to perform publicly in a manner worthy of a music maker.

But the metaphor is even more complicated, bringing with it a host of problematic assumptions. First of all, the metaphor assumes that golfers and bowlers are doing these recreational activities of their own free will. Second, it assumes they are working on improving their game, with the correlate assumption that they are probably practicing frequently. Then, too, they are probably doing it in the context of others; they may practice on their own, but they test themselves with other people. For reasons of their own, these recreational athletes aspire to the same goals that professionals do, to bring the score up or down, depending on the activity.

We run into some problems when we try to help people become part of the musical community. The first thing we have to do is develop their independence, their desire and ability to make their own musical choices. If we want to encourage people to make music their way, if we want them to have frequent involvement in the sense of music being their recreation, that would seem to limit the role of music teachers. I don't think it leaves teachers out entirely; they can still help people feel successful and worthwhile and part of the music community within the bounds of this metaphor.

As for process, I would suggest that whether children sing or play an instrument, the music they are exposed to must be real music, not some contrived music. Or, if they are listening to music, they ought to listen to music that a music community would somehow respect and value. If you're helping children to become involved in the music community, you might think of how to connect them with people who hold these values. Children need opportunities to work consistently with people who are very good at music; they need to know about other people who, like them, are working to break 100 in music.

ROY ERNST: From my perspective as a teacher, I would like to make the observation that breaking 100 is whatever a teacher thinks or says it means. The awesome responsibility of being a teacher is that every day we define success and competence for students in hundreds of ways. It constantly amazes me to think about how uniformly the teacher's views are accepted by students. It indeed would be rare for a student to comment, "What do you mean, you don't like my tone?" or, "What do you mean, that was a bad interpretation?" The labels used and the judgments made by music teachers are generally accepted by students. It is only when the cumulative effects of such pronouncements become devastating that they are questioned, let alone challenged.

During the course of the conference we have heard of instances when a casual comment by a teacher has had a profoundly negative impact on a student — has actually changed a student's life. We've also heard of instances when it was clear that the teacher was reinforcing the student's sense of confidence, where every progressive step was a cause for celebration. Generally, however, I think the tendency is for teachers to be too casual, too indifferent to a student's sense of incompetency or lack of success and self worth. The philosopher, Mortimer Adler, says that teachers should teach the way coaches coach. The coach, when trying to get someone to hit a ball, does not simply throw the ball to the batter and say, "You missed." Rather, he coaches: "Let's try that again, let's have your eye on the ball, let's lower your shoulder." This sense of nurturing and developing the feeling of success and competence is what teaching is essentially about. Working with a student and seeing his/her sense of competence and self worth develop is one of the great joys of teaching.

There are many events that define breaking 100 for students, as for example, playing music for others and having their musicianship validated by the people listening. Teachers sometimes go astray when they pursue their own goals and put their own need for recognition ahead of their obligation to nurture the student's musical progress, or when they seek a polished student performance in order to validate their own skills as a musician. In that context, all too often things happen to students that shouldn't happen.

The panel would be pleased to respond to questions on this topic from the floor. We also can consider other points that have been made during the conference on which you might like to reflect now.

AUDIENCE: Would you recommend that children not read children's books or play children's games, insofar as you recommend that they hear and perform adult music?

SOSNIAK: I would recommend that children not read books on the order of the McGuffie Reader, if that's what you mean. I will not encourage the reading of books which have no substance, books that are written expressly so that they can be organized according to some minimal rules, books which provide little richness, and which are systematically structured to present simplistic environments for young readers. If that's what you mean by children's books, I would recommend that children not read them, in the same way that I'd say that they shouldn't play children's music. On the other hand, if you mean great literature that appeals to children, literature that they can love, like Cinderella, I would support that view. Such literature has broad appeal, it has value and richness, it is part of our heritage. That doesn't mean that one provides children with the most difficult of music at the outset. They should be provided with music that appeals to their age and interests — but it must be real music, not music that has been engineered or somehow contrived to teach them certain skills while missing what it means to be music.

ERNST: I might add my observation that adults absolutely adore good children's literature. It may be children's literature, but it also has content and substance that is deep and speaks broadly to people.

AUDIENCE: Isn't breaking 100 a process rather than a product? And isn't the quality of the process dependent upon the level of involvement?

PRATT: That is precisely what I was trying to convey — that breaking 100 is a process.

PRUETT: It's a process that doesn't require validation. The child can experience an "aha!" or a transcendental insight based on their own capacity, even if the teacher at that moment doesn't say, "How did that sound to you?" or "How did that feel to you?" But I wonder, are you saying that breaking 100 is whatever the teacher says it is? I would certainly hope that the teacher's repertoire includes the phrase, "Is it the way *you* want it?"

COLWELL: It seems to me that there will come a time when the student realizes that the process has not equipped him to do the things that musicians can do, like the ability to read music independently. Process has to lead somewhere. That, I think, is what Professor Gordon is trying to say to us with respect to audiation. I mentioned the reading of music because it seems we must remember the autistic child having an opportunity to play or read music, still lacking the skills that are encompassed by audiation. On the other hand, I think there are a lot of other children out there who read music and are getting a great deal of pleasure from it. Why? Because it's something they want to do.

AUDIENCE: For me, students break 100 when their love of music is strong enough to enable them to continue to love music making after the lessons end. How can teachers help in this process?

PRUETT: I think the coaching metaphor helps here. The coach works from the sidelines. He is penalized if he goes out on the field during a game. It also includes the validation of the children's experience of their own music, the honoring of their attempt to expand the particular piece they are working on in their own direction in ways that are particularly valued by them. When you honor the child's sense of rhythm, of sonority or tempo, and you talk with them about these matters, that generally tends to let the child feel "in tune" or "attuned" with you. It's the kind of support that says to the child, "What you feel is important and valid." We can call that "loving," if you wish.

AUDIENCE: Would Dr. Gordon please discuss audiation some more. I'm not clear whether it is innate or can be taught.

GORDON: Audiation is the ability to give meaning to what one hears; it is a sequential process. The ability to audiate doesn't mean that one knows how to make music, because at any given level one can audiate intuitively, without prior formal instruction. That's aptitude. When one audiates in a formal way, based on what has been taught, including, for example, technical terms, the ability to read music and to recite interval names, that's music achievement. These two, aptitude and achievement, are the basic components of audiation.

There are also five stages of audiation. Very quickly, the first stage is when one perceives the sound. The second is when one begins to give meaning to sound through tonal and rhythmic patterns within a context of tonality and meter. These first two stages represent music aptitude. At the third stage one asks, "What have I just heard?" and begins to find meaningful answers. The fourth stage is marked by the question, "Where have I heard those patterns and sounds before?" and in the last stage one begins to predict what one will hear next. These last three stages are achievement. Generally, one cannot achieve, speaking in a musical sense, without audiating. If one achieves without audiating, it's mechanical. If one achieves in terms of audiation, that's artistic.

SOSNIAK: I'm wondering how Dr. Gordon's comments, as well as those of others, relate to adolescent music and rock music. How do adolescents listen to it? It seems clear that they can identify and distinguish among certain patterns that are common to certain performers, and they can identify the patterns that are unique to a specific group as well as those that generalize across many groups. They can tell which groups share a common style and which groups deviate from stylistic norms. And maybe most important of all, they make value judgments as to which groups they love and those they ignore. They spend a fortune on records! — and represent an enormous musical involvement by a very large number of people.

GORDON: You have raised a poignant issue. We all recognize that rock music is very, very loud and repetitive. My analysis suggests this is so primarily because the average audience member cannot audiate. Because the music is repetitive and loud, it becomes the substitute for audiation; the marketers of such music are well aware of this. Historically, that has usually been the case for bad popular music.

ERNST: I agree with Lauren in that we may be defining music very narrowly. What we really seem to be referring to is art music rooted in 17th, 18th, and 19th centuries. Many of my colleagues, some of whom are very concerned about the level of musical participation in this country, have never been to a concert with 10,000 and more people who pay twenty dollars per ticket to hear some of this country's top rock groups. I certainly would not like to characterize popular music as being inferior in any way.

GORDON: Please remember that I said "bad" popular music. As a trained jazz musician who has had considerable professional experience, I'd be the last one to say that popular music is bad. There's good popular and classical music and there's bad popular and classical music.

AUDIENCE: Won't a child who loves the process also be a child who achieves?

PRUETT: The process has a biologic processing component. Does the music I am making feel good in my hands, my body, and in my sinuses? That's biologic. There is also an interpersonal process between the child and the teacher. Achievement and public performance are two different matters; they require different skills. I don't think one automatically takes a child from process to achievement, particularly if achievement is measured by public performance.

AUDIENCE: Breaking 100 in golf and bowling indicates a score. Scoring in music may mean winning a competition. How does competition enter into "winning"?

JONES: Music competitions in no way bring a student to break 100. That's not at all what music making is about. Competitions happen to be one very small aspect of music making, one which does as much damage as it does good.

SOSNIAK: I'm not sure I agree with that entirely. There are points in children's development where they can thrive on some types of competitions — not necessarily from winning them, but from having someone there to help them see what they are now doing well that earlier may have been difficult or impossible to do. It also is an opportunity for them to test their limits, to see where they fall short and what needs to be worked on next. There was a great deal of richness in the responses of some people I interviewed who took part in competitions. They didn't need to win, probably because they received considerable help in seeing the intrinsic value of the competition as something distinct from winning. It wasn't the competition that was bad, it was the context within which it was presented as an educational experience.

FRANK WILSON: I have enjoyed the complaints about the title of this session, because they mean to me that the metaphor has succeeded in opening a discussion that people here seem to want to have about themselves and their profession. In asking how recipients of the educational process (or *product*) might decide if their investment was worth it, we have also been able to work our way back to another question that any professional eventually has to ask seriously and *regularly*, namely, what kind of a job am I doing? There *should* be some discomfort over the title, because it gets us pretty close to home.

AUDIENCE: I strongly suspect that most of us have had more than one musical 100. The first time I felt that I belonged to the musical world was when I saw a professionally produced opera, from start to finish. Another time was when I was accepted as a singer in a madrigal group. Each 100 leads to another 100.

AUDIENCE: When I think about the breaking 100 metaphor I cannot help but recall that our society is a great multicultural melting pot. In the neighborhoods of many of our inner cities, we can find many who score much higher than 100 in their sensitivity to and appreciation of music. For example, I think of a Black gospel choir, a group of people who come together to perform a particular music with style, sensitivity, and joy. Every choir member, as well as everyone in the audience, appreciates not only the performance, but the work, the necessary process, that preceded the performance. Everyone in that setting will leave it with something that is special.

Now imagine these same people as they enter our public schools; it's like walking into another culture. Who decides what is good and what is bad? Who decides what is and is not taught? The 100 experienced in the gospel choir setting may now be diminished because a music teacher fails to recognize the cultural significance of gospel music, or for that matter, the music of any other culture but his/her own. This is a crucial issue. I don't want us to forget that it exists, nor do I want us to be overly sensitive in talking about it. It needs to be talked about in the light of day.

AUDIENCE: I think we have problems with breaking 100 because we have been overwhelmed by competitions in all phases of our musical experience. We seem to spend a great deal of time worrying about prizes, and not enough time developing people's ability to interpret and appreciate. That's why a very large segment of American society stops making music the day the lessons stop.

JONES: I would like to respond to the issues of competitions and gospel music. There is an alternative. It's something I've used; it's what I call a "playing class." I break the experience down according to the age of the children, from elementary school through college age, giving each child an opportunity, once every three to four weeks, to play in front of the group. The children can play anything they want. It makes no difference if it's rock, jazz, classical, improvisation, or a poem. I also encourage the children to share a record or tape of some music they really love. Kids playing for each other present a wonderfully supportive environment in which to learn the process of critical give-and-take; how to survive and stand tall after someone has suggested that the melody should be louder, or that the performer should do this or that.

Interestingly, the "playing class" concept eliminates the need for competitions, except for those students who ask for them — and there will always be those who ask to compete. In that case, they ought to be allowed to do so.

AUDIENCE: Different kinds of music appeal to different senses within us. I think rock music has a tremendous power and is meaningful to those who are involved with it.

SOSNIAK: For myself, the issue revolves around the notions of breadth and narrowness. What does it mean to be literate in today's society? Does it mean that you can read at the fourth grade level, or that you read regularly? Is reading *Newsweek* every week a good criterion, or is it to read from the

New York Times "top 10" book list? If one is really literate, their reading will encompass a variety of sources.

So, too, with music. If you were musically literate, you might have a particular liking for rock music, but your experience with and understanding of music would be broader that just that. It's a teacher's job to provide students with a breadth of opportunity, to help them discover how rock music fits into music more generally. It's similar to helping students discover how a particular book fits into a broader sampling of literature. Large numbers of people seem to love rock. But it's not enough to be hooked on just that and not be richly involved in the breadth of music.

AUDIENCE: Helen (Meyers), what is your definition of literacy?

MYERS: This is something we would ask from within a particular culture. There is no single answer.

AUDIENCE: Music, for me, is part of recreation. My technical skills are important, but I have many friends who don't have them and still enjoy music. I don't think their lack of technical skills should make them feel that they can't break 100 in music.

AUDIENCE: I've done some research in this area and have developed a test of self-esteem in relation to musical ability. The subjects, children from ten to fourteen years of age, were from Chicago Heights and some of the wealthier suburbs of Minneapolis and St. Paul. The data indicated that the students' musical ability and self-esteem was tied to doing what their music teachers thought they should be doing. When, for example, teachers valued music reading, the students who were praised for demonstrating this ability had high self-esteem. When the better music readers were given more difficult music to read and were appropriately praised for their success, the data again indicated high self-esteem. Simply put, self-esteem was tied to teacher values. If a teacher instills in a child the idea that music reading is a way of "making it," or that being able to read music better than other children is a way of "making it." then the child who demonstrates that ability will believe he or she is breaking 100.

ERNST: I think it's time for concluding remarks from the panel.

GORDON: I see a dichotomy here. There are those who to some degree are interested in standards of achievement that are coincidental with a child's level of development, and there are others who are interested in the psychological or emotional well-being of the child. I don't think an interest in one precludes an interest in the other, nor do we have to defend one or the other point of view. My position is quite straightforward. If you are asked to play a piece of music, or to improvise, or in some way to audiate music commensurate with your aptitude, you will be successful and you will have a good feeling about yourself. So in this sense, I don't see how we can talk about about one without talking about the other. What we need to come to terms with is which precedes the other and is there a sequential relationship between the two.

COLWELL: Earlier in this conference I tried to indicate what I thought the American school of music education was, the essence of which often has been restated in this discussion. Mursell would certainly go along with gospel music and rock; he would also disagree with Pruett and Sosniak that process also becomes product.

I think we also have to consider that education has political ramifications to it. We can't just talk to ourselves all the time. We have to go forth into the world as realists, looking at our product as a part of the political education system. We need to recognize that this system has changed since Mursell defined some of the principles that have been the basis of American music education.

Let me add one thing which follows from Professor Gordon's remarks. He was encouraging all of us to do some research on these topics. I would also like to encourage you in that direction. The only kind of research we have heard about is descriptive; that is, a description of one situation at one time with one group of people. Descriptive research, as important as it may be, is only the very earliest stage of research. It is not a stage from which we can draw meaningful conclusions. At this conference we've heard some conclusions which were interesting. We've heard very few that were both interesting and *important*.

PRUETT: I'm afraid that Ed (Gordon) has raised a chicken and egg question. Biology favors reciprocity over sequence. The biological model that comes to mind is the DNA double helix, which in some ways has neither an end nor a beginning. It is an intertwining continuity. One thing that has been strongly and permanently answered for me by this conference is the need to continually remind and inform ourselves that each element of the suggested dichotomy is really a reciprocal of the other.

Second, a point about literacy. In the little town of Shawnee, Oklahoma (where I spent many summers), the most literate being was a man who could quote Old and New Testament scripture at the drop of a hat. He was revered as the only intellectual in town. Later, when I went to college in New Haven, I found a slightly different view of what characterizes an intellectual. But I was lucky; I had a grandfather who revered his townsman's literacy. I hope that we are not seduced by the temptation to establish national standards of musical literacy.

MYERS: I found this to be a thoroughly fascinating week, one during which I have learned a great deal. While focusing our attention on the child's world of music we have been looking toward the future — the future of our species, of our world, and certainly the future of music. But I suspect that I am not the only one who has taken a moment to reflect on the past, on my own childhood and my own initiation as a child into the world of music. This conference has been a wonderful setting for these private thoughts. I hope the ethnomusicological presence here has helped to call your attention to the diversity of children's musical experiences around the world. We are very eager to share with you whatever insights we may have gained in our travels. I'm afraid that the news we bring you is not simple. We see human creativity taking many different forms; we see a variety of inventiveness; we witness the unending sequence of events by which people invoke and reinvoke their cultures. We can report to you that the world of music is vast, that it has many paths leading to it, and that it has many doors, any one of which a child may open and proclaim with Ravi Shankar, "My music, my life."